ISBN 978-0-260-09648-7

PIBN 10236054

McLOUGHLIN
AND OLD OREGON

A Chronicle

BY
EVA EMERY DYE

FRONTISPIECE

GARDEN CITY   NEW YORK
DOUBLEDAY, PAGE & COMPANY
1924

TO

MY HUSBAND

WITHOUT WHOSE ENCOURAGEMENT THIS WORK WOULD
NOT HAVE BEEN UNDERTAKEN

This Book

IS MOST AFFECTIONATELY DEDICATED

CONTENTS

Contents

McLOUGHLIN AND OLD OREGON

McLoughlin and Old Oregon

I

AN AMERICAN ON THE COLUMBIA

1832

SIXTY years ago, on a green terrace sloping up from the north bank of the Columbia, not far from the mouth of the Willamette, lay old Fort Vancouver. It might be likened to the Dutch stockade at New Amsterdam, or to a rude stronghold of central Europe in the middle ages, with a little village clustered under its guns.

Fort Vancouver was fortified in primitive fashion. There was a stout palisade of fir posts, twenty feet high, sharpened at both ends and driven into the ground. There were thick double-ribbed and riveted gates in front and rear, ornamented with brass padlocks and ponderous keys. A grim old three-storied log tower formed a bastion at the northwest corner, bristling with portholes and cannon. Some rough-hewn stores, magazines, and workshops were ranged inside the enclosure, with an open court in the middle where the Indians brought their game and peltries. Directly opposite the main entrance stood the governor's residence, a somewhat pretentious two-story structure of heavy timber, mortised Canadian fashion, and painted white. Here Dr. John McLoughlin, governor of the Hudson's Bay Company west of the Rocky Mountains, and his chief aide Douglas, afterward knighted Sir James, first governor of British Columbia, dispensed hospitality after the fashion of Saxon thanes or lairds of a Highland castle.

One autumn evening in 1832 a salute was fired at the gates of Fort Vancouver. "Some belated trapper," said the traders in the hall. Guests were luxuries too rare to be anticipated in the far-away Oregon wild. At a word from Governor McLoughlin the porter unlocked the gate and eleven strangers entered, clad all in leather, dripping with rain, and garnished with as many weapons as Robin Hood in Sherwood Forest. Dr. McLoughlin fixed a keen eye upon the wayfarers as Bruce ushered them into the hall.

"Wyeth is my name," said the tall, wiry leader. "Nathaniel J. Wyeth, from Boston: on a trading trip to the Columbia."

"Bless me!" cried the amazed McLoughlin, extending his hand. "Bless me, 'tis a marvellous journey. Few could survive it. Welcome to Fort Vancouver."

Not since Astor's defeat in 1812 had any American tried to trap or trade in Oregon. Unmolested for twenty years, the British fur-traders had reared their palisades and filled their forts with furs. That the young republic on the Atlantic shore might stretch her fingers westward, that a highway might be found across the mountains — these were vague contingencies!

Despite his travel-worn garb, Dr. McLoughlin recognized an honest man in the tall, blond trader from Yankee-land. He and his followers were assigned to quarters among the fur-trading knights at Fort Vancouver. All winter Captain Wyeth lived at the fort, studying methods and evolving plans for future action. All winter Captain Wyeth watched for a ship that never

came. In March he started back on the long journey
overland to Boston. The ship had been lost at sea.
A second was despatched and the Yankee captain
reappeared on the Columbia.

Within sound of the morning guns of Fort Vancouver
Captain Wyeth set up a log fort, palisaded like that of
his rival, on the beautiful island of Wapato, at the
mouth of the Willamette River. Out of that ship, the
" May Dacre," he brought goats, sheep, pigs, chickens,
Hawaiians. The flitting forms of " the Bostons," as
the Indians called them, in their leather pantaloons and
white wool hats, was a constant menace to the occu-
pants of the British fur fort. It brought a breath of
that old battle when Hudson's Bay and Northwesters
fought in the North. While they treated the frank and
manly Bostonian with politeness, with kindness, and
even generosity, they watched him like eagles and
shadowed him like spirits. He built Fort Hall on the
Snake; they set up Fort Boisé to draw away his trade.
Did he send his men to trap or buy beaver? The
Hudson's Bay men were there before him, behind him,
around him. They put up the value of furs to a
ruinous figure. They sold Indian goods at fifty per
cent less than he could afford. Out of an annual fund
put by for the purpose they harassed him on every
hand. "Competition is war, war to the knife, fierce and
deadly," but in this case as usual, it was " concealed under
gentlemanly foils and masks and padded gloves."

Neighborly offices passed between the forts. Governor McLoughlin sent over presents of fresh vegetables.
Wyeth paddled over on rainy nights to join the jolly
boys in Bachelors' Hall. Many and many an hour he
discussed history and government with Dr. McLoughlin.
But underlying all their intercourse was the discovery

of each other's plans — friendship and strategy. Wyeth
concealed his schemes. Nevertheless, whenever his
men were hauling their boats down to the water the
ever-present Hudson's Bay men were already launched
and met the Indians first.

An unprecedentedly rainy winter came upon the Columbia. Heavy mists enveloped the hills; the clouds
came down among the trees; drip, drip, drip went the
rain, surpassing the deluge of forty days and forty
nights. Soft Chinooks blew up from the sea, snow slid
down from the Cascade tips, the very Columbia con-
spired, creeping at dead of night into Wyeth's fort and
soaking his precious bales. In spite of calm and cool
philosophy, Captain Wyeth saw his inevitable disad-
vantage against the hereditary power of the Hudson's
Bay Company, with its hundreds of employés in practice for generations. Bankruptcy shook its finger in
his face. His handsome fortune and the credit of Boston
merchants were invested. Still the fish refused to tangle
themselves in his nets. The Blackfeet killed his trappers, stole his furs. Out of two hundred men, one hundred and sixty had been killed or had deserted to the
rival. Even the superstitious Indians refused to trade,
because, they said, long ago a Boston ship brought the
deadly fever that killed all the people on Wapato.

Once Wyeth referred to Dr. McLoughlin's hereditary
influence with the Indians.

"My hereditary influence?" echoed the doctor.
"Bless you, Mr. Wyeth, bless you, *I* had no hereditary
influence! I made the Indians *fear* me. I compelled
obedience. I studied justice. I cultivated confidence.
It takes time, Mr. Wyeth, it takes time."

"True, Doctor, but you have a great corporation
behind you with unlimited capital. Your servants have

intermarried with the tribes to hold the trade. Our policies are diametrically opposed. Yours is to perpetuate savagism, to keep Oregon as a game preserve, a great English hunting park. Mine would be to fill it with a civilized people."

"How can they get here, Mr. Wyeth? Even India is not so far. Oregon is the very end of the world, a whole year's voyage around Cape Horn or Good Hope. Shut off by rock-ribbed mountains, deserts, savages, the ocean, how can they get here?"

"Overland from the United States," answered the Bostonian.

Dr. McLoughlin laughed incredulously. "When you have levelled the mountains, cultivated the desert, annihilated distance, then and not before. Besides, the United States is too young, too sparsely settled. Look at her miles of unoccupied Mississippi Valley. No, no, no, Mr. Wyeth, if Oregon is ever colonized it will be by sea, from England. We shall not live to see it, but our children may."

The doctor's ruddy face was thoughtful. He knew the secret of Wyeth's discontent. It pained him to feel that Captain Wyeth attributed in any way his failure to the company. The doctor fidgeted with his cane. He spoke his thought.

"What more can I do for you, Mr. Wyeth — consistently with my duty to my company? Have I not treated you kindly? Have I not given your men work when your own plans failed? As for civilization, was I not glad to engage your lad, Solomon Smith, to teach our boys and girls? Did I not hail with joy your good missionary, Jason Lee, and help to establish him in the valley?"

Wyeth was silent. He could find no fault with Dr.

McLoughlin; and yet Dr. McLoughlin had ruined him. The doctor walked up to him. He had a very affectionate, winning manner. McLoughlin, one of the most urbane gentlemen in the world, moreover really liked Captain Wyeth, and was sorry to see him driven to the wall. He took his hand as a father would.

"Business is business, Mr. Wyeth. I like your open, manly way. I find you fair in contracts. I believe you to be a gentleman and an honest man. You support morality and encourage industry. If you — will come over to us — Wyeth, yourself to the fort — join us — then I, myself, will forward your credentials to the house in London by the next express. What say you?"

The sturdy Bostonian reflected, then simply answered, "I cannot join you, Doctor."

"Then I regret that I can do nothing for you," answered the doctor, suddenly stiff and distant and yet with sadness in his eye. "You see my duty to my company forbids it."

Wyeth looked into the benevolent face. Slowly he added, "*But* — I will sell."

So Nathaniel J. Wyeth sold to the Hudson's Bay Company for what it was willing to give, and left the country in defeat.

But though he left, an important man remained. That man was Jason Lee, the missionary.

Long ago, when Lewis and Clark entered the Flathead country, the high chief looked in their pale faces and said, "They are chilled. See how cold their cheeks are; build fires, bring robes."

Before the blazing fires, wrapped in soft buffalo-robes,

the white men's cheeks grew red. Perspiration burst from every pore. The robes slipped off, but the solici₊ tous Indians kept putting them back. General Clark then arose and spoke to the kind-hearted Flatheads of a great people toward the rising sun. "They worship the Great Spirit," he said. "He has made them strong and brave and rich."

"Does he give them wigwams and much buffalo?" asked the Flatheads.

"Yes," answered the general.

Lewis and Clark smoked the pipe of friendship and passed on. The Nez Percé Flatheads talked around their fires. A Hudson's Bay trader came.

"Do you know about the Great Spirit?" inquired the childlike Flatheads.

"Yes; you can learn about him at our school at Red River."

The chief sent three sons to the distant Red River. When they returned they taught their people a rudimentary form of worship.

A great religious movement passed among the Nez Percé Flatheads and on up into the Shushwap country on the Fraser. Old traders record it in their memoirs. By and by an American trapper came.

"Do you know about the Great Spirit?" still inquired the childlike Flatheads.

"Yes," answered the trapper, "there is a book that tells about him."

"Where can we find the book?" insisted the Flatheads.

"Oh, away off in a distant city where the traders go."

The Indians held a council and decided to send for the white man's wonderful book.

After a long and weary wandering two Indians entered the frontier city of St. Louis and asked for General Clark. There was much *wa-wa* (talk-talk) and inquiry for the book. The people gathered and curiously eyed these representatives of a tribe a thousand miles beyond the farthest that had ever appeared in the streets of St. Louis. Shawnees, Pawnees, Arapahoes, Sioux, had come, but never before a Flathead, never before anybody inquiring for a book of the Great Spirit.

General Clark was interested in Indians, in furs, in lands, in wars, and treaties. He banqueted these Indian ambassadors. He sent them with his servant to see the lions of the city. They visited cathedrals and shops and shows, but found no book. At last, tired and disappointed, they turned back and sought the way to their own country.

"Is it true that those Indians came all that distance for a book of the Great Spirit?" said Catlin, the Indian artist.

"They came for that and nothing else," said General Clark.

A young clerk in one of the St. Louis fur-rooms wrote to his friends in the East. It found its way into the papers. The Macedonian cry swept like a trumpet summons through the churches.

"Who will carry the book of the Great Spirit to the Flatheads?"

The chief luminary of the Methodist conference answered: "I know but one man — Jason Lee."

Like the voice of God, Jason Lee heard the Nez Percé call — he thrilled. In a day he tore himself from the entreaty of friends to enter upon a journey that was not ended in a year. With his nephew, Daniel Lee, and two other assistants, he accompanied Wyeth on that second trip in 1834. So came the missionary to the realm of the king of the Columbia. And that tall, angular Puritan, born just over the Canadian border, was just the man Dr. McLoughlin wanted for his settlement at Champoeg. The doctor set his plate beside his own, and before them all discussed the question of location.

"You have no call to go up there among the Flatheads, Mr. Lee, where we cannot protect you. We have plenty of Indians right here. Above the Falls of the Willamette there lies a beautiful valley. Besides the Indians there is a settlement of French Canadians, with their Indian wives and half-breed children. Those Canadians are your own countrymen, Mr. Lee, far from the advantages of school and church. Then, too, I can assist you here with my boats and my influence. Up there in the Flathead country you will be far cut off from a base of supplies and from communication with the civilized world."

These arguments impressed the missionary. Of course Dr. McLoughlin wanted his people at Champoeg instructed. Still more he wanted the mission a dependency of the fort.

Lee went up the Willamette and found a valley fair as the happy land of Rasselas, set between the hills. "I will build here," he said. Out of Wyeth's ship, the "May Dacre," Lee unloaded his supplies, and for a trifle engaged Indian canoe-men to transport them to the site of the future mission.

"I warn you against these missionaries," said John Dunn, a clerk in the Indian shop at Fort Vancouver. "I warn you. Look out for them. They are very meek and humble now; but the time will come when they will rise up to question your authority here, and even your right to Vancouver itself."

"Tut, tut, tut!" laughed the liberal doctor. "Do you grudge the poor Indian a chance? For my part, I think the missionaries show a very good spirit in coming to this neglected coast."

II

THE COMING OF THE WHITMANS

1836

WHEN Wyeth was returning defeated to the States he met a vision in the mountains, a beautiful woman with golden hair and snowy brow, riding like Joan of old to conquest, — Narcissa Whitman. With her rode Eliza Spalding, a slender, dark-eyed devotee, who back in the States had knelt in a lonely wayside inn to consecrate her heart to Oregon. Two brides were on that wonderful journey, farther than flew the imperial eagles of Rome, to their life-work on the Columbia.

Two brides! — there is a romance about modern missions that the apostolic fathers never knew — two missionary brides were the first white women to cross the continent!

Two grooms, knights-errant, rode at their sides: Marcus Whitman, a young physician, strong, resolute, with fire in his deep blue eyes and courage imprinted on every feature to the tips of his auburn curls, he, too, had heard of the Flathead messengers for the white man's Book of the Great Spirit; Henry Spalding, a youth long, lank, prematurely wrinkled and sharp-featured with thought, he, too, was fired with apostolic ardor. While yet a student in a village academy, Henry Spalding had bent the knee and begged the hand of Narcissa Prentice. To him and to every other suitor the beautiful girl said no, until young Dr. Whitman came riding like Lochinvar out of the West.

It was the Sabbath when Dr. Whitman reached his native village in central New York, from his first exploring tour to the Rocky Mountains. In the midst of the sermon, he whom they thought thousands of miles away, walked into church, followed by two tall, blanketed Indians.

"Marcus!" cried his mother, rising from her pew and stretching forth her arms. "Marcus!" echoed the heart of a maid in the village choir. In a few days there was a wedding at the old-fashioned house of Judge Prentice. There was a missionary farewell at the village church. Long after, it was a tradition in that village that when the choir broke down in sobs, the sweet soprano of Narcissa Whitman, the missionary bride, carried the farewell hymn alone, like a skylark to the sky:

> "Scenes of sacred peace and pleasure,
> Holy days and Sabbath bell,
> Richest, brightest, sweetest treasure,
> Can I say a last farewell?"

They started. Cincinnati was a village in the woods; Chicago, unknown; St. Louis, the end of the West. Oregon was foreign land in 1836.

"You can never get the women through," said Catlin, the Indian artist, at Pittsburg. "They will both be kidnapped," said old trappers on the border. "They are white squaws, white as snow," was the word that flew from tribe to tribe as, under the convoy of the American Fur Company, they entered the great, wild land of the West. For miles the enraptured Indians followed in silent admiration.

"This is the end of the wagon route," said the fur-traders, stopping their train of carts at Fort Laramie on the Platte. " We always pack on mules from this point over the mountains."

" But we must take a wagon, on account of the women," said Dr. Whitman. " Did not Bonneville take carts over to Green River? Did not. Ashley haul a cannon to Great Salt Lake?"

" Yes," admitted the traders, " and then Bridger. tried it, but they all gave it up — left their carts in the mountains. Bonneville had no end of trouble — if he had n't had a blacksmith along for constant repairs, he never could have got through. The fact is, it is not considered practicable."

Dr. Whitman had crossed those Alps before. If Bonneville took a wagon across, he could. " I know we can do it — I can almost see a road," said the dauntless doctor, with that positive assurance that always won half his battles.

" Go ahead, then," laughed the traders. " A good wheel route to Green River will double our profits. We will gladly send a man with you to help explore a way."

With the doctor's wagon and a trader's cart the little company pushed on, leaving Fort Laramie, the last outpost of civilized man, on the foothills at their rear. Dr. Whitman made a wagon route his special object of study. With now a tip-up and now a turn-over, and now a long detour among the ragged pines, he followed the way of the Great South Pass through the heart of the Rocky Mountains. Mr. Spalding brought the cows; W. H. Gray, an assistant, drove the packhorses. In smooth mountain meadows the women rode in the wagon; in shelving, rough defiles they mounted their horses, cheering their husbands over this barrier ridge of the world, supposed to forever shut the East from the West.

The magical word flew over the mountains — hundreds of Nez Percés, Flatheads, Snakes, and Bannocks came out to meet them.

Two Nez Percé chiefs went up on the heights to escort them down. There, on the summit of the continent, the flag was unfurled. Under its starry folds, facing the west, the little band knelt, and like Columbus took possession in the name of God.

The moment the two brides alighted at the trader's rendezvous on Green River, scores of Indian women pressed to grasp their hands and kiss their cheeks. A handful of bronzed mountaineers, so long in the wilds they had forgotten the looks of a white woman, pulled off their caps in memory of their mothers.

"Thar!" said Joe Meek, an American trapper, "*thar* are immigrants that the Hudson's Bay Company cannot drive out."

"You must leave your wagon here," said everybody at the rendezvous — everybody but the Indians. They followed with wonder the musical *chick-a-chick* clattering over the rocks. They waved their arms toward the hills, they chattered and jabbered and put their shoulders to the wheels.

"We can take it through," said Dr. Whitman. The Indians went ahead and helped him hunt the road that afterward became the great overland route to the West. Night after night, late and tired, the doctor came puffing into camp.

The wagon stuck in the creeks, it upset on the steep hillsides, and then — the axle-tree broke.

"Leave it, Marcus," said Mrs. Whitman, reining up **her** beautiful bay. "Let us have no more trouble with it."

But no, the doctor made a cart of the back wheels and lashed on the fore wheels. "I shall take it through, Narcissa, in some shape or other," he said.

"You can get it no farther," said the Hudson's Bay men at the cottonwood stockade of Fort Hall — the fort that Wyeth had sold to McLoughlin.

But the doctor went ahead and swam the deep, swift Snake. Cart and mules turned upside down and were almost lost, but with iron grip the doctor brought them out on the other side and safe to Fort Boisé. Then all rose up. "'T is a crazy scheme to take the wagon on," they cried. "The season is late, the animals are failing, the wagon is a source of delay, the route in crossing the Blue Mountains is said to be utterly impassable for it."

"I will send for it by and by," said the determined missionary, stowing the battered vehicle away in a shed at old Fort Boisé under the care of Monsieur Payette, the clerk in charge.

Over the scorched plains of the Snake, with a brigade of Hudson's Bay traders, into the cool groves of the Blue Mountains they rode. Tom McKay's excellent hunters brought down for them the elk and the antelope. On the last day of August, 1836, three days ahead of their party, Dr. and Mrs. Whitman galloped up to the gates of old Fort Walla Walla. Heralds had gone before, a watch was on the ramparts, the gates were open. Monsieur Pierre Pambrun, the courtly chief factor, assisted from her steed the pioneer of all white women across the hills to the River of the West. That night the wearied travellers slept in the west bastion, full of portholes and filled with fire-arms. A great cannon, always loaded, stood behind the door. The water swished by the walls. The wind howled down the Columbia, shaking the driftwood donjon till their voices were lost in the racket. A courier rode post to Fort Vancouver.

"They come," said Dr. McLoughlin, "not as rivals, not as traders, but as allies, to teach our Indians peace and industry."

Seated in the fur-traders' boats with Chief Factor Pambrun and his voyageurs, the Americans glided down the Columbia, beyond the drifting sand, past the log huts of the Walla Walla fishermen, who from point to point stood sweeping their nets in the foaming waters, on into the high dark dikes that shut in the tortuous river. Here they entered an elder, grander Hudson, lacking only castles on the cliffs to give a human touch. But there *were* castles, arrested mid air from the volcanic throat of Hood, in ages long gone by, columns upon columns crowned with towers, columns that swelled like the bastions of ancient citadels — basaltic bluffs, turreted with the pinnacles and shafts and domes that guard this gateway of the floods.

Where the Columbia breaks through the Cascade range they looked where never white woman looked before, on the dark foundations of the hills planted deep in the turbulent water, and rising hundreds of feet in the heavens. The whitecaps rolled as at sea. A gale came up from the west, and the little boats rose and fell like sea-gulls on the surges. Mt. Hood, visible for miles, grew to life size. St. Helens reared her graceful, tapering cone above the distant firs. Within the curving inlets vast amphitheatres with columnar tiers of seats outdid the Roman Coliseum. On every headland grim promontories frowned like forts of some Titanic age.

On the second day they had reached the Dalles.

In three days, hark! the roaring cascades dashed their billows on the rocks. From shore to shore a rapidly declining, irregular sheet of snow-white foam slid to the level below. Grander rose the mountains, four thousand five thousand feet on either hand, cut by livid gashes of ravine exposing the ribs of mother earth. Not a lip moved, not a word was spoken as the French-Iroquois boatman stood at his post and with a skilful dip turned the flying canoe from the point of some projecting rock, while on every side seethed and yawned the great green caves of water. Should a heart fail or a cheek blanch now? No, each face was as immobile as the naked Indian on yonder rock that stood like a statue cut in bronze spearing the passing salmon.

At the portages how the Indians wondered to see the men helping the women over the rough places. Why, they did not even have to carry the baggage!

Fort Vancouver was ready. The flags were flying. Two ships lay in the river,—the "Nereid," a man-of-war just from London and bound for the Northwest coast with bales of Indian goods, and the barque "Columbia," about to sail on her return voyage with furs and peltries. The stirring song of the voyageurs rang over the terraced plain. The stately McLoughlin and the knightly Douglas stood on the shore to welcome these guests whose coming would unfold a world of change. It was an historic time. Mighty men and lovely women stood there, who had trod a continent, bearing the cross, farther than rode the Hun of old, farther than the Helvetian, farther than even the Celt to the verge of Europe. It was a scene to shine on canvas and live in story, like the landing of the Pilgrims, like the march of Constantine, like Augustine in England, like Paul on the hills of Greece. Governor McLoughlin offered his arm to Mrs. Whitman, Black Douglas assisted Mrs Spalding, and all passed into the fort.

It was a welcome rest after the long days on the plains and the mountains, after the camps in dust and sand, after the suns and frost and fatigue. It seemed like a dream to find this roomy old stronghold in the wilderness. Primeval forests swayed and sobbed upon the hills, primeval Indians paddled and chanted along the streams. The long low halls, the echoing floors, the roaring, wide-mouthed chimneys, the weapons of the chase and elk-skin armor on the wall, all told that the fur-traders perpetuated a storied past.

What a change was the bounteous board from buffalo-beef and mountain bread, — flour and water fried in tallow. The best cooks of Canada waited on the fur-trader. Carving was carried to perfection at Fort Vancouver. Salmon, ducks, and geese and venison, the choice of an epicure, was daily fare. And fruit? — through the postern gate they walked in the garden musky with odors of peaches and pears, slender-limbed apple-trees broken with their golden weights, and rows of plum and fig-trees crimsoned in the sun. Between the neat squares the old Scotch gardener had gravelled his walks and lined them with strawberry vines, and at the far end stood the grape-grown summer-house where Rae had wooed his Eloise.

But Dr. Whitman could not rest. Whatever he ought to do, that he must do without delay.

In its great westward sweep to the sea the Columbia narrows at the Dalles into a chasm that a fiend might leap. Here the salmon crowded in such prodigious numbers in their journey from the sea that from time immemorial it had been a famous fishing spot. In the summer season thousands of Indians gathered there and hung enormous baskets from the rocks. The leaping salmon landed in the baskets in schools and shoals, and the watchful Indians hauled up tons and tons a day. It was like a great fair when the tribes of the interior came down to trade for salmon at the Dalles.

"Here," said Whitman, "is a strategic point. Here will I locate my mission."

"No," said Dr. McLoughlin, "the Dalles Indians are fishing Indians, treacherous and unreliable. Go up among the hunting Indians of the Walla Walla. Do you not know that the English troopers are recruited from the fox-hunters of England? The Indians of the chase are the troopers of this continent. They can do anything."

"But can they be tamed?" asked Dr. Whitman.

"The possibilities of those horse Indians cannot be measured," answered Dr. McLoughlin. "They are in a state of nature, uncorrupted, strong and brave and free. These canoe Indians are in the process of decay."

"But how can I locate so far from my base of supplies?" hesitated the missionary.

"I will send your goods in my boats for a trifle. Every summer our brigades go up the Columbia with supplies for the interior. Your credit shall be always good. Our stations at Fort Walla Walla and Fort Colvile are open to your orders."

While their husbands were gone, looking at the upper country, Mrs. Whitman and Mrs. Spalding remained guests at Fort Vancouver. In a day their love unlocked the hearts of Madame McLoughlin and her stately daughter Eloise and the charming Mrs. Douglas. The trader's children crowded about the delicate Mrs. Spalding like bees around a honeysuckle. She

could draw, she could paint, and spin and weave and
knit, and they watched her fingers with curious eager-
ness. Far back on the plains she had cemented a last-
ing friendship with the Indian women by her quick
intuition of their wants and her readiness in learning
Nez Percé, but to Mrs. Whitman the men bowed down
as at a shrine before a golden goddess. The silken
cape that encircled her soft, white neck seemed like
the fluttering of wings, her golden hair like an aureole
of light. When she sang — forty years after, tears
leaped to the eyes of the old fur-traders at the memory
of the prima donna of Fort Vancouver. Quickly the
children and the voyageurs caught from her lips the
plaintive, "Watchman, tell us of the night," to vie
thenceforth with their French chansons in the forest.

At Dr. McLoughlin's request Mrs. Whitman heard
his daughter recite every day. Eloise had the fresh
enthusiasm that has never been cloyed by schools or
tasks. While the girls of New England were patiently
working their samplers, this princess of the Columbia
was embroidering caps and moccasins. While the girls
of New England practised formal scales in music,
Eloise was picking up the tunes of the voyageurs, and
might often be seen in her light canoe darting across
the Columbia, singing as she went the wild songs of old
Canada.

If the missionary-brides instructed the ladies of Fort
Vancouver, they, too, were taught in the lore of lustrous
sables, silky sea-otter, thick brown mink, and soft black
beaver. Eloise could tell them that the fiery fox was a
prize in China, that the Russian would give a hundred
silver rubles for the sea-otter that the Chinook slid
down and speared as it slept on the shore, that the
dappled bearskin would line the coach of an English

noble, that the blue fox went to the czar for a royal cloak, and the silver gray to an Indian rajah.

"And do I care to wear the beautiful furs?" asked Eloise. "Oh, no; you see I know how they get them. I know how our men face winter and summer in the lonely mountains. It is not play. My father says hunting the beaver is the most laborious work in the world."

Never did guests more regretted leave the halls of Fort Vancouver. Had it been possible they would have been detained permanently, but winter rains were setting in, sure sign that storms were whirling around Mt. Hood. They must re-embark for the upper country. Many a token of beads and embroidery was placed in their hands by the skilled ladies of the fort as Whitman and Spalding bore away their brides to the distant mission.

Dr. Whitman had planted his mission among the knightly Cayuses, the imperial tribe of Oregon, who in the long-ago ruled to the mouth of the Columbia and whose herds now covered the plains from the foothills of Mt. Hood to the borders of the Snake. It was on a green spot called by the Indians Waiilatpu, the Rye-Grass Meadow, that Whitman halted on the banks of the Walla Walla.

Chief Factor Pambrun had ridden out with him, both of their horses belly deep in the rye-grass, to decide upon the location. All around lay rolling green prairie, bathing its cottonwood edge in the winding river. Away to the east the Blue Mountains were hazy along the horizon. Far to the west were the snows of Hood, that the Indians pointed out as the mountain near which the White-Headed Eagle dwelt. Twenty-five miles to the west lay Fort Walla Walla on a narrow stretch of sand between the Columbia and the Walla Walla. On the hills around grazed the beautiful spotted horses of the Walla Walla-Cayuses. Here and there the smoke curled up from the conical skin lodges, and thickly gathered all around them were mounted Indians eagerly watching the decision of the missionary. They were clean, well-dressed, noble-looking men, those Walla Walla-Cayuses, with their eagle eyes and fine straight noses, men that looked well worth the efforts of a Whitman or a Wesley. Yellow Serpent, Pio-pio-mox-mox, was their chief, a haughty, handsome Indian fond of dress and parade. By the side of Yellow Serpent rode his little son, a lad of twelve years, baptized by Jason Lee with the name of a bishop of the Methodist church, Elijah Hedding. Already Elijah had studied a year at the mission on the Willamette.

There were present also the Cayuse brothers of Elijah's mother, Tauitau and Five Crows, head men in the council, and Tiloukaikt, a great dark chief with a voice like a brazen trumpet. As soon as the decision was made, Chief Factor Pambrun sent out two workmen from Fort Walla Walla and the Indians all turned in to help build Whitman's adobe mansion.

Spalding had set up his tabernacle one hundred and twenty-five miles northeast at Lapwai, on the Clear-water River, a few miles from the present site of Lewiston, Idaho. Here, among the teachable Nez Percés, the patient, persevering missionary and his gifted wife accomplished a work that has never been surpassed in any age among a savage people. Like Pastor Oberlin in the hills of Alsace, Whitman and Spalding set examples of industry, and ploughed and planted and sowed, and shared the harvest with their people. For a while, wherever they travelled through the country, hundreds of Indians followed to see the white men who brought the Book of the Great Spirit and to hear them preach at night. Spalding's Indians would sometimes spend the entire night repeating what he had taught them in the evening. Gray-haired men and chiefs became pupils of their own little children in learning to read and write.

Did the presence of those women suggest a thought to Jason Lee? No; long since he had written to the Board to select and send him a suitable wife.

III

THE WEDDING OF JASON LEE

1837

AGAIN a salute resounded at the gates of Fort Vancouver.

"Who the devil's come at this time o' night?" grumbled the sleepy fur-traders, turning on their couches. The porter crawled out of his lodge in his nightcap. To the impatient knockers outside a heavy step sounded and a gruff voice demanded, "Who's there?"

"Strangers from the States on the brig 'Diana.'"

The great key turned, the gate swung creaking on its hinges. This time several men entered, with their wives, followed by three fair damsels half revealed by the light of the moon. The old porter led the shadowy figures up to McLoughlin's door.

"Who is it?" inquired the doctor, in dressing-gown and moccasins, holding a candle above his head. The white locks framed an almost youthful face as he leaned, peering into the night.

"A reinforcement to Jason Lee's mission," answered the spokesman of the party.

"More missionaries?" laughed the doctor. "Well, well, surely we'll all get converted by and by. Come in, come in." He took each hand with the grasp of a friend, and turning led into the great dining hall, where a log still smouldered on the hearth.

"Be seated; be seated." The doctor rummaged around, poking the log with his cane, and pushing up a settee. "Burris, Burris!" he called from an adjoining door. In short order the major-domo appeared with candles, that cast weird flickers against the windows and the high dark ceiling.

"And so Congress is still discussing that Maine boundary?" Dr. McLoughlin was saying, when the butler reappeared with a steaming tray. A dusky Kanaka (Hawaiian) poured the tea, while Burris retired to pile Indian blankets on the bunk-like beds of the fort.

Before daylight Dr. McLoughlin called, "Money-coon!" An Indian rolled out of his blanket in the barracks.

"Get the despatch-boat. Take these papers to Jason Lee at the mission as quick as you can."

The Indian disappeared. There was a click at the boat-house door, a gleam on the river. Forty-eight hours later McLoughlin, glass in hand, descried two canoes laboring up the billowy Columbia in a tempest of wind. "See, he even comes in a storm!"

All turned to banter the maiden who now was to behold her future husband. Through all that voyage Anna Maria Pitman had kept saying to herself, "I may not marry him; I may not marry him."

The little company sat with Dr. McLoughlin in a room facing the gate, when it swung back, and a tall, broad-shouldered man past thirty approached at the rate of seventy-five strides a minute. "See the conquering hero comes," whispered the teasing companions.

Anna Maria raised her eyes, and at a glance took in the Yankee make-up, the Puritan face with its long, light hair, spiritual eyes, and prominent nose. Anywhere it was a face to be remembered, but to her poetic mind a certain halo glowed about that high, retreating forehead. Dr. McLoughlin brought them face to face. There was a letter in Jason Lee's pocket saying, " She has been sent out on purpose for you."

" They really took me at my word! " thought the missionary. "Well, well, well! Though a lady should travel the world over to become my wife, yet I cannot marry her unless upon acquaintance I become satisfied that such a step will be conducive to our happiness. Judgment alone, under the influence of an enlightened conscience, must decide this question."

A pale pink suffused Miss Pitman's neck and brow under Jason Lee's scrutinizing gaze. They had met before in New York City, but his recollection had been, " She is not a lady that I should fancy for a wife."

There may have been inward tumult, but outwardly Jason Lee was as calm as on that thirsty day on the plains when he stopped the cows for a cup of milk and was surprised by a band of whooping savages. " Indians! Indians! " cried his comrades. But Lee quietly had kept on till his cup was full. One round little spot of red burned in either cheek.

It was a lovely May morning when the governor's guests started up the Willamette. Bloom and verdure and songs of birds, blue rippling waters and distant peaks of snow smiled on the scene. Governor Mc-Loughlin and the whole household of the fort accompanied them down to the water's edge. With gay farewells and good wishes the boats shot off, bearing, in addition to other baggage, a great Indian basket of provisions from the bountiful larder of Fort Vancouver. By the conniving of their companions Jason

Lee and Miss Pitman were seated last, in a boat alone, with a crew of Indians, not one of whom could speak a word of English.

With a bold sweep Jason Lee sent his canoe far ahead. Anna Maria's hair·rippled from her comb, her cheek glowed, her eye sparkled. Little dappled gray seals, with large, round, gentle eyes, swam on either side, following the boat like mastiffs, now leaping in the water, and now catching at some unlucky salmon as it bumped its nose in its headlong course up stream. At sunset the party camped in an oak orchard grove, where now the city of Portland stretches its stately avenues and rears its palatial homes. The next day they encountered shoals of salmon, literally millions, leaping and curveting and climbing the foamy falls of the Willamette, where now the factories of Oregon City send out their flumes and wheels. On the third day Jason Lee and his assistants landed where the moss-grown cottages of Champoeg dotted French Prairie.

As early as 1827 Étienne Lucier had said, " Governor, do you think this will ever become a settled country? "

" Yes; wherever wheat grows you may depend upon its becoming a settled country."

"What assistance will you give me to settle on the Willamette? I cannot face Canadian cold again. I am getting old." Étienne Lucier had been one of Astor's Canadians, who had never left the Oregon country since the day when the great New Yorker's stronghold was handed over to British traders.

McLoughlin reflected. Here was a case that might become a precedent. It was against the rules of the Hudson's Bay Company to dismiss servants in the Indian country, but by retaining them on his books they might cultivate the land and become a base of supplies for the Pacific posts.

These old voyageurs had Indian wives. They had families growing up around them, born in Oregon and accustomed to its genial climate. To transport them to Canada would be not only a great expense, but a cruel exile. To separate the men from their families — that was not to be thought of. These French Canadians loved their Indian wives. The children had twined about their heartstrings. By permitting them to cultivate the fertile Willamette Dr. McLoughlin could retain them under his control, while their influence on their Indian relatives would maintain continued cordiality between the races.

"What assistance will I give?" said Dr. McLoughlin. "Seed to sow, and wheat to feed yourself and family till crops come. Then I will buy your surplus grain."

One after another had settled in the valley, until now there was a prosperous colony. Jason Lee landed his party at the entrance to this settlement, whose farmhouses were scattered back to the foothills. Rude rail fences ran zigzag around the meadows. Wild roses nodded in the corners and bloomed in the wheat. The Canadians greeted the missionary with friendly welcome, opened their doors, offered their horses. He talked with them in their French *patois*, and could tell as many stories as they of logging on the Ottawa. They were nearly all Catholics. Jason Lee was a Protestant. Nevertheless, they attended his preaching gladly, though sometimes there might be a longing for the showier Catholic forms, and chants, and candles of childhood.

Terra-cotta colored children, some darker, some fair and almost white, dressed in blue and scarlet, were sit-

ting on the stiles and swinging on the lower halves of
the wide barn doors. The dogs slept in the sun, the
cocks crew, and the pigeons cooed in the airy lofts.
The barns themselves, four times as large as the houses,
were still bursting with last year's harvest. The children, true little Frenchmen, left their play to courtesy
to Jason Lee and to watch the wonderful white women.
Their mothers, in calico dresses and leggings and moccasins, with red kerchiefs crossed on their breasts,
nodded and smiled as the strangers passed. These
women, whose mothers had packed teepees and dug
camas all their lives, women who had passed their
infancy strapped on a baby-board, now scrubbed their
little cabins and managed the garden and dairy as well
as any thrifty frau among the Germans. For their
Canadian husbands they deemed no sacrifice too
great, for their children they filled the last measure of
devotion.

" Indeed," Jason Lee used to say, " these happy-go-
lucky voyageurs are fortunate in finding such capable
women to make them homes," and the Canadians themselves would have told you they were worth " half a
dozen civilized wives."

Exchanging the canoe for the saddle, the mission
party galloped across French Prairie knee-deep in
flowers. The larks flew up and sung.

It was not a princely mansion, that humble log mission twenty by thirty, with chimney of sticks and clay.
Jason Lee had swung the broadaxe that hewed the
logs; Daniel Lee had calked the crevices with moss.
There were Indian mats on the hewn-fir floors, home-
made stools and tables. The hearth was of baked clay
and ashes, the batten doors hung on leather hinges and
clicked with wooden latches. Four small windows let

in the light through squares of dried deerskin set in sashes carved by the jack-knife of Jason Lee. Just now every door and window framed a group of copper faces, every eye intent on the flowing garb and satin cheeks of the strange, fair white women.

Jason Lee never talked unless he had something to say. He simply waved his hand, bade them welcome to the humble edifice that marked the beginning of the capital of Oregon and Willamette University.

The rough table, with its battered tin plates and knives and forks, had venison from the hills, bread from their own wheat crushed in the cast-iron corn-cracker. The cattle driven over the plains furnished butter and cheese and cream; glossy cups of leaves held the strawberries that reddened on every knoll.

In front of the mission a beautiful fir grove, historic now, became the Sabbath temple. Thither repaired the missionaries, with their pupils, neatly dressed in English costume. Thither came the Canadians, with their native wives and half-caste children, all in holiday garb, and gathering in the background came the dark Willamettes, picturesque, statuesque, almost classic, with their slender bows and belts of *haiqua*. The hymn of worship rang through the forest aisles. Under the umbrageous firs all knelt in prayer. The July zephyr fanned the drooping cheek and downcast lid. Every Indian knelt in imitation of the white men. When Jason Lee arose every eye was fixed on his flushed face and speaking glance. He spoke briefly, then, to the astonishment of all, walked hurriedly to his congregation, took Miss Pitman by the hand, and led her to the front. Daniel Lee came forward, and there, under the fragrant firs, pronounced the solemn service of the first Anglo-Saxon marriage on the Pacific Coast. There was a

wedding trip up the valley and across the coast range
to the sea; there were strolls along the level beach,
clam-bakes, and surf-baths, a fashion that Oregon lovers
have followed ever since. At harvest Jason Lee was
back, wielding the cradle among the wheat, and his
comrades found that here, as on the river, the bony
Puritan outraced them all.

IV

DR. McLOUGHLIN GOES TO ENGLAND

1838

DR. McLOUGHLIN took pride in his handsome Scotch son-in-law, William Glen Rae. When the doctor found he must be going to England, he chose Rae, the head clerk, to accompany him as far as Fort Colvile on the Upper Columbia. Every year the Pacific accounts were consolidated at Fort Colvile, to be sent across the mountains. Who could do that so well as the head clerk?

Everybody was out with farewells when the doctor left that March morning in 1838. Along the Columbia the Indians watched the progress of the White-Headed Eagle and wondered if Douglas were as brave a chief. They knew that those swift canoes carried letters and papers. Once they stole them. Now they would as soon think of stealing the snows off Mt. Hood. "Cannot the White Eagle throw his medicine beyond the Dalles?" they said. Five days was quick time to Walla Walla in March, but then, who could move camp with McLoughlin? Charlefoux was at the bow. Over and over again Charlefoux had travelled that route, the safest guide if not the boldest. Every summer he conducted the yearly express to Fort Garry on Lake Winnepeg, and there turned back with the new recruits from Canada.

"I will visit you when I pass," had been McLoughlin's message to Dr. Whitman, with a gift of apples, rare as gold dollars on the Columbia.

Then a second courier brought word to the Whitman door: "I cannot stop. Meet me at Walla Walla. We are belated."

Dr. Whitman rode over to Fort Walla Walla, and by the hand of the flying chief sent word to the States of the birth of a little daughter, the first white child born in Oregon.

Next to Vancouver, Fort Colvile was the great Hudson's Bay fort on the Columbia. Behind that palisade, two square towers with portholes guarded the stores of furs. Down in the Colvile valley the traders had a mill. Seventy miles over hill and dale the Spokane Indians came to grind their wheat.

On a three-legged stool in the old log fort Rae added, subtracted, divided, outfit for this post, outfit for that, furs from this, furs from that, balance — a king's ransom, to be divided in that Hudson's Bay house across the sea. Oregon's wealth, three million a year, all went to England. Down by the river, "rat-tat-tat" the hammers flew. Skilled Canadians were building canoes for the spring brigade. Ten days behind the doctor, Tom McKay's Shoshonie brigade set out for its summer hunt. And with it came Jason Lee.

The mission on the Willamette had become crowded. Sons and daughters of the Canadian farmers were eager for books. Distant tribes sent for teachers.

"We must extend the work," said the missionaries. "Some one must visit the States and lay this matter before the churches. We must set up branch stations all over this country." Day and night the question was discussed. All eyes turned to Jason Lee.

"You only can represent us," said David Leslie. "In greater measure than any of us, you have the tongue, the fire, the courage, and the Lord's anointing."

There seemed a struggle in the leader's mind. If possible, Jason Lee had grown even more gentle of late. In his eyes strange beauty had come upon his young wife; her presence was a constant benediction. The Canadians felt new power in his speech, and tears rolled down their furrowed cheeks at his exhortations to a nobler life. In the tents of the Indians he came and went as a brother.

But now, with hesitation quite new in the line of his work, Jason Lee said, "Brethren, I do not see how I can go. It is a long, long journey, the winter and summer of two years. Indeed, I cannot go."

"It is your duty," the brethren said. "And only by starting with the traders in March can you hope to reach St. Louis before the frosts of autumn."

Jason Lee groaned in spirit. "How can I leave you?" he whispered to his bride.

"If it is your duty to go, go," the noble girl replied. "I did not marry you to hinder, but to help you."

With the heavenly countersign, "The Lord watch between me and thee, while we are absent one from another," she bade him farewell. The missionary's bride, like the women of Sparta, sent her hero forth to return "with his shield or upon it."

With nobler sacrifice than ever entered the dreams of ancient ascetic, Jason Lee trod love and ease beneath his feet. In his heart he bore his bride; next his heart there lay a memorial to Congress asking for a United States government for Oregon.

At Fort Walla Walla, one hundred horses were packed with Indian goods for the interior. How easily the Indians might swoop down and capture the caravan! But they will not — the trader is the Indian's best friend, on the lookout, however, with a loaded gun. The brigade wound up the old trail to Whitman's. In two years that had become a favorite halting spot for Tom McKay.

Jason Lee and Tom McKay found the mission gardens green on the Walla Walla. Here and there irrigating ditches intersected the squares, and ran back into the Indian fields, where, in the absence of almost every necessary tool, the Indians had plantations of two and three acres in wheat, peas, corn, and potatoes, An orchard of seedling apple sprouts nodded its tender twigs, and a grist-mill hummed across the river.

The heads of the two missions had a long conference, and Jason Lee passed on to visit Spalding in the upper country. The horse he rode was a gift from his pupil Elijah, son of the great Walla Walla, Pio-pio-mox-mox,

"What are you going to do with William?" inquired Dr. Whitman, patting the dark locks of McKay's little son, the " Billy-boy" of Fort Vancouver.

"I am sending him to Scotland to study medicine He starts to-morrow to join Dr. McLoughlin at Colvile."

"Thomas, why don't you educate the boy in America? Oregon is Uncle Sam's territory, and it won't be long before he takes possession. Take my advice, Thomas. Give the boy a Yankee education, make an American of him."

"I used to think of sending him to John Jacob Astor," said McKay, recalling the time when he himself, a lad of Billy's age, accompanied his father in a birch canoe down the Hudson to join the Astor expedition to the Columbia. "But I have no money. All

my income is in London, in the hands of the Hudson's
Bay Company."

Dr. Whitman's answer was quick. "Do I not trade
with your company at Fort Vancouver? Does not my
money come from the American Board in Boston?
Send the boy to New York, where I studied. I will
pay his bills, and you can pay mine here in Oregon."

The accounts at Fort Colvile were completed. The
annual ship from London arrived at Fort Vancouver,
and a boat with special mail hastened up the Columbia
to hand McLoughlin the latest advices before he left for
England via Canada.

"Dr. McLoughlin sends word for Billy to join him
with the mail express," said Rae, homeward bound,
touching at Walla Walla. But already Billy was with
Jason Lee on the trail over the Blue Mountains bound
for the States.

Rat-tat-tat, the canoes were ready, ten, twelve of
them, and the river was booming. The snows were
melting on the mountains, soon the upper country
would be flooded. Through the timber, over old Indian
trails, the dog-sleds flew, bringing in furs from Kootenai
and Cœur d'Alêne. The patient, exemplary Flatheads
were on hand with buffalo-meat and pemmican for the
up-going brigade, and with buffalo-tongues, buffalo-
tallow and rawhide cords, buffalo-skins, and buffalo-hair
for the down brigade to Fort Vancouver. A touch of
the hand at these nerve centres, a greeting and farewell,
and the traders were scattered by thousands of miles.
One day salutes, bustle, activity; the next, the trader
strolled round his lonely post, his solitary guest the
silent Indian.

April, May, June came. A messenger panted up to
the gates of Fort Vancouver. "Is there any way to get

word to Jason Lee?   His wife and infant son are lying dead at the mission."

Tears leaped to the eyes of Douglas.   The calm, steady, apparently icy Douglas had a heart like a thermal spring, that responded to the touch of sorrow. "I will despatch a messenger," he said.

A solitary boat set out with the details of that saddest tragedy that comes to human life.   The grief-stricken members of the mission consigned to the tomb the bride of Jason Lee.   Under the fragrant firs where her bridal was, the mother was laid, with her babe on her bosom.

"I will send it on to Fort Hall," said Chief Factor Pambrun, when the despatch was laid in his hand at Walla Walla.   At Fort Hall Ermatinger delegated Richardson, a famous American trapper, to overtake Lee on the plains.   July, August, September — the trapper chased an ever-receding shadow.

Far up on the Platte Jason Lee was dreaming of his wife.   By the camp-fire at night he wrote in his journal the story of their courtship, — but he heard no hoof-beats in the rear.   It was late September, at the Shawnee mission on the Kansas River, when a sun-burnt horseman reached the palisade.   " Is Rev. Jason Lee here? "

" Yes," from the gatekeeper.

" I have a message."

Already Jason Lee was at the gate.   He saw not the people around, he saw not Billy McKay looking up into his anxious face — he saw only a horseman with a black-sealed packet.   He took it, entered his room, and shut the door.   God alone heard the cry and saw the heart-break in that rude room at the Shawnee mission on the Kansas River.

Somewhere back in the mountains, Jason Lee had passed a train of trappers. With them rode Captain John A. Sutter, on his way to Oregon. The gay Swiss adventurer, with his broken English and a romance behind him like a fairy tale, captured the hearts on the Columbia. His contagious laugh made Fort Vancouver ring with merriment. The courtly manners of the fortune-hunter, his kind heart and unaffected affability, won admiration, respect, and love. Without a cent, without a prospect, with an avalanche of debt behind him, the very magnetism of his social nature bound friends like cords of silver.

Every one at Fort Vancouver was ready to swear by Captain Sutter. The conservative Douglas gave him letters of introduction to the merchants of Honolulu, to the fur princes of Sitka, to the Spanish governor of California. Sutter borrowed money, credit, clothes. With a free passage on the Hudson's Bay barque "Columbia" he sailed for the Sandwich Islands. Like the prince whose feet with fairy shoes were shod, Sutter danced across the continent, danced into the favor of the great English fur company, danced into the arms of the merchants of Honolulu. Here, all on credit, he purchased cannon, provisions, implements for his proposed rancho in California. Then, on the English brig "Clementine," the gay captain ran up to Sitka, danced with a Russian princess, and figured as the lion of half a hundred banquets. Back at the Islands, still on credit, he chartered two schooners and sailed to California. Governor Alvarado, won by his pleasing manners, energy, and recommendations, granted the adventurer a princely tract on the Sacramento, although contrary to law and the latest orders from Mexico.

"Take a rancho near Monterey," said the fascinated Alvarado.

The shrewd captain knew his own interests too well —the farther away from Spanish interference the better.

"He will hold the American invaders in check," said Alvarado to himself.

"I can ally the Americans with myself," said the sagacious Captain Sutter.

Unlimited wealth seemed at his command. Up the Sacramento his heavy-laden schooners ploughed their way through the virgin waters. At the mouth of the Rio de los Americanos Sutter's adobe fort was built, on the general plan of Fort Vancouver. Forty Indians in uniform made up the garrison. Two Indian sentinels paced ever before the gate. Twelve cannon were mounted on the bastions, the gates were defended by heavy artillery through portholes pierced in the walls. Out of deer-fat, beaver, and wild grape brandy the captain expected to make a fortune. He bought stock and ploughed fields for wheat, and in that sleepy lotus-land of Spain the energetic captain bade fair to accomplish all that he desired.

When André Charlefoux guided back his boat brigade in autumn two Catholic priests came from Canada.

"Drive away those naked Indians," cried the shocked Blanchet at the Dalles. "Drive away those Indians, Charlefoux."

The laughing guidesman tossed his hair.

"Holy father, you come to civilize Indian. Oregon Indian have no clothe. If you no want to see him that way you better turn back home."

But Blanchet stayed and became a famous bishop of the Northwest.

V

THE LONDON COUNCIL

1838

MANY motives had brought about the journey to London. In the first place, Dr. McLoughlin was entitled to a leave of absence. Factors, chief factors, and traders from the St. Lawrence to the Athabasca had taken their turns at a glimpse of the old home in Scotland, or at the familiar hedgerows of some English village. Dr. McLoughlin had never seen the time when he could leave his ultramontane kingdom. From the day he decided to move his headquarters from the restricted grounds at old Astoria to the green, open swell on the north bank of the Columbia, in 1824, scores of hands had been at work building shops, stockades, storehouses, grubbing up trees, and subduing the soil. Then came a reason, and go he must.

Factors in the fur country had said farming was incompatible with the fur trade. From the days of Prince Rupert till that of the Red River settlement every bit of bread had come from England. "Can you raise wheat on the Columbia?" asked the London Directory.

"Oh, no," answered an old Northwester. "It's a bad and barren land. Supplies must come across the mountains, or be shipped around Cape Horn."

In the north-country, trappers and traders fed, like the Chippewayans, on buffalo, whitefish, and moose. Pemmican hung in rawhide bags around the trading posts.

All that North was a land of fat and pemmican, — pemmican " straight " (uncooked), and pemmican fried, pemmican flakes, pemmican soup, and pemmican spiced with berries, — inviting the hungry trader to " cut and come again." On the Columbia it was salmon, fresh salmon, dried salmon, salt salmon.

" ' The country must find provisions,' was Napoleon's motto; let it be ours," said Dr. McLoughlin.

He set his men to ploughing gardens. Out of the virgin mould there leaped such prodigies of grain and vegetables, such an abandon of peas and turnips and all good things, that even five hundred inmates of the fort could not consume it all. Now the first orchard blossomed on the coast, the handful of wheat had become a harvest that filled the bursting granaries, and a few cattle brought up on the schooner " Cadboro' " from California had multiplied into herds that covered the hillsides.

The question of export came up. The doctor's scheme widened.

" Why may not I supply those Russians at Sitka that send half round the world for butter, beef, and flour? "

But there was trouble with the Sitkans. A long strip of Alaska ran down the northwest coast and cut off the Hudson's Bay lands from the sea. One day Peter Skeen Ogden attempted to pass through the Russian shore-strip.

" Boom! " went the Russian gunboats that guarded the Stikine.

" I shall enter the river. I have a right to it," said the Hudson's Bay trader.

" Then I must fire upon you," came Baron Wrangell's answer.

Ogden stormed back to Fort Vancouver, and complaint was sent to England. The London papers were full of "the outrage upon our traders in those distant seas."

Four years Lord Palmerston and Count Nesselrode had been diplomating over the privileges of that shore-strip. Four years Dr. McLoughlin had been piling up supplies that the Russians would have been glad to purchase. "Let us go to Europe and settle it," wrote the governor on the Columbia to the governor at Sitka.

To some who did not understand the doctor's states-manship, — and he kept his secrets to himself and Douglas, — there were other reasons for that long and tedious trip to London.

Some said that Sir George Simpson had complained that Dr. McLoughlin favored the American missionaries. Sir George Simpson, so the Hudson's Bay gossips said, had prepared the London Board to give the doctor a "wigging" for the high hand he held on the Colum-bia; but when that stately form darkened the doors in Fenchurch Street the king of the Columbia was weighed at his true value, — a veritable monarch come out of the West.

It was a stately occasion when the delegates of the Russian American Fur Company of St. Petersburg met the delegates of the Hudson's Bay Company in a Lon-don council and discussed matters usually relegated to the cabinets of kings. The difficulty was adjusted. "And now," said McLoughlin, "we want to lease that ten-league strip of Russian seaboard."

Lord Palmerston and Parliament wondered if the Hudson's Bay Company wanted the earth. Already it controlled an extent of territory greater than all Europe, — of what value could be a barren bit of shore on that lonely northwest coast? Dr. McLoughlin knew its value better than the Russian Directory, better than the London Board, certainly better than the English statesmen, who then regarded those distant realms as vaguely as the phantom deserts in the moon. He knew those rocky islets were rich in priceless sea-furs. For 10,000 land-otter a year the strip was leased, and further reciprocity contracted in furs and flour.

Other great schemes were incubated during that London visit: the Puget's Sound Agricultural Company, to hold that inland sea for England, a plan for posts in California just ready to drop from decaying Spanish rule, and an out-reach to the Hawaiian Islands. In fact, if those American missionaries had stayed over the mountains, England held in her hand the key to commercial empire on the Pacific.

But the English visit was not all diplomacy. At Addiscombe, the East India training-school, a happy surprise awaited Dr. McLoughlin. His son David, the lean, sickly lad of five years ago, appeared in the regimentals of a British officer commissioned to the East Indies. The scarlet coat, bright buttons, and epaulets set off a form as commanding as his own. The Indian tint in his cheek gave bronze enough for beauty, no more.

With pride the doctor looked upon his son. From the cradle he had set his heart upon David, his heir. For him he had planned education, promotion; for him he had built an estate to hand down the name of McLoughlin.

"I cannot spare you, David," said the father, fondly. "I need you on the Columbia. I am getting old. It may be, I would pass the reins of power to you."

The youth flamed an answer back:

"What prospect have I in the service of Hudson's Bay? Does not Sir George bring over his favorites by shiploads from Scotland? Shall I become a packer, a trapper, a leader of brigades? I have no future there. Let me go to Afghanistan."

"Tut, tut, tut, David; I know your prospects better than you do. Great schemes are afoot. Come, pack up."

The strong will of the father prevailed. Purchasing his son's retirement from the army, the two bade good-bye to Dr. McLoughlin's only brother, Dr. David McLoughlin, who had come over from Paris to see them off. The doctors were much alike — Dr. David McLoughlin was younger and less commanding. He had a great name in Paris — a leading physician. Five years ago he had received this Indian-tinted namesake from the Columbia and had given him the best that Paris afforded. Now that nephew had become a man of the world, polished and courtly. When he doffed his regimentals, he donned the ruffled linen and the broadcloth of Parisian fashion, and sailed with his father back across the Atlantic to Montreal.

Since the old French days when the governors-general sat in Indian council in their elbow chairs on the banks of the St. Lawrence, Montreal had been the capital of Canadian fur trade. Hither, now, once a year, Sir George Simpson, Governor of Rupert's Land, came from his London home to superintend the company's affairs in North America.

"Trade with Russia is a hare-brained scheme," had been Sir George's earliest thought, but on McLoughlin's arrival a council was held at Montreal. In it spoke the commercial life of the Dominion. The Hudson's Bay Company and its silent partner, the beaver, practically ruled in Canada. No rival, no competitor dared question their authority. Puget Sound, Alaska, California, Hawaiï were discussed. The merchants of Montreal had not realized there was so great an outlook from that distant land of exile.

"What are you going to do with your Emperor of the West?" asked a chief factor after the doctor's boats with reinforcements for new posts had passed up the Ottawa on their way back to Fort Vancouver.

"Give him free rein," answered the sagacious Sir George.

VI

IT was time for the fall brigade and the Montreal express. They usually came down the Columbia together. Every year the express left Montreal in May. With a sweep and a swing and flying paddles they shot up the Canadian rivers and through the Great Lakes. In July they were at Red River. Through the torrid summer they toiled along the great Saskatchewan. Before the autumn snows came on the voyageurs left their boats and crossed the Rocky Mountains, generations before a Canadian Pacific was dreamed of. There on the western slope at the Boat Encampment stood a deserted hunting-lodge. Twice a year the big fireplace roared and the kettle sung. Tearing off their moccasins stained with blood in the awful solitudes of the mountain pass, the light-hearted voyageurs prepared to re-embark. Leathern bags of flour and pemmican, sugar and tea, were unearthed from a *cache*, hidden canoes were drawn out of the cedar brush, and, launching on the little stream, the express soon entered the head waters of the great Columbia.

Down, down they glided, singing as they went the songs of Old Canada, brought generations ago from the land of the fleur-de-lis. Down, down they glided, past peaks of snow and tangled woody heights, past Fort Colvile on her terrace, past park-like stretches of grove and lake and meadow, past the picketed square of the flat and sandy rock at Okanogan, through miles and miles of Indian empire to Fort Walla Walla at the great westward bend of the Columbia. Here they met the Shoshonie brigade that had come overland on horses from Fort Hall, and all together swept in state down the Columbia to Fort Vancouver.

Vancouver? It was the emporium of the fur-trade on the Columbia, ninety miles from the sea, a fort that, like the castles of mediæval Europe, was at once a defence in time of danger, an oasis of civilization amid barbarism, and a capital from whence its master held baronial sway. Here for a quarter of a Dr. John McLoughlin ruled with the sceptre of a czar the vast territory from Alaska to California from the Rocky Mountains to the ocean. Un- thousands of Indians obeyed his behests, feared his displeasure. On the Upper Columbia the knightly Cayuses laid tribute at his feet, the brave and stately Wallas, the chivalrous Okanogans, the friendly and hospitable Nez Percés, the faithful Flatheads, and loyal Spokanes. Back in the mountain fastnesses the robber Klickitats acknowledged him their chief, along the sandy Dalles the treacherous Wascopams al- lowed his boats to pass in peace. Below the cascades the industrious Molallas, the lazy Callapooias, the lying , the fishermen Chinooks, and their cousins the Clatsops all bent the knee to the White-Headed Eagle that reigned at Vancouver. On all the waters he sent his Canadian voyageurs, through all the woods he despatched his trappers and traders, in and out of the fringing northwest islands to Sitka itself his schoon- ers plied, down through the San Joaquin and Tulare's reedy valley his hunters set their traps, far over into the Shoshonie country, on Salt Lake's borders, and on the Yellowstone his brigades pitched their tents, bringing home rich caravans of skins and mantles.

And who was this king of the Columbia in whose will lay decrees of life and death, at whose bidding the bloodthirsty savage laid aside the tomahawk and entered upon the peaceful pursuits of the hunt? It was a chief factor of the Hudson's Bay Company who had been building on the Pacific a fur-trader's empire. Not for nineteen years had John McLoughlin crossed the ocean to set foot in that old Hudson's Bay house in Fenchurch Street, London; not since the wedding of the rival fur companies in 1820, when he stood up for Canadian enterprise.

That wedding of the fur companies is historic. When the French and English were fighting at Waterloo, two rival fur companies were fighting in North America, — the Hudson's Bay and the Northwest. When the smoke of battle over there cleared away, the British Parliament saw the smoke of battle over here and called a halt: " Here, you rivals! We cannot let you stain the plains of North America with British blood. If you must fight, turn your arms against the Americans or the Indians, — anybody but each other. We cannot afford to lose the few representatives we have over there and abandon the country altogether. Be good children, make up, and King George will give you a wedding present."

So the hoary old Hudson's Bay Company that had slumbered for a century proposed to the young Northwest Company of Montreal, and both sent their best men to London to discuss the marriage dowry. It was plainly a wedding of capital and labor. The Canadian company had nothing but her hands, her courage, and her magnificent exploration. The London bridegroom had the money-bags of nobles and control of the Bank of England. In the midst of the nuptial settlement a young Canadian doctor had startled them all with the boldest speech that had ever rung in those conservative warerooms. He was a study, that courageous young doctor of locks prematurely white and flashing eye, that free-born spirit that had breathed in liberty on the banks of the St. Lawrence.

"My Lords and Gentlemen, I plead for better terms! Since the days of Prince Rupert this monster monopoly has sat supinely on the banks of Hudson's Bay and shut out Canada from her birthright. Did we seek extended settlement? It would drive away their game. Did we attempt to trade in furs? They claimed the only right. Westward, beyond the basin of Hudson's Bay there lay an open field. To this the merchants of Montreal sent out their traders. We scoured the forests and threaded the streams. We sought new tribes and won their friendship. We explored the Saskatchewan and the Athabasca. Our men it was that traced the Mackenzie and planted the flag on the polar Ocean, and turning back found a way across the mountains to the Pacific itself. While the Hudson's Bay Company waited we ran. We built up posts in remotest wilds, we discovered new waterways, we established trade. When the profits began to flow in, the Hudson's Bay Company began to rub its sleepy eyes and claim the fruits of our toil. They claimed our trading fields and shot our traders. To obstruct our work they threw the Red River settlement across our path, cutting communication with Montreal and blockading our supplies. They prohibited their settlers from selling provisions and tried to starve us out. They used their

money to buy over our traders, and when bribes would
not suffice they shot us in the forest. Is this the condition of British subjects? No wonder we fought for our
rights. And now you ask us to 'share equally' the
profits of the trade. I do not object to the union, —
God knows I regretted the war, — but ought we to give
an equal share of those profits they never raised a
finger to obtain, — nay, did all they could to discourage and destroy? What reward have we for those
years of toil and trial if we hand over the moiety
now to a rival? It is not right, it is not just, and in
behalf of the Northwest Company I contend for better
terms."

So spoke young McLoughlin, in that London ware-
room eighty years ago. The very clerks, amazed,
stopped scratching with their quill pens in the dim can-
dle-light to listen. They watched him with breathless
interest, — the Canadian merchants proud of their cham-
pion, the British baronets and stockholders wondering
if of such stuff was made the rebels of the American
Revolution. But he was not yet done.

"Gentlemen, if I contend for better terms for ourselves, what shall I say for our voyageurs, yours as well
as ours, who upon a pittance of seventeen pounds a
year must man our boats and pack our furs? Wading
in icy waters, cordelling canoes in rocky torrents, trans-
forming themselves into beasts of burden at every portage, working eighteen hours out of the twenty-four, cut
off from all refinements of social and civilized life, con-
demned to exile and rapidly sinking to the level of
savages, — all this that the inordinate profits of their
muscles and sinews may pour wealth into the coffers of
this trade. Gentlemen, let us consider the hardships of
our employés' lives and realize that seventeen pounds

a year is beggarly recompense for service such as theirs."

It was a new thing for a factor in the fur company to utter a sentiment like that. But, alas! the doctor was too direct for a diplomat. Even the merchants of Montreal were willing to profit by the serfdom of those French-Canadian voyageurs and thought their philanthropic favorite had gone too far. One vote, one voice, could not bring better terms, but one thing the doctor could and did do. John McLoughlin never set his name to the articles of agreement.

That speech was not forgotten. The Board admired and yet they feared him. He was the most popular and energetic of all the Northwest leaders. He must be quieted, he must be honored, and more than all, the great Northwester must have room for executive sway. He must rule in Canada, or as far as possible from Canada — no intermediate ground would do.

About that time the American Congress had agreed with Parliament upon a joint occupancy of a certain wilderness called Oregon. The very place! a sort of Siberia, far off! Dr. John McLoughlin was delegated with absolute power to the Columbia Department. He knew it was a banishment, but he knew, too, that he would be king in that realm beyond the mountains.

All that was long ago. Now, after nineteen years, Dr. McLoughlin has been to London on business connected with the Pacific. Every year his ships have brought their furs, every year his reports have come in, until from nothing his returns exceed those of any other post in the Hudson's Bay dominion. He is on his way home now. The arrival of his boats may be calculated almost to the hour, for Dr. McLoughlin is nothing if not punctual.

VII

McLOUGHLIN'S EARLY HISTORY

1839

UPON the porch of the governor's residence, one warm October day, there sat two women. Every morning those women were there, from the first bright days of May until the Oregon winter began with the rains of November. Always needle in hand, they were embroidering the caps and scarfs and smoking-bags that were the chief delight of the voyageur's heart.

Madame McLoughlin, the elder, had a marvellous needle; one that might have wrought tapestries in the olden time, so fine and soft and even was her work. And yet, Madame's mother had been a wild little princess on the plains of the North, wooed long and long ago by a Hudson's Bay trader. Madame herself had a touch of copper, that deepened with the years. But her daughter, Eloise McLoughlin, had the creamy tint of a Spanish donna. She had her mother's eyes, and her mother's shining satin hair; but the form and features were those of the Hudson's Bay governor, — imperial, commanding, fair.

Barely twenty-one, tall, graceful, no wonder the beautiful girl was a star in that land of dusky women; no wonder the clerks of the company competed for her hand, and hearts were rent when she made her choice. Indeed, how could it be otherwise in this remote corner of the world — where the governor's daughter queened it on the Columbia? Attired in London gowns, self-poised and sensible, Eloise McLoughlin was too much like her father to submit to the tame self-effacement of the traders' wives. Her mother's humility pained her. She would see her take her place as the *Grande Dame*, the Lady of Fort Vancouver. But Madame herself waived all right to such distinction. By common consent Eloise had become the Lady of that Pacific Coast. The finest horse on the Columbia was hers; a blond Cayuse with pinkish eyes and pinkish-yellow mane and tail, presented to the governor by the great chief of the Walla Wallas. And on state occasions Eloise McLoughlin came forth arrayed in waving plumes and glittering garments, and seated on that steed rode at her father's side, leading the brigade up the Willamette.

For very well her great father, Governor McLoughlin, understood the influence of pomp and color on the savage heart. The horse brigades were gay with brilliant housings; a multitude of tiny bells tinkled at saddle skirt and bridle-rein, bright dresses stiff with beads adorned the trappers' Indian wives, and at the head of this barbaric pageant often sat Eloise and the stately governor, with his long white locks blowing over the cloak of Hudson's Bay blue. As such cavalcades would wind up the valley in the October sun the whole little world turned out to gaze. You would hardly have supposed there were so many Indians in the country until you saw them trooping in to witness the autumn brigade to California. The silence, broken only by the heavy trampling of the fast-walking horses and the tintinnabulating bells; the succession of gleam and color left an impress upon the red man never to be forgotten, an impress of unmeasured wealth and splendor hidden behind those palisades at old Fort Vancouver.

Eloise herself enjoyed these state occasions as a
flower enjoys the sunshine. Ever at her father's side,
taught by him, trusted by him, his companion and con-
fidant, no wonder she repined at his long absence. The
page of Telemachus lay untouched, the page she so oft
had read at her father's knee; and, needle in hand, the
fair bride emulated her mother in patterns of silk upon
the pliant buckskin or the glossy broadcloth.

For Eloise McLoughlin was a bride; and the groom
(so old voyageurs tell me) was the handsomest man at
Fort Vancouver. Reserved, cordial, quiet, William Glen
Rae was at bottom a scholar and a thinker. Six years
had passed since he came from his ancestral home in
the Orkneys, from Edinburgh College honors. His
glance fell on the Lady of the Pacific Coast. The
course of a life was changed. No doubt it was a wise
provision on the governor's part that settled her marriage before his departure, to bind her heart with new
ties, to end the rivalries that grew more pronounced
from year to year. One young trader, who from the
time Eloise was a little girl had joked and sung and
danced to win her, was ready to fight on her wedding
day. But the governor took him aside.

" Wait a bit, Ermatinger, wait a bit. When I come
back I will bring you the fairest lily I can find in
Canada. Then you shall have a wedding, too." Ermatinger stormed. For any other offence the governor
would have shut him up in the butter-tub — as they
called the six-by-nine donjon where refractory engagés
were punished. As it was, Ermatinger betook himself
to Bachelors' Hall and was seen no more till he left with
Tom McKay's brigade for the Shoshonie, ten days
later. He had not even come back in the autumn.
But now it was said that surely he would come — to

meet the governor; for rumor had gone out that Frank Ermatinger had worked himself into an excitement waiting for his Canadian Lily.

So this morning in 1839 the mother and daughter were stitching, stitching; fitting the pink and purple beads into leaves and rosettes, and twining long vines of gray and green along silken sashes. The porch ran entirely across the front of Governor McLoughlin's residence. It had deep-seated windows and benches at the ends. Along fluted pillars a grapevine trailed and tangled; a vine cut from the mother-vine of all the mission grapes of California.

Suddenly Eloise spoke. "Mother, how can you stitch to-day? See, my silks are knotted and my roses spoiled." She tossed her work into the little Indian basket at her side. Unbraiding her hair she let it down, in a shining, shimmering cataract to the floor.

The Madame finished a leaf before she spoke. Then in a slow and gentle tone, "I haf the more patience, Louice. You are like the father, not quiet." French was the family language of the McLoughlin household. With each other the Hudson's Bay gentlemen spoke English; with their families and with the voyageurs, French; with the Indians, Chinook, a trade-tongue that grew up on the Columbia — a polyglot of Hawaiian-English-Spanish-French-Indian.

"Mr. Douglas says my father is like Napoleon. He can out-travel all others. He may surprise us," said Eloise, shaking the loosened waves around her like a camlet.

"That is what I am hoping. But so many ills happen in a lifetime," sighed the Madame. "When one husband haf gone away and never come back again, who can tell about another?" Eloise was sorry her mother referred to that old sorrow.

To one that noted such trifles the Madame's hair was growing whiter, as if a box of powder had been spilled since the governor went away. Quite snowy now, it floated over the back of her easy-chair. She always wore it so, loosely, like her mother and her grandmother before her. Her eyes kept wandering toward the snow on Mt. Hood. Her ears strained to catch the distant boat song; she started whenever the great gate opened and shut.

And who had Madame McLoughlin been before her marriage to the great doctor? Some old voyageurs could have told you that forty years ago the Madame had been the fairest girl in the Cumberland District of Manitoba. Her Scotch father sent her to school with the nuns at Quebec. As a child she heard rumors from the South; scattered fragments of the American Revolution when the Tories came flocking across the Canadian border. As a girl she met Alexander McKay, who had just returned with Alexander Mackenzie from that wonderful tour in which they, the first white men that ever crossed the continent, had scribbled with red ochre on Pacific rocks:

A. MACKENZIE

ARRIVED FROM CANADA BY LAND,

JULY, 1793.

Retracing their steps, Mackenzie went to England to be knighted Sir Alexander and crowned with fame. McKay remained and married Margaret. Two children came to their home at Sault Ste. Marie. A dozen, fourteen years went by. The boy became a sturdy lad, the girl a miss of twelve, while their Scotch father was collecting peltries from Michilimackinac to Detroit in those early days before recorded history began. One summer morning, as he had done every summer for fourteen years, Alexander McKay set out with his brigade of furs for Montreal. That was the last time Madame ever saw him.

For at Montreal McKay met John Jacob Astor. Astor was starting a Pacific fur company. He had come to Canada for men skilled in all the mysteries of the fur trade. McKay pleased Astor — was made a partner. He flew around Montreal engaging his men, and by the return boats to Sault Ste. Marie sent a good-bye to his wife, and a request to the commander of the northwest post to care for her " till his return." It was a sudden leave-taking, but not uncommon in the ups and downs of fur-trading life. Margaret sat day after day with her arms around her little girl — and wept. The boy Tom had gone with his father. How bravely he stood in the boat that summer day, waving good-byes to his mother! In fancy she saw their birchen barks fly down the Richelieu, up Lake Champlain, and down the glittering Hudson. She dreamed that they tossed in Astor's ship around Cape Horn. Then came the war of 1812. The Americans burnt Sault Ste. Marie, and the little house in which Margaret's wedded life had sped so happily. Those blue-coated soldiers waited for the annual fur brigade due from the North; watched and waited and went away. One afternoon a fleet of forty-seven boats, freighted with a million dollars' worth of furs, slid down the Sault Ste. Marie, and passed unharmed to Montreal. She was glad they had missed the furs, — those vandals that had burnt her house! But, to fill up the measure of disaster, word was brought by returning voyageurs that her husband had been killed by Indians on the treacherous northwest coast!

Then the fur companies went to fighting on the plains of Manitoba. How could Margaret know that Tom, safe and sound, in trying to get home to her had reached Red River just in time to take part in that battle fought a year and a day after Waterloo? Tom McKay saw Governor Semple march bravely out of Winnipeg with cocked hat and sash, pistols, and double-barrelled fowling-piece, and his Hudson's Bay men behind him. Tom rode up with the rival Northwesters. There was a rush and a crash, and the governor and some others were killed. Lord Selkirk hastened over from Scotland with a lot of Waterloo veterans, so Tom gat himself back to the Columbia without seeing his mother. But she? She was coming to him in unexpected fashion.

A young Canadian doctor commanded the fort—a strange anomaly. Polished and courtly, he had left the civilized world to bury himself in this uttermost wild. In October, 1784, John McLoughlin was born at Rivière du Loup on the banks of the St. Lawrence. While still a boy his father was drowned. The widowed mother took her children home to her father, Malcolm Fraser. There her boys, David and John, grew up in their grandfather's old stone mansion overlooking the St. Lawrence just where it widens to the sea. They played in those hills, rugged as Scotia's rock-ribbed Highlands. They caught a military presence from the soldier grandsire who had brought a Highland regiment with him to America to colonize these seignioral manors. Here Scottish books were read and Scottish tales retold. Here the bagpipe droned and the kilt hung in the old colonial closet. The brothers were sent over-seas, were pursuing medical studies, when Napoleon began to harry England. Dr. David McLoughlin went into the wars and followed the Iron Duke until Napoleon was caged at St. Helena. Dr. John said, "I can never fight Napoleon — I admire him too much." He returned to Canada.

The world lay before young Dr. McLoughlin. There was a pretty girl in Quebec. One day in spring he was walking with her, when they came to a plank on a muddy street. She was just ahead of the doctor when an insolent English officer, coming in the opposite direction, crowded her off the plank. In one instant that officer, gold lace, epaulets, and all, lay sprawling in the mire. There was danger in store for the young gallant, so he hied him to the Northwest, where his uncles the Frasers were great factors of Fraser's River. That was the whispered tale of how McLoughlin first entered the fur trade. Birth, talent, magnificent presence brought rapid promotion, — already he was in command of Sault Ste. Marie.

And the widow of his friend was in his keeping. As Pythias waited for Damon, so McLoughlin had waited for McKay. His tender heart was touched by the sorrows of one so fair. Her well-bred ways whispered of home. No white woman could go into the Indian country, but Margaret could go because she had Indian blood.

Dr. McLoughlin married the widow Margaret McKay. There was no priest at Sault Ste. Marie, that lonely trading outpost eighty years ago. A brother chief factor said the service. That was all; enough for a loyal heart like John McLoughlin's.

It was not an unusual matter. From the days when King Charles had granted a royal charter to his "well beloved cousin," Prince Rupert, the gentlemen "ad venturers of England trading into Hudson's Bay" had married the daughters of chiefs, — effecting state alliances to facilitate peace, good-will, and commerce. From these had sprung the type to which Margaret belonged, — fair, dark-eyed women, combining the manners and mind of the whites with the daring and pride of the Indian. Such had been Madame McLoughlin's early history.

"How can I know that your father not stiff at the bottom of Lake Superior?" continued the Madame to-day, half to Eloise and half to herself. "He capsize there once, and all but him were lost. Oh, that lake is cold! it quickly numb and drag the swimmer down! I saw them when they brought him through the fort gate like dead man. He had beautiful golden hair, the Indian call it sunshine; but after that it turn white — white as snow. Before he was thirty, Louice, men call your father old."

That incident was when Chief Factor Mackenzie was lost and McLoughlin lived to rule Fort William. Eloise had heard talk of the fogs and storms and flurries of the great Canadian sea; she had heard talk of life at Fort William, the metropolitan post of the Northwest Company on Lake Superior, where the merchants of Montreal used to come in summer like kings on a royal progress. She was a baby then. She could barely remember the journey to the Columbia; one long picnic it was to Eloise and to David her brother, who laughed and crowed and kicked his pink heels in his birch-canoe cradle. He, too, was coming home now with his father; coming from five years' study in Paris and London.

"A penny for your thoughts, Eloise!"

It was the cheery voice of her husband, William Glen Rae, who had stolen up the steps unobserved to the spot where Eloise sat with her unbound hair still rippling on the floor.

" I was thinking," she said, putting her hands in his, — " I was thinking what a family reunion 't will be when the express comes in! We must celebrate this year with a real Canadian Christmas!"

" Yes," answered Rae, the shadow of a cloud flitting over his brow, — "yes, for no one can tell where you and I may be a year from now."

It was the governor's joke when he left: " Wait till I get home, Eloise. Then you and Rae shall have a wedding journey."

Rae looked for promotion, but whether to some wild new Caledonian post on the Fraser, to the sage desert on the Snake, or up the Columbia, he could not guess. For six years, now, he had been head book-keeper at Fort Vancouver. Many a document had Rae filed away in the brick archives of the block counting-house. To take up a new rôle, to control men and manage Indians, might prove less congenial.

The brass bell on its tripod in the centre of the square rang for dinner. The Canadians in the field heard it, and turned out their oxen. The Iroquois choppers heard it, and rested their axes. The clerks heard it, and hurried across the court to brush their coats in Bachelors' Hall. The fur-beaters heard it, and went to their cabins outside the gate. Madame heard it, and disappeared through the door to her own apartments. Unassertive, shy, it was the custom of the traders' wives to live secluded. Visitors at Fort Vancouver saw little of the resident women. Custom forbade their presence at the semi-military table in the

great hall. But children playing about the court attested
the presence of mothers.

"It is worthy of notice," writes an old chronicler,
"how little of the Indian complexion is seen in these
traders' children. Generally they have fair skin, often
flaxen hair, and blue eyes."

Stealing a kiss from the cheek of his bride as she
flew away after her mother, William Rae turned and
watched the other gentlemen of the fort coming up
the semicircular flight of steps to dinner.

Most of them are well known to-day in Oregon story.
There was James Douglas, — Black Douglas they called
him, a lineal descendant of that Douglas who in days
of old was the chief support of the Scottish throne —
tall, dark, commanding, and, next to McLoughlin, the
ruling spirit on the Columbia. James Douglas had left
the storied hills of Lanark as a boy of sixteen to seek
his fortune with the fur-traders of Canada. He crossed
Lake Superior and came to Fort William in the reign
of McLoughlin. Fort William was then in its splendor,
a great interior mart, and chief seat of the growing
Northwest Company. Douglas was there when the rec-
onciliation took place between the rival fur companies.
With joy he watched the late snorting Highlanders, who
had cut and carved and shot and imprisoned each
other, shaking hands under the same flag and setting
out for the uttermost forts in the same canoe. Fifteen years younger than Dr. McLoughlin, his attach-
ment was that of a son or younger brother. Where
McLoughlin went, Douglas went. When McLoughlin
was sent to the Columbia he requested the company
of his young favorite, then a lad of nineteen. Accord-
ingly young Douglas crossed the Rockies and temporarily served at Fort St. James beyond the Fraser.

At Fort St. James, Chief Factor James Connolly, a jolly Irish gentleman, held sway, and dealt out beads and blankets to the Shushwaps for their beaver skins and otter. Chief Factor Connolly had a daughter, who is known in the annals of British Columbia as Lady Douglas. She was not "Lady Douglas" then. A shy, sweet, lovable girl, modest as the wood violet and as fair, it is not strange that Douglas loved Nelia Connolly. It would have been stranger if he had not. In addition to personal beauty the blood of heroes ran in her veins. Old chronicles are full of romance of this pair. Once a renegade Blackfoot murdered a Canadian and escaped. A smoke-dried, skinny old squaw whispered through the gate in Douglas' ear: "He haf come again. He hides in yonder camp." Arming himself, young Douglas walked fearlessly into the Indian camp and shot the renegade. Looking neither to the right nor the left, he coolly walked back to Fort St. James. The daring act awed the astonished Shushwaps — for weeks they were silent, it seemed forgotten. But when Chief Factor Connolly went down the Columbia with a brigade of furs, the mindful Shushwaps roused themselves. "We must have pay," they said, "pay, pay, pay for the dead man." Crowding in at the fort gate one day, two hundred blackened warriors surprised and seized the Douglas and bound him hand and foot.

Nelia Connolly in her little boudoir heard a sound of confusion. The girl of sixteen ran out — she saw every man of the fort tied. A burly fellow was flourishing a knife above the head of Douglas. At a glance she read her lover's peril. Darting upon the Indian she snatched the weapon. Turning to the chief the brave girl cried: —

"What, you a friend of the whites and say not a word in their behalf at such a time as this? Speak! You know the murderer deserved to die. According to your own laws the deed was just! It is blood for blood. The white men are not dogs. They love their kindred as well as you! Why should they not avenge their murder?" Awed by the *skookum tum-tum* (strong heart) of the trader's daughter the Indians fled from the room. As the last blanket flopped through the gate the old chief standing in the door called after them in derisive tone: "You braves! Woman make you run! Go home. Hide in leedle holes!"

Young Douglas married the girl. Chief Factor Connolly read the ritual and gave away the bride. Then over the mountains Connolly went to Canada, where shortly he became the Mayor of Montreal.

As for Douglas, he took his wife down the Columbia, where in the then new Fort Vancouver they took up the quarters they had occupied ever since. The gentle Nelia had grown and ripened with the years, until the comely young matron was only a degree less attractive than Eloise herself. At the west end of that same porch was the door to their sitting-room, where on any Sabbath evening you might find Douglas with the Bible on his knee reading to his wife and little ones. It was a sweet home picture; one of the few, very few, to be found the entire length of McLoughlin's kingdom.

Summer mornings found Nelia the third in that group upon the porch, while her little daughter Cecelia in a pink sun-bonnet played among the flower-beds at the foot of the steps. There Douglas had scattered fine seed, and in floral letters had sprung his little daughter's name — "Cecelia."

There were other things besides flowers at the foot

of the steps. Facing the main entrance of the stockade stood two eighteen-pounders and two swivels, belligerent but rusty, and piled in orderly heaps were pyramids of black cannon-balls that were never disturbed, partly because there was no fighting; more because Robert Bruce, the old Scotch gardener, had piled them there, and woe betide the chick or child that presumed to interfere with anything that Bruce had done. Bruce was far away, now — in England with the governor; but habit had become fixed. In all Bruce's eighteen months of absence not even a dog had ventured to nose the forbidden balls. Neither was the grass trodden. They seemed still to hear the gardener's call, " Meestress Dooglas! Meestress Dooglas! Kap the bairnies aff the grass."

But to continue the dinner company at the fort. Daily, besides Douglas, there was the fort physician, Dr. Barclay; and the clerks, gay young fellows, English and Scotch, whose friends across the sea had sufficient influence to secure them a berth in the opulent fur company. Not that their present salary was at all princely, — twenty to one hundred pounds sterling a year was the most that any received, — but clerks by promotion became traders, chief-traders, factors, and partners. There was not one of them that did not expect to become a chief factor or to retire at middle life to an old-world manor on the Thames or the Dee. Some waited years, some a lifetime, for promotions that never came.

Rae would greet them each as they passed, — Dunn, who wrote letters to the " London Times;" Allen, brother to the physician of the Earl of Selkirk; Roberts, factotum; and all the ever-changing train of voyageurs and traders.

VIII

DR. McLOUGHLIN'S RETURN

1839

HOMEWARD hurrying comes McLoughlin in these October days of 1839. "Ready!" The sun and wind burned voyageurs catch up the paddles, the boat song strikes —

> " Ma—l–brouck has gone a-fighting,
> *Mironton, mironton, mirontaine,*" —

and away they go, glittering down the Columbia. Miles of blue waters sweep behind them before the sunrise breakfast.

It was the doctor's ambition to have the best paddlers in the world, and he did. Never before did there, never again will such bold watermen ride the Columbia. Such order, such discipline! — not the slightest minutiæ escaped the master's eye. Monique, a stalwart Iroquois half-breed, a strong fellow, at home in the rapids, stands in the bow of the doctor's boat. Tawny-skinned, stripped to the waist, and bareheaded, his long hair streaming on the wind, with eye fixed and every muscle tense, this side, that, swift the paddle flies as his quick eye measures the line of safety and sends the signal back to the steersman in the rear. It is a play of life and death, but so skilful are those bowmen that rarely a bark goes tum-tum-tum grazing a rock.

There was a McDonald at Fort Colvile that had a daughter of the rich dark beauty of the Creole type.

Smaller in figure than her Blackfoot mother, better rounded, lithe, and willowy, Christine McDonald was the embodiment of the grace and supple shapeliness of the half-breed girl. The chief factor, with his long locks flowing over his shoulders Indian fashion, was always in the saddle, and at his side rode his fearless daughter, Christine. Handsome as her father and as daring, astride with a serape buckled around her waist, she followed the hounds to the fox-hunt, leaped canyons and fallen trees, and outdid the Indians themselves in her desperate riding.

On such a ride as this they caught sight of the Montreal express and dashed to greet McLoughlin, the chief of chief factors. As in some glen of the Highlands, Scotch plumes and tartans flew. Scotch Macs clasped hands with other Macs famous in the fur trade. Demonstrative Canadians fell on one another's necks with tears and laughter. Indian wives and children clamored for recognition. Delighted voyageurs dandled their terra-cotta babies on their knees with gifts of beads and bells bought in Canadian shops for this happy hour. Within the cedar hall there was roast turkey, sucking pig, fresh butter and eggs, and ale. Spokanes, Kootenais, and Pend d'Oreilles, in all the splendor of paint and feathers, dashed around Colvile on horseback. Some in soft-tanned buffalo-robes peeped through the trading gate. All night old Colvile rang. Outside the drowsy Flatheads heard the droning of the bagpipe.

There was a hush. McDonald had taught Christine the sword-dance. Under the rough rafters in the light of the fire the fair barbarian advanced, invited and evaded the supple blade that glittered round her head. Christine's little moccasined feet twinkled like stars, and her beaded bodice shimmered in the firelight.

Catching a lock of her flowing hair, she threw it across the darting blade — it fell, severed, to the floor. Spellbound the traders watched them. The movements grew swift and swifter, until, in the excitement, Dr. McLoughlin thumped his cane upon the floor and cried, " Enough, McDonald, enough! "

For hundreds of miles the Columbia has a regular descent, broken only at long intervals by steps of rapids and falls. One hundred, one hundred and fifty miles a day, the fur-traders glide, pausing at nightfall to camp. Scarcely has the first boat touched shore before the axe is in the forest. The Canadian cook builds the tiny pile of lighted brush into a pyramid of blazing logs. From a sapling bent beside it the kettle swings and sings of supper.

On one side of the fire the voyageurs carve with pocket-knife and hunting-knife, and never resting in their talk gulp tea, tea, tea. On the other side the cook has spread McLoughlin's kitchen of linen and plate. Catharine Sinclair is that Canadian lily taking her first flight from the Manitoba home. David's laugh rings merrily. Bruce the gardener sips his tea. He loves the camping life; it reminds him of military marches and Waterloo. Two new clerks, McTavish and Finlayson, are keeping copious journals to send home to Scotland. There is a world of difference between the happy-go-lucky voyageur and his more thoughtful Scotch companion. The French-Canadian or French-Iroquois laughs at mishaps, he rollicks and flings out the border song. The Scotchman is grave, solemn, and watchful, the brain and nerve of the Hudson's Bay Company.

Down the Okanogan country the grass is sere. Autumn flames. Sombre Alpine forests climb the far-off heights. Eastward dwell the Spokanes, the Children of the Sun, desolated once by a more than Trojan war over a stolen Spokane bride.

At Walla Walla Chief Factor Pambrun comes down from his tower to greet his chief; there are letters for Dr. Whitman; the Shoshonie brigade sweeps into line with thirty packs of the best beaver of the mountains. The boat song rings in the narrow gorge. The Frenchmen sing in times of danger; the Iroquois are silent and stern as death as they let fly the canoe through the hissing and curling waters like a race-horse. There were times when Monique ran the swift and narrow Dalles; down the Cascades he shot with arrowy wing, but not to-day. Dr. McLoughlin is along and Charlefoux is guide. Many a time McLoughlin said, "Monique is my boldest man, but I 'd trust my life with Charlefoux." On they speed, past Memelose, the Isle of Tombs, the Westminster of the Indian, past Wind Mountain with its Ulyssean tales, past Strawberry Island where the fairies feast in June, to the wild-rushing cascades. Not a feature escapes McLoughlin's eye. Every cliff and crag is a familiar landmark pointing to Fort Vancouver.

Madame and Eloise need wait and embroider no more. Like silver bells shook far away, the boat song heralded the singers. Hood seemed to listen, the Columbia heaved its breast of blue, the very islands smiled with gladsome joy. Eloise touched her finger to her lip. "That is my father's boat song, his favorite because Napoleon was said to hum it when mounting for battle." Again she hearkened; then starting up as the words grew more and more distinct —

"It is just like my father to sing Malbrouck at such a time as this," and as she flew to the gate her own voice joined the strain that so oft had rung in the halls of Fort Vancouver: [1]

[1] "Songs of Old Canada." Malbrouck; *i. e.*, Marlborough.

Malbrouck has gone a-fighting,
  Mironton, mironton, mirontaine,
Malbrouck has gone a-fighting,
But when will he return?

My Lady climbs her watch tower
As high as she can get;

She sees her page approaching,
All clad in sable hue.

"Ah, page, brave page, what tidings
From my true lord bring you?"

"The news I bring, fair Lady,
Will make your tears run down;

"Put off your rose-red dress so fine,
And doff your satin gown.

"Monsieur Malbrouck is dead, alas!
And buried too, for aye;

"I saw four officers who bore
His mighty corse away.

"One bore his cuirass, and his friend
His shield of iron wrought;

"The third his mighty sabre bore,
And the fourth — he carried naught.

"And at the corners of his tomb
They planted rosemarie;

"And from their tops the nightingale
Rings out her carol free.

"We saw, above the laurels,
His soul fly forth amain;

"And each one fell upon his face,
And then rose up again.

"And so we sang the glories
For which great Malbrouck bled;

"And when the whole was ended
Each one went off to bed.

"I say no more, my Lady,
  Mironton, mironton, mirontaine,
I say no more, my Lady,
As nought more can be said."

And with the coming of the express would come all manner of news, and the renewal of contact with the East. Letters, at least, should be in hand. Newspapers for the entire year came in the express, — a year's edition of "Le Canadien" and the "Quebec Gazette," just as in June the barque "Columbia" brought a file of the "Daily London Times" of the preceding year. Packed away in a great chest, every day the traders drew out that date a year, two years ago, to tickle themselves with the fancy that the post-boy called each morning!

They were at hand! "The express! The express!!" rang through the court. Every one was busy. Old Burris ran up the British ensign on the flagstaff. Swinging round the last green headland like the curve of a great wheel, the brigade shot into view. The song rang shrilly out. From the governor's barge fluttered the triangular pennon of the Hudson's Bay Company, with its rampant beaver and the familiar "H. B. C." upon a field of blue.

"H. B. C." — "Here Before Christ," was Ermatinger's translation, and Bruce agreed. "I reeckon ye'll find the coompany's coolers where kirkmen seeldom git." And then there was a struggle to see who could touch the sand first. Paddles rolled on the gunwales, flinging the spray across the voyageurs' faces as they shook the water from the blades.

What rejoicing! Cannon boomed, flags waved, the bagpipes struck up "The Campbells are coming. Hourray! Hourray!" Indians whooped, dogs bayed, Frenchmen ran wild, as the whole fort turned out to greet the arrival — and the chief. The sharp end of the canoes gritted on the sand. Every cap flew off as the familiar form of Dr. McLoughlin arose from the cramped position that had grown so irksome and stepped on shore.

Every eye rejoiced in that majestic presence. With a hand-clasp for Rae and Douglas and a salute for the Madame's cheek he presented her son — "I have brought the boy home, mother." And Ermatinger gave a shout of joy at sight of his Canadian lily, a niece of the Madame, from Manitoba.

In the midst of greetings and tears and laughter on all sides, Eloise, hysterical with joy, clung to her father's arm, and all talking at once, went plodding up the path between the fields of wheat. Behind them toiled the Iroquois packers, rolling the heavy bales on little trucks to the fort.

"The governor has returned with flying colors," remarked Clerk Roberts of the Indian shop, measuring off a fathom of trail-rope tobacco with his arms as he spoke.

"An' richt glad am I," responded Allen, the farm overseer. "There's nae better mon i' the coompany's service. His management o' Indians amounts to genius itsel'. Did ye notice Moneycoon an' the hunters when he called them? The' faces lichted like the sun. An' old Kesano, proud as a peacock wi' a feither in his hair. The verra sicht o' him tam's the red men."

And Bruce the gardener had come again; and Bruce rushed to see his gardens! Reaching England, he had resigned from the Hudson Bay Company. " I 'll neiver leeve i' the wuids again," he said. A few days later, walking lonely in the streets of London, he came unexpectedly upon Dr. McLoughlin. The benevolent face beamed, it touched an aching void — throwing himself upon his knees at the doctor's feet, with tears he begged to be taken back. Despite some obstinate disobediences the doctor valued the old gardener, so back he came, a fixture for life. Bruce looked eagerly, too, for his old musket, that cherished relic of Waterloo. In half an hour he had all the laddies in a row, with flint-locks on their shoulders — " Heids up," " 'Taes out like sooldiers, noo," " Mek reddy," " Tek aim," " Fire ! "

David McLoughlin was like a child again. He seemed to wake from a dream to look upon the weather-beaten palisades, the unpainted stores resting on blocks, the sparks flying from the forge. He strode through his mother's sitting-room, unchanged save that Chinese matting, the first ever used in this country, had supplanted the native Indian mats. Just to see how it would taste, he drew a bucket of water from the deep well never walled, and snipped a handful of biscuit from the bakehouse. Even the big brass bell under its peaked roof sang the same old song, " Pumbrún! Pumbrún! Pumbrún! " that it sang when Pambrun rang it and David was a little boy. Apparently the same furs lay in the same bales in the furroom, the same trappers came in the same boats, singing the same old songs that had been his cradle lullabies. The same ship brought the same goods and departed again on her cycle of sailing. Changes had come to David, and he had expected changes here, but it was like opening a story-book to a page read long ago.

It seemed to him but yesterday, when a lad of thir-teen, he had set out in the traders' care for France. They followed the old route up the Columbia. When he saw the wild Spokanes careering across the plain, his blood leaped as at the recognition of kindred. He longed to mount a fiery steed and ride away with them, far from books and school and gentlemen's clothes. He remembered the hunter's tales of Jemmy Jock, the half-Indian son of a Hudson's Bay trader that became a Rob Roy among the Blackfeet. Watching the daring riders he breathed deeply, and felt within him the stir-ring of savage instincts. It seemed only yesterday that David on snowshoes reached Jasper House beyond the head waters of the Columbia in the heart of the Rocky Mountains. The old clerk Jasper was dead, but in his stead Colin Fraser played the bagpipes and danced at his shadow on the wall. How grateful seemed the blazing hearth and opulent larder of the hermit up there in the Alpine solitude!

That was a land of fat and pemmican. Thirty thou-sand bags, every bag as big as a pillow, hung in the company's forts that year. Every bag represented the pulverized flesh and melted marrow of two big buffa-loes. David had seen pemmican down on the Colum-bia, salmon pemmican, but none like this — with hairs in it an inch long! But in a wonderful manner it stayed the hunger of the voyageur crossing sub-Arctic snow. Never before had David seen such snow, hard and white, compact as adamant, across which the dog-sleds flew to Fort Edmonton on the North Saskatche-wan. All that North had been a realm of fairy-land and every old post a palace. Every bullet-hole in the gayly painted walls of Edmonton, every hack of the tomahawk on the battlemented gateway, had its tale of tragedy and war. The rude fantasies of color and of carving dazzled the boy, as they dazzled the neighboring Cree, the Assiniboin, and the Blackfoot. Five years later, how tawdry they looked! Yes, David had changed. Even Vancouver was not so grand as he had thought. The savage in him slept.

" Bé-be," sang the Indian mothers in the cabins:

> " Bé-be, the governor has come,
> And now there's some fun,
> And a great big feast to-night."

And so came the express from Montreal to Vancouver in 1839, landing Dr. John McLoughlin at home again on the nineteenth day of October — his fifty-fifth birthday.

IX

1839

A YANKEE would have said Thanksgiving was at
hand had he peeped into the spacious kitchen
of the fort when the express came. The fort dining-
hall was a noble apartment, capable of seating five
hundred guests. A huge map of the Indian country
covered the wall. The dinner-bell rang, and the long
tables began to fill. With a wave of the hand the stately
governor seated his guests according to rank. Before
them cut-glass, and silver with the McLoughlin coat
of arms, shone side by side with modern queen's-ware
and rare old china. Dr. McLoughlin presided like a
picture out of the old colonial time, clean-shaven, fair
and rosy, with his white locks twisted into a queue at
the back. At his right sat his faithful aid, who in the
governor's absence had added new lustre to the name
of Douglas. Then came Rae and Dr. Barclay, and factors from other forts, the jolly ship's captain and mate,
trappers and traders, clerks and sailors. The heavy
doors clanged and the plank floor rang. The fire-logs
flickered in the dark old chimney, and the branching
candelabra sent out an odor of perfumed wax. There
was a clatter of cutlery. In peaked cap and ample
apron Burris marshalled his copper-colored, curly-
haired Kanakas with trenchers of venison and tureens
of brown gravies. And sauces? No one ever yet
surpassed Burris in sauces for the Chinook salmon.

These Hudson's Bay gentlemen were a rubicund

set, epicures to a degree. Mild climate, good living, and easy nerves gave them a corpulent habit in striking contrast with the lean and wiry Yankee traders that sometimes touched the coast.

There was once a complaint sent to Parliament that the Hudson's Bay Company made no attempt to cultivate the soil. Dr. McLoughlin broke that old régime. Almost from his coming there had been wheat, flour, bread, on the Columbia, yea, even gingerbread, and of late years apple pie! That fruitful orchard at Fort Vancouver had sprung from a handful of seeds dropped into the pocket of an old ship-captain by a laughing girl across the sea. "Take them and plant them in your savage land," she said. The black satin vest was packed away in a sea-chest. In airing his clothes one day at Fort Vancouver the seeds fell out. "Bless me! bless me! let us start an orchard," said Dr. McLoughlin, picking up the little triangular treasures. Another sea-captain brought a bunch of peach-stones from Crusoe's Island, Juan Fernandez. A little planting, a little care, peaches.

Back of the Fort hummed the old grist-mill, the first ever built west of the Rocky Mountains. William Cannon, the miller, an American, crossed the mountains with Astor's men in 1810. When Astor's people left he elected to remain with the British fur-traders. It was in the day of beginnings, when the post lived on salmon and wapato (the Indian potato) and were just experimenting with apple-seeds and peach-stones. The handful of seed-wheat brought from Canada was increasing marvellously when Cannon said one day, " Governor, let me build a flour-mill."

"A mill? A flour-mill? Bless you, man, where will you get burrs?"

" Make them of granite from the hill back of the fort," said Cannon.

" What power? "

" Cattle power."

" Go ahead then," was the governor's answer.

Cannon worked beneath a mighty fir that stands to-day on the old fort plain. He made his frame of fir, and the cogs and wheels of oak hardened by boiling in seal-oil. He worked his burrs down from rough granite with a cold-chisel.

" What are you making that for? " inquired Tom McKay's little Billy as Cannon smoothed the long main-shaft from a comely fir. Little Billy was three quarters Indian and bright, — bright as a bluejay. " What are you making that for? " again piped the watchful little interrogation point.

" A whip-handle for the governor," answered the crusty miller, making a sharp eye at the little boy.

All was set up. The oxen were yoked, old Brandy and Lion brought up from California in the " Cadboro'." Wheat was put in, the whole fort came out to watch, the main-shaft turned, and lo! it ground out flour, the first flour on the Columbia.

Then Cannon built an old-fashioned over-shot wheel saw-mill. Lumber began to accumulate, so that every summer the Hudson's Bay ship left her Indian goods and taking on lumber went over to the Sandwich Islands. In November she came back for her London load of furs. The same ship was lying there now, furs all laden, her officers up at the governor's banquet.

" And how is competition now, Mr. John? How is competition now? " inquired Dr. McLoughlin of John Dunn just down from the northwest coast.

" Poor picking, Governor, poor picking for the Bos-

tons. We've swept the hocean clean. Hour little
steamer watches the coast like an 'awk. She darts hup
the firths and 'auls in the furs before they hever reach
the coast. The Hamericans 'ave no business 'ere
hanyway." Dunn thrust his fork into the duck with
a savage lunge.

"Tut, tut, tut, Mr. John!" laughed the governor,
"they will come unless we're sharp enough to head
them off."

If there was anything Dr. McLoughlin hated, it was
a Yankee skipper with rum on board. What trouble
they brought! Drunken Indians who would sell for
nothing but rum. All day the shrewd siwashes would
lie on the shore in the sun and watch for Yankee sails.
The company's men watched, too, and ran ahead to
catch the furs before the ship could anchor. When
naught but rum availed, rum was dealt to head the
Yankees off. Then the Yankee captain swore and tore
and sailed away to find another agent — fighting rum
with rum. At last the defeated Bostons almost quit
the coast. Only at long intervals a damaged whaler
ran into the cove at Esquimault. Then the forts cut
off the rum supply. The red men held their furs in
vain.

"Lum! lum! lum!" plead the siwashes, spreading
rich bales of seal and beaver, shiny silver-fox, and glisten-
ing sea-otter around the forts. The traders shook their
heads. "No liquor for the Indians." The angry red
men brandished their tomahawks, but at last, subdued,
were fain to trade their furs for blankets, and soberly
set out on another hunt.

One day a new competitor came — a Boston captain
with a cargo of "Yankee notions." Right up the
Columbia he sailed, and under the very guns of Fort

Vancouver sold out his squeaking cats and dogs and yellow jumping-jacks to the delighted red men. Solemn old sagamores squandered the catch of the season on little red wagons and tin whistles.

How Dr. McLoughlin fumed! The rascally fellow had even followed the Hudson's Bay example and married the daughter of a chief! Something must be done. The governor despatched a messenger to intercept the Yankee captain, and if possible buy him over, cargo, brig, and all. The scheme succeeded; captain, cargo, ship, and crew turned British, and as a chief factor of the Hudson's Bay Company the Boston captain McNeill became the most obstinate John Bull on the books.

The spirited recount of adventure since last the banqueters met filled hours. The candles burned low and began to sputter. "Captain Wyeth has sent a keg of choice smoking tobacco and a copy of Carlyle for you," Rae was saying.

"Just like him, just like him," commented the doctor. "Wyeth was a good fellow. I must write him a letter. Bruce!" The governor pulled a green bell-tassel behind his chair. Bruce opened the door and handed the governor his snuff-box. That was the signal for breaking up.

All passed out to chat and smoke in Bachelors' Hall — all but the governor. He never smoked and seldom trusted himself with snuff — he borrowed of Bruce. As they crossed the court, the wail of the fiddle resounded — the voyageurs danced till daylight. At early dawn the barque "Columbia" left her moorings, and with sails unloosed stood out into the channel.

X

EARLY EVENTS AT FORT VANCOUVER

1812–1829

AND had this handful of whites lived always unmolested in the heart of barbarism? Not always. There was a time, after Astor's people left,
when the Cascade Indians levied toll like the robber
barons on the Rhine, a time when sixty well-armed
men guarded every caravan, a time when the brigades
made the portage at the Dalles with a lighted match
above a loaded cannon. In a dim corner of the furroom there hung a chain armor worn by a Northwester in the early times. One hot night when he
took it off, the skin came with it.

Long after McLoughlin came in 1824, the river
bristled with danger. Once the Dalles Indians, the
banditti of the Columbia, united to make him pay
tribute. One dark night in 1829 their war canoes
dropped noiselessly down upon the fort. But the
sleepless watch was on the walls, the guns were set.
Chief Kesano, a friendly Multnomah, rallied his tribe
to aid the traders. All night the savages blew their
shells and beat their drums. The next morning Dr.
McLoughlin called a council. One by one the hostile
chiefs were admitted. Douglas was there, and Pambrun, and Kesano with his sub-chiefs. McLoughlin
had men concealed, ready to fire at a sign of treachery.
The chiefs were sullen when into their midst came
Colin Fraser, a six-foot Highlander in Scottish kilt

and flowing plume and played the bagpipes. Up and down the great council hall he strode and played an hour while they waited for McLoughlin. " Music hath charms." The savages were so subdued they forgot their warlike errand. While still the piper played, McLoughlin entered with a treaty ready drawn up that they would never molest Vancouver. It was signed, presents were distributed, and the hostiles departed happy.

One night in that same year, Kesano and his people came with shouts and blows to the postern gate, bringing Jedediah Smith, an American trapper, who had escaped from a massacre on the Umpqua. In 1828 Jedediah led the first party that ever crossed the Sierras into California. The Spaniards viewed them with suspicion. Out of the hands of the Spaniards they fell into the snares of the Indians — out of eighteen men three only escaped to the Hudson's Bay Company fort on the Columbia. Dr. McLoughlin was astounded. " Stay! " he cried. " McKay! Tom McKay! This American has been robbed, his party massacred. Take fifty men, ride light, and go down to the Umpqua."

McKay and his Canadians crossed the Columbia that night. Down on the Umpqua the Indians came in, suspecting nothing. Captain Tom counted out the peltries. " There," he said, " for these I will pay you." He handed out their value in goods. " But these with the trappers' mark belong to the men you murdered. Look to the murderers for payment." The enraged Umpquas fell upon the murderers and Tom and his men galloped out of the country. Dr. McLoughlin paid Jedediah Smith three thousand two hundred dollars for his furs. The grateful trapper left the Columbia to rejoin his friends east of the mountains.

In 1829, too, a Boston ship came into the Columbia
for salmon. Was it "the Bostons," as the Indians said,
or was it the first ploughing at Fort Vancouver, that
uncorked the vials of pestilence? For miles the shores
of the Columbia were dotted with villages so near that
a rifle-ball would reach from one to another. The
Willamette was filled with a numerous and powerful
people, a people that had good houses, great fisheries,
and manufactured thread and nets and cloth from the
fibre of the milkweed. The deadly fever came among
them. The simple Indian remedies failed. The jug-
glery of medicine men proved vain. In vain was the
general sacrifice of eagle's feathers and wooden images.
The fated Multnomahs went into their sweat-houses.
Half-suffocated in the vapor-bath, reeking with perspiration, they jumped into the cold Columbia. Barely
crept they back to the wigwam door. In three weeks
Kesano's people perished, and he had been wont to
summon five hundred warriors to the chase. At his
village, Wakanasissi, six miles below Vancouver, the
bones lay five feet high and ten rods long for years,
where the dead were piled in a ghastly open tomb.
With six solitary survivors Kesano moved his lodge to
Fort Vancouver. Here ever after the old chief was
honored above all other Indians with a plate at a side
table in the great hall, with a feather in a silk hat and a
scarlet coat. With his large flat head, bright clear eyes
that could look one through, Roman nose, heavy jaws,
set firm lips, and hair carefully dressed, old Chief
Kesano stalked in and out, an honored pensioner at
Fort Vancouver.

That fever time! From 1829 to 1832 thirty thousand
Indians perished in the valley of the Columbia and
Willamette. In 1831, on the Cowlitz, the living sufficed

not to bury the dead, but fled to the sea-coast, leaving
their homes to the ravens and the wolves. The sun
shone fair as ever — the changeless sun of an Oregon
summer. Not a cloud, not a shower, not a wind, but
the still Egyptian lotus-sky above the changeless days.
Had the boy Bryant of New England divined this when
he wrote, —

> "Lose thyself in the continuous woods
> Where rolls the Oregon and hears no sound
> Save his own dashings. Yet the dead are there"?

Forty men lay sick at Fort Vancouver, and wretched
Indians at the gates plead for "la médecine." There
was no physician but Dr. McLoughlin. His hands
were full. He, too, fell sick of the fever and sent his
clerks among the sufferers with pockets lined with vials
of quinine.

There was an Indian village on Wapato Island at the
mouth of the Willamette. For several weeks no one
had come from there. Chief Trader Ogden arrived at
the fort. "Go over to Wapato and see what is the
matter," said Dr. McLoughlin.

"There is something dead in Wapato," said Ogden,
as his boats neared the edge of the island. There certainly was a sickish, fetid odor in the air. The oak-
trees whispered as they passed. The gleaming alders
fluttered their nervous twigs. The willows shook their
large oblanceolate leaves with whitened under-edges.
The wood-dove mourned in a thicket of young firs.
Canoes lay idle on the beach. Nets hung on the willow
boughs. Dogs watched, birds carolled, insects hummed
and flitted, but no voice came from the village. As
Ogden strode forward he saw them lying dead everywhere, all dead but one little slave-boy to whom the

sweat and the river-douse had been refused.   Thrown out, the boy burned through the fever and lived.

"My legal primer says necessity knows no law," said the practical Ogden, lighting the funeral pyre. Men, now living, saw the grinning skulls of that Golgotha.   Dr. McLoughlin adopted the little Indian slave' and named him Benjamin Harrison, for a member of the London Board.   He was a bright, attractive child, and became a favorite at the fort.

There was another chief, Maniquon, an old man bereft of his people.   Sometimes they could hear him at night walking around the fort, singing a low sad song of death.   Sometimes he would tell of other days, when he rode to the chase or fought in battle.   "Eighty snows have chilled the earth since Maniquon was born. Maniquon has been a great warrior."   The dim eye would glitter, the withered chief would leap and brandish an imaginary tomahawk, then sink back exhausted. "Maniquon is not a warrior now.   He will never raise his axe again.   His young men have deserted his lodge. His sons have gone down to their graves, and the squaws will not sing of their great deeds."   Leaning toward the listener he would ask, "Who has made my people what they are?"

"The Great Spirit, Maniquon."

The old chief would leap like a fiend and fiercely whisper, "The white man did it; the white man did it."   Fierce old Maniquon.   To the end of his days he believed the Hudson's Bay Company poisoned the people of Wapato to get the beautiful island for a dairy farm.   Long ago, in the ancient days of Wauna, the Multnomahs were a mighty people.   All the tribes met them in council under the oaks and willows of Wapato. Now herds of cattle were sent to range where Indian kings once trod. Hogs wallowed in the sloughs or fattened on acorns and wapato. Beneath the oaks of the ancient council grove the herdsman built his hut, and Sauvie, a French Canadian, was given charge of a dairy not far from the site of the deserted village.

An old woman, Waskema, wandered like an unquiet spirit in the valley. Here, long years before the white man came, Waskema was wedded to Canemah the arrow-maker. There he wrought the jewelled arrow-heads of yellow jasper, red jasper, green jasper, and pale chalcedony, or wrought out knives of translucent obsidian carefully chipped down to a glassy edge. Canemah's arrows were famed from Des Chutes to Tillamook. Old Waskema had never forgiven the white man for bringing the fatal fever that carried off her husband and sons. Among the scrofula-stricken fragments of her race she strove to preserve the old superstitions and the old customs, preferring the necklace of claws and teeth and shells to even the gayest of Hudson's Bay beads. Each year as she went up to the fisheries, she tortured her heart with memories of the time when first she toiled with her arrow-maker gathering baskets of agate and jasper and carnelian along the quiet river sands.

In 1828 there was trouble with the Clatsops at the mouth of the Columbia. The " William and Ann," the company's ship from London, was wrecked one dark and stormy night on the Columbia bar. All on board were lost. Goods destined for Fort Vancouver were thrown out upon the beach. Dr. McLoughlin heard of the loss of the ship and sent to demand the cargo. An old broom was sent back in derisive answer. The surmise grew into a conviction that the Clatsops had murdered the crew as they tried to land that stormy night.

The new Caledonian brigade was just in. The doctor despatched them to Clatsop with all the swivels in the courtyard. Boom! bang! boom! down went the wooden huts. The frightened people ran. A few were killed. The Clatsops had buried a quantity of the cargo in the sands on the seashore. The Canadians dug it out.

"Mind ye! Mind ye!" was McLoughlin's message. "Ye cannot profit by disasters to vessels nor murder white men for plunder."

Weeks passed. Peltries accumulated in the hands of the Clatsops. Their ammunition was out, but no one had courage to face the White-Headed Eagle at Fort Vancouver. Dr. McLoughlin divined this and sent Celiast down to conciliate her people. Three daughters had Coboway, chief of the Clatsops, — Kilakóta, Celiast, and Telix, all wedded to white men. Donning her gayest dress and spreading a blanket sail in her little canoe, Celiast and her cousin Angelique glided down to Clatsop.

It was a forlorn little town the Indian princess entered. The cedar logs lay in splinters on the sod. The salmon season had come, and all had been too busy to restore the shattered houses. Celiast sat down with her people on the grassy slope toward the sea. Grave men, voluble women, little children told her the story. "The ship was wrecked on the middle sands and the crew all drowned one windy night in March," they said. "The first we knew of the wreck was when the goods were coming ashore in the morning." With a firm belief in the innocence of her people and a promise of kind treatment when they came to the fort, Celiast made matters right and restored harmony.

About the same time another Boston ship entered

the Columbia, turned into the Willamette, and ran aground at the Clackamas rapids one hundred miles inland. The Clackamas Indians were fishing at the Falls. Around the bend they saw the ship. " King George man hate Boston," said the fishers. " Kill um Boston." They left their fishing and crowded around the unfortunate ship. There was an ominous sound in their scoffing laughter. Already their bows were drawn to the arrow-heads when a crew of boatmen hove in sight. It was McLoughlin's men despatched from Fort Vancouver.

Tom McKay's loud voice resounded, — " The White-Headed Eagle sends word: if you kill one Boston it shall be the same to him as his own King George man. Fall back." The Indians fell back, and McLoughlin's men got out their hawsers and pulled the rash adventurer from the rocks.

XI

BACHELORS' HALL

1839

BACHELORS' HALL was the gossiping place, the clerks' quarters, a long, low, whitewashed log structure on the east side of the court. Here, in the central assembly room, with a rousing fire and tables littered with pens, ink, and paper, the gentlemen often chatted till the stroke of midnight. Hunting, fishing, fowling, these were the sports of summer, but during the long, rainy winter evenings Bachelors' Hall became the nightly theatre of song and story. All grades of employés, the aristocratic Briton, the feudal Highlander, the restless Frenchman, the picturesque Indian, shone in the kaleidoscopic shift of firelight. Here the gay and brusque McLoughlin discussed religion with the funereal, formal Douglas, or joked him on the customs of his Scottish chiefs.

Dr. McLoughlin was a hero-worshipper — Napoleon was his hero. That is the key to his swift flights of travel; it explains his demand for instant and unquestioned obedience, his system of rewards and punishments, and his far-reaching schemes for power. Like Napoleon, his frown was a terror to the culprit, his approbation the delight of his subordinates. An offender would choose rather to flee away to the hostile Blackfeet than to feel again the blaze of that displeasure.

In Bachelors' Hall Waterloo was fought again and again. Bruce had been an actual participant. Clerk

7

Allen saw the French prisoners brought to Lanarkshire
In his native village he saw the bonfires of tar barrels
that celebrated Wellington's victory, and he saw Napoleon's coach that was captured at Waterloo and
exhibited throughout Great Britain.   Once, while dressing a wounded hand for Allen, Dr. McLoughlin became
so excited in discussing the Peace of Amiens that Allen
records in his journal, " The doctor hurt me so that
I wished Napoleon and the Peace of Amiens far
enough ! "

Well bred, well read, were the magnates of Fort Vancouver.   Scholars loved their society.   Many a mile
the library of standard, leather-bound, weather-stained
volumes travelled by canoe, to cheer the lonely traders
around their soughing fires in the northwest forest.
Scott, Burns, Shakespeare, — these were daily food.
The arrival of the American Irving's books created a
great sensation.

" How I should like to write the other side of Bonneville," cried Chief Factor Pambrun one night in Bachelors' Hall.   " He came to Walla Walla.   We gave him
of our best.   As an officer of the United States army
we were hospitable to him, but as a rival trader we had
no favors to bestow."

Pambrun felt he had reason for resentment.   Bonneville distributed presents so lavishly among the Walla-
Cayuses, and paid them so handsomely for their furs,
that he interfered with the Hudson's Bay business.
The Cayuse chiefs came to Walla Walla and demanded
better pay for beaver.   Pambrun refused.   " The rate
is fixed," he said.   Then Tauitau threw him down and
stamped upon his breast until the chief factor cried,
" Hold ! hold ! I leave the decision to Dr. McLoughlin."

The next time Bonneville came, the Indians had been

so instructed by the company that they fled at his approach. Fort Walla Walla was closed against him — not even a dog could be bought on the Columbia. The Indians slunk away as if from a contagion. Bonneville could not get a crew to take him down to Fort Vancouver. He had to give it up, and turning back lost his way in the deep snows of the Blue Mountains. Finally the Nez Percés found him and brought him fainting to the lodge of Red Wolf on the Snake. The Nez Percés nursed him like a brother, gave him horses and provisions, and sent him and his men out of the country. Then Irving wrote the " Bonneville Tales " — commentaries on the days when the Hudson's Bay Company ruled on the Columbia.

When Captain Wyeth was on his way to Oregon he had fallen in with a party of Blackfeet at a mountain rendezvous where Bonneville was and Sublette's trappers. There was a half-breed interpreter in Bonneville's camp, Baptiste Dorion, son of the interpreter in Irving's "Astoria." The Blackfeet greeted the whites. " We have heard of the Americans," said the Blackfoot chief, decorated from head to foot in eagle plumes. He held Wyeth's hand in friendly converse when "whiz" went a bullet from Dorion's rifle. As the chief of the Blackfeet fell Dorion snatched his painted robe and fled. Never a robe was bought more dearly. The outraged Blackfeet pursued the white man from that hour. Four years later one of Wyeth's men smoked the pipe of peace with Jemmy Jock, the Rob Roy of the Blackfeet. Even as he smoked Jemmy Jock gave the signal and Godin fell. Upon his brow Jemmy Jock carved Wyeth's name — " N. J. W."

" The Indian has a double nature," said Dr. McLoughlin, — " one peaceable and friendly, one savage and diabolical. Somebody has stirred up the devil with the Blackfeet."

When Jason Lee was on his journey back to the States, the first steamboat on Missouri waters ran up from St. Louis to purchase furs. Somewhere, in the present Montana, an Indian stole a blanket that had belonged to a man who died of smallpox. The Blackfeet died like flies. Beyond the Missouri the smallpox flew, far up among the Sarcies and Assiniboins, on, up through Alaska to the borders of the Arctic. For years the bones of the Blackfeet lay unburied on the Yellowstone, and to this day decaying lodges of skeletons are found along the Yukon.

"And now, Tom, what is the latest trick of Jemmy Jock?" asked Dr. McLoughlin, who always delighted in his stepson's tales.

"'T was on the Yellowstone," said Tom. "One night I gave strict orders to the Canadians on watch to keep a good lookout. They did so, rifle in hand. Jemmy Jock, dressed as a Canadian, entered the camp unobserved, walked up to the watchman, and said in French, 'I have received orders that the horses shall be turned out to graze.' Supposing the order was from me, he let the horses out. In no time we heard the whoop of the Blackfeet as they mounted our stock and rode away."

It used to be a favorite escapade for Jemmy Jock to steal into a hostile camp, and over the very shoulders of the foe to watch the game of chance. Quietly he walked among them, taking what he wanted, and cutting the hopples of their horses. A gift of wampum dropped, a cap with his feather, and a distant whoop, alone revealed that Jemmy Jock and his Blackfeet had paid them an evening visit. Sometimes in lonely mountain trails the trappers found letters set up on sticks by the joking Jemmy Jock to tell them that he had camped there, to give a useful hint or to lead them into a trap. The Americans offered $500 for his head.

"Jemmy Jock plays no more tricks," said Ermatinger.

"What?"

"Smallpox."

Even hundreds of miles away this carried a shudder to Fort Vancouver.

Dr. Barclay was the new physician; one of the old Scotch Barclays, a Shetlander, born in a manse beside the ocean whose seven foot thick walls had been in the family for hundreds of years. He studied at Glasgow, took his diploma at the London College of Physicians and Surgeons, and went to the Arctic.

"Tell us of your Arctic life," said Dr. McLoughlin in Bachelors' Hall.

The cheek of the young physician flushed as he told of Arctic adventure. Nothing could exceed the interest of an Arctic tale to these servants of the Hudson's Bay Company. Had they not promised to find the Northwest Passage, — Hearne, Ross, Parry, Back — the company claimed them all, and Franklin wintered at their northern posts. Clerk Allen of Vancouver had dined with Franklin the day before he sailed for Hudson's Bay. Rae had a younger brother destined yet to win renown in the icy North.

Old days in Canada were discussed. "Furs, man?" Dr. McLoughlin used to say, — "Lord bless you, man, furs are worth more than mines. While the Spaniard was ransacking Mexico and Peru, France and England were trapping skins, and they made more out of it. Furs led the Russian hunter across Siberia, furs led him along the isles to Sitka. Furs opened Pacific trade. At Nootka Sound Captain Cook's men exchanged trin·

kets for otter-skins for their own use and comfort, but when they reached the ports of China the merchants offered such incredible sums for that accidental stock of furs that they all wanted to give up exploration and turn traders. Cook's men introduced the sea-otter to England. Furs led to the exploration of North America. The first white men on the Great Lakes, the Mississippi, the Missouri, the Columbia, and the waters of the North, were fur-traders." When McLoughlin got started, he was a famous story-teller.

"Once, our magazines were full of unsalable bear-skins. One of our chief factors selected a set of fine large skins, had them dressed in silver with the king's arms, and presented them to a royal duke. His lordship put them into his state coach and drove to court. In a fortnight every earl in England was scrambling after bear-skins." With long whiffs at their pipes they listened. McLoughlin knew the fur trade like a book.

"The Russian Empress Catharine set the fashion for sables — now we have miles of traps, baited with meat and mice. England alone consumes one hundred thousand Hudson's Bay sables a year. But the beaver! I heard old gray-beards tell in my boyhood, that when a Parisian hatter set the fashion, all the young men of Canada left their seigniories and took to the woods. Their farms went back to forests. Du Luth left Montreal with eight hundred men at one time. Nobody knows how far they did go, but when they came back with their fur-filled boats they lived like kings, they dressed in lace, and wore the sword, and made Montreal a pandemonium with their drunken revels.

"Lord bless you, man, the markets of France were glutted, the ships would take no more, every warehouse in Montreal was packed, and still the brigades came paddling down the St. Lawrence. They stacked the bales in empty squares; some became damaged. At last, to get rid of so much beaver, they built great bon-fires, and thousands of pounds were burnt in the streets of Montreal. That was about the time the Americans were hanging witches at Salem and the French were fighting the Inquisition at Quebec. Nobody ploughed the fields in Canada, there was almost a famine, but those men who ranged the woods could never bring themselves to settle down on their farms again. They be-came wild, and cared for nothing but adventure. They settled in the woods, and their children are our Iroquois voyageurs of to-day. You'll not find a full blood among them — their grandfathers were the Frenchmen of that old fur-time!"

XII

THE BRIGADE TO CALIFORNIA

1839

D^{R.} McLOUGHLIN had much to do in gathering
up the threads of routine. "Where is our Spanish brigade?" he asked.

"Ready equipped at Scappoose Point," answered
Michel La Framboise. "We start to-morrow."

There was always bustle when a brigade set out.
At daylight two hundred horses were pawing at Scappoose Point just across the western end of Wapato.
Tom McKay had a ranch there, rich in sleek horses
and cattle, and oceans of grass. A string of boats came
down from the fort with a jolly picnic party to give the
trappers a send-off. The cottonwoods were yellow on
Wapato, sprinkling with gold the old council ground of
the Multnomahs. October russet dotted the Scappoose
hills. The Cascade Mountains lay in banks of crimson
against the sunrise. The ladies from the fort leaped to
their saddles tinkling with tiny bells. The gentlemen
rode at their sides, gay as Charles's cavaliers, with love-
locks round their faces.

As usual, Dr. McLoughlin took the lead on his Bu-
cephalus. Madame rode Le Bleu, a dappled white and
sky blue, that in her day had galloped seventy-two
miles in eight hours, to carry the tobacco, the *sine qua
non* of an Indian trade. David mounted Le Gris de
Galeaux like a Cossack. Rae and Eloise followed on
Guenillon and the snowy Blond, all favorite horses at

Fort Vancouver. Ermatinger with his Bardolphian nose cut a laughable figure on Le petit Rouge by the side of his fair bride Catherine on Gardepie.

After the gentry came La Framboise at the head of his long array of French trappers in scarlet belts and Canadian caps, with their picturesque Indian families, the plumes of men and women dancing and waving in the wind, brilliant as a hawking party in the days of mediæval song.

Michel La Framboise had been a famous voyageur, one of the picked few sent out by John Jacob Astor. He could flip his canoe over the choppy waves where no one else would dare to go. Now, every autumn after the harvest was over, he led the horse brigade to the Spanish country.

The trappers always travelled with their families; the mother bestrode the family horse, with its high-pommelled Mexican saddle; the children jogged along on their Cayuse ponies and slept until night, when down they slid, full of glee, gathering flowers, shooting their little arrows, and listening to tales of grizzly bears and Blackfeet.

La Framboise was proud of his half-breed wife, Angelique, his Grande Dame, in her bloomers of beaded blue broadcloth; Angelique was proud of the pretty white pappoose that dangled from her pommel, asleep in its little *miau* of beads and ribbon. Close behind came the children, with elfin locks and flashing eyes, with one hand whipping their horses to make the bells go " zing-zing-zing," with the other hugging tight the buckskin dollies with blue bead eyes and complexions chalked to the whiteness of the charming missionary women.

The Indian boys brought up the rear, lashing their

unruly packhorses heavily laden with camp equipage
and Indian goods.   All were in fine feather; the caper-
ing steeds, the crisp air, the scintillant sun, the tuneful
meadow lark, harmonized completely with the bursts of
song and gay and lively laughter.

The Willamette was carpeted with green from the
early autumn rain.   Scarlet-flaming thickets of vine
maple glowed along the watercourses.   Every hill-slope
was a bank of burning ash.   The cavaliers were armed
to the teeth; from every belt depended a leathern fire-
bag with pipe, tobacco, knife, and flint and steel.   There
were hunters in that brigade, rough as the grizzlies they
hunted; hunters keen as the deer, suspicious as the elk;
hunters that read like a book the language of tracks.
Leaning over their horses' necks, they could discern the
delicate tread of the silver fox, the pointed print of the
mink, and the otter's heavy trail.   With whip-stock in
hand La Framboise points—"A bear passed last week,"
"An elk yesterday," "A deer this morning."   In a
moment a deer tosses its antlers, sniffs the wind, then
bounds with slender, nervous limbs into the thickest
shade.

A brisk morning ride over the Scappoose hills and
down into the Tualitan plains was followed by a picnic
dinner around a gypsy fire, then McLoughlin dismissed
the trappers into the Indian country.

The parting cavalcades looked at each other from
their curveting steeds.   "Beware on the Umpqua,"
called the doctor.   "If the new men get the fever give
them plenty of broth and quinine."   Again he turned
with a parting word and gesture: "Look out for the
Rogue-Rivers; they'll steal the very beaver out of your
traps."

With gay farewells the fort people galloped back to

the crossing at Wapato. The California brigade followed along the winding trail to the south. La Framboise always touched at La Bonte's, a solitary garden spot in miles and miles of prairie. "How much land *do* you own, mon frère La Bonté?"

"Begin in the morning," the old trapper was wont to say, — "begin in the morning on a Cayuse horse. Go west till the sun is very high, then go south till it is around toward the west, and then back to the river; that is my manor."

And, too, there was always a stop at Champoeg, — every man at Champoeg was "mon frère" or "mon cousin" to La Framboise. Beside his wide hearth for many and many a year La Chapelle loved to sit and tell of the days when he, too, was *bourgeois*, and Madame his wife was the grandest dame that ever bestrode a pony. And for the thousandth time the good dame brought out the dresses stiff with beads that were worn in that gay time when the Monsieur led the hunt to the head waters of the Willamette.

The head waters of the Willamette was a royal beaver republic. There the little colonies cut down whole forests, built up wonderful dams and bridges, scooped out lakes, and piled up islands. With their long sharp teeth they cut up the timber and shaped their houses, plastering them neatly with their broad, flat tails. They had rooms in their houses and dining-halls and neat doorways, these deft little builders, more cunning than the fox, more industrious than the bee, more patient than the spider, more skilful than the Indian. "The beaver can talk," says the Indian. "We have heard them talk. We have seen them sit in council on the lazy ones. We have seen the old chief beat them and drive them off."

Two hundred miles south of the Columbia, La Framboise descended from a high ridge of mountains down to a little plantation on the banks of the Umpqua, the fortalice of old Fort Umpqua. Carronades peeped from the donjon tower. Tom McKay built it after that disaster to the American trappers — sometimes they called it Fort McKay. Here a solitary white man ruled the Umpqua. Jules Gagnier was a Frenchman, the son of an honorable and wealthy family in Montreal. In vain they made efforts to reclaim him from his wanderings and his Indian wife. Hither, twice every year, La Framboise came, twenty miles off his trail, to bring Gagnier Indian goods and to carry away his beaver. Here, summer and winter, year in and year out, the jolly, genial Frenchman traded with his red friends and cultivated his little patch of garden. Such were the first white men who broke the way for pioneers on the northwest coast.

La Framboise's brigade wound along gorges and canyons, through the Rogue River valley with its orchards of sunlit manzanita and hillsides of gnarled madrono and chinquapin, into the Switzerland of America, where Mt. McLoughlin on the summit of the Cascades was the most conspicuous landmark on the southern trail. One more pull — over the Siskiyous — and they have crossed the Spanish border. As a rule the brigades started early, to avoid the snows of Shasta, where once they lost the whole of their furs and three hundred horses. All day long, for days and days, the triple peaks of Shasta watched them winding down the Sacramento. La Framboise set his traps. Sutter's men began to look with unfriendly eye upon the intruders from the Columbia, but the Hudson's Bay Company had a permit from the Spanish Governor Alvarado.

XIII

DR. McLOUGHLIN AT HOME

1839

ELOISE at the door was stitching as usual. Little Cecelia on a cricket at her feet was untangling the many-colored skeins of silk.

In the doctor's room they were discussing the Russian question. Now and then she could distinguish a phrase: "along the coast," "ten leagues," "a lease," "ten thousand otter-skins." Somehow, half-dreamily putting two and two together, Eloise understood that the company had leased the Russian strip over which they fought five years ago. She knew that scores of Canadians had come to man the new posts on the Russian strip.

"Now, daughter, you and Rae shall take your bridal trip." Dr. McLoughlin came out on the veranda and laid his hand on the thick, glossy braids of Eloise.

"Where? To Canada?" asked Eloise, with a quick glance toward her husband, who, pulling at the grapevines, seemed absorbed in thought.

"Worse yet, to rainy Stikine," said Rae, looking away from his wife.

"Tut, tut, tut, my son. Don't quarrel with your promotion," said Dr. McLoughlin. "The most dangerous post in the service is the most important just now."

"I am satisfied," explained Rae, "but Eloise — I hate to expose her." It was the old fear, — a white woman in an Indian country.

"William," said Eloise, rising like a queen, "do you not think I shall be safe if you are there? Do not hesitate if my father thinks it best. Perhaps you can do more than any other toward reducing that district to order. They send only the most trusted men to posts like that."

"Spoken like McLoughlin's daughter," said Douglas, coming through the door. "These Hudson's Bay girls inherit heroic blood." The words were both a compliment to Eloise and a tribute to his own brave wife, who at that moment approached from the other end of the long veranda.

So during that winter preparations were made for the trip in the early spring. Arrangements for the lease were yet to be perfected, so an opportunity offered for Rae and Eloise to accompany Douglas to Sitka before settling to the dangers of dreary Stikine. Rae carefully completed his accounts to hand over to Dugald McTavish, his successor in the head-clerkship. Douglas looked after sundries for the new forts. Mrs. Douglas assisted Eloise in overhauling her boxes of London dresses preparatory to meeting the Russian grandees at Sitka castle.

How did they dress when Eloise was young? Vandyck puffs and wing bretelles, everything just as it is now, was in fashion sixty years ago. Noah's ark, a massive cedar chest bound with copper and lined with zinc, was hauled out of a capacious closet of the governor's residence. Noah's ark came from over the sea, packed full of carefully folded and perfumed dresses of made-up silk from the hands of London dressmakers. Everything lovely was in that old cedar chest, — "silken hose and satin shoon," Indian shawls and Canton crêpes, brocades and French embroidery, old-time ruffs and stomachers and caps, velvet cloaks and Parisian bonnets, odds and ends of chemisettes and under-sleeves, silken-fringed bretelles, and even the tie of her father's old peruke that he used to wear in the dance at Montreal. Ten or twelve breadths were in the skirts of those dresses; neat-fitting bodices ran down to a point; all sorts of bell sleeves flared like the cups of convolvuli. If there was anything the fur-magnates were proud of, it was their daughters, and they had the money wherewith to gratify that pride.

All winter the axe of the Iroquois chopper rang in the woods; all winter the little saw-mill hummed. Roderick Finlayson had been put in charge of the new grist-mill. At the end of the week, Saturday night, he walked home to the fort, five miles, in the heavy winter rain. It was late. The gate was locked. The new clerk beat on the wall. Bruce looked out.

"Ye're brakin' the rooles a-coomin' this time o' nicht," said the crusty old gatekeeper, letting him in. The quick ear of Dr. McLoughlin caught the sound. Finlayson was summoned.

"Why are you out contrary to regulations? Are you not aware that clerks must be inside the fort at ten o'clock? I am afraid we shall have to discipline you young gentlemen from the East."

Finlayson explained, some accident at the mill. "And," he added, "after my work was done I had to walk five miles, sir."

" Yes, yes, I know all about that," said the doctor. Finlayson was only eighteen. When Dr. McLoughlin saw the boy, cold, wet, and hungry, whose only crime was zeal in doing his duty, he spoke kindly, and turning to Douglas said, "You had better let him have a horse, James." Finlayson bowed his thanks and walked away. " A horse," cried Dr. McLoughlin after him, " a horse; but mind ye, no saddle; ye must furnish your own saddle."

Monday morning Finlayson selected a spirited horse and bought a good saddle with Mexican spurs and gay trappings. Saturday night came again. The dashing cavalier, seeing the gate open, reined his prancing steed within the palisade. " Who the devil is that daring to break the rules of the establishment by coming into the square in that fashion ? " roared Dr. McLoughlin, levelling his spectacles.

" Roderick Finlayson, at your honor's service," answered the gay young clerk, reining up before the governor.

" Dismount, sir," cried the governor in a tone of thunder. " Do you suppose the court is a parade ground? Do you suppose we want half-broken colts in the presence of these women and children? This is a private square, sir, and not a public horseyard. Baptiste, take the horse. Young man, you may walk hereafter." So poor Finlayson had to wade through the mud the rest of the winter.

Discipline was strict at Fort Vancouver. In the semi-military life idleness was unknown. For weeks the Canadian voyageurs, laid up for the winter, thwacked with the flails in the barns, thrashing out the harvest of Canadian peas. All winter the ploughs followed the furrows. " Mind ye make them straight," said the doctor. The straightest furrows ever drawn at Fort Vancouver were by the unerring eye of the Iroquois, perfect as a surveyor's line. Spades dug in the ditches. When nothing else offered, decayed pickets in the palisade were pulled out anj replaced with fresh ones from the forest.

XIV

1839

WINTER rains followed the departure of the brigade to California, — the still, steady rain of Oregon, that falls straight down. The grass revives, buds swell, moss runs rampant. One morning Dr. McLoughlin watched the sun swinging his chariot of light above Mt. Hood. " 'T is like the suns of Napoleon, propitious," he said. " Charlefoux ! "

" Oui, oui, sire," answered the guide.

" Let us get to Champoeg before the next rain."

" Oui, oui, sire."

Sometimes in summer Dr. McLoughlin took Madame to visit Champoeg and the mission. His fleet of canoes brought beds, bedding, tea, coffee, sugar, bread, cakes and wine, a numerous suite, and a cook. He camped beside the mission, and took a lively interest in its work. " The doctor's urbanity, intelligence, and excellence of character made his visits very agreeable," say the old chronicles.

To-day he sped with only his Iroquois. At the Falls of the Willamette, where the blue sea tide came up to the foaming cataract, he made a portage. Dr. McLoughlin had a house there, two of them, holding the claim to the site of a future city that he dreamed of. Forty miles from the Columbia the shrill " *Rouli, roulant, ma boule roulant*," rang over French Prairie.

Wherever the Frenchman's heel has danced from polar snows to San Diego, the Frenchman's oar has cut each lake and stream to this favorite song of the forest, —

" Rouli, roulant, ma boule roulant,
En roulant ma boule roulant,
En roulant ma boule."

The deep rich orotund " roll, rolling " from the chests of the canoe-men rang an endless round that sixty years ago made Oregon waters vocal. The moon had risen over the tree-tops. The deep, swift river slid like a dream between her umbrageous banks. The gentle dip of the oars broke the water into a million diamonds, trailing behind in a wake of silver. As they neared the landing at Champoeg the song was answered from the shore — even the tiniest child could sing " *Rouli, roulant.*" The voyageurs gave a last repeat to the ever-repeating chorus as they leaped into the water and dragged the boats upon the shore. Many a night in the marshy muskegs of the North had they presented their shoulders to carry Dr. McLoughlin dry shod to shore.

While Charlefoux pitched the tents Dr. McLoughlin strode rapidly up the bank toward the mossy-roofed houses of old Champoeg. The barns loomed duskily. From every parchment window there came a glow of firelight, sparkles danced over the chimney-tops like fireflies in the dark. There was a smell of southern-wood and sweet marjoram as the governor climbed the stiles and crossed the pole-picketed gardens. The long-horned Spanish cattle were lowing around the well-sweeps in the neighboring corrals.

" Félicité," the doctor called. He had halted in the mossy porch of a double log house. Étienne Lucier's charming daughter sprang out with a glad laugh. The governor kissed her on the cheek. "That's a good girl. Tell your mother to bring on the gingerbread," he said, as she led him into an immense room with a huge fireplace occupying the entire opposite end.

It was a sight for gods and red men when the pompous governor, six feet three in his moccasins, entered the low-raftered room and threw off his ample blue cloth cloak on a leathern chair before the fire. His obsequious vassals, the father and sons, bowed down to the chair-tops, quite overcome by the honor of his visit. The children courtesied from their corners. If King George himself had entered, the good dame could not have felt more flattered. A horde of slaves were summoned. The heavy fir table was loaded with fruits of the hoe and the hunt, hams of venison, and wheaten cakes. Of nothing were the Canadians more proud than of their wives' skill in bread-making. Under the tuition of the Methodist mission, the women of Champoeg vied with one another in this useful art. Nearly every time the bateaux went down to Fort Vancouver some Canadian carried to Dr. McLoughlin a sample of his wife's baking, neatly browned and rolled in a towel. And to every one the encouraging governor said, "Bless me! Bless me! The best bread this side of London" — a compliment the proud housewife stored ever after in her heart.

"'Ee eat no more tan te sparrow," urged the host, pressing upon the distinguished guest the Madame's choicest dried huckleberries. The slaves in their buckskin dresses peeped and peered until their dusky mistress "shooed" them back into the shadow.

Reverence fails to express the depth of feeling these Champoeg settlers entertained for the indulgent Hudson's Bay governor. He, together with the gentlemen at the fort, constituted the *noblesse* of the forest, linking the red men with the London nobles. No less was it a bond of kinship that Dr. McLoughlin was Canadian-born and spoke provincial French. Almost fabulous tales were told of his power, his wealth, his benevolence. Some to this day regard him a saint not yet canonized on the books of the clergy. This was partly Dr. McLoughlin's natural philanthropy, partly his habit of reading prayers to his people and lecturing on their morals.

"Eh? begosh! Eef mon 'ave more nor one wife de hol dogtor will 'ang eem," whispered the voyageurs.

McLoughlin donned his bright chintz dressing-gown. His feet were on the fender. His clean-cut face looked almost classic in the firelight as he watched the hurrying slaves clearing out the room for a dance. Indian slavery was no exotic in Oregon; it had grown into Champoeg with its Indian wives and aboriginal traditions. Back of every manse their cabins straggled like quarters of the blacks in Georgia. Every autumn still the Klamaths came over the Calapooias, bringing their captives to trade for ponies and three-point blankets. Five blankets would purchase a boy, fifteen a girl. Beads, blankets, and guns would buy a wife, some captive princess from Rogue River or the Shasta land. Even as they jostled one another in futile haste to move tables and settees, up the back path through the onion bed came the toot-a-toot-toot of André's squeaking fiddle. Never a voyageur was there who could not make his own fiddle and draw from it, too, the good old tunes his father brought from France when the fleur-de-lis flew over Quebec. In short order, neighbors of every complexion were treading the night away in honor of the guest. The fire burned low and the moon was pale

when the governor was escorted back to his camp.
The dark boats tied to the shore rocked idly on the
glassy Willamette.

The bell in its frame on Father Blanchet's new chapel
rang in the Sabbath. In every direction the habitants
were wending their moccasined steps to the house of
worship. Last night's dancers brought their numerous
children packed three and four in a bunch on horseback. Graceful young half-breeds on their Cayuse
ponies came loping in with a long and easy swing.
Some sweethearts sat in pairs upon the sturdy little
steeds. Everywhere the gayest garbs brightened the
picturesque prairie.

White-headed Dr. McLoughlin, in his blue cloth
cloak adorned with double rows of silver-gilt buttons,
stood on the steps with a hearty hand-shake for each
father and son and a cordial kiss for each wife and
daughter. No wonder he stole their hearts away, this
gallant governor of early Oregon! Among those
weather-beaten faces were some of the first white men
that ever crossed the continent; faithful Canadians, who
in 1792 paddled and poled that homespun old baronet,
Sir Alexander Mackenzie, from Montreal to the Fraser;
men who came with Lewis and Clark; and Astor's
trappers, who had drifted into the old Northwest before
the war of 1812. In the fur-service they had grown
gray. Now with their native wives and half-breed children they had come to a halt in the incomparable valley
whose fruitful acres invited repose.

They seated themselves quietly on the rough benches,
the men on one side, the women on the other, devoutly
kneeling and crossing themselves as Father Blanchet
went through the Catholic service. There was a rat-
tling of beads as toil-stiffened fingers counted the

rosary. Weather-cracked voices joined in the canticles learned long ago on the banks of the St. Lawrence.

Liberal as he was in religious matters, Dr. McLoughlin felt a peculiar home feeling in that rude little church with its tawdry pictures of the saints and its candles before the Virgin. It carried him back to his native hamlet at Rivière du Loup among the maples of Canada. These old servants were indeed his brethren. He loved them as he loved the memory of his mother and the pictures of childhood. After mass the children lingered for a word of recognition, the old men loitered to consult about private affairs and recount losses and trials to the patriarchal governor, who took a personal interest in every one of them. Whatever he told them to do, that they did. Obedience is one of the first virtues of the French Canadian, learned long ago at the foot of Mother Church. If they were industrious he praised them, and let them have whatever they needed from the stores at Fort Vancouver. If they were shiftless and wasted the harvest season in horse-racing and idle games, he came down with denunciations that frightened them back into rectitude. Hearts stood still like a whipped school-boy's when they heard Dr. McLoughlin's loud voice bidding them, " Go to work! Go to work! Go to work! " There were no written laws; the governor settled their disputes arbitrarily. Whatever he said, that was law in the valley Willamette.

They were a careless, thoughtless, happy people, these Canadian farmers of old Champoeg, quiet, simple-hearted, free from fear and envy, temperate, — for the governor allowed no ale in the valley, — honest, for there was nothing to steal. Free from cares of Church and State, no political issue troubled them, no church schism. There were few books and less English. Their great galas were weddings. A wedding lasted a week at old Champoeg. Everybody far and near came and danced, danced till they wore out their moccasins, then pulled them off and danced in their stockings.

"Don't 'e recollect? I danced at your wedding," was the open sesame to almost any favor. Long winter evenings were spent around the ample hearths, while the rain went drip, drip, drip outside, recounting over and over their boyhood days in Montreal, dog-sled tours to Athabasca, and canoe-brigades on the Saskatchewan. Covering the fire, for coals were precious and not to be lost, they retired to sleep without locks on their doors or ambition in their hearts.

In a solitary cabin across the river from Champoeg there dwelt a lonely Tennesseean. He had come from California with a herd of Spanish horses only to find French Prairie blazoned with his name:

"BEWARE OF EWING YOUNG THE BANDIT."

In wrath he tore the placards down. "Who dares," he cried, "who dares insult an honest man!"

The timid Canadians avoided the tainted stranger. Their doors were shut. In need of clothing, he sent a pack of beaver down to Fort Vancouver. Dr. McLoughlin declined the beaver, but sent a gift of food and clothes to the supposed bandit. In a towering rage Ewing Young hired Indians and a canoe and journeyed to Fort Vancouver.

"Before you arrived, sir," exclaimed Dr. McLoughlin in the hot, explosive interview, "before you arrived I had warnings of you. Our schooner 'Cadboro'' returning from Monterey brought word from the governor of California that Ewing Young, journeying to this country, was chief of a gang of banditti, — horse-thieves, sir;

that is the word he used. As head of a great company trading to California, what can I do in face of such a charge and from such a source?"

"Do?" cried Young, white with rage, "why, give a fellow-man a chance. Demand the proof. I myself will probe this thing to the bottom, if I have to go to Monterey to do it."

In view of this indignation and this stout denial, Dr. McLoughlin himself began to be half convinced of Ewing Young's innocence. Letters of inquiry in time brought back a retraction of the charge. "Not Ewing Young himself, but some of his followers," the Spanish governor explained.

Nevertheless the outraged Tennesseean could not forget the insult. At his ranch in the valley he continued to nurse his wrath and his herds of horses. Hate, hate, hate of the Hudson's Bay Company and distrust of its every move became the keynote of the life of Ewing Young. He talked it to every American that entered the valley; with Jason Lee he wafted a breath of it to Boston and to Congress.

1839

DECEMBER arrived. Basil's Christmas fires kept up incessant roaring. The rafters of the provision house creaked under the weight of birds picked smooth and white. The high-backed settees took on a knowing air as Dr. McLoughlin walked through the kitchen. The tin and copperware winked on the wall. Even the kitchen had Christmas greens.

Burris set all his Kanakas in a whirl. Some turned the plovers on the spit. Some set the quails on the gridiron. Burris kept an eye on the sun-dial, and every now and then took a sly nip of ale behind the buttery door. With a thump of the rolling-pin he announced the Christmas dinner. Fat goose, cranes, swans, so fat they swam in grease, plum-duff crowned with holly, ducks, showing the rich red after the knife, and baked quails, white to the bone, — these the Oregon epicures ate for Christmas dinner in 1839.

The tables were removed, and the governor in flowing peruke and ruffled waistcoat led the dance with Madame. The hall blazed in greenery. The tall central posts were wound with the holly-leaved Oregon grape, the Christmas candles were wreathed in ivy. A Yule-log of fir beaded with globules of resin snapped and sparkled. Scotch clerks and English kissed the pretty girls beneath the mistletoe, plucking each time a pale gray berry from the bough.

And who were the pretty girls? Eloise, of course, and Catharine — the Canadian Lily. Six weeks Ermatinger duly courted her; and then they were married. From the mouth of the Columbia there came the handsome Birnie girls, whose father, James Birnie, a genial, jolly Aberdeen Scotchman, kept the only hostelry from Vancouver to the sea and from Sitka tó San Francisco. Old Astoria, renamed Fort George, had been abandoned; but after the Clatsop trouble Dr. McLoughlin had sent Birnie there to keep a lookout for passing ships. Here he cultivated a little garden, did a little Indian trading in salted salmon and sea-otter skins, kept a weather eye out on the bar over which at long intervals a ship came into the river. Astor's old post was burned; only the scarified and blackened chimney stood among the ruins that were overrun with brier and honeysuckle. The latchstring of Birnie's log house on the hillside was out to the trapper, the trader, the Indian, and the sailor. More than one old missionary has paid tribute to the housekeeping virtues of his pretty wife, the daughter of a Hudson's Bay trader in the north country. Her blazing hearth, clean-scrubbed fir floor, and neat pine table of snowy whiteness, offered cheer and comfort to all the early wanderers who came "the plains across or the Horn around." Sole Saxon of the forest, Birnie's flag was first to welcome the incoming ship, and last to wave a farewell from the shore.

Chief Factor Pambrun, the *tinas tyee* (little chief) that held in check the upper tribes, sent down his fair Maria, the pride of Walla Walla. Pambrun himself was a blond with thin light curls. This in his child developed into peach-bloom red and white, blue eyes, and the midnight hair of her mother rolling in her father's curls. Very well Miss Maria remembered the urbanity of that accomplished Captain Bonneville who came riding so gayly over the mountains, and then — rode back again. With his feet under Astor's table in New York City, he told Irving a pretty tale of " Pambrun's attractive wife and her singularly beautiful children."

The chief factor's daughter had seldom passed beyond the stockade of Walla Walla except to the neighboring mission, where she became the favorite pupil of Mrs. Whitman. The good Chief Factor Pambrun himself was a great friend to Dr. Whitman, — more than once he called the Indians to task for some act of discourtesy to the devoted missionary. There was a young American at Whitman's, Cornelius Rogers, an enthusiastic missionary, and the finest Indian linguist in the upper country, who madly lost his heart to the curly-haired daughter of the chief factor. Maria was a beautiful singer. Rogers taught her music. Her visits to the mission became events in his life — she seemed a child of joy and beauty. The pensive, studious young missionary watched her from afar as she rode with her father after the fox-hounds, like Christine of Colvile, like Eloise of Fort Vancouver.

This feudal life of the Hudson's Bay Company reproduced in the western wilds the feudal age of Europe. The chief of nearly every post had a beautiful daughter who sat behind her casement window, harp in hand, and sang the songs of France. Many of the chief factors took pride in the education and companionship of their children, the nearest links to the Saxon world from which they came. The sons were sent abroad to be educated; some of them are influential chief factors in the North to-day. The girls were sent to Red River or Montreal. Even Maria had once started for Montreal. It was during one of her father's long absences that the fur-traders were sometimes obliged to make. An uncle sent for the little girl to come to Montreal for her education. For her child's good Mrs. Pambrun consigned her weeping little daughter to the care of the east-bound brigade. Somewhere in the north country, on Rainy Lake, Lake of the Woods, or contiguous waters, the little girl lay sleeping in the bottom of the canoe. Suddenly she heard a well-known voice, her father's voice, crying his orders. Up popped the curly head. The west-bound brigade was flying past them toward the sunset. "Papa," she screamed.

"Why, Maria, is that you?" exclaimed the astonished chief factor. "Where in the world are you going?"

"They are sending me to school at Montreal."

"I guess not. Come," said the chief factor, holding out his arms. With one leap the lovely child cleared the intervening space and nestled her head on her father's bosom with a little cry of joy. From that hour they had never been separated.

Poesy and song found its way into those old forts; it was no rare thing to find a chief factor's daughter far better instructed than many an Enid or Elaine of Tennysonian song. The clerks went wild over these beautiful girls, so fair in contrast with their dusky surroundings. Cornelius Rogers, the missionary, went to the chief factor.

"Marry her? Marry my daughter?" ejaculated the chief factor. "With all my heart, young man, with all my heart. I shall be proud to call you my son-in-law."

But Maria's blue eyes flashed, "Father, I do not care to marry, and when I do I prefer a Hudson's Bay man."

" Do not urge your suit now — time will do wonders," said the chief factor to the impatient American. But that Rogers should marry his daughter became the chief wish of the factor's life. He discussed it with Dr. Whitman, he consulted Dr. McLoughlin; he made a will bequeathing a thousand pounds sterling to Cornelius Rogers.

Every autumn of her life Maria Pambrun had walked the ramparts of Fort Walla Walla, watching for the Montreal express. Somehow, in her romantic little heart, she believed that a knight would come out of that north from some castle beside a distant sea, and then — then — Day after day she sat there and dreamed, beading the moccasins in her lap. Along the northern wall rolled the wild Columbia, sucking in the lesser Walla Walla in its mighty sweep to the sea. Eastward, the Blue Mountains purpled in the sun. The bunch-grass prairies were covered with horses. Close around the fort lay the ever drifting, shifting, changing sands of the peninsula, darkening the sky in summer and sweeping in gales at night. And now, with such dreams in her head, she had come down to Christmas at Fort Vancouver.

At this Christmas festivity, Douglas and his wife Nelia, Rae and Eloise, Maria and the clerks, and the Birnie girls and Victoire, the daughter of La Bonté from the valley, all whirled in the dance together. Dr. Barclay lifted his eyes to the unexpected beauty of Maria Pambrun " in her kirtle green and a rosebud in her hair." She danced with David McLoughlin. David's long black locks had a careless grace; he had his father's fine, straight nose, and his mother's square-set mouth; there was a ring on his finger and a sword at his belt. Dr. Barclay's eyes followed the pair with a strange surprise, and David — cared for no one yet.

"Ah, I beg your pardon." It was unusual for David to do an awkward thing, but he trod on Bruce's toes, and Bruce had corns. Snuff-box in hand, the old Scotch warder reposed from the care of the flags, the guns, the garden, and the gate, sleepily watching the weaving dancers and thinking — of Waterloo, perhaps. Burris, portly and rubicund, resplendent in a huge roll of colored neckerchief and horn spectacles astride his nose, slipped out again — to take a nip of ale behind the buttery door.

To be the governor's guest at Christmas was no light honor. Monique and Charlefoux were there in their gayest dress, fine green cloth coats and silver buttons, crimson caps and golden tassels, cutting pirouettes and pigeon wings, stamping in the noisy rigadoon, and heeling it and toeing it on air. Tom McKay alone made no change in dress. With the free, frank manners of the Scot and the grace and affability of the Frenchman, he came in his hunting outfit. Scorning the effeminate foppery of the Canadians, he wore as usual his leathern belt, from which depended the powder-flask, the bullet-pouch, and the long scabbard that concealed the sword-like hunting-knife. Tall, dark, powerful, Tom McKay acknowledged no master save McLoughlin. No other man could do what McKay did at Fort Vancouver or on the trail. His name was a terror in the mountains. The Indians believed this Hudson's Bay cousin of theirs bore a charmed life; the whites knew him to be an unerring shot. But with all his fierceness Tom McKay had the gentle heart of a woman.

Past midnight the dance, half Highland with a dash of Indian, ceased, and the dancers disappeared. Old

Burris returned in his peaked nightcap and carefully bore away the last brand of the Yule-log to light the next year's Christmas fire. And he took a nip of ale behind the buttery door.

From Christmas to New Year's, feudal hospitality reigned at Fort Vancouver. The servants' rations were doubled, and they danced more madly. On New Year's every employé put on his best and mounted the flight of steps to the governor's door. Madame and her daughter stood at the heaped and laden tables, and with gracious air dispensed English candies, cakes, and coffee to the governor's guests.

Far away in the dim recesses of the Oregon woods an altar was reared that Christmas night. Before a green bower lit with candles and hung with garlands stood the Jesuit Father, De Smet, among the Flatheads. A hundred lodge-fires burned, a thousand red men slept. At a signal gun the Indians rose. The midnight mass, the mystery, the swinging censers, the decorated altar, the solemn ceremonial awed the savage heart. Indian voices chanted the Kyrie Eleison and the Te Deum, Indian fingers signed the cross and took the beads. The baptismal rite was read with the rising sun. The neophytes knelt with fluttering hearts. " Receive this white garment," said the smooth-shaven priest. " Receive this burning taper." The red hand received it from the white, robed in a flowing sleeve. One by one the untutored red men retired, proud of the white vestment and deeply impressed with the Black Gown's method of making medicine.

So ended the Oregon Christmas of 1839.

XVI

THE grizzlies were waking up from their winter naps and the drumming of the partridge in the woods gave token of returning spring. A thousand crystal streams leaped from the glaciers of Mt. Hood. In March Bruce was out with a scythe, laying low the thick swaths of grass. On every hillside the scarlet currant invited the gay little Nootka humming-bird to sip its hidden sweets. In March, too, Chief Factor Douglas and Finlayson, and Chief Trader Rae and Eloise, embarked, along with fifty Canadian assistants, to man the new forts on the Russian strip.

Often had Eloise seen the fur-ships come and go, often had she watched the brigades, dimly remembering the time when, as a little child, she came down the Columbia; but to-day, for the first time, she was really bent on a journey. Dr. McLoughlin held his daughter's hand, while tears ran down his cheeks. Her mother sat wailing on the shore.

Dr. McLoughlin turned to Rae. "My son, to you I intrust my child. Never betray that trust." Then the disciplinarian came uppermost. "You are going to a dangerous post, William. With Indians, firmness and management can do everything. Avoid offence. Soothe irritation. Deal honestly. Be kind, be patient, be just but remember Napoleon's motto, 'Be master.' In a subject country always expect an attack. Look for it. Prepare for it. Crush it. Trust nothing to chance." In these few words Dr. McLoughlin outlined his own life policy with the Indian.

David lingered at his sister's side, but to Eloise, to-day, more than father or mother or brother was the tall young Scot whose fortune henceforth was hers. The barque spread her wings, and with fluttering farewells, sped like a sea-gull out of sight.

During the winter there had been great excitement at old Wascopam, by the Dalles. Daniel Lee had preached to the fishing Indians until a thousand fell on their knees to Christ. Now, in early spring, Daniel Lee followed down along the Columbia to the sea, preaching as he went. He reached a Chinook village.

Naked little pot-bellied, bow-legged Chinook children, with wedge-shaped heads and goggle-eyes, were rolling in the sand. No white man ever looked upon the queer little Chinook children without a shudder — there was something so elfish, so impish, so almost inhuman in the distorted little faces. As soon as a baby was born it was swaddled in moss, its poor little forehead was pressed down with cedar bark and tightly corded to a board. The child cried all the time — presently it stopped; sensibility seemed deadened. The swelled cheeks and bulging black eyes reminded one of a mouse choked in a trap. The pitiful little attempts to smile under the frightful pressure resulted in grimaces, funnier than Palmer Cox's funniest brownies; but to the end of life, all subjected to this cruel practice had the most aristocratic and flattest of heads.

"Great canoe! Great canoe!" cried the Indians. The Chinook chief, his copper highness Chenamus,

rose from his rush mat at the door of his cedar house
and looked out. Sure enough, a ship was crossing the
bar. He wrapped his rat-skin toga around him, put on
a conical bear-grass hat, slipped a scalping-knife into
his sheath, and called his runners. They launched the
royal canoe that lifted her prow like the beak of a
Roman galley, and Daniel Lee, Chenamus, and his
two squaws were off. With a monotonous "Ho-ha-ho-
ha-ho-ha," to keep time, the Indian crew sent the cedar
barque like a wherry through the water.

Safely the mate in the masthead cried his orders,
safely the sailor hanging far over sounded the misty
breakers, safely the good ship crossed the bar. The
little canoe touched her side, then all clambered up,
just as the Indians had clambered into the Boston ship
of discovery forty-eight years before (1792). Pressing
his nephew to his bosom, the ever-directing, guiding,
energetic Jason Lee lingered but a moment, then char-
tering the crew and canoe of King Chenamus, set out
for the mission, to make arrangements for the reception
of his unexpectedly large reinforcement.

All that time Dr. McLoughlin was toiling abroad for
the aggrandizement of England on the Pacific, Jason
Lee, the missionary, was lecturing in the States. He
woke up Congress, suggested that a mile square of land
be offered to immigrants. He stirred the entire country.
Through him Caleb Cushing, of Newburyport, conceived the idea of trading in the Columbia. In response to his call for men and money, the Methodist
Board granted $40,000, and a mission colony of fifty-
three persons, ministers, mechanics, farmers, and teachers, sailed out on that ship "Lausanne" from New York
harbor. At Honolulu, Jason Lee arranged a treaty of
commerce with the king of the Sandwich Islands.

Fifty miles an Indian runner sped to Fort Vancouver. Back came McLoughlin's compliments in the schooner "Cadboro'," bringing milk and vegetables, a bag of fresh bread, and a tub of Sauvie's fresh-churned butter. The "Lausanne" anchored at Vancouver with the largest company of missionaries that had ever left an American port. Dr. McLoughlin came on board — his momentary surprise at their numbers passed, as with the courtesy for which he was famous he invited them all to the hospitalities of the fort.

"Pest take it all!" grumbled the clerks. "The governor goes too far when he turns us out of our comfortable bunks to make room for these Americans."

The same day four ragged boys came down the Columbia in a canoe. "Well! well! well!" ejaculated Dr. McLoughlin, unprepared for this second accession. "And where do *you* come from?"

"From the States, across the plains," answered the boys.

"At this time of year? And where did you winter, pray?"

"Among the Indians."

"They are certainly runaways," said the missionaries.

"No," said the boys, "we heard Jason Lee's first lecture when he reached the States, and we resolved to meet him here and grow up with the country."

With very round eyes the benevolent doctor sent them to the dairy to get some bread and milk.

"It won't be long before others will follow in their footsteps," said Josiah Parrish, the mission blacksmith.

"Tut, tut, tut!" laughed the doctor, waving his arm with grandiloquent air. "For all coming time we and our children will have uninterrupted possession of this country."

"Before we die we shall see Yankees coming across the mountains with their teams and families," insisted the missionary.

"As well might they undertake to go to the moon," laughed Dr. McLoughlin, in his genial way, feeling that he had the best of the argument.

XVII

THE BRIGADE FROM FRASER'S RIVER

1840

JASON LEE sped up the Willamette. All night he rowed, watching the fires of wigwams on the shore where naked savages passed between him and the light. "He be faster nor Dogtor Magloglin," said the Canadians, as he galloped through Champoeg. The children were at play, the dogs slept in the sun. He heard as of old the crowing cocks and the cooing pigeons in the barn lofts; again he waded knee-deep in flowers, again the larks flew up and sang. He arrived at the mission unannounced, opened the door of his own room, and paused upon its threshold. There hung the dresses of his wife, her books, her portrait, everything just as he left it two years ago. Through the wind-swayed muslin curtain he saw her garden in the rear, blooming just the same.

"Ah, God, why did they leave it so to break my heart? It seemed so long ago. Now it is but yesterday."

"Do not weep. She is gone from you entirely," said David Leslie, hurriedly followed by the tearful household. With an effort in their presence Jason Lee suppressed his grief.

"Public duty will not wait upon my sorrow. We must make place for a great reinforcement. Here is the list." Jason Lee passed the day in action, but night found him kneeling in the dewy grass under the firs.

Again Jason Lee came toiling down the Willamette. As he neared Vancouver he saw the people watching, he heard the cry, "The brigade! the brigade!"

The flag of the traders' barge, with its legend "Pro' pelle cutem," "A skin for a skin," fluttered down the Columbia. Every canoe shook out its beaver-painted bannerol. The boatmen in full song rose and fell with the heavy sweep. Jason Lee paused with the rest to watch the glittering pageant. These were the golden days of Fort Vancouver, when wealth poured in on every passing tide. Nearer came the swish of waves and the measured rap of the paddles on the sides of the canoes; nearer came the slender vessels, laden, heaped, and sunk to the gunwales with their precious freights of furs.

With only less *éclat*, it was a repetition of the splendid panorama of the governor's return eight months before. Again the bastions roared a welcome; even the mission ship caught the enthusiasm, and waved her flags and fired her guns. The fort gates opened to receive not knights in armor clad, but the brigade of gay and happy trappers with their winter's catch of skins.

Dr. McLoughlin, with an eye to business, lingered a moment. Clerk Roberts called, "Pack in the bales, pack in the bales." The voyageurs leaped to the task and trundled up the furs.

Chief Factor Ogden, homely and kind, passed on up to the fort with Dr. McLoughlin and the other factors of his fleet. His good wife Julia and his daughter Sarah Julia followed at a distance with Archibald McKinley, a tall, red-headed Highlander, second in command at Fort St. James. All the way down the zigzag rivers of the North McKinley had sailed and sung with Sarah Julia.

"Mons. Pete," as the voyageurs called Peter Skeen Ogden, was of the Ogdens of Ogdensburg and the Skeens of Skeensboro. Away back sometime his ancestors had founded those cities in New York, but when the Revolution broke out the Tory Ogdens crossed the border, — "saved so as by fire." Peter Skeen was born in Canada. As a lad he returned to what would have been his native State and entered the service of John Jacob Astor. Astor sent him to Astoria, on the far Pacific. He reached there just in time to find the post in the hands of the British. Of course Ogden became British again. He it was that explored the Yellowstone, the Utah and Shoshonie countries, made his winter rendezvous at Ogden's Hole in the Bear River Mountains, paddled his canoes on Great Salt Lake, and discovered Ogden's River, that Fremont renamed the Humboldt. He raided the beaver dams of Colorado, and following Jedediah Smith over the Sierras, trapped on the Sacramento. He it was that built the first forts to the north, stirred up the trouble with the Russians, and now ruled Fort St. James, the capital of all that region from the Fraser to the Russian border.

"Here, August." He handed one his wet moccasins, who flew away to hang them up to dry. Little Cecelia balanced on her arm the pretty feathered pouch that contained "Mons. Pete's" shot. Little Benjamin proudly bore the beautiful embroidered sheath that held "Mons. Pete's" big hunting-knife. Sarah Julia fled past her father into the arms of Mrs. Douglas. The women withdrew into the Douglas apartments.

"I don't want to get married," cried Sarah Julia, throwing off her sun-hat and bursting into tears.

" She too young," said Princess Julia, her mother.
" She fifteen summer."

" I want to stay with my mother," sobbed Sarah Julia.

"Who want to marry you, my child?" inquired Mrs.
Douglas, slipping her arm around the sobbing girl.

" Monsieur McKinley. He say he leave the service J
do not."

" He can wait," suggested Mrs. Douglas.

" No, he will go with my father."

" And where is your father going?"

" To Canada when the brigade go."

Mrs. Douglas understood. Lifting the tear-stained
face, she said: " My dear, your father do not like to
undertake a journey and leave you unsettled. If anything should happen to him, what would become of you?
Mr. McKinley may be chief factor some day. Have
you seen him much?"

" Every day — every evening — at Fort St. Jame —
my father — taught — me," came between the sobs.
" When he gone — Mons. McKinley taught me till I
read and write. We have read books together."

" And do you care for him?"

"Ye — s," Sarah Julia admitted, still tearful, "but
how can I leave so good a mother?"

And she had a good mother. Princess Julia made
the fortune of Peter Skeen Ogden. Long ago he went
into the Flathead country and was drawn into a quarrel.
The chief sent for him. " What!" cried the impulsive
Ogden. " Do you demand my life for a paltry pony?"
Ripping open his shirt and pointing to his breast — " Do
you think you sent for an old woman? Fire!"

" The Flathead never killed a white man," calmly
answered the Indian chief.

A council was in session; in the council sat the chief's

daughter. She ruled the council; she demanded restitution for the stolen pony, and Ogden had to pay it, —
but he saw the power of that Indian girl and resolved
to win her. She proved to be a high-priced maiden —
Ogden sent fifty ponies before there came any sign of
acquiescence. Then the chief's daughter came out and
mounted the last one — that was the wedding. He
called her Princess Julia. There was a great feast con-
summating the nuptials of the son of Isaac Ogden of
Montreal, Chief Justice of Canada, to the daughter of
the chief of the polite and unobtrusive Flatheads.

This marriage was distinctly a business transaction,
a state alliance. Ogden married the chief's daughter
for her influence, but in time he valued her far more for
personal bravery, for distinguished talents, and undying
devotion. With the form of an Indian squaw Princess
Julia had the head of a statesman. One day there
came a little pappoose to Ogden's tent — he named her
Sarah after his mother in Montreal, and Julia after his
Flathead spouse. Mrs. Ogden had much finery about
her pappoose-cradle, — embroidered coverlets, bird-
wings, and hoops of bells that jingled as they rode.

Once a party of American trappers came near the
Ogden camp and began selling liquor to the Indians to
get away their furs. In the hostile state of feeling that
ensued there was a stampede among the horses. Along
with a packhorse loaded with furs Mrs. Ogden's Cayuse
pony dashed away into the hostile camp with Sarah
Julia hanging to the saddle.

"The prize is ours by the laws of war," said the
Americans. At that instant Princess Julia ran into
their midst, clasped her child, leaped upon her pony,
and leaning down seized the halter of the packhorse.
"Shoot her, shoot the damned squaw," was the cry.

"Stop! She's a brave woman! Let her go," cried the captain, as Princess Julia and her baby galloped out of camp.

As long as she lived Mrs. Ogden retained her influence over the Flatheads, and her services secured her husband's rapid promotion among the fur-traders. On both father and mother's side she was related to all the great chiefs of the Northwest, making it safe for them to travel where no one else would dare to go Once at Salt Lake the trappers were away. The faithful Julia, mistress of the lodge, heard the dreadful war-whoop and ran out to secure the horses. Like a Scythian horde the enemy came dashing down upon the defenceless camp. Gathering up the halter straps, Princess Julia turned — and faced the hawk's eye and the Roman nose of a Crow. The war-bonnet of eagle plumes trailed in his hair.

"Ah!" said the feathered chief, leaping from his horse, "is that you, my sister, that is camped here? Let your horses eat; we will not trouble them;" and the rascals of the mountain, deadly as the Blackfeet, passed like the whirlwind.

Many a time she kept the Indians from going to trade with the Americans. "Bring the furs to me," she said.

Never was the wife of the chief factor idle. Into her husband's work she threw the full ardor of her nature. When the strong, swift Snake was at its highest notch and no horse could cross it, she tied a rope about her waist and towed to the other shore a raft of priceless furs. Once in March she swam the Snake for a goose for her sick child. When she returned to camp, there was a necklace of ice around her neck where she held her head above the water. What the Hudson's

Bay Company owes to Indian women cannot be told. In a few cases they acted as spies, to shield the wrong-doing of their own people, but as a rule they became faithful allies of their white partners, persuading the Indians to bring in their trade and settling many a difficulty to the satisfaction of both parties.

Dr. McLoughlin introduced Mr. Ogden to Jason Lee. "By my faith, it's not a bad thing to have a minister here just now," exclaimed the chief factor. "Never before these later days have I heard of sermons or prayers either in a Hudson's Bay fort. But remember, my friend," said Ogden, with an impressive shake of the finger, " remember, gunpowder is stronger than prayers."

Jason Lee was astonished at the effeminate voice of Peter Skeen Ogden, a voice so out of harmony with the hunter's rough external make-up.

Chief Justice Isaac Ogden was the greatest lawyer in Canada, and Peter Skeen, too, had been destined for the bar, — but that voice! As a boy in Montreal he pored over the yellow tomes. He set them back on his father's bookshelf. "I can never plead in this falsetto, father. The very clerks would snicker in their sleeves." So that harsh, squeaking, unmanageable voice drove Peter Skeen Ogden into the fur trade. Instead of devoting his life to tracing the seigniorial subdivisions of Canadian property, the son of the chief justice became a Nimrod of that primitive age fast slipping into fable. So long had Ogden been among the Indians that his manners resembled theirs. There was the same wild, unsettled, watchful expression of the eye, the same gesticulation in conversation. Never did he use a word when a sign, a contortion of face or body, would indicate his thought.

"Let me introduce you to my *kloochman* (wife),"
continued Ogden, in the same squeaky voice. "She's
the best moccasin-maker this side of Winnipeg, Mr.
Lee, — not so handsome as some, but I tell you she's
a goddess. And to-morrow I want you to marry this
young man to my daughter," turning toward McKinley.
Sarah Julia had yielded to her fate.

"It was due to the company," Mrs. Douglas said.
That was a great consideration. Everything was due
to the company. And Peter Skeen himself, — he
would not have the company lose a promising young
man for want of a bride, even if that bride were to be
his own daughter and the groom a much less desirable
man than Archibald McKinley.

These Hudson's Bay men, living in the vast solitudes,
seeing, hearing, knowing little but the fur trade, naturally looked up to "the company" as the one great
power next to England's queen. Its interests were
their life. Their devotion to it became a mania. As
contrasted with Indian wigwams, their substantial log
posts took on palatial splendors, their governors were
kings, their chief factors high nobles, and their daughters fit consorts for the best-bred young gentlemen the
company could employ.

The gentlemen from the various posts assembled
at Fort Vancouver viewed with apprehension the host
of missionaries within their domain. Right there in
Bachelors' Hall Jason Lee made appointments to
stations at the Dalles, Puget Sound, the Falls of the
Willamette, and at Clatsop-by-the-Sea. Dr. McLoughlin, a model host, with boats, provisions, and packhorses,
was there to speed the parting guest. But before they
separated Sarah Julia became the bride of Archibald
McKinley.

XVIII

DEPARTURE OF THE BRIGADE

1840

JULY brought the shining days of Oregon summer, beginning with twilight two hours after midnight and ending again in twilight. The clerks were fitting the brigades for their return to the interior. Indian goods were packed for transportation. The black-smiths were preparing axes, horseshoes, bridle-bits, beaver traps. The newly gummed boats were lying at the shore. The freshet had reached its climax, and the governor came out to set up his graduated, painted pole to note the number of feet. Old Waskema, the squaw, watched from under her shaggy brows and said: "The flood is over. It will stop now. The White-Headed Eagle has set out his stick to stop the river's rise."

The Indians looked with awe upon the old crone. Sure enough, the river did cease to rise. "She talks with the dead at night. She understands the white man's magic." In their eyes old Waskema was wise as the chiefs at Fort Vancouver.

The voyageurs were dressing for the launch, devoting an unconscionable amount of time to the decoration of their legs. The fringed buckskin trousers were tied with beaded garters and knots of gaudy ribbon. From their silken sashes hung fire-pouches like ladies' reti·

cules, with pendent tails embroidered with beads and silk.

"My canoe is my castle," laughed the electric-eyed Monique, strutting in the bow of his boat under a bonnet like the headpiece of a drum-major.

At ten o'clock Dr. McLoughlin summoned them in to take the parting cup of good-fellowship. Some songs, some tears, and repeated hand-shakes wafted the half-wild, Arab-like voyageurs upon the wave.

"Good-bye! Bon voyage!" The New Caledonian brigade shot gracefully into the current. All the up-river boats fell in. The cannon boomed, the trading guns sent back a parting salute. The boat song struck, and Sarah Julia turned in a paroxysm of tears from the last, fond look of her Indian mother. No more she travelled up the zigzag rivers of the north.

The brigade bore straight toward the base of Mt. Hood. No mountain in the world looms like Hood beside the Columbia. Although twenty-five miles away, it appears to approaching boats to rest on the broad water, and towers pyramidal into the clouds.

The brigade turned to the left and was lost amid the hills. At Okanogan they transferred to horses, and to boats again on the upper Fraser. It was a thrilling sight when the caravans of two hundred and fifty and three hundred horses, laden with merchandise, wound through the pack-trails of the North. Merrily, as amid the lochs and bens of their home across the sea, the hardy Highlanders sent the skirl of bagpipes screaming from hill to hill. At old Fort Kamloops the rout and revel rang, as the trading brigades drove through the gates and hung their saddles on the wall.

Fort St. James, 54° North, on a peninsula in Stuart's Lake, was Ogden's castle. Here the humorous, eccentric, law-defying chief factor ruled absolute among the red men and sent his dog-sleds over the snow to still more northern forts. Every April he left St. James, with his family and retinue, for the summer trip to Fort Vancouver, reaching home again in late September. This time, however, the chief factor bade his brigade adieu in the warm and fertile Flathead country, and turned his face toward the Rockies.

Ogden carried a breeze across the Rockies.

" What does Dr. McLoughlin mean by encouraging so many missionaries? What does he mean, I say?" exclaimed Sir George Simpson, the most arbitrary Hudson's Bay governor since the days of Prince Rupert. " I'll checkmate this American move if I have to depopulate Red River."

Sir George recognized the resources of Dr. McLoughlin — he did him the honor to overestimate them. Despatching his agent, he made this promise to the prosperous farmers of the Red River valley:

" To the head of every family emigrating to the Oregon country we will give ten pounds sterling in advance, goods for the journey, horses and provisions at the forts en route, and on the arrival at Puget Sound the company will furnish houses, barns, fenced fields, fifteen cows, fifty sheep, oxen, horses, farming implements, and seed. On the other hand, the farmers shall deliver to the company one-half of the crops yearly for five years and one-half the increase of the flocks at the end of five years."

In the chilly autumn nights the farmers talked it over.

" Not every day does such a fortune fall into our laps. Charlefoux says it rains and the grass is green all winter. Never is there a thunder, never a lightning, never a blizzard, drought or hail. Let us go," they said.

So twenty-three families of eighty persons altogether agreed to accept Sir George's offer, and meet at rendezvous the following June on the White Horse Plain west of Fort Garry.

10

XIX

DR. WHITMAN AND HIS CAYUSES

1837–39

DR. WHITMAN'S Indians were proud of their little farms. He bought them ploughs. The first time they broke ground for planting, a strange sickness broke out among the Cayuses. They were filled with consternation. Dr. Whitman attended from lodge to lodge. When over-eating and unnecessary exposure brought on a relapse, "This medicine bad, bad, bad," they cried. "Go bring the *tew-at* doctors."

The wife of the oldest chief fell sick and came near dying. Umtippe cried in a rage, "Whitman, my wife die to-night, I kill you!" Dr. Whitman was nearly sick with the excitement and care of them all.

Umtippe sent for the great Walla Walla *tew-at*. He came. He muttered and mumbled and waved his wand and pronounced her well. Umtippe gave him a horse and two blankets. The next day she was the same again. "He bad, bad, bad," cried Umtippe. "Ought to be killed."

All through April the Cayuses groaned in their teepees. Umtippe himself was stricken and sent for Dr. Whitman. The doctor thought he would die; fortunately the medicine relieved him. Just then the Cayuse war chief died in the hands of the great Walla Walla *tew-at*. The same day Umtippe's younger brother rode to Walla Walla, arrived at twilight, and shot the *tew-at* dead. That is Indian fashion. The medicine man is responsible.

Sticcas, a sub-chief, fell sick and came to the mission for care and treatment. Late at night Mrs. Whitman sat by the sick Indian with her seven weeks' baby on her lap, writing to her mother. Utterly worn out, Dr. Whitman had thrown himself down to sleep. Sticcas was the most enlightened man of his tribe, but because he was not well in a moment he became restless and uneasy. He rolled in his sleep and muttered, "The *tew-ats*, the *tew-ats*, send for the *tew-ats*."

In a few days he was better; soon he was well. When the warm Chinook blew in the May all the Cayuses recovered. Then great was the fame of Dr. Whitman.

That baby born at the Whitman mission was named for two grandmothers — Alice Clarissa. Her advent created great excitement among the Cayuses. The whole tribe of the Walla Wallas moved their teepees nearer. Far away to the buffalo country the tidings flew, up among the Nez Percés and to the distant Flatheads. The next day after she was born Chief Tiloukaikt called at the mission.

"Ugh-úgh!" he grunted, at sight of her ladyship. "Ugh-úgh! fall to pieces! *Tecast! tecast!*" he cried, dropping his buckskin robe and waving his arms so wildly that Mrs. Whitman thought something must be the matter.

The old chief knelt down and poked the baby's clothes with his big red fingers to see if under the dainty flannels there might not be indeed a hidden *tecast* (baby-board).

Pio-pio-mox-mox came, and Five Crows and Elijah, all worshippers at the shrine of the little white child. Five Crows remained a long time, smoking in the

Indian room and asking strange questions of Dr. Whitman.

The house became such a highway for every passing band that Dr. Whitman had to put up a stockade fence to keep them out. Sheets had to be hung to keep them from peeping through the windows and keyholes and crevices. They dug the moss out of the chinks to get a little glimpse of the mysterious chamber within, so much they wondered at this respectful care of a white wife in childbirth, when their own women at such a time were turned out of the lodge to live or die alone.

Every day the chiefs and headmen came to marvel at the baby that was not lashed to a *tecast* and yet did not fall to pieces. Indian women thronged the house continually to get a glimpse of the little stranger.

"She Cayuse *temí*, Cayuse girl," said Tiloukaikt, "born on Cayuse land."

"Yes, yes," laughed Dr. Whitman, "she is a Cayuse girl."

"Ugh-úgh!" grunted Tiloukaikt. "I not live long. I give all my land to her."

How she stole their hearts away, that little Cayuse girl! Every day she saw the dark faces around her. By and by she began to prattle in the Cayuse tongue.

"Ugh-úgh! Cayuse girl talk Cayuse." They were wild with joy. The chiefs would sit for hours teaching her Cayuse words.

Dr. McLoughlin sent up an orphan Indian girl to assist Mrs. Whitman. She became the baby's nurse. Mrs. Whitman's kitchen was full of little Indian children morning and night, learning to read and write and sing. At one year little Alice's size and strength astonished the Indians. She was as large and active as Indian babies two years old.

"Because she was never tied to a *tecast*," said the Indians.

"Because she has better food and better care," said Mrs. Whitman. How she pitied the poor Indian women, struggling along with burdens greater than they could bear and a little baby tied on top of all. No wonder they did not thrive when the overworked mother herself was ready to sink with exhaustion. And the little graves — it was shocking how many died from pure neglect.

In those days it was a familiar sight to see Dr. Whitman riding from plantation to plantation with little Alice on the horse before him. She was fair as her mother, and her flossy hair hung in silky yellow curls. Mrs. Pambrun sent a present of a rocking-chair to Mrs. Whitman and a little chair for Alice. Like a fairy queen the little girl sat in her chair in the Indian school, beating time with her tiny hands and singing the Nez Percé hymns. Her readiness to learn amazed them, but not more than the aptness of the Cayuse children amazed Mrs. Whitman.

"They are good-looking, quite handsome children," said Mrs. Whitman. "To sit at a little distance and hear them sing one would not think he was in a heathen land."

Sometimes Mrs. Whitman took baby Alice and went to Tauitau's lodge to help them sing. It was a compound lodge, — several lodges together, made into a long hall of skins and rush mats, with a fire in the centre. Here Dr. Whitman talked to the Indians and Mrs. Whitman sang with little Alice on her lap. In the old New York days Dr. Whitman could not sing, but here he discovered a new talent, and in rich tenor, led the Indian chorus.

The Oregon Indians moved with the seasons. When the wapato lay ripe under the last drip of winter rain, the women went waist deep into the marshes to dig this Indian potato. When the summer sun killed the stem of the star-flowered camas down to the ground, they dug in the prairies. Before the spring freshet subsided the salmon came sliding up the streams; while yet their opaline hues were glancing on the wave, the ripening berries called the squaw-mothers to the hills and the hunter to the buffalo beyond the Snake. September brought the salmon back to the sea, roots again filled the smoky October. So the Indian had his fishing trip to the Columbia, his summer residence in the mountain, his autumn camp on the prairie, and his winter home in some sheltered hollow contiguous to water, fuel, and winter pasture. For a time these roving habits threatened to render nugatory every effort of Dr. Whitman to settle the Indians on farms of their own, where he could superintend their education.

"Come, Narcissa," said the doctor one day, "let us go a little while and live with the Indians in their own lodges. It will give us better access to their language and more opportunities for instruction."

So one January morning the doctor and Mrs. Whitman mounted their horses, and taking little Alice before them, rode fifty miles over the sun-dried plain to the Cayuse camp on the Tucannon. The Indians received them with delight and entertained them in the best lodge. Mrs. Whitman conversed with the women, the doctor mingled with the warriors. The little children lay around on the ground, with their elfin locks in their eyes, listening to every word and drinking in the beauty of the flossy-haired little Alice. Every morning at dawn, every evening at twilight, the song of worship

arose. At midday the doctor addressed the attentive
throng. Again at evening, with the moon shining in
full splendor, the dark, eager faces gathered around the
great fire in the open air. With a shawl around her
shoulders and a handkerchief on her head, Mrs. Whitman sat in the door of her tent facing the fire in the
foreground, with little Alice asleep in her arms. The
air was clear and cold, but the cheeks of Alice were
never so rosy. Now the doctor related the parable of
the rich man and Lazarus, anon it was the tale of the
Crucifixion. Sobs and cries burst from the Indians,
women buried their faces in their hair. Almost as
weird a scene as on that night in Calvary, was enacted
on the banks of the lonely Tucannon.

Sometimes the missionary dwelt on their own sinful
lives, their hearts, "deceitful above all things and
desperately wicked." Then their faces grew stern and
they drew back.

"Don't, don't, don't tell us that. That talk is bad,
bad, bad. Now give us some good talk. Tell us about
the Bible country."

In summer the squaws had filled hundreds of rush-
bags with dried roots, and berries, and salmon pemmican, that they had worked hard to pulverize on the
rocks in the sun. They buried them at night in
caches, and went to the hills with the hunters to chase
the deer. While they were gone other tribes came
down and robbed their salmon caches — those cellars
where their winter stores lay hid — and great suffering
resulted.

"Ah, my poor people," said the sympathetic doctor,
"I see some of your discomforts. Some of these days
I shall have you all off the ground, out of the smoke,
living in nice comfortable houses of wood. And you

must all have farms, so you need not depend on the precarious living of roots and fish."

And they treasured these things in their hearts.

"Margaret, where is Alice Clarissa?" said Mrs. Whitman to the Indian nurse one day in June after her second birthday. Never could the fond mother bear the child out of her sight.

"I go see," said nurse Margaret. The Hawaiian servant also went out and returned. "There are two cups in the river," he said.

"How did they get there?" asked Mrs. Whitman, imperiously.

"Let them be," said the doctor, "and get them out to-morrow."

"How did they get there?" insisted Mrs. Whitman, "and what cups are they?"

As in a dream she recalled a glimpse of the curly-haired sprite — "Mamma, supper is most ready. Let Alice get some water." Going up to the table she took *two cups*, hers and Margaret's and disappeared. Like a shadow it passed across her mind, passed away and made no impression. Mrs. Whitman did not recollect it until she reached the river brink where the child had fallen in. No Alice could be seen. Turning toward the house, they saw an old Indian preparing to enter the river. They stopped to see him swim under the water.

"She is found," he cried, holding aloft the lifeless form.

Mrs. Whitman ran, but the doctor passed her and snatched the baby to his arms. The precious life had taken flight.

Four days they kept her. "Then," says Mrs. Whitman, "when she began to melt away like wax and her visage changed, I felt it a great privilege that I could put her in so safe and quiet and desirable a resting-place as the grave. Although her grave is in sight every time I step out of the door, yet my thoughts seldom wander there. I look above, where her joys are perfect."

In a home-made casket the stricken parents and the weeping Indians consigned to her grave the golden-haired Cayuse *temi*, the light of the Whitman mission.

XX

THAT WAGON

1840

CHIEF YELLOW SERPENT, old Pio-pio-mox-mox, sat on a buffalo-robe at the door of his tent, smoking his calumet and watching the horses. Far out as the eye could see the hills were covered with horses, coal black, cream white, spotted white and roan and bay, Cayuse horses, well-knit, deep and wide at the shoulders, broad-loined, fleet-footed. At the slightest hint of danger the wild beauties would lift their heads with a shrill neigh, dart in air their light heels, and speed with horizontal manes and tails across the hills.

The young men had gone to hunt the buffalo far away. Out in the meadows the Indian women, with long crooked sticks, were busily digging the camas, the queen root of the Columbia, and tossing the bulbs into baskets slung on their backs. Some were baking them into figs to pack away for winter use. Others pulled the conical kouse, the biscuit root, to bake into sweet little cakes for the winter's bouillon.

As the old chief sat there he heard a sound unlike the hum of insects or the whir of grouse. 'T was not the bleating of the kid nor the plaintive call of the fawn. Far out beyond this city of conical teepees something was following the horse-trail through the grass.

Yellow Serpent turned and bent his eye upon the approaching wonder. Some of his people were gathering around a vehicle that rolled on the grass. Yellow Serpent stood up. "Chick-a-chick," said the Indians, imitating the phenomenal sound. "Horse canoe," cried Yellow Serpent. Round and round the Indians walked and gave it up. Yellow Serpent bent and peered and touched it with a stick. The horse canoe paused for a moment, then rolled on over the grass to Whitman's mission. It was that wagon.

Beaver had grown scarce in the mountains. Jo Meek, the American trapper, and his "pard" had decided to settle in the Willamette valley. They went to Fort Boisé and got Whitman's old wagon. Into it they packed their Indian wives and babies, and drove by a recently discovered trail over the Blue Mountains to Waiilatpu. Dr. Whitman and his wife came out to meet them. These trappers they had met in the mountains seemed like old friends.

"'Twar a hard trip over the mountings," said Jo Meek. "Back thar on the plain the sage-brush war over the mules' backs and the flippers a'most cut off the axletrees. I war a'most sorry we undertook to bring the wagin."

"Oh, no," said Dr. Whitman, "you will never regret it. You have broken the road. When others see that one wagon has passed they too will pass, and in a few years the valley will be full of our people." A Delaware standing by heard these words, and told the Indians. Like wild-fire it flew from mouth to mouth.

Dr. Whitman killed the fatted hog for his trapper friends and they had a feast. Jo Meek left his little half-breed daughter Helen Mar to be educated at the mission. "How did you get that famous name?" asked Mrs. Whitman, smoothing the tangled locks of the little girl.

"Waal," he answered, with a twinkle in his eye, "we war reading the 'Scottish Chiefs' in the mountings when the little gal came, so I named her Helen Mar." The trappers passed on and took up farms west of the Willamette, where their descendants live to this day. Soon after, the famous Captain Bridger sent his little Nez Percé daughter Mary Ann to the Whitman school. On his first journey Dr. Whitman had cut an Indian arrow from the back of Bridger, a feat of surgery that gave him great fame in the mountains.

At the Indian camp a little half-breed Spanish boy abandoned by his Cayuse mother lay in a hole in the ground. The Indian children were amusing themselves lighting sticks in the camp-fire and burning spots on his little bare body. An old squaw passed by heavily laden with her lord's saddles and bridles and blankets; with a jerk that might have dislocated the infant's arm, she snatched him away from his tormentors, tossed him on top of her burden, and running across the Walla Walla on the teetering foot-log laid him down at the door of the mission. So now the Whitmans had three adopted half-breed children to take the place of the flossy-haired Alice.

XXI

A TRIP TO SITKA

1840

WHEN Douglas and his crew and Rae and Eloise left Vancouver that March morning in 1840, they slid down the Columbia to the confluence of the Cowlitz. Entering this river, milky with volcanic ash from St. Helen's, they soon came to its headwaters and crossed overland on horses to Puget Sound. All the storied beauty of Scottish lakes, Italian skies, and Isles of Greece seemed centred here, on these unsung shores that commemorate the name and fame of Lieutenant Peter Puget. Here the little black " Beaver," the first steamer on Pacific waters, took them out on their northern journey.

For miles and miles, interlacing the northwest coast, rocky islands, like the summits of submerged mountains, hold their green fringes down to the sea. In serried rank, the Douglas spruce — " the tree of Turner's dreams," the king of conifers, the great timber-tree of the world — stands monarch of the hills. Once, twice, thrice, they ran up rivers where Hudson's Bay forts held subject the clans of red men. " Reports from these posts form the most agreeable part of my library," McLoughlin was wont to say.

One evening the little " Beaver " rounded a rocky point and, quite unexpectedly, the Bay of Sitka burst into view. Beside Mt. Edgecumbe it lay, dimpling in the sunset. A few Russian ships lay at anchor in the Norse-like fiord close under the guns of Sitka Castle.

On either side of the bay, precipitous walls of rock
dipped into the emerald waters and waved their plumes
of pine-trees far above. As soon as word went up to
headquarters, a salute rang from the brazen guns, and
Governor Etholine, in his gig, ran out to greet his
English guests. Only three weeks since, Adolphus
Etholine had arrived from Kronstadt, bringing with
him a blond bride from Helsingfors. The events of
the London council were fresh in Etholine's mind, as
he greeted the envoys of the potentate on the Columbia.

On a high rock overlooking the Indian village of
Sitka old Count Baranoff had built a castle, — built it
strong, of heavy hewn cedar, pierced by copper bolts,
— and on the terrace, commanding land and water, he
planted his batteries of a hundred cannon. At the top
he ran up a lighthouse tower, that flashed the first
beacon ray on Pacific waters. Above it waved the
Russian flag and the eagles of the czar. For twenty
years the bearded old Baranoff ruled Alaska, and despatched home shipload after shipload of furs, that sold
for fabulous sums in the markets of Russia. The count
was a shrewd old tyrant, bold, enterprising, with a heart
of stone, nerves of steel, and a frame of iron. Under his
vigorous rule, seals, sea-lions, beaver, and sea-otter perished by millions, and the overworked Alaskans dwin-
dled away to a few sad-faced, cringing slaves.

When Astor sent his expedition to Oregon in 1810,
Baranoff was in the prime of his power, alternating days
of toil with nights of revelling on raw rum and fiery
vodhka. Setting out the foaming camp-kettles, he
would sing and shout like an old Norse viking, " Drink,
children, drink," till every serf and slave in Sitka Castle
lay sprawling on the floor.

But he was a great manager. Sea-furs and walrus

ivory were to be had for the taking, so that when the Russian-American fur-ships came home, nobles and princes and the czar himself took shares in the stock, and dreamed of one day controlling, not only Alaska, but the entire coast of California.

One day Baranoff died. The Directory at St. Petersburg sent out Baron von Wrangell, and now the baron's successor, Adolphus Etholine, a young admiral of noble birth, had come to live in viceregal splendor in the stronghold that guarded the strip of shore, the tundra moors and mountains of rainy Alaska. The business had greatly fallen off, yet Etholine was able to despatch every year to St. Petersburg peltry valued at half a million silver roubles, and his returning ships, commanded by officers of the imperial navy, brought back the luxuries of Italy, Spain, and France. Could plain old Baranoff have looked in upon their mirrors and carpets and curtains and candelabra, he would have torn his beard in Russian rage and sworn a big round oath at these degenerate days.

At dawn Governor Etholine and several officers assisted Chief Factor Douglas and his companions to disembark. Sitka was a dirty village, full of drunken Indians, reeking with all imaginable smells, through which they hastened to the steep flight of steps leading up to the castle.

Etholine's drawing-rooms, with portraits of the czars, decorated walls, damask-draped windows, waxed floors, and heavy carved furniture, quite surprised the Hudson's Bay officials, who, in their plain quarters at Vancouver, had studied comfort rather than display. Here was a fur company that certainly had no greater income than their own, yet everywhere were signs of extravagant display and costly living.

" Perhaps they need it to reconcile them to this awe-inspiring, silent Sitkan land," thought Douglas, as he mentally counted the cost.

Through parted curtains, Etholine's petite child wife entered; like a fairy she approached the stately daughter of the magnate on the Columbia. She spoke in French. Thanks to her father and "Telemachus," Eloise had a fluent command of French. There were other ladies, maids and companions, and, yes, there really was a princess, Madame Racheff, who had renounced the gayeties of the Russian court to accompany her husband to the far Pacific exile.

Long they lingered at the state breakfast in the resounding banquet-hall. What unexpected viands! Wines from France and fruits from Spain, hyperborean pickles and caviare, flanking and interlarding long arrays of sauces and chevreuil. There were toasts and jokes and laughter, not so wild, perhaps, as in the old Baranoff days, but enough to prove that the Russian and English fur companies were no longer at war.

"By the way," exclaimed Etholine, "the Russians came near appropriating the Columbia long before you fellows took it."

"How is that?" inquired Chief Factor Douglas.

"It was in 1802 that the Directory met at St. Petersburg to consider the post at Sitka. Some complaints had reached them against Count Baranoff. It was a ticklish thing to deal with Baranoff — he was autocrat here. In general, they left him to his own way. But Prince von D. said, 'We ought to extend the business.'

"'We need a better base of supplies,' said Baron X.

"'What we really need is to send a responsible man to look after Baranoff,' added Count T.

"'Why not take lands farther south and start an agricultural colony?' suggested Baron von Resanoff.

"Everybody stared at the young baron who had come up for the first time to take his seat in the Directory. He returned the stare with the additional suggestion, 'Why not make the Columbia a base of supplies for Sitka?'

"After a good deal of talking it was decided to send Von Resanoff himself as the Russian Imperial Inspector of Alaska. 1805–6 found him at Sitka, laying plans with Baranoff, one of which was to expel American traders from the North Pacific. All too numerous had become those Boston skippers on this northwest coast. Frequent complaints had been made to the American president that his people were selling fire-arms to our Indians, but all to no purpose. Von Resanoff said it was an outrage, and we were justified in using force. Supplies went low at Sitka that winter. No ship came. No flour, no fish, not even seal blubber for the garrison could be bought or caught. Just then, when all the cannon were loaded to sweep the Yankee skippers from the sea, a little Rhode Island ship sailed into Sitka harbor.

"'Shall we expel these American traders from the North Pacific?' said Von Resanoff.

"'For the love of God, no,' cried Baranoff. 'That little ship is our saviour.'

"Into the starving garrison the Yankee captain brought bread and beef, and raised the famine siege at Sitka Castle. Baranoff bought that little ship, the 'Juno,' that saved their lives, and sent her down the coast to cruise for supplies. Von Resanoff sailed with her, trying to find the Columbia, to plant a Russian colony. Those exploring Americans, Lewis and Clark, were just leaving their winter post at Clatsop, but Von Resanoff knew nothing of that. The whole coast might have been ours, but he could not get across the bar. Beastly river, the Columbia. Tried it three days and gave it up and went on down to California. There he found supplies, and fell in love with the Spanish commandant's charming daughter, Doña Conception.

"The matter was brought before the commandant — would he give to the baron the hand of his daughter as a seal to the compact for future supplies to Sitka?

"Don Arguello, the commandante, considered and consented, but a dreadful lion lay in the way! Von Resanoff was a Greek Catholic, the donna a Roman Catholic. Von Resanoff laughed at the lion: 'I'll go to St. Petersburg. I'll beg the consent of the czar himself; then to Madrid, and doubt not, I'll conciliate the King of Spain.'

"They parted with tears. Far out from shore his handkerchief fluttered farewell. But alas! in his haste to cross Siberia, Von Resanoff fell from his horse and broke his neck. The girl is down there yet, somewhere. But England forestalled Russia on the Columbia."

After breakfast the gentlemen went away to attend to their commission. Lady Etholine and the Princess Racheff led Eloise out on the promenade around the castle. Below them lay the low, square, rough-hewn huts of the half-breed Sitkans. Yonder were the officers' homes, three-storied, lemon-yellow houses with iron-red roofs and stained-glass windows. The green roof of the bishop's house shone in the sun, and the green dome of the Greek church, surmounted by its oriental spire. Behind the castle, the princess pointed to the living green flanks of Vestova, where the Muscovites held their summer picnics.

"All the year round the glaciers glitter on those heights beyond," she said. "And you can read, at night. You can read all night in these Sitkan summers. The midnight sun just dips behind Edgecumbe, and before twilight is gone the dawn is here."

Edgecumbe rose like a snowy cone beyond the island-studded harbor. A fleet of skin bidarkas moved in and out among the ships. The steamer "Alexander," from Okhotsk, was landing the mail from St. Petersburg, whereat the princess flew away for letters.

"And do you like it here?" asked Eloise of the dainty Lady Etholine.

"One always likes the home of the honeymoon," answered the bride of Etholine. "My husband says the grandest scenery of the world lies along this coast. I love to fancy this is Naples, with its cliffs by the sea and its lava cone. It lay like this long ago before the Romans built their villas on its shores."

"And do you think some Virgil yet may write an Æneid here?" asked Eloise, smiling.

"Who knows? Baranoff would be a worthy hero. They tell great tales of him in his battles with the Sitkans. Some dark tales, too. When at night I hear the roar of the sea-lions and the pitiful cry of the seals, I tell Adolphus it sounds like the moans of all the dead Alaskans."

Governor Etholine and his lady were model hosts. Sumptuous dinners and courtly balls followed each other in swift succession. At sunrise the reveille sounded, at sunset the drums beat, and the great light blazed in the tower. The heavy Muscovite padlocks were turned in the gates, and all night the sentinels paced the promenade, guarding the life and treasure of Sitka Castle.

Meanwhile Douglas and Etholine were discussing provisions and boundaries and tariffs for the Indian trade. Douglas took part in all the gayeties of the fort; at the same time he criticised them in private.

"It is not our way of doing things," he said to Rae. "These Russians are squandering all they make. What folly to appoint naval officers to the command! They know nothing of the business, yet draw pay from both the fur company and the government. Look at these establishments crowded with idle officers and men, fifteen vessels afloat, and thousands spent every year on provisions for Sitka alone. You never saw such a lazy crew around Vancouver — the doctor would·n't have it."

Too soon the week rolled by. The ten-league transfer was made according to the London agreement, and exchanges concluded in grain and furs. Farewells were quickly said, salutes were fired, and the little "Beaver" sped down the coast to the sandy flats of Fort Stikine. On the self-same spot where a few years ago the Russian gunboats had threatened Ogden, lay a Russian brig of thirty-two guns, ready to hand the redout over to Douglas and the English. As Rae marched out with his detachment of eighteen Canadians the Russian officer drew back.

"What! hold this fort with eighteen men! I required fifty, and you can do with no less."

"Other forts we rule with twenty men, and we can hold Stikine," said Rae, setting his lips in the firm way habitual to him.

At the mouth of the Stikine River, on a strip of sand that was an island at high tide, stood the old Russian redout, St. Dionysius, near the present Fort Wrangell. Over the log fort Rae hung out the English flag and the

Hudson's Bay pennant, and with his wife and eighteen Canadians saw the Russian brig set sail for Sitka, and the "Beaver" and Douglas depart to build Fort Takou.

Scarcely had the Russians disappeared when the Indians began hostilities. It was not a pleasant outlook, on that bank of sand scarce large enough to hold the fort, with only the rising and falling tide to break the monotonous days.

In the inner gallery a watchman paced, ever on the outlook, with a loaded swivel above the gate. In the bastions eight nine-pound guns and an armory of Hudson's Bay flintlocks lay ready for action. The wood-boats plied back and forth with musketoons on their gunwales.

Here, there, everywhere, rolled the smoke from savage camps. Canoes came over with beaver, beaver, beaver, until the fort was packed with beaver, but all the pay they would take was drink, making night hideous with their orgies. Years after Eloise spoke of this time with a shudder. Once, at midnight, the savages attempted to scale the stockade and take the fort. A thousand bidarkas came down from the north and shot their arrows at Fort Stikine. The brave girl stood by her husband's side, beating them back with the carronades.

In autumn the "Beaver" passed as she gathered in her furs, but no one came when the dark and rainy winter sent the waterfalls tumbling down the mountains and swept the white foam out to sea.

Meanwhile events were occurring at Fort Vancouver that led Dr. McLoughlin to recall Rae to take charge of another important post.

XXII

ERMATINGER GUARDS THE FRONTIER

1840

CONSUMPTION was eating away the vitals of Tom McKay. This was not strange, in view of the winter bivouacs on the Missouri, the dog-sled journeys to Colvile, the fights and flights at Okanogan long ago, the days of wet moccasins and nights of damp blankets, the weeks of sand-dust and alkali along the Shoshonie. His brigade was handed over to Ermatinger.

"Tom will spend the winter in California," said Dr. McLoughlin.

There were reasons for despatching Ermatinger to the Shoshonie. More and more St. Louis trappers were crossing the Rockies and disputing grounds with the Hudson's Bay Company and the Blackfeet.

"This opposition must be frozen out," said Dr. Mc-Loughlin. "We must fight fire with fire," said Douglas. So Ermatinger rushed over the twisted aromatic sage-brush of the upper country, snuffing the air for rivals. Witty, skilful, affable, he was the trump card, and they played it.

How kind Ermatinger was, how insinuating! How hospitably he received a rival camp! — inspecting their outfit from the corner of his eye. He knew to a skin how much the Americans carried. He counted every gun, and reckoned up the value of the goods. How trickily he misled them! — worse than Jemmy Jock.

How deftly he planted the seeds of discontent! — "Your leader pays you ha beggarly rate; hour men would never put hup with it." How he fomented disputes, how disinterestedly he conveyed word to the Indians, how he played on their superstitions! — "These Bostons bring trouble. If you deal with the Bostons we shall sell you no more smoke-smoke. These Bostons hare swindlers. They charge ten dollars for scarlet that just falls to pieces. We charge honly thirty-two shillings for cloth that will last a lifetime."

But when the missionaries came Ermatinger was in his glory. Gray, Walker, Eells, Griffin, Munger, and their wives, all passed under his convoy. "Surely there is no danger in missionaries," he said; "they come not to trap nor to trade nor to make settlements, they come only to teach the Indians." Ermatinger flew around among his men. "Company to-night. Company to-night. Put hon your best faces, boys. Serve up the supper hon has clean ha mat has you can find, Baptiste. Let them see that we live on civilized fare. More cakes, Gabriel, plenty of fried cakes."

The quick Canadians, trained to obey, turned camp over at his call. Cook Gabriel, blowzy at the fire, dropped ball after ball of flour and water dough into the boiling tallow, stirring it afar off with a pointed pole to avoid the blistering heat.

Skipping out to meet his guests, the little man bowed profoundly — "Come, ladies hand gentlemen, let me hintroduce you to the chairs hand tables hand hedibles."

There was something almost homelike in Ermatinger's companionable camp, with regiments of buffalo ribs propped up before the blaze on dress parade, and savory fumes of fleece meat bubbling in the kettles. There

had been a great hunt; even now the buffalo runners
were restless in the camp, the hills east of the Snake
were black with shaggy herds, and their deep-mouthed
bellowings rolled like thunder far away. Some of the
Canadians were still busy with hatchets, cracking the
marrow-bones, to lay bare the rolls of trappers' butter
contained within; others had cleaned the intestines,
turned them inside out, and tucked them full of strips
of salted and peppered tenderloin, and beside the ribs
these long, brown festoons of trappers' sausage snapped
and crackled with their juicy contents.

The missionaries, young men just out of the semi-
naries, and their rosy-cheeked brides, sat down on the
Indian mats spread on the grass. Ermatinger kept up
incessant chatter.

"I'm 'ungry's a grizzly. Pour the coffee, Baptiste.
Notice hany trappers this side hof the Rockies? 'Elp
yourselves, 'elp yourselves. Don't stand hon ceremony.
To-day hit his buffalo 'umps hand marrow-bones, to-
morrow hit may be mice. We starve when we must, but
when we 'ave plenty we heat the best first, for fear hof
being scalped by han Injun before we 've henjoyed it."

On their brushwood beds the wandering missionaries
slept in this early Oregon time. The wolves howled
them to sleep every evening, howled them awake every
morning; all the night long the wolves bayed at the
moon as she rode in a cloudless sky. Under their
heads they hid the meat for pillows, to keep it away
from the wolves — even then some sly old gray-back
would come in the night and pull it out.

"Harise! Harise! Harise!" was Ermatinger's daylight call. "Hi'll be 'anged hif the wolves 'aven't
grown so bold hand saucy they've come to the fire to
warm themselves!"

There they sat, three great gray wolves, with noses pointing to the fire. One touch, over they toppled, dead, set up by this joking hunter in the night to frighten the tenderfeet from over the Rockies!

"Hi'll be 'anged if the dogs 'ave n't heaten my moccasins," was the next discovery. Perhaps the remnant of a cap chewed out of recognition lay under a tent edge. More than likely one leg of a pair of buckskin pantaloons was all that was left of somebody's apparel.

The missionaries laughed, laughed, laughed as at holiday. How could they look for guile when all went merry as a marriage-bell under the lead of this good-humored, winsome host? To Ermatinger they confided their plans and acted on his advice. He slapped them on the shoulders, lounged round their tent doors, and sat in their secret councils. He penetrated their inmost hearts, warned them against trespassing the regulations of the great company.

"What are the regulations of the company?" asked the incoming missionaries.

"Hamericans must not trade with Hinjuns, they must confine themselves to hagriculture hand mission work, hand keep to the south side hof the Columbia," was the answer, impressed like a solemn law. And he tricked them, tricked them out of their tame cattle for long-horned Mexican heifers that needed to be caught with a lasso and held for milking, tricked them out of their gentle American horses for wild Indian ponies. Even at Whitman's he tried his wiles.

"You live too plainly. You dress too plainly. Splendor wins the Hinjuns. You must put hon more style hand get all the hinfluence possible. The Hamerican Board agrees to give you your living; that living must not be mean." Then the tempter passed, leaving a worry in the heart of Dr. and Mrs. Whitman, for to some extent they knew his words were true.

Sometimes the conversation fell on politics. Then Ermatinger fired:

"If the Hunited States tries to drive hus from the country the Hudson's Bay Company will harm 'er height 'undred mixed bloods, and with their knowledge hof the mountain fastnesses we can 'old Horegon hagainst the world. Ham hi not ha marvellously proper man to go a-soldiering?" The little man drew himself up, and his big nose shone. Of course everybody laughed, "It is only Ermatinger."

Even Dr. McLoughlin would laugh, "Bow-wow-wow! It's only Ermatinger."

"Ho, no, this country can never be settled," said Ermatinger, slyly taking the missionaries through the most difficult goat-trails over the mountains. "'Ow could wagons hever get through these jungles?" Over sharp-cut rocks he led them, through dense woods, and over mountain patches of snow where never man or beast had trod before.

Long since, the Indians had revealed to Dr. Whitman wide, comfortable trails that the company had hoped to keep secret. But Ermatinger, leading the new-comers a thorny chase, laughed, laughed, laughed because he had fooled the missionaries.

"Be silent, exclusive, secret," said the company, "lest the furry folk be frightened away. We shall be undone if colonies of people supplant our colonies of beaver. Mill-dams break up beaver-dams; they never flourish in the same water."

"Why have you never taught the Indians agriculture?" inquired Dr. Whitman.

"Hoh, beaver is hour business. Why meddle with the plough?" was Ermatinger's careless answer.

"How came the Spokanes, then, to plant and plough?"

"The Spokanes 'ave planted for twenty years. Hastor's men built Spokane House hand made ha little garden. The Hinjuns watched them, tasted their vegetables. When they left the squaws saved the seed hand tried their 'and hat gardens."

" Does n't that prove that all the Indians want is a chance — that they are ready to take up civilization?" Dr. Whitman was standing by that historic wagon with his foot on the hub.

Ermatinger knocked the ashes from his ever-burning pipe with an impatient snap.

"Yes, too ready, if anything. We don't want 'em civilized — we want 'em to catch skins. That is why the company gets along better with the Injun than you Hamericans do — we leave 'im to 'is own ways. You try to change 'im. All along your border states you say, ' 'ere, take a farm and settle down like white folks, or get hout.' That 's no way to get halong with Hinjuns."

" Exactly." Never before had Dr. Whitman grasped so clearly the difference of the two policies. Then began the nervous walk in which he indulged when under the pressure of exciting thought. " It 's here in a nutshell, Ermatinger. The fur-hunter meets the Indian half-way, he intermarries, he perpetuates barbarism. The American brings the rifle, the axe, the home. For the beaver-dam and buffalo-range he substitutes the plough, the mill, the school, the railroad, the city."

Ever after Dr. Whitman seemed to hear a voice soughing in the wind like the worried ghost of the great company: "Away! away! You must not civilize our Indians. Away! away! Your mills, your ploughs and schools and shops must not frighten our beaver."

Silence brooded over Oregon, the silence of the grave. England looked upon the great fur preserve as a waste, a desert where a few wild beasts gained a scanty living. As the fur-traders tramped the forest they knew of coal, but they never told it; they knew of marble and iron, but they kept it secret; voyageurs discovered ledges of gold, but were enjoined to silence; the Indian was not more quiescent. To publish to the world these vast savannas and belts of a greater Britain would bring in people, and people frighten away the game. So Oregon slept behind her battlements, waiting for the prince at whose magic kiss the gates should fall, the forest trails expand, and her thousand industries leap to life.

In November again Monique's brigade glanced like a shadow down the River of the West.

"Time? time?" he called at Fort Colvile. Chief Factor McDonald gave him the time. Monique scribbled it on his orders.

"Time? time?" he called at Walla Walla.

"Time? time?" at Fort Vancouver.

Dr. McLoughlin looked at his watch. "Five minutes past ten o'clock in the morning." Monique scribbled it on his papers and passed them in.

Dr. McLoughlin looked over the record in the quiet of his office. With drooping head the Iroquois stood like a weary race-horse. Dr. McLoughlin came to the Colvile paper.

"You scoundrel, you!" he cried, leaping to his feet. "You have run every cascade this side of Colvile!"

Up flew his cane, but Monique dodged and darted through the door. The proud Indian had reached the goal that Kennedy missed, the fastest time ever made from Colvile to Fort Vancouver.

When December rains were beating on the hills, James Douglas and Tom McKay took a run on the Hudson's Bay Company barque Cowlitz down to Monterey. The company's ships had become frequent visitors at that southern port, buying up sea-otter and paying a handsome fee for the privilege.

On New Year's day they anchored. The warders of the old Spanish castle on the coast were not backward in collecting customs.

With lifted beaver Douglas returned their civilities. "No, not sea-otter to-day, thank you, gentlemen; we wish to see the governor."

With a shade of disappointment the Spanish officials conducted the Hudson's Bay ambassador to the home of Alvarado. It was an unpretentious mansion, luxurious only in windows overlooking the sea, windows upon windows in those California days when glass was worth its weight in solid silver. The common people had no glass, only wooden shutters and outdoor verandas, that were the actual living rooms.

When La Framboise came home from the Spanish land he had brought this word from Captain Sutter: "The Hudson's Bay Company need not come down here to trap any more. I have engaged these grounds." No attention was paid to it. In autumn La Framboise set out as usual. Now Douglas, in the presence of Alvarado, after the usual salutations, inquired, —

"Did you authorize Captain Sutter to order our brigade to leave the Sacramento?"

"Captain Sutter was authorized to act for the government, not in one hostile way, but merely to request the withdrawal of your partie on account of the new settlements," said the Governor Alvarado.

"Very well, then," replied the haughty Douglas,

"when *your* wishes shall be officially communicated they shall be followed to the letter. For the present I suppose the old agreement stands."

"*Certano*, Signor, *certano*," answered Alvarado, somewhat puzzled, somewhat flattered.

Douglas found it hard to bend the knee and sue for favors from this southern potentate, but he did it. In the end his courtliness quite undermined the gallant Captain Sutter.

In the bay of Saint Francisco the fur company wished to establish a post to capture the Spanish trade — perhaps the Spanish state.

"*Certano, certano*, Signor, by payment of suitable duties."

"And we want sheep to stock our farms."

"*Certano, certano*," said Alvarado.

All Douglas wished and more he got, — a post on the bay, trappers' rights renewed, and five thousand sheep from the old missions, three thousand to be driven overland, and two thousand to be brought by sea.

Tom McKay, tall, dark, long-haired, standing hat in hand, had been a silent auditor. As negotiations progressed mutual esteem mounted high and higher. With fluttering flags of Spain and England at the mast Douglas dined and wined the Spanish grandees on his ship. He lent the impoverished Californians powder to fire a salute from the old castle and departed amid a shower of, "*A Dios! A Dios!*" leaving McKay to recruit his health and superintend the sheep brigade.

XXIII

AN AMERICAN EXPLORING SQUADRON

1841

THE New Year of 1841 opened a new act in the drama on the Columbia. In his lonely cabin on the Willamette, Ewing Young, the Tennesseean, lay dead. Outside, his herds grazed on the hillsides, without a visible heir. The little handful of Americans, scarce thirty-six all told, gathered at his funeral. Jason Lee deeply felt the situation. No law, no court, no government, nothing from the Spanish land to Sitka, but the arbitrary will of Dr. John McLoughlin. " He is a good man," said Jason Lee, " but the one man power is not American."

They carried the Tennesseean out and buried him under the oaks on his ranch, and then returned to discuss the disposition of his property.

" We must have some sort of organization," said Jason Lee. "We must draft a constitution and frame a code of laws."

The committee sat, with pens in hand, when, presto! change! an American exploring squadron came sailing into the Oregon waters bearing the banners of Uncle Sam.

The Hudson's Bay Company on the Columbia had paid little attention to the young republic at the east, they sometimes forgot there was a United States; but this sudden apparition startled them with its possibilities. Conciliatory, urbane, troubled, the doctor and Douglas visited the American commodore on shipboard. The yards were manned, salutes were fired, the flags of both nations flew at the international banquet where the two governments met on the disputed Columbia.

"Come right over to the fort," was the doctor's cordial invitation. "Rooms, boats, guides, whatever you need is at your service."

Commodore Wilkes set up his tents outside the British stronghold, but like all others who passed that way, he, too, was enchanted with this old feudal host and hospitality. Like Whitman, he viewed the fields and farms, like Sutter he tasted the wine and heard the song, like Lee he ascended the charming Willamette. Under the roof of the new mission house George Abernethy, the mission steward, entertained the commodore.

"Do you advise us to establish a government?" he asked.

"Not yet," said the commodore; "wait. The British interest already feels itself threatened by the presence of this exploring squadron. Any action on your part may precipitate trouble, in which case you are too few and too far away to be properly supported. Wait till your numbers augment."

"Dr. McLoughlin's wine has affected his judgment," said the men of the mission.

In the purple twilight, Commodore Wilkes walked in the fields of wheat. The crescent moon hung over Mt. Hood. "A lovely land," he murmured; "charming by day, enchanting by night. Tell me, what do you Americans think of the Hudson's Bay Company?"

"The Hudson's Bay Company is Great Britain's instrumentality for securing Oregon," was the answer.

" But," urged the commodore, " the missionaries have received untold favors from the Hudson's Bay Company, and if they are gentlemen, it is their duty to return them."

The missionary faced about in the commodore's path. " Return them? Certainly. I will exchange favors with Dr. McLoughlin or any other man or set of men, but *I will not sell country for it.*"

Wilkes was almost angry with this blunt missionary. Presently he inquired, " What was that bleating I heard at sunset — flocks of the mission? "

" It is the company's sheep brigade, being driven overland from California, to stock the country on the Sound. That is part of the plan for holding Oregon."

Eloise stood at Vancouver's gate as the sheep passed by. Already she had been summoned from Stikine, and Rae had been sent to the South. California had a new meaning for her now; even the shepherds might bring a message from her husband at the company's new post on the bay of Saint Francisco. As the bleating of sheep died out in the west the beaver-painted bannerols of Ogden's brigade came fluttering in from the east. Among the gayly decked voyageurs the quick eye of Eloise noted the drooping curls of her old play-fellow, Maria Pambrun.

" Maria is an obedient girl," Chief Factor Pambrun had been saying six weeks before, as he rode with Cornelius Rogers on the flowery meads of Walla Walla, — it was the old topic, the marriage of his daughter, — " and skilled in housewifery."

At that moment the half-wild Cayuse pony lost the rope from his mouth and ran and surged, throwing Pambrun over the high-pommelled Mexican saddle. In

a moment Rogers knelt by his side.   Indians came running to the rescue, and carried the injured officer home
to the fort.   Dr. Whitman was summoned, but in vain.
Four agonized days the piteous appeal resounded, —

"O Doctor, Doctor, give me something to kill me
quick!"

Then Pambrun's strength failed.   All was hushed
save the labored breathing and the lapping waters on
the northern wall.

"Cornelius."   Cornelius Rogers bent to support the
dying   head.   "Cornelius — I — give — you — my —
watch — and — my — gun."

The sobs of Maria and her mother were all that
broke the death-bed silence.

"Cornelius — in — secretary — find — will — made —
in — your — favor —   Take — care — of — my —
family."

With falling tears Cornelius Rogers smoothed the
clammy brow.   "Yes, yes, dearest friend.   I will see
to everything."   A look of peace settled on the ashen
face.

Pale as death Maria Pambrun sat on the bed with
one of her father's hands pressed close in both of hers.
The other hand Madame, her mother, pressed close to
her heart.   The chief factor fixed his glazing eye upon
his child —

"Maria — darling — marry — Mr. — Rogers."

The anguished girl dropped her head upon her bosom
— the chief factor interpreted it as a sign of assent.

"God — bless —"

"He is dead," said Dr. Whitman, bending low to
catch the last pulse.

Maria Pambrun slid from her perch on the bedside.
With uplifted face and hands clenched in her wild dis-

ordered curls she gave a shriek, the terrible death-wail that has rung for ages in the tents of the dead. The Indians waiting outside caught it up, till it rolled in one long reverberation over the plains of Walla Walla. It reached the home of Mrs. Whitman before her husband did, and she knew the good Chief Factor Pambrun had gone to rest.

They buried him there in the drifting sand. Ogden's brigade came by and Rogers accompanied the mourning family down to Fort Vancouver, whither they had been summoned by Dr. McLoughlin.

"I cannot marry him," sobbed Maria Pambrun, hiding her face on the shoulder of Eloise. Dr. McLoughlin looked on in compassion. The face of Cornelius Rogers was paler than Maria's, set as marble.

"I will not ask it," said Rogers. He heard the din in the court as the doomed man hears the hammer of the executioner. "I will not take advantage of her helpless situation. Let the will be void. I return the property, but the watch I would like to keep as a memento of my dead friend."

His own voice sounded far away and dead. Maria ceased her sobs and breathless waited — she only heard a departing step and the shutting of a door. When she looked up Rogers was gone. Dr. McLoughlin stood there, looking at the closed door. The arm of Eloise was still about her waist, and the sun through the grape-vine cast checkered shadows on the Chinese matting.

"That is an honorable man," said Dr. McLoughlin, picking up the torn fragments of the will at his feet. "He is worthy of an excellent wife. But remember, Maria, you and your mother and the younger children can have a home here as long as you live. I adopt you all."

Maria had scarcely time to murmur her thanks when a shuffling was heard outside.

"Boston ship at Fort George, laden with liquor," announced a Frenchman, hat in hand, suddenly breaking up the tableau in the doctor's office. Dr. McLoughlin went out. In ten hours he stepped from his barge on the sands at Astoria. The "Thomas H. Perkins" looked up grimly, demoniacally, from the water.

"How many barrels on board?" demanded Dr. McLoughlin of the captain. "What is it worth? I will take the whole cargo." And in the end Dr. McLoughlin chartered the ship itself, to put a stop to the business.

"It's cheaper to buy 'blue ruin' out of hand than to deal with a riot of drunken savages," was the doctor's explanation to the inquiries of Commodore Wilkes. The liquor was stored in the basement of the governor's house, where it lay untouched for years.

Commodore Wilkes sent exploring parties all over the country. Everywhere the Indians fell into convulsions of laughter at the useless labors of these lunatic scientists, who came squinting around at rocks and soil and hills and stars, and never once asked for beaver. Did the geologist use his hammer — "Ho! ho! ho! no kernel in that nut! Indian know better than that!" Did the botanist creep along picking flowers like precious gems — "He! he! he! see the grass man?" All flowers were grass to the Indian.

"Come over and see us celebrate the Fourth of July, Doctor. We have the finest warship in the navy there," said Commodore Wilkes, setting out for that portion of his squadron anchored in the Sound.

"Tut, tut, tut! Ask *me* to celebrate the Fourth of

July?" laughed the doctor. "I have business over that way and may run down to look at your ships."

A few days later Dr. McLoughlin went over to the Sound, arriving, however, a day too late for the celebration. At this moment, while the doctor was gone, the Rupert's governor, Sir George Simpson, came sweeping down the Columbia with his retinue of fancy voyageurs and his buglers and bagpipers on his journey around the world. Douglas did the honors of the fort.

Sir George had been head of the old Hudson's Bay Company before the coalition, and, naturally, had never acquired perfect confidence in this independent northwester who never took the trouble to cross the mountains to his annual council at Norway House on Winnipeg.

"Ah!" was Sir George's mental comment as he took off his tall felt chimney-pot hat and scratched the bald spot on top of his head. "Last year McLoughlin entertained the missionaries. This year I find him hobnobbing with Americans in their gunboats on the Sound."

Everything encouraged Sir George's suspicions. He was angry on account of the squadron, angry on account of Dr. McLoughlin's courteous hospitality to it, angry on account of the banquet to which the Americans were invited on the doctor's return to the fort. Sir George, in narrow-waisted, swallow-tailed coat, occupied the chair of honor. There was an aristocratic scantness to the tight-fitting sleeves; a corresponding fulness to the immaculate puffed and ruffled shirt-front above the waistcoat of salmon-colored satin. Behind his chair the pipers played. Dr. McLoughlin kept up the conversation. Under the rim of his gold-bowed glasses

Sir George eyed the commodore from an immeasurable distance of formality and reserve. His temper cast a damper on the festive scene, despite the magnificent table garnished with venison and rosemary, grouse and salmon and cygnets.

"The dinner was a funeral," said the clerks that night.

"It was like a feast of feudal times," said Commodore Wilkes.

"Those Americans are spies," said Sir George, reproving the doctor in private.

"You are not to encourage Americans in any way," said Sir George, in the positive tone bred of years of command. "The United States will never possess more than a nominal jurisdiction west of the Rocky Mountains, nor, if you do your duty, will it long possess even that. You make a great mistake in assisting these missionaries. Let them take care of themselves, refuse them favors, drive them out of the country as soon as possible."

"But," interposed the doctor, standing up beside Sir George — he could look down upon him like a little boy — "what excuse can we have for driving them out of the country? They are peaceable, industrious, helpful to the Indian. By the terms of our treaty with the United States they have as good right here as we have."

"The Hudson's Bay Company was not chartered to educate the Indian," curtly responded Sir George, hitching up the wires of his glasses in a few once curly locks behind his ears. "That is no part of our business. I would not give them even a spade to till the soil. We want furs, not farms. We must tolerate nothing that interferes with our business."

"Sir George prays only to mammon," was a well-known saying in the upper country.

The doctor kept his temper. Better than any one else west of the mountains he understood the policy of his company, and never had that company a more brilliantly cold and calculating manager than Sir George Simpson.

"By your management already you have lost us all that country south of the Columbia," continued Sir George.

"*I* lost that country?" cried Dr. McLoughlin, bristling at this unexpected charge. "England never claimed it. The company never expected to hold it. The Joint Occupancy Treaty was in itself official notice to that effect. As for these missionaries — when they come bringing passports signed by the Secretary of War, dare I treat them like Yankee skippers or overland traders?"

Sir George by his John Bull obstinacy was fast driving the doctor into an American advocate.

He saw his error, and with the quick diplomacy for which he was noted Sir George grasped the angry doctor's hand.

"I beg your pardon, Chief Factor McLoughlin — I beg your pardon. Your situation is indeed a complicated one. I shall take immediate measures to press this Oregon question to an issue. England cannot afford to lose this territory."

How he pressed this question is hidden in the English archives. A few days later Sir George left with Douglas to inspect the northwest coast and visit Sitka.

When Ogden went back up the Columbia he took with him Cornelius Rogers to the Whitman mission,

and his son-in-law, Archibald McKinley, whose young
wife, Sarah Julia, the first woman of white blood born
on the Snake, was destined now to become mistress of
the driftwood fort at Walla Walla.

Failing to secure the hand of Maria Pambrun, Mr.
Rogers became discouraged over the work of the mission. He, who never before could see an obstacle, began to say, "Religious truth can never be taught in
the Indian tongue. They have no words for spiritual
thought. How can the Indian unacquainted with law
be made to understand a broken moral law?"

"This reasoning is delusive," said Dr. Whitman.
"The Indian knows the right and wrong. That is the
basis of all moral law."

Nevertheless Cornelius Rogers left the mission and
settled in the Willamette valley.

Before a year had rolled away there was another
wedding at Fort Vancouver. The bride was Maria
Pambrun, still in mourning — the groom was Dr.
Barclay.

One October morning, after Sir George's return from
Sitka, a mist hid the Columbia from view, but up the
terraced plain rang the familiar

" *Sur la feuille ron — don don don*," of the voyageurs.

Far back on the Saskatchewan, months before, Sir
George had passed a lengthened cavalcade toiling westward under the broiling sun of a northern July. And
now those bronzed, determined men, those women and
children have crossed the Assiniboian plains in ox-
carts and wagons, and scaled the mountains on packhorses; they have arrived to claim Sir George's
promise.

Sir George paled slightly under the doctor's ques-
tioning glance.

"No doubt it is those half-breeds of Red River," he said. "Possession is nine points of the law, and actual possession is now conclusive in our favor. You must help me meet them."

"Certainly," said the doctor.

The leaders and headmen of the Red River immigrants came up to the fort. The people camped on the plain below. Sir George Simpson, Dr. McLoughlin, and James Douglas met them in the hall. Sir George knew he had to face an ordeal, and nerved himself with a glass of wine. He saw the hope on every face — and shattered it at a glance.

"I am sorry to tell you that we cannot fulfil our agreement," began Sir George, hesitating at the disagreeable truth. "We have neither horses nor barns nor fields for you, and you are at liberty to go where you please. You may go with the California trappers and we will give you an outfit as we give others. If you locate south of the·Columbia we will help you none. If you go to the Cowlitz we will help you some. To those who will go to the Sound we will fulfil our agreement."

For a moment the Red River immigrants were struck dumb with amazement. Then wrath arose, some oaths escaped. Sir George with utmost coolness declared the interview at an end. Dr. McLoughlin was greatly distressed at the plight of the poor people who had sold their homes and travelled to a wilderness two thousand miles away, on the strength of such great expectations. He followed them out to their encampment, and in every way helped them to their destination with food, clothing, boats, and horses. Slowly, wearily, disheartened, heaping imprecations on the company's head, they toiled over to the woods on Puget Sound. After a winter of ineffable suffering most of them moved to the Willamette valley, where their descendants still live, loyal citizens of the United States.

From that hour the coolness increased between Sir George and the doctor. Sir George was angry because Dr. McLoughlin was not prepared to furnish houses, barns, and fenced fields to all these people. The doctor was astonished that such a promise had ever been made.

"I will go back," said James Sinclair, the leader of the northern immigrants, "and I will tell the Red River people this latest fraud of Sir George Simpson's. It is not enough that the company has throttled that colony in its cradle; it is not enough that they have subordinated every interest there to the fur trade; it is not enough that they have frustrated every effort at traffic by enormous freights and jealous regulations until they have driven our best men over the border into the United States, but now they must needs practice on the credulity of those who remain and rob us of our last little all."

When next Sir George went back to Red River he fled by night from the threatened rebellion, and he disarmed the leader, James Sinclair, by despatching him to the Columbia — promoted at once to the honors and emoluments of a chief factorship.

XXIV

"*THE STAR OF OREGON*"

1841

THERE was an animated discussion among the Canadians in the court at Fort Vancouver. "What is it, Baptiste?" inquired Dr. McLoughlin.

"Begosh! Dat w'at we not know, Dogtor. Dey say hit be for ferry-boat, but Antoine, 'ere, sir, 'e tink hit for be keel of a schooner."

"What looks like the keel of a schooner?" inquired the doctor.

"Dat boat, w'at de Hamericans buil' hon de islan'. Dey 'ave borrow w'ip-saw an' tools on de mission. Dey buy hall hour hol' Dutch 'arness-rope an' want more."

"Who are they?" persisted the doctor, with sudden interest.

"Josef Gale, 'e ees de boss. Felix 'At'way, 'e ees de 'ead builter. Dere be five hall togedder."

"Joseph Gale! Hathaway! Joseph Gale! Hathaway!" exclaimed the doctor, excitedly turning toward the office where the head-clerk sat. "The very men! The very men! They were mad because we had a monopoly on cattle. They tried to get passage on the 'Cadboro'' to buy cattle in California. I refused to let them go, but offered to help them settle. They appeared to agree and got supplies. Let me see, McTavish, let me see what Gale and Hathaway have bought."

He began turning over the yellow leaves. "Here is their bill: Draw-rope, Draw-rope, Bagging, Draw-rope, Sails and rigging as I live! Gale is a renegade sea-captain, Hathaway a deserter from the 'Convoy.' I've no love for Hathaway; he's the rascal that built a house on my island at the Falls. I sent him word, but he paid no attention to it."

Dr. McLoughlin reappeared in the yard.

"Dere be one of dose mon now, Dogtor," said Baptiste, pointing to a young man just entering the gate.

"And what do you want now, Mr. Woods, what do you want now?" Dr. McLoughlin abruptly inquired, walking toward the young man. Sir George's rebukes had temporarily affected the doctor's urbanity to Americans.

"Why, Governor, some of us fellows are trying to build a schooner to go to California to get some cattle. If you will trust us for chains and anchors and rigging, we can pay you by and by."

"How? how? how, I'd like to know, — how, sir?" cried the doctor.

"In furs and wheat, sir," answered the American.

"A schooner to go to California on this iron-bound coast? Tut, tut, tut! You'll all be drowned, and I'll not be party to such a transaction. You had better settle in the valley, as I told you, and take up farms. I'll lend you all the seed you want, but chains and anchors don't grow in this climate."

"But, Doctor, cattle —"

"Tut, tut, tut!" impatiently the doctor waved the petitioner away. "A hare-brained scheme! a hare-brained scheme! Who ever heard of a trapper-sailor? You've no idea of the danger you venture into. No slipshod schooner can live on this rock-bound coast."

"And you won't advance supplies, sir?" asked the young man, whitening.

"Did n't I tell you it was a hare-brained scheme? Why, boy, don't you know that without papers you are liable to be captured as a pirate, and how do I know you do not intend to become one?" said the doctor, looking very fierce and nodding his head.

"Well, Doctor," shouted the enraged Yankee, "you may keep your paltry rigging. You carry matters with a high hand now, but it won't last always. Remember, sir, I have an uncle in the States, that, rich as you are, is able to buy your great company out and several more such. He 'll come along here some day when you ain't thinking of him and send you all packing."

"Tut, tut, tut!" cried the doctor, reddening. "I am glad to hear so rich a man as your uncle is coming to this country. Who is it, Mr. Wood? What is his name, Mr. Wood? I should like to know him, Mr. Wood."

"Why, they call him Uncle Sam, and he 's liable to come out here looking after us fellows most any day," retorted the angry American, making a bee-line for the gate.

"The persistency of these Americans is amazing," said the doctor, as he watched the retreating figure. "If I tell my Canadians to stop, they stop, but these Americans keep right on."

And the Americans did keep on. On Wapato Island they found material fit for a keel and a frame of swamp white oak. They grubbed up red fir roots for knees, put up beams of red fir timber, and planked their boat with cedar dressed by hand. Parrish, the mission black-smith, made the spikes and irons.

When Commodore Wilkes went up the Willamette he saw the unfinished craft.

"Yes, we've got so far," said Gale, "but Dr. McLoughlin refuses to sell us supplies. Can you?"

"I cannot sell to you," said the commodore. "I am not in the trading business, but I could give you cordage and anchor out of my ship-stores in case of distress. I'll interview Dr. McLoughlin when I get back."

"They are making a coffin for themselves," said the doctor, when Wilkes approached him on the subject. "Now there is Gale. He has been in our employ for several years as a hunter and trapper. Now what does he or the rest of them know about managing or navigating a vessel at sea?"

"I have tested Gale's knowledge. He is an old sailor, and I have given him papers," said Commodore Wilkes.

"You have?" exclaimed the amazed doctor. "But do you think that vessel is strong enough to make the voyage to San Francisco?"

"It's stout enough to double Cape Horn," said Wilkes. "Gale knows what he is about and Hathaway worked in a shipyard in the States. If you have such things as they need you will oblige me by letting them have them. If they are not able to pay, charge it up to me. I shall need considerable cordage and canvas myself."

"Oh, well, well," exclaimed the doctor, "they can have whatever they want." So the store was thrown open, and the delighted Americans hastened to get all they needed before Commodore Wilkes got out of the country. The commodore gave them a flag, an ensign, a compass, an anchor, and a hawser one hundred and forty fathoms long, and a log-line and glasses.

The little schooner, clinker-built on the clipper model, painted black with a white ribbon running from stem to stern, was in the eyes of her builders the cutest little craft that ever sat upon the water. With flying sails she dropped down the Willamette, and for pure buncombe crept up to Fort Vancouver. The little clipper ran so close to the barque "Vancouver" that it nearly touched her side.

"Helm-a-lee!" cried Captain Gale.

As she spun around on her keel the stars and stripes were flung in the face of the British tars and they read on her side in full-face letters, "The Star of Oregon."

Dr. McLoughlin was absent. Gale sent word to Douglas:

JAMES DOUGLAS, Esq.:

SIR, — I am now on my way to California. If you have any letters or commands that you wish to send to Mr. Rae, residing there, I will with pleasure take them to him.

Yours,   JOSEPH GALE.

"Talk of their getting to California — that's all braggadocio," said Douglas, as he penned the answer.

MR. JOSEPH GALE:

SIR, — As the schooner "Cadborough" will leave for that port soon, we will not trouble you in that particular.

Yours, etc.,   J. DOUGLAS.

Again at old Fort George (Astoria) the daring little crew unfurled the stars and stripes for Birnie and his men to see.

"Oh, ho!" cried the British tars, "as soon as you see the Pacific your hearts will fail and you'll all be back again."

"I'll go to Davy Jones's locker first," cried Gale, spreading his sheets to the wind.

Gale had a quadrant epitome and a nautical almanac that some one had brought to the country. He set out with his crew of four and a little Indian boy, not one of whom knew the compass. After giving his men a few lessons in steering in a seaway and by compass, they crossed the bar, and just at sunset, September 12, 1842, turned their faces to the south. The wind freshened to a tempest, the little barque skipped like a stormy petrel on the surface of the sea, the crew fell seasick, and for thirty-six hours the dauntless captain stood at the helm and steered his flying ship.

On the fifth day the little "Star" shot through the portals of the Golden Gate, and just as the sun went down dropped anchor abreast of the old Presidio. Not the Spaniards when they found the new world felt prouder than the youthful crew of the little ship.

"Oregon, Oregon," mused an officer in port when the little "Star" touched Yerba Buena the next day. "I'll be hanged if there's any port by that name on any of our charts."

"Are there letters for me?" asked Rae, amazed at the sight of the little craft.

"No letters," said Gale; "they'll come creeping in by and by on the 'Cadboro'." This delivery is a trifle too swift."

The boys sold the little "Star" for three hundred and fifty cows. They trimmed up a cottonwood tree and ran up the stars and stripes. Under it forty-two Americans gathered to emigrate to Oregon. The next season the boys came back, bringing with their settlers three thousand head of sheep, six hundred head of horses, and twelve hundred and fifty head of cattle, forever breaking the stock monopoly in Oregon.

The little "Star," the first ship ever built on the coast, remained in the South, where she ran on the Sacramento in the days of gold. But Joseph Gale never parted with the dear old flag that floated from her masthead. He made it into a canopy, under which he slept, and was buried with it around his coffin.

XXV

McKINLEY AT WALLA WALLA

1841

SOON after Archibald McKinley took charge at Walla Walla, a younger brother of Elijah, rambling around the place, came upon a pile of birch seasoned for pack-saddles.

" Put that down," demanded the clerk.

" The wood is ours," retorted the boy, defiantly tucking it under his blanket.

The clerk stepped out and struck the lad. Swelling with rage, the little savage fled through the gate to his father's lodge. Archibald McKinley was busily sorting and matching furs, when he caught sight of the Walla Walla chieftain and a dozen warriors filing into the court. There was something grim in the old chief's lofty look.

"What will you have this fine day? " inquired the politic trader, advancing and shaking hands.

" *Him*," roared Yellow Serpent, shaking an ominous finger at the clerk. " Big Boston say ' Indian strike white man, whip him. White man strike Indian, whip *him*.' " The chief's attendants advanced and seized the clerk.

"What does this mean? " inquired the chief trader. The Indian deigned no reply. One drew out a lash.

" Stop ! " cried McKinley, wheeling through the door of the Indian shop and returning with a copper keg of gunpowder. Knocking out the head and crossing a flint and steel — "Touch him and I'll fire," said McKinley, with determined look, yet trembling with excitement.

Pio-pio-mox-mox threw up his hands. His men loosed their hold and fled precipitately. The old chief, with eye on the powder, backed out after them.

In that hour old traditions passed away. At one bound McKinley became a "great big brave of the *skookum tum-tum*" (strong heart).

"How long, sir," roared Dr. McLoughlin, when next the clerk appeared at Fort Vancouver, — "how long, sir, do you suppose we could hold this country, with our feeble forces, if you are going to get into a row with every boy over a paltry whip-handle?"

XXVI

DELAWARE TOM

1841-5

WHEN the Cayuse Indians dashed on their fleet ponies through the Grande Ronde, they often noted a smoke curling on the Blue Mountains, and said, "There is the lodge of Delaware Tom."

It was in a mountain pocket, rich in trout and beaver. Occasional herds of elk wandered into its green plateau, and the salmon of the Columbia ascended into the little mountain lake. Here, in a lodge of deerskin, with his Nez Percé wife, dwelt Tom Hill, an educated Delaware Indian, once a student at Dartmouth, now an independent trapper in the mountains. His knowledge of English made him valuable to the white man. For several years he was employed as an express between the trading posts of Bent, Laramie, and St. Vrain. No runner could surpass him, no obstacle lay in his way as he took his swift courses over mountain height or foaming rapid. Alone, without a horse or a dog, he first came to Oregon, into the Grande Ronde where the Nez Percés were digging camas.

Indians as well as white people are conservative to strangers. Gradually the Delaware worked into their confidence. He heard that white men had penetrated even here.

"I know the white man," he said. "He came to the Delawares a welcome guest. We invited him to the best lodge, seated him on the best robe, smoked with him the calumet. He came again and killed off all our game. A third time he came and took our lands. So it will be with you. We are but dogs, to be driven from his path. I have come step by step across from tribe to tribe and watched the Americans. They begin by sending missionaries, who say all men are brethren, you must live in harmony. When you live in harmony then they want to buy a little piece of land. Then more come, and more and more, until they have occupied all the land."

The Nez Percés began to be deeply interested in this strange Indian who had seen so much. The Cayuses came around and the Walla Wallas listened.

"I am acquainted with missionaries," said Delaware Tom. "It is only a way of making property. There is nothing in religion only to make money. You can see that. Look how they are selling everything they raise on your own lands. You cannot get anything from them without paying for it, not so much as a piece of meat when you are hungry."

The Nez Percés invited Delaware Tom to go with them and visit Spalding's mission at Lapwai. Mr. Spalding was very busy attending to the wants of his people and paid no attention to a single stranger. It piqued the pride of Delaware Tom.

"See," he said, "if these were true men of God, they would supply every one of you with food and clothing. God gives you all things free of charge. The Indian shares his wealth; the white man gets it all for himself."

They took him to visit the school.

"I know schools," said Delaware Tom. "White men have books to describe great scenes of the West. We have the scenes themselves. White men measure mountains. Does the Indian measure a mountain that he can climb?"

Mr. Spalding had been explaining the use of the compass.

"What care we for the compass?" scoffed Delaware Tom. "We follow the stars. The trail leads to the hunt. The shores guide our canoes. The green leaves tell us when it is spring; the yellow, when to pitch our winter teepees. White men have the locomotive — what need, when our own fleet feet out-travel the horse? The missionary teaches you to weave cloth. Has not the buffalo spun a robe for you? The white man tears up the soil, it becomes full of worms and weeds. He makes a garden. Are not your meadows full of camas, your rivers full of fish, your father's hillsides stocked with game? Who would obstruct the streams with bridges? Does not the beaver build bridges enough for you?"

This talk drove the Nez Percés into a frenzy of excitement. Tom Hill would gallop down from the mountains, talk around a few days, then go back for weeks of solitary hunting. He refused to wear anything made of cloth; day in and day out his squaw sat beating the buffalo skin to make it soft and pliant for the couch of her lord. Mr. Spalding heard of the Delaware's instructions and warned his people against them. But the Indians looked up to Tom Hill as a mighty *tyee*, learned in the secrets of the white man. A few left the main tribe and camped with the Delaware on the mountain. The Nez Percé chiefs only laughed, and went on cultivating their farms and gardens.

Mr. Spalding went to the mountains for material to

build a mill. The childish Indians saw him rolling down the stones. It annoyed them that these inventive white people could find uses for even the stones on the hills.

"Bad, bad, bad," said the disciples of Tom Hill. "Mr. Spalding, we going to kill you."

"Oh, no," carelessly responded the missionary, rolling away at his stone.

"Yes, we are."

"Oh, no; you would n't do that. What would you gain by it? If you do I have many friends over the mountains who will come and destroy you all and take your wives and children and horses."

This awful prospect quieted the discontents. Some spoke with McKinley at Fort Walla Walla.

"What say you? Shall we drive these missionaries away from our lands?"

"You are braves," said McKinley, "and there are many of you. It would be easy to kill two men and two women and a few little children. Go quickly and do it, if you wish. But, remember, if you do, I shall have you punished."

Delaware Tom and a few Nez Percés came down into the Walla Walla valley to visit Dr. Whitman. For a long time the doctor had heard rumors of the Delaware and had formed an unfavorable impression of the supposed renegade. Quite surprised, then, was he when an attractive Indian of prepossessing appearance approached him with excellent English and in a cordial manner said, "I am glad to meet you, Dr. Whitman."

The black locks two and one-half feet long were dressed with uncommon care. The eager, flashing eye was lit with intelligence. Dr. Whitman had heard that the Delaware was vain of his learning and approached him through that medium.

"Ah, Mr. Hill, I am pleased to welcome you to our mission. I am told you are a student of Dartmouth — a great institution."

Pleased, flattered, the Indian became easy and talkative, revealing a surprising acquaintance with the politics of Europe and America. He dwelt on his school-life, describing again and again the walks and groves of Dartmouth.

"Why do you leave civilized life for the precarious life of the wilderness?" inquired Dr. Whitman.

"For reasons found in the nature of my race," answered the Delaware. "Never again shall I visit the States or any other part of the earth torn and spoiled by the slaves of agriculture. The pines of the Connecticut look on an age of decay. Only the Indian is strong and free. I shall live and die an Indian."

"What do you mean by strong and free?" inquired the doctor, curious to investigate this riddle.

"I mean the white men are too many. Population is increased to an unnatural extent. They crowd one another. That necessitates laws, it curtails liberty. There is no freedom among the whites. You break a law, they lock you in a jail or hang you on a tree. They have laws to punish murder. My own arrow can do it better."

The Delaware began to speak of his own tribe — a certain scintillant gleam began to coruscate in his eye as he dwelt on the wrongs of his people. Dr. Whitman wisely cut off the discussion by announcing a feast in honor of his guest.

An immense kettle of mush — cornmeal cooked in

tallow — was set in the centre of the school room. The
principal chiefs of the neighborhood, Pio-pio-mox-mox,
Five Crows, Tauitau, and Tiloukaikt came in and sat
down on the floor. The tallow dips were lighted and
Mrs. Whitman brought in the tea. The Indians dipped
in sugar, four, five, six teaspoonfuls to a cup. They
ate without a word, sipping noisily, as Indians do; now
Dr. Whitman and now a chief dipping his big wooden
spoon into the kettle. Other Indians came in, until
every bench in the school-room was crowded. At last
the Hawaiian servant carried the kettle away, and for
two hours Tom Hill spoke eloquently in the Cayuse
tongue on the benefits of education.

"I like Dr. Whitman better than Spalding," he said
to the Nez Percés on reaching home. "He asked me
into his house sometimes."

But spite of all, Tom Hill did the mischief with the
Cayuses. Pointing to the mission house —

"See," he said, " big house, big barn, big mill, grain,
all out of Cayuse land. All belongs to you." Pointing
to their graves he affectionately asked, "Where are all
your principal men who were alive when these pre-
tended teachers of God came among you? Is not Dr.
Whitman a great medicine to let your people die in that
fashion?" Mr. Spalding wrote to a friend: "God has
interposed in a wonderful manner to prevent this
calumny from taking effect upon Dr. Whitman."

At a joint meeting of the missions the question was
debated whether danger from that source had not become so great that duty required them to leave. But
on their knees Dr. and Mrs. Whitman resolved to com-
mit themselves anew to the work.

"God does not understand Injun language," was the
next report from the oracle in the Blue Mountains.

The distressed Nez Percés were shocked.   Of all known
tribes they were most inclined to prayer.

Dr. Whitman wrote to a friend in the valley: "The
question of worship or no worship is now before the
minds of our people as urged by Tom Hill, a Delaware
Indian.   I am in hopes we can turn his influence to the
best account, not only in regard to religion, but in
regard to the intercourse of the whites with Indians, as
he is well acquainted with the border history."

Delaware Tom visited Fort Walla Walla.   From the
corner of his eye he scrutinized every lock and barri-
cade.

"Since these skin buyers have come we can do nothing without their guns and ammunition," he said.

The Delaware visited the Willamette and shook his
head at the signs of white men.   He came to Fort
Vancouver — Dr. McLoughlin kicked him from the
gate.   The Delaware picked himself up and gave one
look.   Dr. McLoughlin never forgot those eyes, —
strange eyes, wonderful eyes, glittering, scintillating
with inward fire.   Back in the Blue Mountains the
Delaware ground his teeth.

"Why do not all Indians band together and fight
for the independence of their native land?   We are
like the partridge wounded by the hunter.   They have
given us guns until now we have forgotten the use of
the arrow.   They alone have the secret of gunpowder.
Could we plant the powder and make it grow, could
we gather shot like pebbles on the shore, we might be
free.   Now we are slaves."

Walking nearer and shaking his finger in the solemn
faces of his auditors — "White men bring diseases.
Look at the Willamettes, dying year by year; yet once,
like you, they were brave and free and rich and inde-

pendent. Look at the Blackfeet, fleeing to the mountains to escape the contagion of white men." Slowly and yet more solemnly spoke the Delaware: "Disease will come to you and you will die, and they will take the land. I have warned you. Beware. Have nothing to do with white men. They scorn us. They kick us from their gates. We are but dogs."

Again the Delaware spoke: "They judge us by the border Indian degraded by the vices of white men. They call us drunken. Who brought the fire-water? We drank from the rill and the spring. They say the Indian fights. Has the white man never fought? The savage red man burns his enemy at the stake. Did the enlightened white man never burn his kindred, even helpless women, at the stake? I have read it."

Some one ventured to remark, "Dr. Whitman is good to Indians." The Delaware blazed. He leaped from the ground and strode back and forth, talking and gesticulating to the Indians that squatted before the camp-fire.

"A white man good to the Indian? Never. It is not in the race. Do I not know? Did they not come to my home on the Susquehanna? Did not the white man want a little land to till and we let him have it? And did not more white men come, and more and more, until the Delawares were driven west and west, and no longer had any home? Does not Whitman say this land belongs to the Americans? Is he not encouraging immigrants to come this way? In a little while they will come in a great tide, and the poor Indian may slink like a dog away."

The Delaware raised his hand — "Never let the Americans settle on your lands."

"NEVER," said the Cayuses, "*never*, never."

For a long time Tiloukaikt had shown good evidence
of conversion. He longed for the beautiful and mysterious rite of baptism. But Dr. Whitman put him off.
"Too many wives, Tiloukaikt, too many wives. God
says one man, one wife."

"Ugh-úgh!" said Tiloukaikt. "Ugh-úgh!" echoed
the Indians. Then he went away and stayed for weeks.

"He has talked enough about your bad hearts,"
said a priest at Walla Walla. "He ought to have
baptized you long ago."

One day Tiloukaikt rode to the mission on his
spotted Cayuse, opened the door, walked in, and sat
down on the mat before the fire. "Well, Tiloukaikt,
are you going to put away your wives?" asked Dr.
Whitman. The Indian continued gazing into the bed
of driftwood. He spread his taper fingers before the
blaze. His hands were smaller and more shapely than
the squaws' who dug the camas.

"Cannot — cannot," said the savage, slowly shaking
his head. "One old wife — no work any more, old,
old. She mother of sons, tall sons," gesturing high
above his head. "I take care her. One young wife
— she strong. She take care me. Three wives —
dig camas, tan robe, pick berry, pack salmon, take
care all."

"You can be married to one and take care of the
rest until they find husbands," suggested Dr. Whitman.

"Ugh-ugh-úgh!" grunted the old chief, shaking
his head again and again. "Much squaw — much
camas."

"Must be white men," said Five Crows at the lodge
that night. "One wife, wood house, big plantation,
cattle."

Tiloukaikt wrinkled his vinegar face. On Sundays

the Indians came to the mission for ten and fifteen miles around, except a few to watch the lodges. Sometimes hundreds met after the buffalo hunt. Tiloukaikt stayed away.

"It was good when we knew nothing but to eat, drink, and sleep. Now it is bad, bad, bad," growled Tiloukaikt, poking around the hoes and shovels in the lodge. "Prayers no bring guns and blankets. Me no pray for nothing."

He kicked every implement of civilization out of his lodge. He trampled up his garden in a rage. He struck the bread out of the women's hands — bread they had learned to bake at Mrs. Whitman's. "Bad, bad, bad. Lazy squaw, get kouse, camas, salmon," raising his frightful double-thonged whip, "Go."

Jason Lee had said, "My Indians are so anxious for civilized food that they will even dig up potatoes after they are planted and eat them." Tiloukaikt kicked the potatoes into the river.

The old chief watched Mrs. Whitman with jealous eye. "Doct' Whit'n, why you take you wife where you go? Why not go alone? See, I leave my wives, they work, pack fish, camas, skins. Why you treat her so like big chief?"

"It is good for her to go with me," said Dr. Whitman. "We are one. Wives are given us for companions."

"Ugh-úgh!" growled Tiloukaikt. "That was Adam. God made him wife from rib. These wives not our rib. These not one with us."

In a wretched little hut constructed by herself a pretty young squaw lay dying in childbirth. Dr. Whitman heard of it, snatched his surgical case, hastened to the spot.

"Te-he-he-he," tittered the Indians. "Squaw-doctor! squaw-doctor! squaw-doctor! Te-he-he-he!"

Year after year Dr. Whitman went quietly on in his work of mercy, but his Christ-like forbearance seemed lost upon the savage.

"Ha knock-down with a club would hinduce more respect," said Ermatinger.

"It takes time, time," said Dr. Whitman. "Civilization is not the work of a day."

Above his squaw, above his pony, the Cayuse prized his gun. He ornamented the rough flint from a London smithy with streaks of red ochre and studded it with brass nails. He slid it into a mink-skin case and slept with it over his heart. To him that old gun brought food and furs and security from the hated Blackfeet. And the greatest hero in Indian eyes was the finest shot. That youth that could bring down the eagle on the wing was in the line of chieftainship.

Tom McKay had an old-fashioned rifle heavily ornamented with silver. Ermatinger called it "ha gingerbread gun."

When McKay came up the Walla Walla with his favorite gun, the clans followed him like sheep. The Indians believed he bore a magic life. They trusted and admired his coolness and bravery. None but he would have dared to trounce the impudent chieftain at the Dalles, none but Tom could have killed a boastful Walla Walla and escaped the Avenger of Blood. At one hundred paces he could drive a dozen balls through a Spanish dollar or knock off a duck's head at one hundred and twenty yards. "I always shoot a bear in the mouth to save the skin," he said.

Dr. Whitman seldom touched a gun, only now and

then to shoot a pony in his corral for horse-steak.
The grouse and the gray hare looked in his face and
laughed.

"Te-he-he-he!" laughed the Indians. "Doct' Whit'n,
he put up he gun so — shut he eye so — go bang.
Poolalik (the rabbit) — nibble — nibble — nibble just 'e
same."

"Dr. Whitman, you are too indulgent with your
Indians," said McKinley at the fort. "Indians cannot
be controlled except by fear. You must learn to use
your gun."

"Doct' Whit'n," said Tiloukaikt, "I am mad at
you. Before you came we fought each other, killed
each other, enjoyed it. Before you came the spot
where Walla Walla stands was red with blood. You
have taught us that it is wrong, and we have in a great
measure ceased. So I am mad at you, Doct' Whit'n
I am mad at you."

The young chief Elijah had shot up into the teens
straight as a fir and beautifully fashioned as the Apollo
Belvedere of Canova. Those who remember him best
say he had the face of a Roman, at times lively and
laughing, at times solemn, even sad. When he looked
upon the scrofula-smitten children of the Willamette his
dark, luminous eyes spoke volumes. As a lad he played
among them in his embroidered tunic of deerskin and
his little band of eagle plumes. His small, swift feet
outsped them in the race, his shapely hands outshot
them with the bow. "He is very bright," they said at
the mission. Sometimes the boy boasted: "My father
and my father's father were chiefs. My mother is a
sister of chiefs, and I am a chief."

At seventeen, in his war-cap of eagle feathers and his
robe wrought in porcupine, the young chief Elijah was

every inch an Indian king. Already he had been sent
to Spirit Hill in the Grande Ronde to learn his destiny;
already he led the braves in the buffalo hunt.

In October the Walla Walla-Cayuses came home
from the summer hunt laden with spoils of buffalo-beef
and hides. The nights were cold and the driftwood
fires blazed merrily.

Walking there in the soft twilight with the hum of
the lighted lodges around him, Elijah heard the gossip
of the Indian village. Here it was the whisper about
his uncle, Five Crows, who wanted a white wife. A
year ago he had asked the missionaries for one; he had
been down to Vancouver to negotiate, and at last dis-
missing his five present wives he had gone in great
state of fine horses and blankets to Fort Walla Walla to
propose to Chief Factor Pambrun for the hand of the
lovely Maria. To his astonishment, the suit was rejected with a kick, and the discomfited chief returned
home and married a Modoc slave to the great scandal
of the tribe.

Here the talk was of some trouble at the mission.
The Cayuse horses had broken into the mission field
and damaged the growing grain. When Dr. Whitman
reproved the Indians, Tiloukaikt said: "It is not your
grain, it is ours. The land is all ours, and the water
and the fuel."

One threw mud on him and pulled his ears, one
snapped a gun at him, and another aimed an axe that
the doctor dodged.

"What Indians did that?" demanded Elijah, turning
sharply.

"The ones that talk so much with Delaware Tom,"
was the answer.

"And did not Dr. Whitman punish them?"

"No, but Mr. McKinley heard of it and made them beg his pardon."

Elijah passed on frowning. "That renegade Delaware will get us into trouble yet. I wish he would go back to his own people. Why need we fear the whites? Is not my father a very great chief?"

XXVII

THE HUDSON'S BAY COMPANY IN CALIFORNIA

1841

IN wintry mist and flying cloud, Dr. McLoughlin and Sir George Simpson, on board the Hudson's Bay barque " Cowlitz," dropped down the Columbia on the way to California, and with them went Eloise Rae to her husband. Following the swells toward the whitened strand, the ship entered the Golden Gate, still quiet in the age before commerce discovered that auriferous highway. The little square Presidio, with its Mexican flag, was fast asleep. Horses and cattle dotted the hills around the bay. There was a handful of houses at Yerba Buena cove, and, yes, there was Rae, glass in hand, watching for the ship to bring his bride. It was on the last day of 1841 that Dr. McLoughlin, Sir George, and Eloise landed on the sand-dunes where in a few short years should rise the magic city of San Francisco.

The New Year's holiday was quietly spent, then followed diplomatic visits to the Spanish grandees. It was a radiant morning when they set out across the bay to Sonoma, the home of General Mariano Guadalupe Vallejo, the Prince of Northern California.

" Their castanets do not click together," the Spaniards said of Sutter and Vallejo. But they were far enough apart. In California, as in Oregon, these old feudal chieftains counted their land by leagues instead of sections. Before 1836 Vallejo had been commandant at Sonoma, where the old mission stood. Now, since the confiscation of missions Sonoma belonged to Vallejo as chief of the colonial army. It was his strong arm, more than anything else, that had seated his nephew, Alvarado, in the governor's chair at Monterey.

Vallejo's house was the finest on the coast. Eight thousand cattle bore his brand on the hills; his leagues of wheat yielded eight hundred fanegas for every eight sown. Indian serfs without number tilled his lands and toiled in his house.

Vallejo sent mounted horsemen to bring in his guests. As Dr. McLoughlin, Sir George, and Rae and Eloise galloped under the arched gateway, his retainers fired a salute under the Spanish flag. Vallejo's young brother, Don Salvador, led the way in jingling spurs and serape. The handsome general came out in his dark-blue broadcloth cloak, the señora bowed in her silken gown and spangled satin shoes, and a star like a coronet in her hair.

Everything had an old-world air, — gilded mirrors, square old Spanish sofas, even the spindle-legged pianoforte, the only one in California. The carpets were made by Indians of Mexico. Vallejo, and his nephew, Alvarado, had collected the only libraries west of the Rockies. The señora sparkled at dinner, and the señora's charming daughters. Indian servants sped to and fro with frijoles and tortillas, olives, stewed beef with red pepper, and onions and native wines.

General Vallejo, of old Castilian stock, born in California, foresaw the building of a great commonwealth. All the world knew that Spanish rule was trembling in

the balance.   To Vallejo's feet France, Russia, England
sent suitors, as if in his hand lay the disposal of this
fair Pacific province.

Naturally the conversation turned on the future of
the country, its independence of Mexico, whether
feasible, and could it be maintained by the few whites
then in California, the idea of a French protectorate,
the extension of the Russian claims to this free and
lovely land, and Sir George's suggestion in a quiet
way that England could make it to Vallejo's advantage
to favor the queen.   Vallejo was used to this — had he
not a hand full of propositions?   With due Spanish
etiquette he listened to all, entertained all, drew out
the various phases of advantage, yet held himself
uncompromised.

Evening brought on the fandango.   Don Salvador
and his troopers played the guitar, the Alcalde paddled
over the bay with the fierce, fat little commandant of
the Presidio, round as an apple dumpling.   One or
two padres, not loath to taste the general's wine,
dropped in on their way to San Dolores.   The people
at Vancouver were dancers, but even they had never
seemed to so melt into the liquid poetry of Terpsichore
as did these sinuous Spaniards.

"Let this not be the last of your visits," said General
Vallejo, as his guests departed after a round of festivity.
"When these pretty señoritas are married there will be
whole weeks of fandango and bull-fights, and no end of
drinking sweet wines."   In truth, the California days
promised to be far from depressing.

A few days later Eloise sat in the Hudson's Bay
House at Yerba Buena, when a jingling cavalier rode
up to the door.   He seemed a typical Spaniard, in
broad-brimmed sombrero, with silken cord and tassel,

profusions of lace and embroidery and buttons, and
pantaloons split on the side and laced to the ankle. A
long sword was thrust into the right boot of untanned
deerskin, a silken sash drooped at the side. Eloise
looked for the fierce mustachios and piercing eyes of a
Spaniard, and beheld — Ermatinger!

With lifted sombrero and laughing face he called,
" Are Sir George and the doctor here? "

" They sailed five days ago for Monterey, sir," answered Eloise.

" And Rae? "

" Is with them. Where is your brigade? " she asked.

" Camped with La Framboise beside the old mission," and with a jingle he was gone, galloping down
the trail to Monterey.

It was the work of a moment for Eloise and her
maids to saddle, and set out for the first time to meet
the California brigade from the other end of the route.
They heard the Spanish women singing and thrumming
guitars in the whitewashed adobes on the scattered
farms. Now and then they passed a gilded and painted
horseman, in steeple-crowned sombrero and fiery serape, flying to the race-track. Eloise hastened on over
the sandy hills covered with dwarf oak and strawberry
trees, past San Dolores walled in with skulls of slaughtered cattle, scarce noting the mouldering pile where once
the Indian converts carded wool, and wove blankets and
cloth with home-made looms. A few Indians lingered,
still chanting canticles traced by the early fathers in
the great choir books of sheepskin. She scarce noted
the narrow windows deep set in the wall, or the gaping
roofs whence the lazy Californians had stolen the tiles
for their farmhouses on the bay. Her heart thrilled as
children's will when all at once the full brigade burst

into view, — La Framboise in his Hudson's Bay buttons, Angelique as of old on her beaded palfrey, and all the long line of bearded men and butternut-colored belles like some far caravan on Arabian hills. Around the camp, fisher, beaver, and marten were stretched to dry, and through the door of a gypsy tent she caught a glimpse of Catharine Ermatinger lying on a couch of skins.

"Where have they all been to-day?" asked Eloise.

"On dress parade to Sonoma," she said.

So much they had to tell.

"Yes, my husband saw Captain Sutter and he is very angry," said Catharine. "He and the Americans think Sir George and Dr. McLoughlin are down here not only to monopolize the trade but to get possession of California. Do you know that Captain Sutter has bought the Russian post at Bodega Bay for $30,000?" added Catharine.

"Why," exclaimed Eloise, "the Russians offered that to the Hudson's Bay Company when we were at Sitka and Douglas thought the price too high."

"Money is no obstacle to Captain Sutter," said Catharine. "He has bought the post and hauled its cannon down to his fort on the Sacramento."

"Catharine, are you not afraid here?" asked Eloise.

"Why should I be, with our people all around?"

"Because," answered Eloise, "they told us at Sonoma the mountains are full of banditti. When the missions broke up some of the Indian converts became servants, but the bolder ones fled to the mountains. They hate their Spanish oppressors and come down to steal their horses and cattle. Once they tried to kidnap Señora Vallejo's beautiful sister, but she was rescued. Now the Spanish lancers go out, and when they come to a strange village they spear down men, women, and children. I have heard them tell it."

Catharine shuddered.

"The Spaniards hunt them like cattle," continued Eloise. "The story is told that one governor drilled a company of Indians as soldiers; they became so proficient the governor became alarmed and ordered them all to be shot!"

"It is not strange these California Indians have that hunted, haunted look. Whenever we approach they flee away and hide," said Catharine, thinking of the flitting shadows of the Shasta route.

"England has no rival on this coast but the Russians," said Sir George as he sailed to Monterey. "Now Mexico owes to British subjects a debt of more than fifty millions of dollars. By assuming a share of this debt on condition of being put in possession of California —"

Sir George looked what he did not say. Dr. McLoughlin was silent. He too had his dreams.

Again the warders of the old Spanish castle at Monterey looked out and saw a Hudson's Bay barque approaching the shore.

Governor Alvarado, "grown in four years from a thin and spare conspirator into a plump and punchy lover of singing, dancing, and feasting," as Sir George expressed it, also beheld them from his balcony. The "A Dios!" of Douglas still rang in his ear, but the doubloons had long since gone from his pockets.

Whatever Monterey could afford was shown to the doctor and Rae and Sir George. Whatever trade was suggested was welcomed, but State affairs — Alvarado was silent. He was jealous of his own seat at the head of Spanish power; he was even jealous of his Uncle Vallejo at Sonoma, with whom he divided the province.

"Monterey is the kitchen to Santa Barbara's parlor," said Sir George, after they doubled Point Conception and landed at the latter village. Evidently Sir George was not satisfied with Alvarado. They were enchanted with the lovely dons and doñas of Santa Barbara, rich, even in that day, in linen and lace and damask and satin. At the Spanish mission they were served by a middle-aged nun in black.

"Doña Conception, a famous lady hereabouts," said the padres, as she passed from the room with a plate of cakes.

"What! Doña Conception who would have been the bride of Baron von Resanoff?" asked Sir George, who had just been to Sitka.

"The same," said the padres. "He never came, so she devotes herself to the instruction of the young and the consolation of the sick."

"What!" exclaimed Sir George. "Is she not aware that Von Resanoff is dead?"

"Dead?" shrieked the nun in black at the open door.

"Yes, my lady, he fell from his horse and was killed at Krasnoyarsk on his road to Europe more than thirty-five years ago."

And the nun who had mourned her lover for thirty-five years went away and wept in a cell of the mission at Santa Barbara.

Rae returned with Ermatinger to Yerba Buena. The doctor and Sir George sailed away to interview the king of the Sandwich Islands. Kamehameha III. made the same promises he had given to Jason Lee, and presented Sir George with a feather mantle for Lady Simpson. Dr. McLoughlin returned to the Columbia, and Sir George went on across Siberia in his journey around the world.

XXVIII

THE FIRST IMMIGRANTS

1842

IT was September, 1842. Dr. Whitman was talking Cayuse at the top of his voice, directing his Indians, when he caught sight of a small pack-train. " 'T is early for the Shoshonie brigade." Shading his eyes to scan more closely — " No, there 's not a red belt nor a Canadian cap among them. They are not trappers. They are not Indians."

"Why, Marcus, see those women! They must be immigrants!" cried Mrs. Whitman at the door. With three bounds Dr. Whitman cleared garden, field, and irrigating ditch. Mrs. Whitman flew to greet these women who had followed her to the farthest West. Fifty men, a dozen women, with children in their arms, sat upon their jaded horses.

"Where are your wagons?" was Dr. Whitman's first inquiry.

"Broke them up for pack-saddles on Green River. The rest are at Fort Hall. The Hudson's Bay agent told us no wagon could cross the Blue Mountains."

"Left your wagons? All a mistake, all a mistake. Come in, come in," said Dr. Whitman, hurriedly, helping the women down. "Any accidents by the way?"

"None, barring that our two lawyers here were captured by the Indians and we had to buy them back again with tobacco. The rest of us were sharp enough to keep out of their clutches." Everybody laughed at the expense of the lawyers.

"Hasten, Sticcas; bring corn and flour for these people." The obedient Cayuse started for the mill.

"Roll up some melons, Aps." The Walla Walla backed into the melon-patch, his eye still on the doctor helping down the women. This deference was a strange mystery; Indian women bundled off alone.

Mrs. Whitman escorted them to the house. How gladly their tired eyes took in the poppy garden and the curtained windows. "A house! a house! How good it is to see a house!" they cried, wiping away an involuntary tear. "We have lived so long in tents we have almost forgotten what homes are like." They glanced from room to room, — Indian matting, hand-made chairs, a table covered with white — "Can we ever realize the preciousness of home again!"

Dr. Whitman called, "Bring bread, Narcissa. The men will camp in the field." Mrs. Whitman gathered up the loaves of a fresh baking, the first bread the travellers had seen since leaving Fort Laramie on the Platte. In fact, Mrs. Whitman's pantry was swept. Her hoarded jars of yellow butter went with the rest, and Dr. McLoughlin's latest gift of apples, and the pickled tongues from Colvile — nothing was too good for the doctor's fellow-countrymen. Some one suggested pay.

"Pay?" echoed the doctor. "This is not an inn. You are my guests to-day." Dr. Whitman was all in a fever. "What of immigrants?" he asked.

"They are talking of Oregon all along the border," answered one. "These came this year, more will try it next," said another.

Ever since the Red River immigration Dr. Whitman had been uneasy. At a glance he had penetrated Sir George's design in the English race for occupation.

"What is Congress doing? Is the boundary settled? Will government extend its arm over us soon?" These and a thousand other queries fell from the lips of the energetic doctor. "Oregon don't count in politics so long's the nigger question's on the boards," answered one of the lawyers. "I believe Webster was talking of trading it for a codfishery when we left," he added by way of a joke.

Oregon was no joke to Dr. Whitman. Setting his lips firmly and looking the speaker in the eye — "Do you think it possible for me to cross the mountains at this time of year, Mr. Lovejoy?"

"I think you can if you start immediately," replied the lawyer.

Again that studied, anxious look that had led Mrs. Whitman so often to say, "Marcus, you are a bundle of thoughts." He spoke again: "You see, Mr. Lovejoy, I have adopted Oregon as my country, the Indians as my field of labor. But there will be a great immigration next year. Some one must superintend it. There can never be any great influx of settlers to this country until they learn to bring their wagons. Such a wagon train, safely carried through, will lay the foundation for speedy settlement. If it fails, it will discourage any further attempt for years to come. Meanwhile, Oregon will be lost. My idea is to go back, meet these immigrants, pilot them through, and, if possible, go to Washington and present the needs of a military road across the continent. In that matter you could be of great help to me. Will you accompany me?"

The question was unexpected; the lawyer requested

time. The next day he brought his decision, — "I will accompany you." Aged men, yet living (1899), say that in answer to their responses concerning Congress, he kept saying, as if talking to himself, "I'll do it; I'll go, I'll go to Washington."

This was no sudden impulse. "This vast and fertile country belongs to us," Dr. Whitman was wont to say. "Congress had delayed too long, while England gains a foothold. Bring in people, build houses, plough up the soil, and Oregon is ours."

There was another reason for going. A letter had been brought from the American Board at Boston: "The Indians are so intractable that we have decided to discontinue the mission."

"Discontinue the mission!" That would be taking the heart out of Dr. Whitman. "Have I toiled here six years to abandon the field at last? It must not be. Why, these Indians have their little farms in every direction, and are every year extending them farther. Is that nothing in six years? Suppose they are unruly at times, — what else can be expected of wild, untamed Cayuses? Men are not civilized in a day. And is not this on the highway of all future immigration? The very gateway and the key?"

An Indian courier flew over the hills to Lapwai, another to Tschimikain, near the present Spokane, where Walker and Eells had built a station. In the little library at Whitman's they met for consultation. In an agony of grief Mrs. Whitman begged their intervention. Even imperious little Helen Mar stamped and cried.

"You must not go," said Spalding.

"No man can live upon the plains in winter," said Walker.

"You will be lost in the mountains; you will perish in the snows," said Eells.

"My first duty is to my country. I am not expatriated by becoming a missionary," said Whitman, rising before them.

"Doctor, Doctor, it is madness. Even the trappers remain in camp until the snows are gone. Think of the famished wolves on that wintry waste; think of the frozen streams, the lack of food, the howling storms, the hostile tribes that will cut you off. Doctor, three thousand miles — "

"Say no more," cried the hero of that winter ride, closing his eyes and shaking his hand at the speaker. "I am ready, not to be bound only, but to die at Jerusalem, or in the snows of the Rocky Mountains, for the name of the Lord Jesus or my country. I must go, even if I sever with the mission."

Who could stand against the will of Whitman! He bore down every objection, just as six years before he bore down every objection to his coming on a mission to the Indians. Through her tears Narcissa Whitman smiled. "He is right. He is right. Let him go," she said. Reluctantly, seeing that he would go anyway, they gave consent. Like Samson of old, he snapped the withes that bound him and passed from their control.

"It will never do to let the Hudson's Bay Company know what I am after," said Whitman in a lower tone, as if the very walls might hear and tell the message. "Delegate me to Boston. I'll take care of the rest."

There was a day of hurried preparation. There was a ride to Fort Walla Walla to purchase certain necessaries. "I am going to Boston on business, Mr. McKinley. I would like to leave my wife in your care. I have sent to the Willamette for Mr. Geiger to assist in the mission. He will be here shortly."

A wish from Dr. Whitman was a command with the chief factor. The warmest friendship subsisted between the two. His young wife, Sarah Julia, had become Mrs. Whitman's most intimate friend, neighbor, and pupil.

There was little sleep that night at Waiilatpu. With tears silently falling Mrs. Whitman put the last stitch in the buckskin garments. The food, the axe, the rifle, the medicine, horses, — all were ready. Spalding and the rest had departed for their stations.

"The board may dismiss me, but I shall do what I can to save Oregon to my country," was Dr. Whitman's parting word.

With a single companion, Lovejoy, the lawyer, the intrepid doctor undertook a journey that well might daunt a less courageous heart.

What apprehensions surged through the soul of Mrs. Whitman as she turned from the farewell at the gate! She heard the hoof-beats die on the sod — the riders melted into the tawny shadow of the grass. She re-entered the lonely home; she paced from room to room. "Why do you cry?" said Mary Ann Bridger. "Will father be home to-morrow?" said Helen Mar.

Dr. Whitman set out on his famous ride October 3, 1842. In eleven days he reached Fort Hall. The Indians were returning from buffalo-hunting. Once, twice, thrice, the doctor sent letters to his wife. Each day she wrote a line to him, hoping for an opportunity to send it. Let us make a few extracts:

Oct. 4, 1842. MY DEAR HUSBAND, — The line you sent me to-day by Aps did me great good. . . . Night and day shall my prayers ascend in your behalf, and the cause in which you have sacrificed the endearments of home at the risk of your life.

Oct. 5. In arranging the cupboard to-day I found that you had not taken the compass as you had designed. . . .

7*th.* My DEAR HUSBAND, — I got dreadfully frightened last night. About midnight I was awakened by some one trying to open my bedroom door. I raised my head and listened awhile. Soon the latch was raised, and the door opened a little. I sprang from bed and closed the door again, but the ruffian pushed, and I pushed and tried to latch it, but could not. Finally he gained upon me until he opened the door again, and, as I supposed, disengaged his blanket (at the same time I calling John) and ran as for his life. The east dining-room door was open. I thought it was locked. I fastened the door, lit a candle, and went to bed, trembling and cold, but could not rest until I had called John, the Hawaiian servant, to bring his bed and sleep in the kitchen. Had he, the intruder, persisted I do not know what I should have done. I did not think of the war-club, but I thought of the poker.

Chief Trader McKinley, at Walla Walla, heard of the attempt to break into Mrs. Whitman's room. Without delay he sent a runner saying, " Come to us. We will fix you a comfortable room. It is not safe for a woman to be there alone."

Oct. 12. My DEAR HUSBAND, — I am now at Walla Walla. I could not refuse, as Mr. McKinley came on purpose to take me in the wagon. The Indians did not like my leaving very well, seemed to regret the cause. I felt strongly to prefer to stay there if it could be considered prudent.

Oct. 22. My DEAR HUSBAND, — The word is given that the Express is arriving, and I hasten to write you my farewell, praying earnestly that we may be permitted to meet again and spend many years together. . . . Indeed, much as I shall, and do, want to see you, I prefer that you stay just as long as it is necessary to accomplish all your heart's desire respecting the interests of this country, so dear to us both — our home.

Dr. McLoughlin sent me a keg of fresh apples from Fort Vancouver, and ever since we have been enjoying apple pies.

The Indians that met you beyond Grande Ronde appeared very happy to say they had seen you, and to hear something about your plans for returning, from yourself. Sticcas really mourns about you, that he did not come and see you before you left. I believe it is a great comfort to them to see me left behind. They tell me they are waiting to see where I go, before they decide where to go for the winter.

Almost three long weeks have passed since we exchanged the parting kiss, and many, many long weeks are yet to come before we shall be permitted, if ever, in this world, to greet each other again. . . . I follow you night and day, and shall through the whole journey, in my imagination and my prayers. My heart is as your heart in this matter. I confidently believe you will be blessed in the object of your visit to the States.

Read this letter, my husband, and then give it to my mother. Perhaps she would like once more to take a peep into one of the secret chambers of her daughter's heart. . . .

NARCISSA.

Even while Mrs. Whitman was writing, the Cayuses were fishing in the Walla Walla. Dr. Whitman had just thrashed, and the straw lay in a pile by the mill. They built a fire to roast their fish. That night, while the careless Cayuses slept, the sparks crept from straw to straw until they reached the pile. At midnight the flames of the burning mill cast a lurid glare on the walls of Whitman mission.

It was enough. "I dare not go back," she said. The Methodist mission sent an invitation for Mrs.

Whitman to come down to the Dalles, so, when the
Montreal express came singing by, she embarked with
a heavy heart, full of foreboding.

The weather-beaten voyageurs recognized the prima
donna of Fort Vancouver. They heard the story of her
flight. Was it the delicate sympathy of those brawny
Canadians that prompted the thought? The song she
taught them six years ago thrilled with pathetic melody
the evening air: —

> " Watchman, tell us of the night,
>   What its signs of promise are,
> Traveller, on yon mountain height,
>   See that glory-beaming star.
> Watchman, does its beauteous ray
>   Aught of joy or hope foretell?
> Traveller, yes, it brings the day,
>   Promised day of Israel."

A solitary star twinkled above the cliffs that rose per-
pendicularly on either hand. The music reverberated
from wall to wall of the narrow gorge. Never in arched
cathedral or gilded choir rang out that old hymn as on
that night in the Dalles of the Columbia.

The mission at the Dalles received Mrs. Whitman as
a sister. After the solitary life at Waiilatpu, it was like
a home-coming to see again white men, white women,
white children. She noted not the tall Indians passing
and repassing and peering in at the windows; her soul
was with the rider on the plains.

The flight of Mrs. Whitman, and a rumor that the
Indians were coming down " to kill off the Bostons,"
created a panic in the Willamette valley. The handful
of settlers loaded their guns and barricaded their doors.

Scarcely a month had Dr. Whitman been on his way
when an Indian subagent, who had come with the immi-

grants, invited Tom McKay to go up with him to quiet the Indians. Cornelius Rogers accompanied them. Chief Trader McKinley joined them at Fort Walla Walla. They rode out to Waiilatpu — it was deserted. The charred mill lay on the river bank. One hundred miles northeast they galloped through a beautiful, undulating country, to the lodge of Red Wolf on the Snake.

"See my trees," said the chief. By a creek at his door grew a tiny orchard, planted by his own hands. Mr. Spalding had presented the sets that blossomed into the first fruit raised by an Oregon Indian. Following the great Nez Percé trails that terraced the hillsides for hundreds of miles, they spied across the Clearwater River a low, irregular roof, with wings, sheltering an establishment of eleven fireplaces. It was Spalding's mission at Lapwai.

In the schoolroom two hundred children were busy with books and pens, printing like copper-plate in the Nez Percé tongue. In the weaving and spinning room, Nez Percé girls were knitting and making cloth. In the kitchen, Nez Percé women were cooking and sewing and shelling peas. In the fields one chief had just harvested one hundred and seventy-six bushels of beans, one hundred bushels of corn, and four hundred bushels of potatoes. Forty others had raised grain, eight had ploughs. Several exhibited with pride a few cows, some pigs and sheep and poultry.

Early in the morning the Indian children ran to the mission, and without being called, began teaching one another, and continued so until dark. The chiefs governed the school; taking the books home at night, every lodge became a schoolroom.

"Yonder sits my most promising pupil and our first

convert, Chief Joseph," said Mr. Spalding. " The one
beside him is the Cayuse chief, Five Crows, — they are
half-brothers on the mother's side. Three winters now
Five Crows has driven his herds over here and attended
our school. That one with the hawk's nose is Lawyer,
my teacher. With his aid I have been able to translate
the four gospels and many hymns into Nez Percé. We
have a printing-press now, the first one west of the
Rocky Mountains."

A little boy sat on Chief Joseph's knee, the image of
his father, even to the band of feathers in his hair.
Every day the child came to school with his father at
the mission. Who then dreamed that little Joseph
would one day lead our troops a bloody chase of a
thousand miles, twice crossing the Rockies, fighting
pitched battles from point to point, retiring each time in
masterly retreat with his women and wounded, until his
name should be written in the scroll of great military
leaders?

" Have you no trouble with the Indians?" inquired
the agent. "We are agitated with strange rumors in
the valley."

" Yes, we have trouble," was Spalding's answer. " A
renegade Delaware has been exciting their fears. Indians are children, and easily influenced. Just now
they are excited over Dr. Whitman's going to the States.
They have been told that he will bring back an army of
immigrants to take their lands."

It was decided to summon a council on the plains at
Lapwai. Twenty-two chiefs responded. Dark-eyed,
long-haired men and women poured thickly over the
hills. Silently, stoically, the Indians listened, until an
old chief, father of the famous two that journeyed to St.
Louis, tottered to his feet.

"I speak to-day," he said. "To-morrow I die. I am the oldest of the tribe, was high chief when Lewis and Clark came to this country. They visited me, honored me with their friendship. I showed my wounds received in bloody battle with the Snakes. They told me it was not good, it was better to be at peace, gave me a flag of truce. I held it up high. We met and talked, but never fought again. Clark pointed to this day. We have long waited. Sent our sons to Red River to school to prepare for it. Two of them sleep with their fathers. One is here, can be ears and mouth and pen for us. I say no more. I am quickly tired. I am glad I live to see you and this day. I shall soon be quiet in death."

He ceased. The Nez Percés were moved as by a wind. The instructions of forty years were voiced by that old chief. The memory of Lewis and Clark was a potent spell. Distrust of the Americans gave place to confidence. Ellice, the old man's educated son, was that day elected High Chief of the Nez Percés nation.

Among those who accompanied the subagent up from the Willamette valley was Baptiste Dorion, a half-breed interpreter, the same Dorion that shot the Blackfoot chief and stole his painted robe. Dorion's mother, the heroine of Irving's "Astoria," had brought him as a child over the Blue Mountains to the camp of Pio-pio-mox-mox, the Yellow Serpent. He came now to visit his benefactor.

The Walla Walla-Cayuses were preparing the ground for winter wheat. Dorion's ever restless eye, "the lurking home of plots and conspiracies," fell upon their rude husbandry.

"Why do you make farms and build houses? It is no use," said Dorion. "Dr. Whitman will come in the summer and bring an army. Then the whites will destroy everything, take your lands and kill you, or make you slaves."

Dorion returned to the valley, but the words of Dorion flew from lip to lip. The young men grew wild for war. " Let us rush to the Willamette," they cried.

"Be cautious," counselled the old men. " The season is late. The trail around Mt. Hood is deep with snow. Let us wait — see. We do not wish to go to war, but if the Bostons come to take away our lands we will fight to the last drop of blood. Yellow Serpent is a wise and careful chief. Let us send him to talk with the White-Headed Eagle at Fort Vancouver."

Directly after his return with the subagent, to the Willamette, Cornelius Rogers went up the valley to wed the daughter of David Leslie at the old Methodist mission. The bridal party came down the laughing river. A thousand rainbows danced that February morning, when the bride and groom were landing at Willamette Falls. And at that moment, while friends waited with congratulations, the boat veered into the current. Resistlessly it tore the rope away from the Indians on shore. Only inanimate rocks answered the despairing shriek, as Cornelius Rogers and his bride and her sisters swept over the Falls and into the yawning gulf together. The cruel waters whirled and hissed and curled, but the seething maelstrom never gave up its dead.

XXIX

WHITMAN'S RIDE

1842

SCARCE an hour had Dr. Whitman ridden from his door at Waiilatpu when the Cayuses fiercely gathered and barred his progress.

"Back, go back," they cried. "You cannot go."

"You promised to build houses."

"You promised fences."

"You promised a saw-mill."

"You promised sheep."

"You promised cattle."

On every side arose the clamor recounting every improvement the doctor had ever suggested. When the doctor said, "We will do so and so," the Indians construed it into a promise, and to the Indian a promise is a sacred thing.

"Yes, yes, yes, my boys," said the doctor, pleased at this sudden recollection, yet impatient to be off. "I'll do it. I am going now to see about it. Look for me back; meet me at Fort Hall when the corn is ripe."

Still they delayed and detained him, — they feared he was leaving entirely. After repeated assurances and promises they let go his bridle-rein and regretfully watched his departure.

To avoid the hostile Sioux, to strike a warmer clime, and to gain the trail of the Mexican traders, Dr. Whitman turned south by way of Fort Wintee, Salt Lake,

Taos, and Santa Fé. A Siberian winter set in. Stormed in on the mountains, imprisoned in dark defiles for days, feeding their horses on cottonwood bark, yet on, still on. The multitudinous cry of coyotes followed on their track. Blizzards obscured the winter trail, the guide lost his way in the darkened air; their steps must be retraced, but whither? Even the morning trail was lost in the blinding drift. There in the wild mountain, with the wintry tempest howling loud and louder, all seemed lost. Dr. Whitman threw himself upon his knees and committed his wife, his mission, and his cause to God. The half-frozen mule began to prick his ears, and turning about led them back to the morning fire. After days of weary waiting the wind lulled, the sun broke through the dun clouds, and through the dazzling snow the travellers broke a path to Grand River. Here again the sides were frozen. A black current dashed down the middle.

"Danger. Cannot cross," said the Indian guide in the sign language of his race.

Dr. Whitman set his lips as Washington did that night on the Delaware, and rode to the edge of the ice. He tried to force the animal in, but he sat back on his haunches.

"Push," commanded the doctor.

Lovejoy and the guide pushed. Down, down they went, the doctor and the horse, completely out of sight, then rising like Poseidon on the foam, they battled with the current. Sweeping far below they reached the other shore, and the doctor leaped upon the ice. With his master's aid the dripping steed clambered after. Lovejoy and the guide followed with the packhorses, and all soon melted their coats of icy mail before a blazing bonfire. Another month of cold and hunger, of mule-meat and dog-flesh, took them over the Sierra Madres to Taos in New Mexico. Rest, supplies, then a final charge conquered the main ramparts of the Rockies. Safe on the plains beyond, the exultant missionary could no longer restrain his impatience to reach Bent's Fort on the Arkansas. Leaving Lovejoy and the guide to follow, he set on ahead. Bleak Arctic wind rolled down upon the rider in his lonely saddle. Again he was lost, bewildered, and Indians directed him down the river to the Fort. Lovejoy followed him and gave up at Bent's Fort, but Whitman pushed on, until one cold February morning he stood in the streets of St. Louis surrounded by mountaineers entreating him to tell the story of his winter trip.

" Not now; I cannot stay, I must get to Washington."

Stopping not even to change his clothes, with frost-bitten ears and feet and fingers, with the very flesh of him burnt with cold, the heroic Whitman paused not till he stood in the presence of Daniel Webster. In his shaggy great buffalo-coat and hood and fur leggings and moccasins, he was certainly a curiosity. Daniel Webster looked at him with those historic lion's eyes and said: " You are too late. The treaty has been signed."

" So I heard in St. Louis, but Oregon — "

" Lies untouched," said Webster, with unmoved countenance, still curiously eying the man in the shaggy great-coat.

" Then I am not too late," said Whitman, " not too late to tell you that Oregon is a treasure worth our holding, a land of broad rivers and fertile valleys."

Webster was tired. The " intricacies and complexities and perplexities" of this boundary question had worried him for years. New England was dissatisfied with his settlement of the Maine boundary, the west was howling about his Ashburton Treaty. Senator Linn had introduced a call for information as to why Oregon had not been included in this last treaty. Fifteen days ago Linn's bill was carried in the upper and lost in the lower House — and now here comes this Oregon man to reopen the whole discussion.

Webster was not a foe to Oregon, but had he not heard, time and again, that the Americans must be crazy to think of trying to cross unbroken wastes of desert and impassable mountains to occupy a country fit only for the beaver, the bear, and the savage? Had not the "London Examiner" said the whole territory in dispute was not worth twenty thousand pounds to either power? Had not the Senator from South Carolina just said in the Senate that he would not give a pinch of snuff for the whole territory? That he thanked God for his mercy in placing the Rocky Mountains there to keep the people back? With all this in mind Webster was inclined to misinterpret that rapid utterance and that positive tone.

"You are an enthusiast, Mr. Whitman; you certainly are an enthusiast. Sir George Simpson says wagons can never get over the Rocky Mountains, and he must know. He has traversed those wilds from his youth. Besides, the country is good for nothing, the papers are full of it."

"All from English reprints," added the doctor, quickly. "The Hudson's Bay Company has flooded Great Britain with such reports to keep the land to themselves. It is to their interest to keep it a wilderness."

Secretary Webster endeavored to change the subject.

"How did you get to Oregon, Mr. Whitman?"

"With two women and a wagon across the Rocky Mountains."

"How did you return?"

"On horseback over the snow."

An hour they talked, but the subject was ever the same, — Oregon, the paradise by the sea.

"I want the President and Cabinet to hear what you have said to me," said the great statesman, visibly impressed with the heroic effort of Dr. Whitman.

They were called together, and Dr. Whitman spent an evening answering their questions on Oregon, its importance and its resources.

President Tyler listened attentively. "Dr. Whitman," he said, "your frozen limbs and leather breeches attest your sincerity. Can emigrants cross the mountains in wagons?"

"My own wagon went across."

"Is there likely to be an emigration this year?"

"They are already gathering on the frontier. I am publishing a pamphlet to help it on. I came to the States for that express purpose."

"Very well," answered the President. "Go ahead with your wagons. This question can rest till we see if you get them through."

"That is all I ask," said Whitman, rising.

Promising to forward to his old school friend, the Secretary of War, a synopsis of a bill for a line of posts to Oregon, he hastened away.

Twenty years before, Senator Benton had urged the occupation of the Columbia. "Mere adventurers may enter upon it as Æneas entered upon the Tiber, and as our forefathers came upon the Potomac, the Delaware, and the Hudson, and renew the phenomenon of individuals laying the foundation of future empire."

Now Benton said, "Thirty thousand rifles in the valley of the Columbia is our surest ground of title."

"What are you here for, leaving your post?" gruffly inquired the Secretary of the American Board, eying his shaggy visitor as Dr. Whitman entered the office in Boston.

"I came on business to Washington," answered the doctor, unabashed.

"Opening up new territories to settlement is not a part of our business," was the Secretary's comment on his scheme to pilot emigrants over the mountains. "Here, take some money and get some decent clothes; then we 'll talk."

"Marcus came to father's house in sorry plight," says his sister Harriet in a letter to this author. "He had been so chilled in coming over the mountains that he was suffering all the time. He was the grandest man in overcoming difficulties and executing the most improbable things. Yet his heart was tender as a woman's."

By order of Congress Senator Benton's son-in-law, John Charles Fremont, was despatched to accompany the proposed immigration. When the first grass sprung the emigrants crossed the border with their rifles on their shoulders. Already the long train of wagons was far out on the Platte when Dr. Whitman joined them in May, so far out that Fremont barely caught up and followed in their wake to Oregon.

Long after Webster remarked to a friend, "It is safe to assert that our country owes it to Dr. Whitman and his associate missionaries that all the territory west of the Rocky Mountains and north of the Columbia is not now owned by England and held by the Hudson's Bay Company."

XXX

A PROVISIONAL GOVERNMENT

1843

CAPTAIN COUCH, sent out by the Cushings of Newburyport, opened trade with the Sandwich Islands and sailed his brig up the Willamette. American sentiment began to crystallize. The handful of settlers had long looked with jealous eye on the commercial aristocracy of the Columbia. Now, hither into their midst came the democratic corner grocery, with its tea and flour and Yankee notions, with its free discussions, long-spun yarns, and political caucus.

The immigrants of 1842, winding over the pack-trails of Mt. Hood, were soon ensconced on the dry-goods box and nail-keg. " Is not the country ours?" they said. " Did not an American discover the river? Did not Lewis and Clark explore it? Did not John Jacob Astor found Astoria at the mouth of the river? Did not England admit all this when she restored Astoria after the war?" So they argued.

As early as 1829 Dr. McLoughlin had taken a claim at the Falls of the Willamette, the town-site of the future Oregon City. " I may want it for a home in my old age," he said, thinking of that future far-away time when he might be too old to serve the Hudson's Bay Company. Already some adventurous American had jumped his claim to a mill-site on an island at the Falls. Now the immigrants had come, the doctor sur-

veyed his claim and offered lots for sale. The pot began to boil.

"What right has Dr. McLoughlin to this town-site?"
asked the jealous immigrants.   "He is head of a
foreign monopoly and he does n't live here.   There is
no question that he is holding this town-site and water-
power for the Hudson's Bay Company."

"Fur that matter," chimed in a mountaineer, "ther
ain't a town-site er water-power in all the valley wher
the company ain't built a shed an' sent a man to hold
it daown."

"Yes, and if they dared they would set up a great
'No thoroughfare' board to keep us immigrants out,"
added another.   "Were it not for that Joint Occupancy Treaty, a settler would have no more right to
enter Oregon than to trespass on the lawn of a private
gentleman in Middlesex, England.   The company
designs to hold Oregon, as it holds all British North
America, like a vast estate, exclusively in the interests
of the fur trade."

"Don't be too hard on the company," suggested
one of the more conservative.   "We live here under its
protection and in comfort."

"We live here!" exclaimed a tall, gaunt man astride
the counter.   "Yes, as the lamb lives with the lion, to
be swallered up.   Under their protection? Yes, because our own country refuses to give it.   Like a great
octopus the Hudson's Bay Company has us in its claws.
No private trader has ever ben able to compete with
this 'ere monopoly.   They claim every fish in the
stream, every beaver in the dam.   Look at Wyeth,
Bonneville, and the trappers that venture to cross the
Rockies — defeated every time."

"I move that we draw up a petition to Congress to

protect American interests in Oregon," said Robert Shortess, a native of Ohio. "This salmon-skin aristocracy has ruled the country long enough."

"'T will do no good," said a missionary. "Uncle Sam is dozing while England takes the country. We have sent petitions by the yard, — Jason Lee took one, Wyeth wrote a memorial, we sent one by Farnham, we have begged and plead, and prayed, but Congress pays no attention. She is too much engrossed in the nigger business to notice an obscure little settlement on the northwest coast."

Nevertheless Shortess and Abernethy, the mission steward, did draw up a document bristling with charges against the Hudson's Bay Company and despatched it to the States. Dr. McLoughlin heard of it — it cut him to the heart.

The people in the valley feared the restless chiefs beyond the mountains. Their own Indians began to mutter, "These Bostons are driving off our game and destroying our camas-fields."

The woods were full of painted faces. Tomahawks and scalping-knives glittered in the grass. The whites had scorned these valley Indians; now a secret dread took hold of every heart. Outlying ranchers came in with frightened whispers —

"The Clackamas Indians are on the move."

"The Molallas are defiant."

"The Klickitats are collecting back of Tualati Plains."

A Calapooia chief crossed the Willamette, shaking his finger toward the settlement by the Falls. "Never will I return till I bring back a force to drive out these Bostons."

"Should these Injuns combine, we are lost," said the settlers.

"Dr. McLoughlin will not help us on account of that memorial to Congress. There's no ammunition except in the stockade at Fort Vancouver."

"We are without defence," said the settlers. "We cannot wait for Congress, we must organize."

"But how?" queried the timid. "The French Canadians of Champoeg will oppose. They are not afraid of Injuns. They will stand by the company, and they are more than we in number."

"We must find a basis of common interest, — how about wolves?"

Wolves? How they laughed and cried around the mission! With what long howls they struck the midnight hour beside the Falls! What multitudinous reveilles rang along the valley at the first red streak of dawn! How the fine bark of puppies staccatoed the hoarse bass of big gray grenadiers! How they ran down herds of elk and horses and cattle! How they dined on pigs and poultry and calves!

"Yes," was the unanimous response; "let us call a wolf meeting!"

So, on the first Monday of March, 1843, every American that could muster a boat landed at old Champoeg at ten o'clock in the morning. They proceeded at once to the house of Joseph Gervais. Telix, faithful housewife, had scrubbed her floor and swept her hearth and hied her away to plant her onion bed.

The long-haired Canadians, indulging in their favorite vice of smoking, discussed the bears and wolves and panthers with these astute Americans. For fifteen years these Frenchmen had depended each on his own old rusty trade-gun, and the wolves were bad as ever. Every night the good wife heard the squawking in her chicken-coop, and the farmer ran out bare-legged at the squealing of his pigs. But these Americans — one loss was enough to set loose relentless war against the " varmints."

" How is it, fellow-citizens," cried the ringing voice of an immigrant when bounties had been fixed upon the scalps of wolves, " how is it with you and me and our children? Have we any organization upon which we can rely for mutual protection? Is there any power or influence in the country sufficient to protect us, and all we hold dear, from the worse than wild beasts that threaten and occasionally destroy our cattle? Who in our midst is authorized to call us together to protect our own and the lives of our families? True, the alarm may be given, as in a recent case, and we may run who feel alarmed and shoot off our guns, while our enemy may be robbing our property, ravishing our wives, and burning the houses over our defenceless families. Common sense, prudence, and justice to ourselves, demand that we act consistently with the principles with which we commenced. We have mutually and unitedly agreed to defend and protect our cattle and domestic animals; now, fellow-citizens, I move that a committee be appointed to consider the civil and military protection of this colony, and that said committee consist of twelve persons."

Canadian and American, the ayes were unanimous. The founders of Rome were suckled by a wolf. Out of a wolf meeting grew the government of Oregon.

May came. Knee-deep in flowers, the delegates gathered again at old Champoeg. The larks flew up and sang. The Canadians made big eyes at one another. " The old régime is good enough," they said. " Wait until the sovereignty is decided."

The Americans groaned in spirit. Some opponent unknown had passed from house to house in old Champoeg and said to the Canadians, "Vote no, vote no, vote no to everything." The Canadians were out in force — hope flickered against hope that some of them might favor American institutions.

They stood in the open air. The river ran by and laughed, as when the red man held his councils on the bluff. The report of the committee was read.

"Shall we accept the report?" said the chairman.

"No!" thundered the Canadians as one man.

The hearts of the Americans thumped against their ribs. Confusion prevailed. The eye of the Secretary measured the crowd — "We can risk it; let us divide and count!"

Scarce had the second passed when Jo Meek the trapper stepped forward with stentorian call: "Who's for a divide? All in favor of the report and organization, follow me!"

The lines marched apart, swayed a moment, hesitated at deadlock — then — after a moment of heart-throbs — *two Canadians* crossed to the American side. Fifty-two against fifty!

"Three cheers for freedom!" again rang out the trappers' call. A shout went up that summoned the dusky dames to their doors a mile back on French Prairie. The river ran by and laughed, but Oregon was not the same.

"These Americans fatten on politics," said the clerks at Fort Vancouver. "Why, it was as good as 'Punch and Judy' to see the fun go on. And they were so solemn and earnest about it, too."

The Canadians looked on and wondered. Dr. McLoughlin could hardly realize that out of these appar-

ently trivial proceedings had arisen the fabric of a
State, that the infant settlement had donned the *toga
virilis*.

Dr. McLoughlin was walking in the garden at Fort
Vancouver, musing upon the troubled state of affairs.
The stronger grew the American colony the weaker
seemed his influence over the Indians. The last returns of each brigade grew less and less. The beaver
were disappearing. Added to this, a contest between
England and the United States seemed imminent, in
which a single misstep on his part might precipitate a
bloody war. The usually erect form was bent. A
light breeze dallied with his hair. A footstep at his
side attracted his attention. He turned and faced the
stalwart form of Yellow Serpent. The Walla Walla's
long black hair rippled over his beaded buckskin.
The eagle-plumes in his head-band gave a regal touch
to the haughty face.

"Ah, my son!" said Dr. McLoughlin, "I am glad
to see you here. What news from the Walla Walla?"

"Bad news, my father. My people are full of fears.
I have come a long journey to show you my heart.
Dorion says Dr. Whitman will bring white men to take
our lands and kill us all."

"Tut, tut, tut! Why does the naughty Dorion
frighten my people? The white men will do no harm.
They are your friends. They come to help you, to
teach you."

Yellow Serpent was even taller than Dr. McLoughlin.
Approaching him closely he bent forward and looked
him eagerly in the eye.

"Will Boston man fight King George man?"

"Certainly not," answered the doctor; "we are at
peace."

"What for then you strengthen your stockade?" said the Indian, majestically waving his hand toward the wall. "What for another big gun? What for big ship guarding you all winter?"

"Our stockades were old. We renew them often," answered the doctor. "The ship was a visitor, not a defender."

The Indian went on: —

"We hear Boston man making laws. Getting ready to become great people. Dr. Whitman will bring many, many people. He say this America land. He take all our land. Poor Indian will have no horses, no land, no home by and by."

"You must do as Dr. Whitman tells you," said McLoughlin. "Build homes on your land. Cultivate your ground, and you can keep it like white people."

"My people fear King George man and Boston man join together and kill all Indian." Again that bent face, that eager, searching, flashing look.

Dr. McLoughlin saw the real trouble in Yellow Serpent's soul. Truly he had shown his heart. Stepping toward him and taking the Indian's two hands in his own the benevolent doctor said: "My son, is this what troubles you? Go home and fear no more. No white man will harm you. Dr. Whitman is your true friend. He will not see you injured. If any American should make war on you the Hudson's Bay Company would never join them. Have we not been your friends for thirty years? Do you think we could bring our hearts to harm our brothers? Go home and work in your little gardens as Dr. Whitman taught you. Drive the wicked Dorion away. He will bring my children into trouble."

" I will tell your words," said Yellow Serpent, turning away.

But though Dr. McLoughlin had quieted the chief, he himself was not quieted. In considerable mental distress he dismissed the friendly chief and retired to his office. An hour later Douglas entered.

" What have you written?" inquired Douglas, as the doctor looked up.

" I have written to the Hudson's Bay Company that if they would not lose the country they must protect their rights here; that immigrants hostile to British interests are coming in, made more hostile by the publication of Irving's 'Astoria' and 'Bonneville,' — these immigrants really fear we will set Indians upon them; that by kindness we are striving to overcome this prejudice; that, however, we have enemies here trying to make trouble, — threats have been made against Fort Vancouver, and really, the people have been encouraged to make an attack, by public prints in the United States, stating that British subjects ought not to be allowed to remain in Oregon; that there is no dependence in the servants about the fort to do sentry duty beyond a few nights, nor are there officers enough to be put upon guard without deranging the whole business; that our forces are not sufficient in case of attack, and that in the dry season the fort could easily be burned. So I have asked for a government vessel to protect Fort Vancouver. The great question with me is, how to keep the peace till the sovereignty is decided. I think that covers the case."

" I think so," said Douglas. The chief and his second always consulted each other and always agreed. The letter went by express to Canada and on to

London. Dr. McLoughlin mounted more guns and waited for a reply.

A Catholic priest from the upper country brought word to Fort Vancouver: "The Indians say they are not mad at the King George men, only at the Bostons, because they take their lands."

"Very well, then," said the irritated doctor. "Let the Americans take care of themselves."

"The Indians of the interior are endeavoring to form a coalition for the purpose of destroying all the Boston people," wrote the missionaries from the Dalles to the Indian subagent. "They construe the language you used last autumn into threats. The wicked Dorion has told them that ships are coming into the river with troops."

"I must go up there again at all hazards, and meet those Walla Walla-Cayuses," said the subagent. He engaged twelve Frenchmen to accompany the expedition, but when the day came every one sent word, "We have decided not to go."

Not to be daunted, the subagent set out with four companions from the Methodist mission. At Champoeg Dr. McLoughlin's long boat met him with a despatch, — "I entreat you not to undertake such a dangerous expedition. In all probability you and your party will be cut off." But the subagent went on.

At the Falls a second runner met him with a second letter from Dr. McLoughlin. "I advised my Frenchmen to have nothing to do with this quarrel. Keep quiet, keep quiet. The excitement will soon subside."

Madame and Mrs. Douglas were at their embroidery when they heard loud voices in the fort: "Is it true that you refuse to grant supplies to the Americans who signed that memorial?"

" I have not refused supplies to the *signers*, but the *authors* need expect no more favors from me," answered Dr. McLoughlin, in a tone that made the household tremble.

" Then, as we had nothing to do with it, you can let us have Indian goods on the credit of the United States for our journey up the Columbia, can you not? " persisted the subagent.

" I am astonished that you think of going up there among those excited Indians," roared the doctor, looking hard at the venturesome four. Dr. McLoughlin's usual tone was low and slow. This thunderous key he sometimes used to his servants in reproof or command, never before to Americans.

" Not all the people of the valley signed that paper, Dr. McLoughlin. Not all of them approved of it. It was puerile and childish. I shall tell the commissioner of Indian affairs in my next report that if any one not connected with the fur company had been at half the pains and expense that you have been to to establish a claim at the Willamette Falls, there would have been few to object. Under the Joint Occupancy Treaty you have as good a right as they."

This statement quite mollified the doctor's wrath. " I thought my character as an honest man was beyond suspicion, but when I heard of those charges, — well, really, really, the citizens themselves are the best judges if I have injured them or not."

The governor seized a pen and hastily scribbled some orders.

" Here, Roberts! McTavish! Let the gentlemen have whatever they want. God bless you, gentlemen, God bless you. May your errand succeed."

Mrs. Whitman joined them at the Dalles. Rogers,

beloved of the Indians, Rogers without whom Mrs. Whitman felt the meeting could not be held, was dead.

The Indians were watching for the subagent and the subagent was watching for the Indians. Each expected to see an enemy. When three or four whites entered their midst unarmed, their fears gave way to wonder.

"Yes; Yellow Serpent was right," they said. "We were mistaken." Ever since the chief's return they had been working on their little plantations. Corn, peas, and wheat were peeping through the mould.

"I actually found the Indians suffering more from fear of the whites than the whites from fear of the Indians," was the subagent's report on his return.

The Walla Walla meadows were purple with camas, the plains a moquette of multicolored phlox. The Cayuses were camped along the base of the Blue Mountains. Three thousand Walla Wallas were camped on the Umatilla. A thousand Nez Percés came down from the North on their best horses. The mounted Cayuses and Walla Wallas rode forth to meet their guests in sham battle. In front of Dr. Whitman's the entire plain was a glittering cavalcade of prancing horses and plumed warriors, gay as when the monarchs of old met on the Field of the Cloth of Gold. Elijah, Tauitau, Five Crows in splendid array led their several bands.

Yellow Serpent sounded the war whistle. Chief Joseph answered with the Indian bugle. The spirited chargers dashed as in deadly combat, imitating a recent battle with the Blackfeet. There was a rush and a roar, a whirl and confusion, and shouts and flying foam, as the savage cavalry swept the plain. Even the chiefs began to fear an actual battle, when Spalding, from Lapwai, said, "Let us retire to the doctor's house for worship."

Chief Ellice rose on the back of his splendid charger, waved his hand over the dark mass, and all was still. The horses, gay with scarlet belts and head-dresses and tassels, were led away. The trampling of many feet resounded in the mission house. Like a vision Narcissa Whitman glided into the dark assembly. The fair brow, the golden hair, the clinging dress, riveted every eye. When they sang her clear soprano soared like a bird above the Nez Percé chorus. Ever since her return there had been a constant stream of Indian women, calling with little gifts to show their love.

The next day the chiefs in paint and plume assembled at the Council.

"You have heard a talk of war," said the subagent. "We are come among you to assure you there is no war. We come to regulate your intercourse with white people. If you lay aside your quarrels, cultivate your lands, and receive good laws, you may become a great and happy people.

"Hear! hear! hear!" cried the Walla Walla-Cayuses.

All that day and the next the chiefs discussed the laws. "And do you accept them?" said the agent.

"Ay," said all the Indians.

At this point excitement rose to fever heat.

"Who shall be our High Chief?"

Some said Tauitau. In former time Tauitau had been head sachem of the Cayuse nation, but after his attack on Chief Factor Pambrun that officer had broken up his power, encouraged his young men to insubordination, and had advanced the influence of the younger brother,

Five Crows. Tauitau wore a rosary and a crucifix and there was a blue cross embroidered on his moccasions.

"He is a Catholic. We do not follow his worship," roared Tiloukaikt.

"I cannot accept the chieftainship," said Tauitau. "I have tried to control our young men in former time, but I am left alone to weep."

Some mentioned Five Crows. "He is a strong heart," said one. "He will not change," said another.

"Our hearts go toward him with a rush," cried all the people.

Five Crows, the most ambitious chief of all the Indian country, did not respond at once. He only bowed his head and wept. By inheritance the chieftainship belonged to Tauitau, now by election it was his.

The wind blew the tempting fragrance of a barbecued ox toward the scene of deliberation. A fat hog hung hissing over a pit of fire, and the hungry throng soon gathered around a feast on the flowery field. The sharp teeth of the Walla Walla-Cayuses and their Nez Percé brethren made quick work of the savory menu. Chief Ellice brought out the Nez Percé peace pipe, three feet long with a bowl like a porringer, and laid upon it a coal. The chiefs puffed first, and then the whites. As each one drew a whiff he spoke, — Five Crows, Ellice, Tauitau, Yellow Serpent, — one by one, as the fragrant aroma curled up by the still Walla Walla. One by one they took each other's hands — and went out from the council and faced their antelope-footed horses homeward. Late at night the fires still smouldered, but where the nations camped that day only one solitary old Indian remained to boil up the feet of the barbecued ox for his next day's dinner.

XXXI

WHITMAN RETURNS WITH A THOUSAND PEOPLE

1843

"TRAVEL, *travel, travel,* — nothing else will take you to the end of your journey. Nothing is wise that does not help you along. Nothing is good for you that causes a moment's delay." The commanding voice and clear-cut face of Dr. Whitman passed from wagon to wagon of that great procession on the plains.

Back, far back as the eye could reach the line extended, a thousand souls, one hundred and twenty wagons drawn by oxen, and following in the rear fifteen hundred loose horses and cattle trampled up the dust. Like the Greek anabasis, like the exodus of Israel, like the migrations of northern Europe, this little army of emigrants broke all previous record, as they toiled on westward two thousand miles in one unresting march. At every dawn the bugle woke the night encampment. At every dusk the tents were set and supper fires were kindled. Old rocking-chairs were brought out. Grandams knit by the cheerful blaze and babies toddled in the grass. Under the mellow moon the old men met in council, and young men and maids tripped the toe to " Pretty Betty Martin" on the velvety plains of the Platte. Many a lover's

vow was plighted in that westward march from Missouri to the sea.   Hunters swept in from the buffalo-
raid and scouts reported the trail of Indians.   Future
senators, governors, generals, divines, and judges were
in that train; founders of cities and carvers of empire.
Burnett, a brisk lawyer, good-looking and affable, became the first governor of California; William Gilpin,
the first governor of Colorado.   Nesmith sat in the
national Senate; McCarver, the founder of Burlington,
Iowa, became the founder of Sacramento, California, of
Tacoma, Washington, and missed by only ten miles
the metropolis of Oregon.   Journeying leisurely in the
rear, by a somewhat different route, came Lieutenant
Fremont with fourteen government wagons, following
the emigrants out to Oregon.

Here, there, everywhere, Dr. Whitman attended the
sick, encouraged the weary, and counselled with the
pilot over the safety of the route.   He was patient with
complaints.   "The best of men and women, when
fatigued and anxious by the way, will be jealous of
their rights," he said.   For them he sought the smooth-
est route, the shallowest ford, the most cooling pastures
for their fainting cattle.

Men were in that train who had inherited a hearty
hatred of the British, men whose fathers had fought in
the Revolution, and to whom 1812 was fresh in memory.
Burnett, the lawyer, struck a responsive chord when
he cried: "Let us drive out those British usurpers,
let us defend Oregon from the British lion.   Posterity
will honor us for placing the fairest portion of our land
under the stars and stripes."

Along the Big Blue in the sweet June weather,
ferrying the Platte in their wagon-box boats in the July
sun, sighting the Rockies in August, they camped and

marched and marched and camped toward the sunset. In the buffalo country the Indians peeped like blackbirds over the hills and disappeared. In September, dashing across a cut-off, Dr. Whitman reached Fort Hall three days before the train. Thither to his great joy he found his faithful Cayuses had packed a quantity of provisions on their plump little ponies. There they were, riding and swaying and swinging, clinging with their legs under the ponies' bellies and waving their arms in greeting—the poetry of Delsarte before Delsarte was heard of.

We can well imagine Dr. Whitman's first words, "My wife?" and the answer, "Watching for you," in Indian pantomime. Something of the May-feast he may have learned and of the burned mill as he shook hands with his red retainers.

Against the crackling sage-brush the dust-covered train came rolling in.

"What are you going to Oregon for? You cannot get the wagons through," said Captain Grant, the Hudson's Bay factor at Fort Hall. "'Tis a physical impossibility. A small immigration passed through here last year. I told them as I tell you, wagons never have passed, never can pass through the Snake country and the Blue Mountains. They believed me, left their wagons, bought pack animals, and got through safely. My advice to you is the same, get pack animals and go through, but I advise you to go to California. The route is shorter and safer, and there is the better country."

"Can't get the wagons through," was the word that passed from lip to lip.

"No," said Captain Grant; "there you see the ones abandoned last year."

Sure enough, there in a corner of the stockade stood five battered old wagons left by the venturesome party last year. Along with them were ploughs and other implements that could not be packed on horses. At this apparent proof the men looked solemn. The women began to cry.

"Both the Snake and the Columbia are deep, swift rivers," continued Captain Grant; "no company has ever attempted their passage but with a loss of life. Besides, several Indian tribes in the middle regions have combined to prevent your passage. Why, the Willamette is a thousand miles from here. The distance is so great that winter will overtake you before you reach the Cascades. I am astonished that you ever scaled the Rockies, but the Blue Mountains are much more formidable. From here to the Blue Mountains the plain is a cut-rock desert — without water. The Snake River runs at the bottom of a deep canyon — if you have read Irving's 'Astoria' you remember how Hunt's party wandered along the brink, and yet almost died of thirst because they could not reach the water. There is absolutely no food to be had — unless you eat gophers and ground-hogs you will die of famine. I wouldn't undertake it; the short cut to California is much safer."

Groups stood here and there, talking in great excitement, when Dr. Whitman returned from his conversation with the Cayuses.

"What! Can't get the wagons through!" exclaimed Dr. Whitman. "That's all bosh. My wagon went through three years ago, and where one went a hundred can. Bring the wagons by all means. You'll need them. There's a great demand. What can farmers do without wagons? — and most of you are farmers. Here, my friend, sell me that light dearborn and I'll prove what I say. My Cayuses are here, they know the trails; they are the safest guides in the world."

Six months had passed since that gallant company crossed the border with their rifles on their shoulders, headed for the end of the West.

"The Sioux will oppose you." "Look out for the Crows." "Beware of the Blackfeet," had been the warning from point to point. No foe had troubled them. They had forded many a rushing stream, had followed the wagon route of two women round and round and over the Rockies. As to Dr. Whitman, some of them had heard his bugle-call along the border, some had read his pamphlet as far away as Texas. More had heard of the previous immigration, for Oregon was in the air, and the settlers of the then isolated Missouri believed that their crops might find a better market by the seaboard. Of Whitman they knew nothing. All they saw was an immigrant, like themselves, who had almost recklessly exposed himself in hunting fords for their wagons and cattle. His past they knew not, his future not, nor his plans; he spoke seldom, and to the point, and always hopefully. He was worried, perhaps, with the expense of that winter ride, that the Board would not meet and he must. He was anxious, perhaps, for future food for that army. Flour at Fort Hall was selling at mountain prices, — a dollar a pint, forty dollars a barrel, or four cows a hundred weight. The immigrants had spent thousands of dollars for provisions at Laramie and Fort Hall — he knew they were short of money. If worst came to worst they had their cattle, perhaps the mission plantations had raised enough to last them down to Fort Vancouver. These cogitations the immigrants saw not, but they did see an American,

His positive manner, his honest face gave them confidence.

"He has led us right so far," they said. "He has been over the road. He lives here. These Injuns know him. They have come to meet him. We will follow Dr. Whitman."

As the groups closed round their leader again, Captain Grant expostulated.

"You Americans are running an awful risk. There's not a particle of pasturage on the Snake; your cattle will all die. All I have seen convinces me 'tis a beggarly country. The buffalo starves there, even the wolves are so thin you can count their ribs. As for wagons, the pack-trails are of sharp, cut rock, and narrow and steep. You will be stranded in some lonely gorge, if you persist in this attempt to take them through the tangled woods and rocky cliffs and canyons of the Blue Mountains. But I wash my hands of your destruction."

It was not the last effort of the Hudson's Bay Company to divert immigration away from Oregon.

Dr. Whitman gave the whole of the provisions brought by the Cayuses to the immigrants, reserving only scraps and bones for himself, and with a body-guard of axemen and his trusty Indians, set on ahead. He tacked up notices at every difficult place, and set up guide-poles in the dusty desert. Night by night tents were set at oases of buffalo-grass, and the Indian guides by day became night guards and herders. The Snake was forded at Salmon Falls, then over the future battle-ground of the Chief-Joseph-Nez-Percé-War, through the deep sand and tough sage, thirteen miles a day, they came to the Burnt River canyon. On every side lay tangled heaps of burnt and fallen trees, but with the

genius of a Cæsar Whitman led his battalions in the
centre of the river-bed for twenty-five miles. Over
the rough hills, on the first of October, the main body
of the immigration entered the Grande Ronde valley.
Hundreds of Indian women were digging and drying the
camas. A second party of Cayuses, on their plump
little horses adorned with streamers, came out to meet
them with a feast of bread and berries and elk meat.
In their long-laced leggings, and deerskin jackets, and
flying hair, the Cayuses welcomed Dr. Whitman with a
thousand extravagant antics, circling about and about,
and flinging themselves over and under their ponies like
circus boys.

The Indians offered their native roots. The white
people gingerly touched the bulbous camas. It flaked
off like an onion. "Better than licorice," said the
white children. The snowy kouse, the biscuit-root, was
tasted. "Sweet potatoes," shouted the little Yankees,
and later most of them learned to like the starchy
wapato.

While yet feasting, a courier rode into the Grande
Ronde and stopped at the doctor's tent.

"Mr. and Mrs. Spalding are very ill. They send for
you."

Dr. Whitman turned to the faithful Cayuse that had
met him at Fort Hall, " Sticcas, my boy, can you guide
these people in?"

" I can," answered the sub-chief, who was never
known to refuse a request of Dr. Whitman.

The doctor struck across the country to Lapwai.
Sticcas went ahead, with forty men, cutting a road
through the heavy timber. The Applegates, the Daniel
Boones of Oregon, Burnett, the future governor, and
Nesmith, the senator-to-be, walked all the way through

the Blue Mountains, with axes in their blistered hands, hewing a wagon-way through the crossed and criss-crossed fallen trees.

Nesmith says, "Sticcas was a faithful old fellow, and although not speaking a word of English, and no one in our party a word of Cayuse, he succeeded, by panto-mime, in taking us over the roughest wagon-route I ever saw."

A heavy snow fell in the mountains, the warning of approaching winter. Descending the western slope, there lay before them the great valley of the Columbia. At their feet the Cayuse lodge-fires curled on the green Umatilla. Miles away the sinewy Hood, and his sister St. Helen's, swam in light, Mt. Adams lay like a couchant lion, and winding 'mid her battlements, the Columbia, a long line of liquid gold, blazed in the setting sun. Fatigue was forgotten in this glorified glimpse of the promised land. Exultant, the train of wagons rolled into the plain.

High on a spur of the Blue Mountains one stood and watched the moving caravan. A dark scowl of hate disfigured his face, his clenched hand, lifted, sunk again. Too well the Delaware knew the story of American immigration.

For miles the Indians came to view that caravan, that, farther than Cæsar bore the Roman eagles, had come to claim a land. But the feature that most engaged the Indians was the wagons, the mysterious "horse canoes," that rolled along over the obstinate bunch-grass, bearing women and little children into Oregon. On, on they came, it seemed to the Indians a never-ending train, as if that great mysterious land to the east was pouring itself into the vales of the Colum-bia. All their doubts, all their fears, all their terrors leaped anew. "Yes, it is as Dorion said; they have come to take the country." But no hand was lifted against the new-comers — surprise absorbed all other emotions.

Dr. Whitman, the Nestor of them all, had already despatched from Lapwai a train of Nez Percés, with grain and potatoes, that the immigrants might purchase needed supplies before advancing down the Columbia.

"I said I would bring an immigration over the mountains, and I have done it," said Dr. Whitman, bringing his hand down on the pommel of his saddle.

"Yes, but mind, now, Doctor," said Spalding, as the pack-ponies set out, "I furnish those provisions only on condition that you accept pay for them. Of course let nobody suffer, but remember, we are not in a condition to give out of hand to every immigrant as you did last year. I know your generous nature; you would give your last ounce of flour and live yourself on the bran. The missions are compelled to be self-supporting. The very toil we expend in raising these supplies is that much taken out of our time for preaching and teaching."

"Not so, brother Spalding," cheerfully answered the doctor. "With the plough, the spade, the hoe, we teach. When the Indians see us work, they are more willing."

"I know, I know," said Spalding, "my Nez Percés often laugh and tell me, 'Before you came we never worked. Now we are become a nation of squaws.'"

The worn-out oxen dragged the worn-out wagons down to the Dalles. The herders drove the cattle by the trail around Mt. Hood. Some cut timber and fashioned log rafts to navigate the perilous river. Driving on their wagons and piling on their goods and families, down they glided, Indians assisting, and stealing now and then, till the seething cascades rendered the crafts useless.   On one of those rafts a child was born.

Pitching their tents, the men struck into the forest to cut a wagon-road around the Cascades.   It was toilsome work.   The stormy season had come.   Cold rains set in.   High winds from the sea sucked up the Columbia, blowing down the tents at night, drenching the sleepers in their beds.   Provisions gave out.   On the very threshold of their Canaan the Oregon immigrants of 1843 seemed likely to perish of cold and hunger. The hardships of the entire journey seemed concentrated at the Cascades of the Columbia.

Below, at Fort Vancouver, the Canadians were busy, as usual, beating furs in the court.   The dull thud of their batons kept time with snatches of song, and tilts of wit and repartee.   The furs were out for their last airing, to be sorted and packed for London.   Bales of beaver, bales of bear, bales of otter were dusted and folded in a certain way for their long journey to the dim old warerooms on Fenchurch Street.   The barque lay in the river taking on her precious freight.

"Dose Engine say Bostons camp by Mt. Hood, der odder side," exclaimed a Canadian in from the court. "Dose Engine say women and wagons—"

"Oh, nonsense, nonsense, Gabriel.   You're like Father De Smet, who roused the whole camp crying 'Indians! Indians!' in his dreams," said Dr. McLoughlin, sticking his quill behind his ear, and holding the paper he was writing at arm's length.

"Dose Engine say—" but the doctor waved him off impatiently.

"Bah! Indian bugaboo! Indian bugaboo! Don't tell me."

Nevertheless, when Gabriel reluctantly withdrew the doctor called him back.

"Say, say, Gabriel, send those Indians here."

A few men in a canoe shot the Cascades and hurried down to Fort Vancouver.

"A thousand people? Lord! Lord!" exclaimed Dr. McLoughlin, crossing his breast. "What manner of men are these that scale the mountains and slide down the rivers as the Goths of old down the Alps?"

He heard the tale of distress. Dr. McLoughlin thought not of the company, not of rivals; he only knew that women and little children were perishing at the Cascades.

"Man the boats," he cried. In fifteen minutes every boat was on the water.

"Take provisions, — twenty-five pounds of flour to every small family, fifty to every large one, one quart of syrup to every small family, half a gallon to a large one; take sugar in three and five pound packages and a pound of tea to every family. If any can pay, let them, but don't stand on ceremony. Make haste, reach there to-night."

The boats shot out on the errand of mercy. The doctor was greatly excited. He ordered the servants to bring great piles of brush and fuel for bonfires on the morrow.

The boats arrived at the Cascades none too soon. With tears streaming down their cheeks aged women yet living say fervently: "God bless Dr. McLoughlin!"

Little children danced for joy. Many had not had a square meal for weeks. So starved were they, some cooked and ate all night. The next day they set out for Fort Vancouver. The overloaded boats rocked on the tempestuous river, cold brown clouds wrapped the hills, wheeling eagles shrieked and screamed, the winter rain beat in their defenceless faces. Mothers wrapped their babies in their shawls, and fathers with lips set, as the Pilgrims of 1620, looked toward the blast.

Dr. McLoughlin had been up since daylight and was watching on the bank. There were Indians all around. The doctor noted the angry, excited glance that fell upon the approaching boats. As the first boat swung toward the shore a big Indian flourished his club and shouted to his comrades, —

"It is good for us to kill these Bostons."

Dr. McLoughlin's quick ear caught their meaning. One word from the Hudson's Bay Company and those Indians would rise as one man to cut off the incoming Americans. The possible tragedy seemed about to open with all the horrors of tomahawk and scalping-knife. Rushing upon the savage, with uplifted cane, the doctor grabbed him by the throat, —

"Who is the dog that says it is a good thing to kill those Bostons?"

That awful tone, that made the red men tremble, seemed doubly awful now. Fire blazed from his eye. The white locks flew like a bush around his head, giving him a fierce and terrible aspect. The craven slunk back in abject fear.

"I spoke without meaning harm, but the Dalles Indians say so."

The doctor gave him a shake as a terrier would a rat. "Well, sir, the Dalles Indians are dogs for saying so, and you also. If I hear another such word, I'll put an end to you." With that he flung him to the ground.

Crestfallen the Indian crept away.

Returning to the landing, Dr. McLoughlin anxiously

took the hands of the immigrants. Bonfires were blazing all along the shore, where the wet people hastened
to dry their drenched garments. In five minutes the
friendly doctor in his cap and cloak seemed like an old
acquaintance, meeting them there as a matter of course.
" Go right up to the fort to dinner," said Dr. McLoughlin. Some went up, glad again of the shelter of a house
and a civilized meal.

The indoor servants were busy, sweeping, replenish-
ing fires, dusting clothes; but at a word from the Governor all turned in to wait on the multitude of guests.

" And what did you have for dinner?" was asked of
one now white with eighty years.

" Salt salmon and potatoes, hot biscuit and tea. It
was a splendid meal, the best I ever ate, and we were
thankful to get it."

" And did Dr. McLoughlin eat with you?"

" Oh, no, he stayed all the time at the river-bank
watching the boats come in. It was raining hard, and
the wind blew his long white hair around his shoulders,
but he would not leave the boats. After dinner we
went on up the Willamette, but the last we saw was Dr.
McLoughlin, there in the rain, watching the boats."

" How the wind howls!" said Dr. McLoughlin that
night.

" 'T is time noo to lock the gates," answered the old
gatekeeper, pulling down his hood and buttoning up his
great capote.

" Leave them a little, Bruce. Some one else may
come. 'T is a stormy time for immigrants. I am sorry
for those poor families that went up the river."

All day, and into the night, and for days thereafter,
Dr. McLoughlin stood by the river, never for a moment
relaxing his vigilance, personally superintending the

reception of the immigrants, as if they had been his own invited guests. Many a hostile intent was disarmed, and to the end of their lives the heroes of 1843 cherished a brother's regard for Dr. John McLoughlin.

In a day or two the mission blacksmith came down to the fort. The doctor caught sight of him on the steps, and that prophecy, "Before we die we shall see the Yankees coming across the Rocky Mountains with their teams and their families," flashed through his mind. Rapidly crossing himself, Dr. McLoughlin exclaimed, "God forgive me, Mr. Parrish, God forgive me, but the Yankees are here, and the first thing you know, they will yoke up their oxen, drive down to the mouth of the Columbia, and come out at Japan."

The servants were turned out of their beds, every available niche and cranny of the old fort was filled with immigrants. The Montreal express came in, bringing Billy McKay home from the States, a young M.D. "I found the fort full of immigrants," says Dr. McKay, "and my father's house at Scappoose, and all the Canadians' at Champoeg. There were only six houses at the Falls; they were crowded, and all the posts of the Methodist mission." Through the long autumn the immigrants continued passing at Fort Vancouver.

"How they ever get here is what confounds me," said Dr. McLoughlin. "These Yankees seem to be able to drive a wagon where our men can only lead a packhorse."

"Can't we devise some method to head them off to California?" suggested James Douglas, annoyed by the constant arrivals.

"Who cries 'head them off'?" said the doctor, flushed and tired. "The very effort would precipitate trouble. Too many Boston ships have visited this coast for us to hide her riches now. America is not asleep. If we hold north of the Columbia 't is all that we can hope."

Black Douglas was angry. He thought the doctor's philanthropy excessive. Ogden felt again the baleful star of his birth that gave him no rest between the rival powers. Ermatinger put on the cap with, "Why, Doctor, I believe you 've a bit of Yankee blood yourself."

"Thirty miles north of the Maine border lacks little of it," growled the doctor, nodding his shaggy mane. Somehow McLoughlin, born on the St. Lawrence, never could see through the partial eyes of a Thames-born Briton.

He walked back and forth with excited stride, kicking now and then a chair with his cane. Absolute in his rule, he was not accustomed to being crossed, least of all by strangers. Many things had gone wrong. Despite his well-meant kindness, some rough fellows of the baser sort had spoken rudely. He caught the contemptuous epithets, "Money bags," "British," "Monopoly." His companions reminded him of these things. Turning with that eye of his, that cut to the marrow, — "Because an ill-bred puppy barks shall I blame a whole people?"

Stung, harassed, annoyed on every hand by the perplexities of the situation, the doctor had one mentor that always led him right — his faithful wife, the Madame. Composed, apparently imperturbable, she sat with her knitting, soothing him with her soft French, — "There, there, Dogtor, he low-bred fellow. Gentlemen not heed such thing."

So always it had been. Frequently the doctor's quick temper had ignited over some recreant servant, and he had stormed in a rage, "I'll thrash that rascal. I'll —" until the Madame's crooning, "There, there," fell upon his ear. "He, poor ignorant boy, he not know any better, he not understand, he tired, he too much work," until the wrath cooled out of the doctor's heart.

Lieutenant Fremont hastened down to Fort Vancouver to purchase supplies for his overland trip to California. He records in his journal: "I immediately waited upon Dr. McLoughlin, the executive officer of the Hudson's Bay Company, who received me with the courtesy and hospitality for which he has been eminently distinguished, and which makes a forcible and delightful impression on a traveller from the long wilderness from which we had issued. . . . Every hospitable attention was extended to me, and I accepted an invitation to take a room in the fort and to make myself at home while I stayed.

"I found many American immigrants at the fort; others had already crossed the river into their land of promise — the Willamette valley. Others were daily arriving, and all of them had been furnished with shelter, so far as it could be afforded by the buildings connected with the establishment. Necessary clothing and provisions (the latter to be afterward returned in kind from the produce of their labor) were also furnished. This friendly assistance was of very great value to the immigrants, whose families were otherwise exposed to much suffering in the winter rains, which had now commenced, at the same time that they were in want of all the common necessaries of life."

A month after the immigration was in, Dr. Whitman came down to Fort Vancouver — he felt it his duty to come in person and thank Dr. McLoughlin. These men, of opposite religious faiths yet of equally noble hearts, had always entertained for each other the warmest friendship.

Whitman was always direct in speech. "Doctor McLoughlin," he said, "I come to Vancouver to thank you in the name of humanity for your kindness to my countrymen. That very act disarmed that company of a thousand prejudices that had worried me all the way. By a single act you turned presumptive foes into the warmest friends."

Dr. McLoughlin reddened. It was hard to stand thus and be thanked by one who had just returned from the errand of a rival, and that, too, for succoring the very ones who, confessedly, came to take the country from the government to which he owed allegiance. And he, himself, had he been loyal to Britain? Banish the doubt. There is a law above all personal consideration, the law of common humanity. In feeding the hungry and clothing the naked, in saving fellow-men from the tomahawk of the savage, no mere worldly policy but a divine principle had governed his action.

Justified of God, he smiled and grasped the hand of Dr. Whitman — "Do not thank me, Doctor, I could not help it. I could not see those people in want while I had stores of plenty. But there was another reason, a more potent one yet. I stood on the shore that day and saw your first stragglers coming up in their canoes, and I read in the looks of the excited Indians that there was danger. I said to myself, 'If these savages see that the Hudson's Bay Company receives these people as friends they are safe,' so I did what I could. I was racked with fear that if your excitable countrymen learned the situation there would be fighting, and so, without concerted plan, they would all be cut off. Fortunately my ruse succeeded. I thought some of our rascally Iroquois might have sprung this scheme, and investigated the matter afterward, but found no light on the subject."

" Oh," said Whitman, " I know all about it."

" You do, Doctor? " ejaculated the governor.

" Yes, and I have known it for two years."

" You have known it for two years and have told me nothing! Pray, who is at the bottom of this mischief? Who is making you trouble? If it is a graceless Iroquois I will tie him to the twelve-pounder and give him a dozen."

Dr. Whitman saw in fancy the irate governor already in quest of a guilty Iroquois and said: " No, it is not an Iroquois. His name is Thomas Hill."

Dr. McLoughlin knit his brows in thought, gazing at Whitman. " We have no one by that name in our service," said Dr. McLoughlin.

" No, it is Tom Hill, the Delaware Indian, educated at Dartmouth College in the States. He has urged the Indians to allow no Americans to settle on their lands — my Cayuses are greatly agitated over the matter. I have told them white men will pay them for their lands, but they no longer believe me. I think, however, the trouble will blow over and they will set to work again. Some of my faithful Cayuses met us at Fort Hall, others at the Grande Ronde. The immigrants owe a great debt to the sub-chief Sticcas."

" Doctor, take the advice of a friend — come down to Fort Vancouver. Some one has been exciting those Indians, and the consequences may be immediate and awful. You know while you were gone we had a great deal of trouble. Yellow Serpent came to me for advice and told me the same tales. My brother, I tremble for your safety."

Dr. Whitman sat in a large, leather-covered chair in the doctor's sitting-room. Dr. McLoughlin had risen and laid his hands upon his shoulders. Entreaty shone in his eyes and in every line of his noble countenance. "Listen to me," continued the governor. "Indians are not to be trifled with. Leave them. Come here and stay. By and by they will invite you back. Then you can go in safety."

The Indians seemed friendly; they had welcomed him back with joy. He could see no danger, and yet Dr. Whitman was not unmoved by his friend's solicitude. He recognized the motive of the generous heart that would shield him from possible harm, but he said: "I cannot leave, Doctor. My duty lies with the Indians. I cannot desert my post. I must stay and do what I can."

Dr. Whitman had risen. Two heroes stood face to face. The early sunset cast its slant shadows across the wall, lighting up the silver locks of the Father of Oregon, and resting in a halo on the brow of the future martyr. Catholic and Protestant, British and American, yet brothers in a common fidelity to God and humanity.

Yes, from her mission door Narcissa Whitman, watching on the Walla Walla, had heard the returning hoof-beats of that rider on the plains. From that door she saw the wagons rolling in, that were to turn the rocking balance forever in favor of her country. There were immigrants with a new-born babe in her bedroom, immigrants with four little children in the room east of the kitchen, an immigrant family with six little children in the Indian room, immigrants slept on the dining-room floor. Little Mary Ann and Helen Mar, tucked in their trundle-bed in the doctor's room, asked, "Mamma, mamma, where so many people come from?"

A village of Indians camped outside, eager to explain to the doctor: "We no burn the mill. We no do such thing."

"I know it, my boys, we'll build another;" and the doctor brought out his blackboard, and printed the lessons as if nothing had happened. At the ringing of the hand-bell the feet of little Indians came tracking up the yellow pine floor, and musical voices joined the Nez Percé,

"*Nesika papa kláxta mitlite kopa sáh-a-le.*"
Our   Father   who   art   in   the above
(*or Heaven*).

It was nearly Christmas before Dr. and Mrs. Whitman were fully settled to the old routine at Waiilatpu But the larder was bare, as if swept by a swarm of locusts. Everything went to the immigrants. The mill with its grain was gone. Nothing was left but potatoes and salt, and even salt was two dollars a pound at Fort Walla Walla. "Never mind, Narcissa," said the doctor, "next year we will plant enough for all that come. For the present I think the Indians will sell us some ponies for steak."

Just after the arrival of the immigrants a heavy cloud rose over Mt. St. Helen's, and continued to enlarge. A copper haze, heavier than Indian summer, hung over the Columbia. Mt. Hood was hid in shadow. The sun glared red as blood.

"Why, this is equal to a Christmas fog in London," said Dr. McLoughlin, noting the increasing darkness.

"Has the mountain fire-bug been out again?" inquired Douglas.

"Cannot be," said Dr. McLoughlin. "September rains extinguished the mountain fires long ago."

Old Waskema, returning with berries from Mt. Hood, had seen the immigrants in bateaux going down to Fort Vancouver. Hastening to a camp of Molallas who were fishing for the late run of salmon, she startled them with the Cassandra-cry, "Woe, woe, woe the poor Indian!"

"Lou — wala — clough smoke," said the old crone, shading her eyes with both skinny hands and looking toward St. Helen's.

The superstitious Molallas trembled and put aside their fishing. Still with the hollow "Woe, woe, woe" upon her lips Waskema set out for Fort Vancouver.

It was a phenomenally dark and heavy day. Not even when the great forest fire came down and threatened the fort had it been so oppressive. Dr. McLoughlin went out to observe the lurid sky. Candles were lit in the hall, and the cattle came lowing up from the marshes at midday. The air was full of fine, light ashes that fell over a radius of fifty miles. For the first time in the memory of man the white robes of St. Helen's were blackened with dust.

Down by the boat-house Dr. McLoughlin saw old Waskema, landing from her canoe. With the kindness of heart that would not slight even a withered old squaw, he advanced and took her hand, "Well, what's the good word, grandmother?"

The decrepit figure tried to straighten itself. In spite of her taciturnity the White-Headed Eagle had won the heart of old Waskema. A smile, that was a pathetic contraction of leathern muscles long unused to laughter, danced over her face and was gone. In a sepulchral tone, shaking her bony finger, she pointed to the erupting mountain.

"Lou — wala — clough smoke! White-Headed Eagle beware. Um too much Boston! Um too much Boston! Um drive King George man out. Um drive poor Injun out."

The attitude, the tone, the darkness, all corresponded with the gloom of the doctor's spirit. Only too well he knew that with this influx of Americans the Hudson's Bay régime was over. A wind loaded with frost blew down from Mt. Hood.

"Ugh-úgh! Walla Walla wind freeze," chattered Waskema, drawing her blanket closer and crouching beside old Kesano's camp-fire by the gate. Dr. McLoughlin watched the pair, withered and thin, bent and gray, the last of two distinct tribes in the once populous Willamette. "So will it be with them all," he thought sadly. "The beaver and the Indian will perish together."

St. Helen's poured her molten lava over the beautiful white snow. Moneycoon, the hunter, was up in the mountain and found his return cut off. Taking a run, he tried to leap and fell, one foot in the glowing torrent. The moccasin was singed from his foot, and the flesh so burned that he came near being a cripple for life. Crawling miraculously back to Fort Vancouver, he was put in the hospital, where Dr. Barclay nursed him back to health.

"Oh, lovely Oregon!" cried the immigrants as the green pastures appeared along the Willamette. Nothing surprised the new-comers more than the tropic luxuriance of vegetation. Beyond the storm-swept Cascades a new world appeared. The moist Chinook nurtured the trees to mammoths. Shrubbery, like the hazel, grew to be trees. The maple spread its leaves like palm fans; dogwood of magnolian beauty, wild cherry, crab-apple, interlaced with Oregon holly, black-berries, rose-bushes, vines of every sort and description, and ferns, ferns filled the canyons like the jungles of the Orinoco.

"We will all own dukedoms now," said the immigrants, picking out the fairest tracts, a square mile each of land, that might have been the pride of an English manor. Six hundred and forty acres to each family was the bill in Congress.

For seeds, wheat, implements — they all applied to Dr. McLoughlin. "Yes, yes, I will loan you wheat and implements, and you can pay me when you harvest," said the doctor. "Plant all you can. Another such immigration will bring a famine."

To those without stock he loaned cattle for a term of years. To those without provisions he loaned a supply for the winter, and then loaned the boat that carried them to their destination. The commissariat was kept busy weighing out salmon, the clerks kept busy measuring out cloth. "I can't have them suffering for what we can supply," he said. "The best thing for them and for us, too, is to forward them to their destination and get them settled and self-supporting as soon as possible." About the same time Ermatinger was despatched with a cargo of goods, to open a Hudson's Bay store at the settlement by the Falls.

During that winter of 1843 a village sprang up at the Falls of the Willamette — Oregon City. Out of the books brought over the plains a circulating library was formed, a lyceum was organized, a Methodist church was built, — the first Protestant church west of the Rocky Mountains.

"Scissors! Scissors!" grumbled Ogden, taking a run up the river. "These colonies of people are driving out our colonies of beaver. I think I'll beg a leave of absence and take a trip to England."

XXXII

McLOUGHLIN AND THE IMMIGRANTS

1844

BOTH parties watched for the immigration of 1844. The Americans wanted news from the States. The Hudson's Bay ship brought word of impending war with the United States. With an incoming army of hostile immigrants what might not happen at Fort Vancouver? "If they are destitute as last year, they will pillage the fort," said Douglas.

Dr. McLoughlin set his Canadians to building another bastion, and strengthened again the ever decaying stockade. "What for do you this?" asked a Canadian.

"To guard against the savages," Black Douglas answered with a frown. The Canadian nodded his head. "Sabages prom de Rocky Mountain!"

"They are afraid of us over at Fort Vancouver," was whispered in the valley. "Nay, indeed, they are preparing to make war on us," answered another. Still, when the first wagons appeared, far up the Columbia came McLoughlin's word — "Do not let the poor people suffer. Help them along. Teach the Indians to do so also."

The men of 1844 started with extravagant dreams of the velvet prairies by the sea. That blessed country! "The trees forever bend with fruit," they said. "Camas-bread grows in the ground." "Salmon crowd each other out of the streams." "Money? Why, man alive, money grows out there." "Yes, and feather-beds grow on the bushes."

With gay hearts they started as on a summer holiday, some with only the clothes they wore and a blanket slung over the shoulder. The spring was late. It rained and rained, and the camps were long and frequent along the swollen Platte. Provisions melted away.

"Courage," they said to one another. "Did not our ancestors come in six weeks' journeys from the seaboard to Ohio, to Kentucky, to Missouri? Oregon is but another journey a little farther west."

But it stretched away and away, six months and more, and still the road ran on. No one supposed that Oregon was so far, no one realized that there were no hospices through all that fearful stretch of travel. Buffalo eluded the immigrant trail. Provisions gave out. Clothing wore out. Some were sick. Infants were born on the way. Without a mentor to bid them "travel, travel, travel," winter came down upon them unprepared, and from Burnt River to the Dalles the caravan became a panorama of destitution.

Pioneer printers, pioneer lumber-kings, pioneer merchants and manufacturers, poor enough then, barefooted broke the path over the Blue Mountains through the deep, untrodden snow. Oregon is dotted with their granite pillars; for one of them California has reared a statue-crowned shaft on the spot where four years later he found the gold of Eldorado. Dr. Whitman taught his Indians to go far out and build their bonfires on the hills to guide them in. They "packed" provisions to the Grande Ronde, and yet the end of October came with five hundred people still beyond the mountains. Whitman's mission became a great inn thronged with the passing tide.

" The crowd and confusion almost drive me crazy," wrote Mrs. Whitman to her mother. " The doctor is as if a hundred strings were tied to him, all pulling in different directions."

With almost superhuman effort Dr. Whitman had extended his fields; to lighten his labors Mrs. Whitman herself had gone out to superintend the Indians gathering the garden stores.

" Can you look after an orphan family of seven children?" inquired the captain of a company at the Whitman door. " Father and mother died on the way, the youngest a baby, born on the Platte."

Dr. Whitman looked at his wife. Already they had adopted four children.

" Where are they?" he inquired, reaching for his hat.

" Back on the Umatilla."

" Have they no friends ? "

" Not a relative in the world."

" Bring them on," said the doctor.

Two days later their wagon rolled in, — two little boys weeping bitterly, four little girls huddled together, bareheaded, barefooted, a wee little baby, five months old, almost dead. For weeks the compassionate immigrants had cared for them and shared with them the last crust.

" We can get along with all but the baby. I don't see how we can take her," said Dr. Whitman.

" If we take any I must have the baby," cried the mother-heart of Mrs. Whitman, lifting the mite of humanity out of the arms of a tired old woman. " She will be a charm to bind the rest to me."

Little Helen Mar ran out, in her pretty green dress and white apron, and peeped at them, timidly, under her sunbonnet. " Show the children in, Helen," said Mrs. Whitman.

" Have you no children of your own, Madame? " inquired the captain.

" All the child I ever had sleeps yonder," she answered, dropping a tear on the baby's forehead.

In four days Dr. Whitman sent word to the captain: " Take no more concern for the children. We adopt them all."

" Who ever saw such herds of horses! Why, there are thousands! " exclaimed the immigrants as they passed along the Walla Walla. " And see the cattle! the finest kind of stock. These Indians will soon be rich."

Pio-pio-mox-mox, Five Crows, and Tauitau rode with the Indian herders on the hills, and watched the immigrants' lean and worn-out cattle. Every head they could, they bought. This annual influx of stock almost reconciled them to the immigrants trampling down their pastures. The Indians talked of nothing but cattle in those days.

" Let us go down to California and buy more cattle," said the young chief Elijah to his father. " The white men in the valley go down to Sutter's fort and bring up hundreds."

Immigrants camped near the Walla Walla heard the sweet notes of a chant steal out upon the air at twilight. In the morning the Cayuses rose up early and prepared for worship.

" Quite civilized Indians," said the immigrants, looking at their little plantations. " They make their grounds look clean and mellow as a garden."

"Yes," said Dr. Whitman. "Great numbers of them cultivate, and with but a single horse will take any plough we have, however large, and do their own ploughing. They have a great desire for hogs and hens and cattle."

At the mission, Dr. Whitman addressed his Indians upon the duty of peace and providence for the future. Tiloukaikt, "court crier," fickle as the wind, but now loyal again, rehearsed after him in that voice like a brazen trumpet.

"Ugh-úgh," responded the Indians, "ugh-úgh," like Methodist amens.

The choir flipped over the leaves of their Nez Percé hymn-books and struck the key like old-fashioned singing-masters.

As might be expected, the immigrants of 1844 came prejudiced against the British and itching for the honor of driving them out.

"We dread meeting that old barbarian in his den on the Columbia worse than anything else," said the immigrants at the Dalles.

"If the Hudson's Bay Company does n't conduct itself properly we'll knock their old stockade about their ears," said Gilliam, an ex-captain of the Seminole War.

Again winter rains were beating up the Cascades. Already December snows were whirling around Mt. Hood. Snow-bound cattle were famishing on the mountain trails, weary mothers were dragging their children along the slippery portages. Emaciated, discouraged, exhausted, the silent tears dropped down their hollow cheeks as they thought of the comfortable homes they had left in the States; but as a rule the women were brave, braver than the men. The dogs were killed and eaten, the last spare garment was traded for a sack of potatoes. Wet to the skin, shivering around their green camp-fires while the damp flakes fell "as big as a hat," they even envied the comfort of the Indians, lying flat on the clean sand under the huge projecting rocks, secure from the storm, with fires in the foreground. Mt. Hood and St. Helen's were hid in fog that rolled opaquely to the sky. Men in the prime of life sat with bowed heads among the rocks, groaning as if about to die. "Hello!" There were shadows in the fog.

"Here, gentlemen; you were so late in getting down Dr. McLoughlin was afraid you might be in trouble. He has sent a bateau of provisions, also some clothing."

"But—" hesitated one, thankful, yet abashed.

"Do not apologize, sir," said the agent, kindly; "take what you need. Those who can pay may do so. Those who cannot must not be left to suffer. Such are the doctor's orders. Boats are on the way to help you down to Fort Vancouver."

Such was the greeting from that "old barbarian" in his den on the Columbia.

Ragged men, tired men, grateful men, piled their wives and children and their household goods upon the welcome bateaux. With violent-beating hearts they struck into the troubled water. The wind whipped the blanket sails, eagles screamed and circled, storms swooped and dipped the spray, on frowning heights the owl and the wolf answered each other, unaccustomed hands were toiling at the oar, but miraculously, out of it all, they landed at Fort Vancouver.

"What can we do?" they asked.

"Go to the fort. The old doctor never turns people

away hungry," answered the boatmen. Some had cut off their buckskin pants time and again to mend their worn-out foot-gear, so with garments scarce covering their knees, with ragged blankets tied with a string about their necks, " tatterdemalions worse clad than the army in Flanders," they knocked at the gate.

" Where can we get some provisions? "

" Goo to Dooctor Maglooglin," was the Scotch warder's answer, pointing to the office.

A large and dignified elderly gentleman with magnificent head and benevolent countenance came immediately forward and shook one after another by the hand. " Are there many left behind? " he inquired, plucking some grapes and handing them to his guests.

" Hundreds, hundreds. This is only the vanguard," was the answer.

" So many? " exclaimed the doctor, nervously. " The season is late. I fear the poor people will suffer, but I will do what I can to prevent it. Come in. Come right in." Hurriedly turning into the office he sat down at a small table.

" Stand in a line," he said, tapping the desk with a quill pen. The men stepped into place — the line reached nearly around the room.

" Last year," said the doctor, " I furnished the immigrants with food and clothing here at the fort, but now that we have established a trading-house at Oregon City, you can get most of your supplies there. Provisions for immediate necessity you can obtain here."

" But, sir," broke in several, " we have no money. We don't know when or how we can pay you."

" Tut, tut, tut ! Never mind that. You can't suffer," said the doctor. Glancing at the head man, — " Sir, your name, if you please. How many in the family? What do you desire?" and so of each the questions were asked and orders made out.

"Here, gentlemen, take these to the clerks; they will supply your immediate needs. The rest you can obtain later. All can be paid at our house in Oregon City when your crops come in."

Profoundly moved, one by one they bowed themselves out from the presence of that "old barbarian in his den on the Columbia," whose generosity had rescued them and their families from suffering, starvation, and possibly death.

Standing on the porch of his residence, Dr. McLoughlin beckoned to a group of young men waiting irresolute below.

"Our ship sails to-night," he said. "If any of you wish to write home, you'd better do so. It's the last chance you'll get for six months."

"Thank you," answered John Minto; "we would like to write, but we have no material."

"Go over there," said the doctor, pointing to Bachelors' Hall. "The clerk will furnish stationery." Pulling out his gold watch — "You have just twenty minutes before dinner."

In Bachelors' Hall the lads indited the first letters since leaving St. Joe in May, letters to apprise the dear ones at home of their safe arrival at Oregon-by-the-Sea. Scarcely had they finished when a servant entered with roast beef and potatoes, and the boys dined like guests in the home of a friend.

Says one of those boys, a gray-haired grandsire now: "Mr. Douglas was urbane, civil, gentlemanly, but he could not disguise his chagrin at each addition to the number of American settlers."

In after years James Douglas was knighted by Queen Victoria, "but," adds the honorable commentator, "John McLoughlin held the patent for his honors immediately from Almighty God."

Dr. McLoughlin so bestowed favors that the recipient felt honored by the contact. The warm hand-grasp, the personal interest, the *bonhomie* and gayety, made him seem a good fellow among them as he went out to be introduced to their wives and children. Dr. McLoughlin never forgot those pioneer women. Years after, if he met them in the grassy paths of Oregon City, his hat was off, and with the salute of a courtier he stepped aside and waited till they passed.

The immigrants prepared to embark for the Willamette. At the river-bank Dr. McLoughlin was storming at a boatman — "Here, you scoundrel, what have you loaded that bateau with wagons for? I gave strict orders to bring down nothing but people, and to leave none behind."

Even as the doctor spoke the immigrants piled in, on top the wagons, under the wagons, and into every nook and cranny, till all was full. The bateau swung into the current; he looked to see it sink, but no, with three cheers from the boat-load the doctor laughed and waved his hand. "All right! all right! all right! sir," he said.

A Missourian slid down the Cascades in a canoe, and arrived in time to see the annual ship about to sail for London. Without ado, he clambered on board and began to look around. By and by he blundered into a little room where the captain sat, busy with his log-book. The captain looked up, and eying him with a calm surprise inquired, "Young man, who are you, and what do you want here?"

"Sir, I am an emigrant, just come down the river. I do not wish to intrude, but I wanted to see the ship, as I never saw one before to recollect."

The captain wrote a moment in silence, then said, "Where do you come from, and why do you come here?"

"*We've come from Missouri,*" answered the boy, "*we've come from Missouri across the Rocky Mountains. We've come to settle in Oregon, and rule this country.*"

The captain scanned his unkempt hair, his corduroy clothes and worn-out shoes.

"Well, young man, I have sailed into every quarter of this globe, and have seen most of the people on it, but a more uncouth, at the same time a bolder set of men than you Americans, I never met before."

Just in time to meet the immigrants, Captain Couch re-entered the Willamette with another cargo of merchandise. With him came Lieutenant Cushing, the son of Caleb Cushing, to investigate the Oregon question and report to his father in Congress.

Captain Couch, a jolly New England tar, wedded to the most beautiful girl in Newburyport, broke the Hudson's Bay rules of exclusive trade like brittle twigs, traded with Indians and Frenchmen, and bought wheat and skins at his own prices. His little corner grocery had become a formidable rival to the square trade-window of the Indian shop at Fort Vancouver.

The watchful Hudson's Bay Company grew uneasy as it saw the rich territory of Oregon sliding from its grasp. Overland from Canada there came Lieutenants Warre and Vavasour, of the Royal Engineers, ostensibly to strengthen the defences at Fort Vancouver. Into their ear Sir George Simpson had whispered, "Watch the doctor."

They saw the advent of the immigrants of 1844.

The great spirit that could not see suffering, and that sought to conciliate and ward off war, was beyond their comprehension. Unknown to Dr. McLoughlin a secret report was sent to London.

XXXIII

ELIJAH

1844

" WE want cattle, much cattle," said the Walla
Walla chief in the Indian council. They all
knew the gallant Captain Sutter; he passed through
their country when he came to Oregon. And now,
when he heard those eastern chiefs were in need of
cattle, he sent them an invitation to visit his fort
on the Sacramento. Pio-pio-mox-mox, Tauitau, and
certain chiefs and sub-chiefs of the Nez Percés and
Spokanes, agreed to go down there together, to make
a trade with skins and ponies. This Walla Walla expedition constitutes one of the most remarkable commercial exploits in Indian annals. Conceived and
planned and manned entirely by the chiefs, it bade
fair to be a great success.

The morning sun poured over the Blue Mountains
in a cataract of gold when the chiefs set out in English
costume, magnificently mounted, to visit their white
friend, Captain Sutter. Behind them followed a pack-
train, heavily freighted with beaver, deer, and elk skins.
A bevy of beautiful girls, on their Cayuse ponies,
accompanied the expedition a few miles up the John
Day River. Their little grass caps fitted closely over the
smooth-combed hair. Their long, black braids hung
over their breasts, and the chalk-whitened deerskin
dresses glistened in the sun. Their noses were fine

and straight, and the skin pure copper, like the statues in some old Florentine gallery. At Elijah's side rode Siskadee on her white Cayuse. The tiny, glove-fitting moccasins were laced high up the ankle. As Elijah talked the expression of her oval, oriental face changed like the play of wind on a meadow.

"When we come with the cattle I will build you a house like the white man's," he was saying. "Then we shall be married like white people. I spoke to Jason Lee and he promised. And I shall never let you carry burdens; the white men never do. You shall ride always on a pony and be my *klootchman* [wife]."

"And take me with you everywhere?" asked Siska-dee, "as Dr. Whitman does his klootchman?"

"Yes," said Elijah.

The tall rye grass, high over their horses' heads, sometimes tangled the path, and Elijah pressed on ahead, clearing the way to an opening. The autumnal sun was past midday before the girls turned back.

"I will return when the camas blooms," said Elijah, at parting.

With Indian calls, and farewells, and gypsy laughter, the maidens galloped home. The young men followed the trail, east of the Cascades, to Spanish California. The dreaded Klamaths, the warlike Shastas, were passed in safety. Several weeks of steady travel brought them eight hundred miles over the Sierras to Sutter's fort on the Sacramento.

Six years Elijah had been to school at the Methodist mission. He could read and write and speak the English well, better even than Ellice, the accomplished head chief of the Nez Percés.

Siskadee, daughter of Tiloukaikt, was a typical maiden of the upper Columbia fifty years ago, closely

covered, chaste, and modest. Tradition says, she wore
the classic dress of deerskin down to the ankles, whitened and beaded and fringed and soft as chamois,
ornamented with long, wide sleeves and a belt of
haiqua.

Siskadee's mother was a cook and a basket-maker,
learned in the camas-beds. "Observe, my child," she
was wont to say as she shaped the biscuits of kouse
for the winter bouillon, "observe how neat the deer and
the antelope, how industrious the beaver and the bee,
how cleanly the plumage of the bird. The dress of a
Cayuse maid should shine like snow."

Siskadee was very industrious now. She had a marriage dress beaded to the value of a Worth gown.
Every day she sat with her maids embroidering sheaths
and moccasins and cradle wrappings. There was a
basket of beads at Siskadee's side. In her bosom there
were coils of fine dried sinews of deer that she pulled
out one by one. She was embroidering a shot-pouch
for Elijah. As she sat, a marriage procession passed,
solemn and slow, bearing flambeaux of cedar to a spot-
less new tent. She heard them sing praises of the
bridegroom's valor against the Blackfeet.

She thought, " So it will be when Elijah comes."

She heard the exhortation to the bride, —

" Be chaste, industrious, obedient, silent."

Siskadee's shapely head drooped lower at her work.
The copper fingers flew over the beaded shot-pouch.
Poolalik, the little gray hare, hid under the sage. The
wild hen cackled and scratched in the sand.

Over in the mission fields Dr. Whitman, in slouch
hat, buckskin trousers and moccasins, was wielding the
cradle.

" No Indian is yet able to use the cradle." said Dr.

Whitman. " I must do that myself, except as a white man helps me."

The Indians followed behind him, raking, binding, and bearing the shocks to the threshing yard. Crowds of Indians were trying to help. He could not keep them from working. They drove their ponies into the rail-fenced enclosure to trample out the wheat. They gathered up the grain, and women and girls with willow fans winnowed away the chaff. It was slow work, but Indians have infinite patience. A smart breeze comes down the Columbia after dark. All night the Indians stood there, pouring and repouring the yellow grains, winnowing in the wind. At last the wheat was in the granary. Every night Dr. Whitman paid them, shirts, ammunition, fish-hooks. The women wanted needles, thimbles, rings, beads. Some in the yard were sawing and splitting wood, — pine and cedar logs that they had helped the doctor raft down from the mountains when the river was high. The women carried great arm-loads and piled them in the wood-house. That meant more needles and needles from Dr. Whitman.

Then came the corn-gathering.

" Hold up your hands," said Dr. Whitman; " count ten fingers. Now, for every ten bushels you husk and bring to the house I will give you one."

Then the corn-gathering began. It was done in one day. It would have been one day had there been ten times as much, such multitudes of men, women, and children flocked into the fields to pick and husk. Every lodge-pole along the Walla Walla was hung with ears of yellow corn.

Once the Walla Walla-Cayuses talked only of war; now they talked of corn and cattle. Once the squaws

dug kouse and camas.   Now they began to neglect the
camas-beds to hoe in their little gardens of pumpkins
and potatoes and corn and carrots.

"Thank the Lord, my farm-work is done for this
year," said Dr. Whitman.   "My Indian trade-goods
are about used up."

"I wish we could get rid of this soul-belittling, piety-
killing farm-work and give our whole time to teaching
and preaching," said Spalding, riding over the hills
from Lapwai.

"Brother, brother," said the doctor, "'t is a part of
our work.   Agriculture and the gospel go hand in
hand.   Christianize an Indian, give him a home and a
farm, and he has too much at stake to go to war with
the whites."

"Yes, yes, yes," said Spalding.   "You have said that
before.   They must have hoes and homes.   We cannot
teach them on the wing.   I passed the cabin of Five
Crows to-day.   He has it complete, with floor and fireplace and doors and windows, but he can't live in it.
He says it is too close, and has set up his old lodge.
There they stand, the cabin and teepee side by side."

"That Indian desires civilization more than any
other I ever knew," said Dr. Whitman.   "He is insane
now on the subject of a white wife.   He thinks it would
help him to become like white men."

"I know; he has talked with Mrs. Spalding about it.
Three winters now he has driven his herds to the Clear-
water and come with Chief Joseph to school.   Both of
them have made remarkable progress; they read and
write with considerable fluency.   Why did n't Five
Crows accompany Elijah to California?"

"Mrs. Whitman thinks he stayed to meet the immigrants.   Every few days he goes out to meet them, and

tries to buy a white wife. And he would treat her well, too. He is a kind-hearted and wealthy Indian, the richest Indian in this country."

"Yes, but —" and they both laughed at this hallucination on the part of Five Crows, head chief of the Cayuse nation.

"How are your congregations, Doctor?"

"Two hundred to four hundred in spring and fall, about fifty when the young men are gone to hunt buffalo. And you?"

"Better than ever. Not less than two thousand have gathered for instruction at Lapwai. Eighty to one hundred families have planted gardens. The outward forms of Christianity, prayer and singing, are observed in almost every lodge."

"You have the most promising field in Oregon, Brother Spalding. Your Nez Percés are more docile than my mettlesome Cayuses. These are like spirited race-horses, hard on the bit, sometimes. But I know you have trials as well as I."

"Trials?" echoed Mr. Spalding. "I think so. The Indian's never-to-be-satisfied desire for property is one. He thinks the white man's stock of goods is inexhaustible. That comes of this pernicious present system. Give an Indian an egg and he wants an ox. They seem to feel that all whites are in debt to every Indian. But regular pay for regular work will develop self-reliance."

"Yes; we must throw the Indian on his own resources," said the doctor; "make a white man of him. That will cure this childish habit of expecting presents."

"But even after I have given them presents and presents, they expect pay for every little thing they do," said Spalding. "They even expect pay for the water, earth, and air. They even wanted pay for the stones I brought down the mountain for my mill."

"Very likely. Dr. McLoughlin once told me of a similar case. He was ballasting the barque 'Columbia' for a trip to the Islands. A chief stepped up and demanded pay for the stones they were lading. The tribe looked on. With quick wit the old doctor grabbed up a stone and chucked it into the chief's mouth. 'Pay! pay!' he roared, 'here, eat this.' The chief backed out amid the jeers of his people. Dr. McLoughlin has established the precedent that what they cannot eat or wear he does not propose to pay for. Remember, Brother Spalding, we would have trials even in teaching white children; Indians are only children, but they desire civilization and we cannot let this noble disposition expend itself in fruitless effort." Thus comforting and encouraging one another the missionaries entered the house where Mrs. Whitman sat instructing a class of bright little Indian girls, and every one had a rag dolly.

"Ha! ha!" laughed the gentlemen, "ha! ha!"

"Well," expostulated Mrs. Whitman, "I was tired of seeing them carry sticks around on their backs for babies. Wouldn't mother wonder what looking objects Narcissa could make?" holding one up with a laugh. "No matter how they look. So long as it is a piece of cloth rolled up, with eyes, nose, and mouth marked with a pen, it answers every purpose. They caress and carry them around at a great rate."

Siskadee, with her beads, at the lodge door, saw the missionaries walking across the plain, but she only thought of Elijah; thought of him when as a child he wagered gravel-stones that he could shoot the little gray hare; thought of that day when he played he was a wolf with the wolf's hide on **and** ears erect; thought of that day when he sat on the hillside and calmly watched a wounded bear tear up the sod around him.

"No young brave so brave as Elijah," she said to herself.

XXXIV

AT SUTTER'S FORT

1844

"THESE are my friends, the chiefs of eastern Oregon," said Captain Sutter, taking the hands of his red guests. "I have invited them down to trade in cattle."

The packhorses were driven into the fort and the beautiful peltries unrolled. The spotted Cayuse racers tried their gait on the green. The long-horned Spanish cattle were inspected, and the trade consummated to the satisfaction of all concerned. Elijah, the head and soul of the whole enterprise, was jubilant. In the soft autumn twilight Sutter's Indian boys bound fillets of leaves about their heads, and danced and sang in the soft-flowing vocals of the South. A schooner lay in the river, ready to proceed to the Columbia for a cargo of supplies. The moon rose over the Sierras, and red men and white slept in peace at Sutter's fort.

California was still in its primeval beauty. The inroads of Spanish civilization scarce scratched her vast savannas. Whole valleys and mountain flanks and forests were sacred to the Indian, the beaver, and the elk. "Let us hunt in the mountains and get more peltries," said Elijah, as they arose, refreshed from slumber. The woods were alive with game that the lazy Spaniards disdained the trouble of hunting. Their chase was with the lasso among their own herds.

The Oregon Indians rode to the hunt. Back in the mountain fastnesses they fell upon a band of Indian robbers, renegades, who swooped into the valleys, corralled herds of horses, and, under cover of the hills, retreated to some hidden pocket of streams and pastures. The suspicious banditti, anticipating pursuit from their recent raid, fired upon the Walla Walla-Cayuses. A sharp skirmish ensued, in which the mountain free-booters were worsted, and the victorious Walla Wallas galloped back to Sutter's fort, driving before them twenty-two head of captured horses.

" Ah, there are our horses," said the men at Sutter's fort, coming out to claim each one his property.

"No, no," remonstrated Elijah at this peremptory proceeding. " We took these horses in battle. By the laws of war they are ours."

" No," cried the white men, " they were stolen from us. You must give them up." Yellow Serpent sat on his horse. Elijah had dismounted.

" In our country," said Elijah, " six nations are on terms of friendship. If any one of these six nations steals a horse, the tribe is responsible. But if our enemies, the Crows or the Blackfeet, steal a horse, it is lost beyond recovery. Now at the risk of our lives we have taken these horses from your enemies. By the laws of war they belong to us."

At that moment an American, seeing his mule in the band, sang out, " There is my mule, and I shall have it."

" Will you?" said Elijah, glancing at a tree and passing into the lodge pitched close at hand. He came out in a moment with a loaded rifle. " Go now and take your mule," he said.

"I hope you are not going to kill me," quavered the American.

"You? No. I am going to shoot the eagle perched on yonder oak."

The American looked at the bird, and the unerring shot, and retired to the fort.

The next day was Sabbath. Captain Sutter invited the Indians up to the fort to church. After the service, Elijah and his uncle, Tauitau, were invited into another apartment. The American of yesterday began to berate them.

"You hounds, you dogs, you thieves of the upper country! I heard of you on the Willamette. Yesterday you were going to kill me. Now you must die." Drawing his pistol he aimed at Elijah.

"Let me pray a little first," said Elijah, falling on his knees.

"Dare you, an Indian, presume to preach to me? Take that and that." With a quick jerk the American shot the kneeling boy through the heart.

A look of horror passed from face to face as the kneeling form fell back with prayer upon its lips. Blood gushed from the nose, one convulsive sigh, and the lad was dead.

Sudden terror seized the white men, lest the Indians should attack them. The death-wail had hardly sounded when the Indians turned to flee before the guns of the frightened inmates of the fort. One wicked desperado had put them all in peril. The Indians leaped to their horses. One, only, lingered a moment, and covered the face of the dead with a blanket.

"Boom! boom!" went the cannon of Sutter's fort tearing away the tree-tops above the heads of the fugitive red men. Tents, provisions, and the purchased cattle were left, as they fled before the pursuers sent out by Captain Sutter. Six weeks later, worn and torn and bent with rage and grief, Pio-pio-mox-mox reached his lodge on the winding banks of the Walla Walla. Riderless beside him galloped Elijah's horse. Siska-dee came out, and put her arms around the good steed's neck and whispered in his yellow mane. The shot-pouch was done. She handed it to Yellow Serpent and said nothing. But the warriors heard her wail on the hills at sunset, and they heard the wail of Elijah's mother, sister of the great sachems of the Cayuse nation.

A raging fire burned in the tribes on the upper Columbia. Never the death of an Indian had created such an uproar; the six allied nations had lost an idol. Apprehensive of danger, Chief Trader McKinley strengthened Fort Walla Walla and loaded his cannon with nails and grapeshot. Dr. Whitman wrote a friendly letter to Ellice, head chief of the Nez Percés, and another to the Willamette.

"Our Indians are enraged on account of the treacherous and violent death of their educated and accomplished young chief Elijah, and also on account of their own great hardships and losses. Disaffected scamps, late from the Willamette to California, calling them dogs and thieves, have made the Indians think they have been slandered by your settlements."

The six nations, the Walla Wallas, Cayuses, Nez Percés, Spokanes, Pend d'Oreilles, and Snakes met together in council.

Seven hundred Walla Wallas stood ready to march on the Willamette, but were stopped by Tauitau.

"No," said Tauitau, going before their horses and waving them back. "The Willamette whites were our young chief's best friends. They are not to blame."

"Let us raise two thousand warriors, invade California, and sweep the coast," said Spokane Garry.

"Let us send Ellice down to see if the Oregon whites will interfere," said the Nez Percé Chief Joseph.

"The Americans are responsible. An American killed Elijah. Let us cut off the Americans," cried the Snakes.

"Blood for blood. A chief for a chief. Let us take Dr. Whitman," hissed the Cayuse Tamahas.

All looked toward Yellow Serpent. Afar off, strange, and mournful sounded the old chief's words.

"Dr. Whitman is our friend. Let him not be injured. My voice is as the voice of a pine-tree full of snow. I say no more."

At that moment, leaping from their fleet horses, Dr. Whitman, Mr. Spalding, and Chief Trader McKinley walked into the dimly lighted council lodge. For a moment there was tumult, but the three white men stood firm and fearless.

"What has the Great Medicine to say?" inquired Yellow Serpent, looking at Dr. Whitman. The doctor stepped forward and the Indians all craned their necks to listen.

"Chief, you have lost your noble son. We all mourn with you. I hear you want me to go away. When I came among you, you had no farms, no gardens. I have taught you to read and to work, and to live like white folks. Now I can go. I am getting old. You must tell me at once. If a majority wish me to leave I will go in three weeks' time. If you want me to stay, say so. I cannot change when I am old."

"Go! go!" cried Tamahas.

"Go! go!" brayed Tiloukaikt, in that voice like a brazen trumpet. But the other chiefs bade them be silent.

Dr. Whitman arose and went out of the lodge. Chief Trader McKinley talked to the Indians. Mr. Spalding talked. The chiefs talked. The auditors evinced their attention by now and then a pithy and sympathizing, "Ugh-úgh!" like their Amen after prayer. Then Yellow Serpent sent for Dr. Whitman.

A strange pallor, blent with wonderful resolution, seemed fixed upon the almost haughty face that re-entered the council lodge. So we might imagine John Knox stood, or Luther went to the Diet at Worms. The doctor seemed to expect a sentence of banishment. To his surprise old Yellow Serpent himself advanced to meet him and took his hand.

"My brother," he said in Nez Percé, "we have decided that you must stay. When you came we had no ploughs, no hoes, no axes, not anything to work with. Now we have all these. We used to be hungry every winter. We used to have only the camas. Now we have cattle, corn, potatoes, beans, peas, wheat. Now we are no more hungry. We want you to stay and live with us always."

"Stay, stay, stay," cried the fickle Cayuses.

"Stay, stay," echoed the Walla Wallas.

Tiloukaikt brought the long-stemmed pipe of peace. Yellow Serpent placed a live coal on the tobacco, puffed it, and passed it to Dr. Whitman.

"I admit there is danger," said Dr. Whitman to his friends that night, "but I am become accustomed to danger. I should not feel to stay among the Indians in itself considered, but as we are here now I do not see how we can leave without exposing the cause of religion to reproach and repulse. There are so many things involved in our situation in this country, that I do not see that we should be discontented. I feel that vast

results have followed us. To leave would be wrong
indeed, for now, we must, as far as may be, see the end
of what we have begun, both in regard to Indians and
whites."

During the winter Dr. McLoughlin summoned the
chiefs to Fort Vancouver, and by pacific counsel
shielded the Oregon whites from any consequences of
the outrage.

XXXV

DEATH OF JASON LEE

1845

TWELVE miles below Oregon City, in a little swale in the muffled, silent forest, a rival town was laid. A missionary hauled timber to build a church. A wandering printer set up a newspaper that he called the "Oregonian."

"The head of ship navigation, the outlet of a fertile valley, must become a metropolis," said the far-seeing Pettygrove, a Yankee merchant who had brought a cargo around the Horn from Portland, Maine. "And what shall we call our metropolis?" said Pettygrove to Lovejoy, the lawyer, as they laid out lots in the timber.

"Call it Boston," answered Lovejoy, the Bostonian.

"No, Portland," said the man from Maine, and the two wandering Yankees tossed up a penny for "heads or tails," and "Portland" won.

"Hah, Doctor, Hi did not suppose Hi should be hable to find you hout hof bed," cried Ermatinger, gayly landing at Fort Vancouver a few days later.

"Why so?" inquired the doctor.

"'Ave n't you 'eard? Dumbarton of Big Pigeon 'as made the speech hof the epoch, ha great big-tree talk, ha real Hamerican stumper, you know."

"What was the subject?"

"You.   Hit was in regard to that contested mill-site at the Falls.   Listen," — Ermatinger rose, blew a blast on his bandana, and swelling with pomposity gave a mock recital of a spread-eagle speech he had heard the day before.

"Friends, neighbors, hand Hamerican citizens [through his nose], han hopportunity his now given through this hinsignificant controversy to settle the title hof the whole country hand to hexpel the governmental trespassers from every point and position hof its dominions. This will bring war between the Hunited States and Great Britain, Hireland will revolt, Canada will secede, the monarchs hof the Hindies will throw hoff their slavish yoke, Russia will snap hup Turkey, hand, hin short, the whole world will be revolutionized, hand the balance hof power haltered by the controversy hin relation to this little strip hof land."

Ermatinger paused from his elocutionary effort.   To his surprise the doctor did not laugh; he did not even smile, but arose in a nervous way and left the room.   Some time after, one of his clerks ran upon him, kneeling in his office.

"I beg your pardon," said Ermatinger, humbly, that evening; "I did not suppose you took the matter so to heart, Doctor."

"The possibility of a war is what distresses me," said the doctor.

The Provisional Government, born at Champoeg and cradled in the primitive State House at Oregon City, developed with the colony.   Somebody was known to be in Washington working for a steamboat route across the Panama.

"Hah," said Ermatinger through his nose, "we shall soon be sighing for the Hindian days, the squaws hand skins hand savages. But there, now, Hi ham ha good Hamerican, you know," he added with a wink, — so good, indeed, that he was made Colonial Treasurer at the next election.

George Abernethy, the steward of the Methodist mission, an upright man, of smooth face and agreeable manner, became Oregon's colonial governor. On a green point overlooking the Willamette and within sound of the Falls, he built his modest mansion, with gable roof, French windows, wide porch, double parlors, and fireplaces, and the American flag floating above. The streets in Oregon City were only trails, and the new governor whitewashed the stumps that he might find his way home on dark nights through the timber. Here his apple-cheeked wife gave parties in the hospitable days of early Oregon.

The governor's house was on the very spot where old Canemah once shaped his arrow-points. One night Waskema came back. There stood the governor's residence, with its pillared porch and windows of glass. She went around to a favorite Balm-of-Gilead that clapped its silver leaves in the summer night. The white chief had dug him a well, throwing out the sand on countless clippings and fragments of imperfect arrow-heads. Like a lover who looks for a lock of his mistress's hair where he dropped it long ago, so old Waskema had been wont to return to gather broken chips from the arrow-maker's shop; but now they were covered, mixed with the sands, and the brick-walled well seemed not deeper than the grave in her heart. She clutched her hands and looked up at the windows. There were lights in the governor's windows — she drew near and saw the ruddy glow of the fire lighting up the fair faces of white boys and girls. Even so in the long

ago the red men's children met in social converse on
the selfsame spot. She pressed her withered face too
near the glass.

"Ugh," shuddered the flaxen-haired daughter of the
host, "there's a horrible old Indian woman peeking in
at the window."

Frightened glances turned that way, but the face was
gone.

"She was here, just this minute. I saw her," said
the girl, going out on the porch to look, followed by
her companions; but nothing could be seen.

"Never mind. 'Twas only an old squaw. Let's
play that game again," cried the merry-hearts.

Old Waskema had retreated to a rock in the governor's garden. By dint of some digging and some
pushing she turned it over. Beneath, in a little cache,
lay a bunch of obsidian knives, some strings of copper
beads, and a handful of haiqua shells. Gathering up the
rusting treasures, Waskema stole away. The next day
Governor Abernethy wondered who had been digging
at the stone in his garden.

The Methodist mission had not prospered. In fact,
while Jason Lee was lecturing in the States, unforeseen
influences had been at work in the valley. The most
casual observer had noted the frightful growth of the
mission graveyard. It may have been scrofulous inheritance, it may have been the sudden caging of these
wild birds—the Indian children perished like leaves
of the forest. Jason Lee in distress had taken some
favorite pupils to Fort Vancouver for treatment—in
vain. At this juncture some ran away; the rest were
withdrawn by their superstitious parents. The history
of Indian schools at Dartmouth and Hamilton repeated

itself here — the Indian mission on the Willamette, the centre of so many hopes and prayers, became the seat of an embryo university re-dedicated to the numerous children of incoming whites.

In the midst of this toil and endeavor Jason Lee stood again at the threshold of his bridal chamber; a second wife lay dead, with an infant in her arms — but the infant lived.

" ' Though he slay me, yet will I trust in him,' " said the anguished missionary as he looked on the cold, white lips of his second love.

He crossed to the Sandwich Islands with the precious, flickering little life so strangely left in his hands; then came another blow, — he had been superseded in the superintendency of the Oregon missions.

The waxen face of his child was flushed now with health. Turning, he laid the daintily draped morsel of pink and white in the arms of one who had received her from the bed of death.

"Take her back to Oregon," he said, " and keep her till I return." Then he sailed for Mazatlan, and struck across Mexico for the United States.

They knew he was collecting funds for the projected university that lay so near his heart, they knew that consumption had fixed its fangs upon his giant frame; still he wrote from his old home of the gray gables at Stanstead: —

" Wait, brethren, and watch, — some day you may see me threading my way up the Willamette in a canoe, as I used to do; " but the hand that penned it fell nerveless, the noble eyes closed in death. With the winged sail came the parting prayer for the little Lucy Anna, —

" Brethren, under God I must hold you responsible to train that child for heaven."

Jason Lee's body rests where he played when a boy on the shores of one of the beautiful lakes of Lower Canada, and in coming years that motherless waif, the little Lucy Anna, became the first preceptress of Willamette University. Love, life, hope, youth, — all were given to Oregon. Who shall say the light has failed?

XXXVI

THE BEAR FLAG AT SONOMA

1846

LIFE glided smoothly with the hospitable, light-hearted Spaniards of California, but not so smoothly at the Hudson's Bay trading-house at Yerba Buena. There were pleasant guests; Vallejo came often, and Don Salvador. The fierce, fat little commandant came up from his ruinous Presidio; the Alcalde came, and the padres, who wandered now like vagrants in the land they used to rule. Yerba Buena was a great resort for trappers and Englishmen for trade and supplies. La Framboise camped near in winter, and the servants of the Hudson's Bay Company constituted almost the entire population of the place.

From the very beginning there was trouble with the Yankee ships from New York and Boston. Some of the unavailing anguish of Wyeth on the Columbia came to Rae as he saw the Yankee clippers sailing from port to port, vending their wares and carrying off great cargoes of hides and wheat and tallow. Sometimes weeks would elapse without a single fanega of wheat or arroba of tallow at the Hudson's Bay house. It made Rae desperate. Once he said to a Yankee captain that spread his wares on the very threshold of Yerba Buena: "It has cost the Hudson's Bay Company £75,000 to drive the Americans from the North-west trade in furs, and they will drive you Yankees from California if it costs a million."

The Yankee only laughed, and put up his calico to ten dollars a yard and hauled in the wheat and tallow.

And the careless Spaniards went on singing and dancing, horse-racing and gambling — everybody gambled in Spanish California.

There was a new governor in California. A new governor in a Spanish-American State generally means a revolution.

"This new governor, Micheltorena, is partial to the Americans," said the Spanish Californians.

"His course is a menace to English interests," said Rae.

The Spaniards hated the Americans as much as Rae did. They often gathered at Yerba Buena to talk the matter over.

"We must depose him," said the Spaniards.

"We must fight them to the death," said Rae.

So the insurgents came to Yerba Buena for arms and ammunition. But the insurgents lost, and Rae lost.

"Curse it all! why did I let them have the arms and ammunition without a cent to show?" cried Rae, despairing. "And how shall I answer for mixing in this Spanish trouble?"

The proud chief trader groaned. He had done the best he could for his company, but the best he could would not avail. Already Sir George had sent recommends to shut up the house at Yerba Buena as a profitless venture. But Dr. McLoughlin held firm. And to disappoint the doctor now —

"What if the Hudson's Bay Company is driven out of California? Am I to blame, with all these rival Yankees like the swarming rats of Hamelin nibbling on every side?" The servants heard a shot in Rae's room.

Eloise saw her husband fall with the smoking weapon in his hand, then she fainted.

When Eloise opened her eyes again she lay on a couch in a darkened room. Through the lattice she saw Don Salvador leap to his saddle, cutting his horse with the long and rusty rowels of his spurs. She heard the hurried voices of Spaniards, forgetting somewhat the customary stately and measured tone. She heard the voices of women skipping from consonant to consonant. She knew La Framboise had come over from the camp. Then all was dark again.

Again it seemed like morning. Through the lattice Eloise saw the Spanish dames go by to mass, with their high combs, necklaces, and earrings hidden under the "beautiful and mysterious mantilla." There was a sound of marching, and she knew it was the funeral.

La Framboise's brigade bore sad tidings up the Willamette to Fort Vancouver. David and Dugald McTavish came down in the little "Cadboro'." The business was closed, and the Hudson's Bay house was sold for a song.

Eloise took a last look at the Spanish land. The Alcalde was chasing his herds. The señoras were sewing and singing in their verandas. The Indians were ploughing the Spanish gardens, after the fashion of old Mexico in the days of Cortez.

The fierce, fat little commandant peeped out of the tile-roofed Presidio as the schooner sailed through the Golden Gate.

With the fading of Mendocino, the fandangoes, boleros, and barcaroles of old Spain faded from the life of Eloise McLoughlin, but not the face of him who was buried in the little graveyard at Yerba Buena, — it lived again in her infant child.

Already immigrants on the overland route had rendezvoused at Sutter's fort. Strange rumors were current there —

" The Mexicans are negotiating with England for the sale of California."

" General Castro intends to expel us from the Sacramento. He is already on the march."

They whispered with Fremont.

Scarcely had the little " Cadboro' " disappeared through the Golden Gate that day in June of 1846, when General Vallejo was captured at daylight in his house at Sonoma, along with nine brass cannon, two hundred stands of arms, and tons of copper shot.

" Fly ! " cried the Señora, sitting up in bed in her night-robe.

It was too late to fly.

The Americans ran up the Bear Flag, and with Fremont's cognizance took General Vallejo and Don Salvador prisoners to Sutter's fort on the Sacramento. Vallejo did not resist. Long since he had seen that a change must come, and he favored the United States. He quietly gave up the keys, and in succeeding actions a thousand of Vallejo's best horses went under the saddles of American riflemen.

For twenty days California was a republic, then Captain Montgomery, by order of Commodore Sloat, raised the stars and stripes on the plaza at Yerba Buena. A flag was sent to Fremont, camping on the Sacramento, and was raised over Sutter's fort.

Hark ! Who is this winding along the trail to California ? It is Pio-pio-mox-mox, going to avenge the murder of Elijah. Warlike Walla Wallas and dark frowning Cayuses on their swift steeds bending to avoid the boughs of semi-tropic forests are following the old trail to the South. Delaware Tom is there, dressed like the rest in a robe of skins, going to avenge the death of the accomplished young chief of the Walla Wallas.

There are only forty men, but a courier flies to Sutter's fort. Breathless he passes the Indian guards —

" A thousand Walla Wallas are marching from Oregon to avenge the death of their young chief."

The guests leap from their wine-bowls. Artillery is primed and mounted. Runners gallop to Sonoma for reinforcements. Word even reaches Monterey. Commodore Stockton hastens to San Francisco, and preparations for defence are hurried to the North.

Meanwhile, Pio-pio-mox-mox, whose numbers have been so greatly exaggerated, is defiling down the canyon with vengeance in his heart. But his eyes are open. He hears for the first time that the old régime is over, that Sutter is out of power, and the Americans rule on the Sacramento.

" Then if the Bostons rule, to the Bostons will I present my claim for justice," said the indomitable old chief of the Walla Wallas.

Colonel Fremont met him in council, and promised redress. Under this persuasion the Walla Walla chief and his followers enlisted under Fremont's banner, and Delaware Tom, valued for his fluent use of English, became a trusted bearer of despatches and a member of Fremont's body-guard.

General Castro retreated to the South. Fremont followed on his trail and marched into Monterey.

The anxious Spaniards beheld a cloud of dust roll up beyond the city. From behind their grated windows the timid women beheld the long line of mounted Americans advancing up the street with Fremont at their head, shaking the ground with the tread of conquest. Nothing escaped the fierce eye of that wiry leader in blouse and leggings and Spanish sombrero. Around him closed his Delaware guard. Nothing escaped the eye of his wild followers, two and two abreast, with rifles cocked on the pommel of their saddles.

The Spaniards love a spectacle. Here was power. As they watched the stern-featured horsemen with sinewy limbs and untrimmed locks flowing under their foraging caps, as they caught the gleam of pistols and the glitter of knives, a thrill shook the throng, then arose a faint, " *Viva ! — vivan los Americanos !* "

The latest governor, Don Pio Pico, fled by night from his capital at Los Angeles and escaped to Mexico with his secretary. Tradition says they carried away and buried the government archives.

The next January the Alcalde sent forth his pronunciamento changing the name of Yerba Buena to San Francisco.

Had Rae but lived he might have ruled the richest post under Hudson's Bay control. As it was, he was forgotten by all but the Spanish nobles.

XXXVII

"FIFTY-FOUR FORTY OR FIGHT"

(1845-46)

THREE years had passed since Dr. McLoughlin wrote that letter for protection, and now word arrived from the Hudson's Bay house in London: "In the present state of affairs the company cannot obtain protection from the government. You must protect yourselves in the best way you can."

Many difficulties perplexed Dr. McLoughlin as well as the Provisional Government. Outlaws from the States found their way to Oregon. One, Chapman, boasted, " I came all the way from the States for the purpose of burning Fort Vancouver."

"Such a step would precipitate war in Oregon," said the settlers. Applegate was sent privately to Dr. McLoughlin.

"We are troubled," said Applegate to the doctor. "We want to protect you, but we cannot unless the company agrees to the articles of compact. To do that you must pay taxes and comply with the laws of the Provisional Government, which promises protection only to its adherents. Otherwise you will stand alone. Restless spirits from the States will consider you lawful prey. You need to join us. It is for your own interest."

"But how can I?" insisted the doctor. " I am a British subject, and this is British property."

" We have altered the form of oath to meet that very point," said Applegate. " Now the compact reads ' to support the Provisional Government so far as is consistent with our duties as citizens of the United States or subjects of Great Britain.' That lets you in, you see, without interfering with your allegiance."

The doctor sat with his head on his hand, thinking. Now and then he tossed back the white locks that fell around his face.

Applegate went on: " You see, Dr. McLoughlin, it will secure the property of the company. And it will conduce to the maintenance of peace and order to have it known to the American people that the two nationalities are united in Oregon. There will be a large immigration again this fall, and you may depend upon it there will be many to annoy you."

" I realize that, I realize that," said the doctor, despairingly. " Let me call in Douglas. He has a level head."

Douglas came in, tall, dark, and formal. He did not get on so easily with people as the doctor did, and especially these Americans he held at arm's length. But if he unbent to anybody it was to the cultured Applegate, the " Sage of Yoncalla." Again the whole subject was canvassed.

" Our taxes, if assessed at their real value, would outweigh all your colony," said Douglas.

" Of course you would tax only our sales to your settlers? " suggested the doctor.

" That is fair," said Applegate.

" Very well, then, we will join you," said the doctor and Douglas after some consideration.

Mr. Applegate returned to Oregon City and put the measure through with a rush. Dr. McLoughlin and

James Douglas signed the articles and became members of Oregon's Provisional Government.

"I don't see that we could do anything else," said the doctor, snuff-box in hand, a few days later. "I am glad the suspense is over, James. If we must live with these Americans we must live in peace."

"Yes," agreed Douglas. "The property is safe now. The fact that England paid no attention to your appeal for protection justifies the step we have taken."

"I am glad they elected you Judge of this Vancouver district," added the doctor. "That was handsomely done."

Just then the gate-keeper stuck his head in at the door.

"Eh, what, Bruce?" said the doctor, rising. "Ogden back from England, and strangers, did you say?"

Dr. McLoughlin turned and met face to face the scarlet coats and gold lace of two English officers advancing up the steps.

"Lieutenant William Peel, son of Sir Robert Peel, Prime Minister of England," said Peter Skeen Ogden, advancing and introducing the taller one, a fine young fellow, well bronzed, who advanced to meet the doctor.

With quite colorless face Dr. McLoughlin shook hands with the Premier's proxy so suddenly set down on the Columbia.

"Captain Parke of the Royal Marines," turning to the other.

Captain Parke handed Dr. McLoughlin a pack of credentials.

The doctor's color rose as he broke the royal seal and read.

"What! What! What! Brother of the Earl of Aberdeen here with a fleet to protect us?"

Douglas gave an involuntary start. " Protection! Now!"

" Gentlemen, where are your ships? " inquired the doctor.

" Anchored in Puget Sound. There are fifteen warships on the coast, carrying four hundred guns," answered Lieutenant Peel.

Dr. McLoughlin's face was a study.

" Where is your ship? How did you get here? "

" Overland by way of the Cowlitz. The ' Modeste ' is entering the Columbia with twenty guns. Do you think that will be sufficient? She will soon be here."

" Sufficient? I should think so! " ejaculated the doctor.

With the intuitive grasp of situation for which he was noted, Dr. McLoughlin provided for his distinguished guests, thinking mightily all the time.

" The devil's to pay now," he whispered aside to Douglas. " What have they come for? If they had only arrived six weeks sooner I should n't have signed the compact. Now we have recognized the Provisional Government the ships are not needed. Indeed, they are likely to stir up a d—l of a row by rousing the suspicions of the Americans."

" 'T is well to have them here till we try the temper of the next immigration," said Douglas, to soothe the spirits of his chief.

" Don't you think we can bring troops overland from Canada? " inquired one of the officers, as Dr. McLoughlin re-entered the room. " If it comes to blows we will hit these Americans a good deal harder than we would other people."

" Oh, Captain Parke! Oh, Captain Parke! " ejaculated the distressed doctor. " The country is not worth a war."

"Then what are the Americans coming here for? Just speak the word and we'll give them a hint that'll take the carts all off the wheels from here to the Rocky Mountains."

"That would be savage!" said the doctor.

Peel set his lips. "The United States is not going to euchre us out of Oregon. My father has said in Parliament, 'England knows her rights and dares maintain them,' and she will."

"The claim of the United States to this coast is absurd," said Lieutenant Peel. "Captain Gray was only a private speculating trader, dodging along this coast bartering for furs. He only went twelve miles up the river, he did not explore it; and as for taking possession — the poor coaster never thought of such a thing. Vancouver explored a hundred miles. We have as good a right to this river as to the Thames or the Humber."

"Why, of course," laughed Parke. "The Columbia has always belonged to us. This American talk is mere bravado, like the so-called 'Patriot War' of Canada — some noise and a good deal of smoke."

A sip of wine had warmed the guests, and all laughed merrily.

That Patriot War of Canada (1838) touched a tender spot in McLoughlin's heart.

"The effort of an oppressed people to free themselves is not a proper subject for merriment," he said.

"Whatever comes to pass," remarked Douglas, "these whittling Yankees talking politics are here, and more are coming. I hear that one of them is in Washington now, trying to get a steamboat route by the way of Panama."

"So? Next they'll be talking of a railroad right over the top of the Rocky Mountains!"

At this another "ha! ha!" went round the table.

"Enemies need bayonets," said Captain Parke, as they rose from their wine-cups.

"But, my dear fellow, these are not enemies," insisted Dr. McLoughlin. "They are simply settlers, quiet, peaceable, industrious."

"And like their fellow-countrymen always smoking and chewing and spitting, eh, doctor? I'd rather meet a grizzly than a settler."

That night Dr. McLoughlin wrote a letter to some one high in British authority, pleading against war. Somewhere, still, that letter may lie in English archives.

At the instance of the officers additional guns were mounted. The night-watch was doubled. The hourly "All is well" sounded like a cry of danger.

For eighteen months Her Majesty's warship "Modeste" lay like a policeman in the river. Five hundred men, sailors and marines, performed their daily evolutions on the green esplanade in front of the fort. A barrel of silver dollars dealt out for their pay was the first money ever seen in Oregon. Before that, barter ruled in skins and wheat.

The red-coats, running over the country with their glittering arms, might have made trouble had not Dr. McLoughlin kept up a constant counsel of peace.

"Whatever we do here will make no difference with the final outcome of the question," he kept saying. "It is better for us to keep on good terms with the settlers. These inoffensive, peaceable people are not the ones to fight."

Nevertheless the colonists had their fears.

"They'll turn the Indians loose upon us yet. I've seen their blacksmiths working all winter. They say they're making axes for the trappers. No such thing;

they 're tomahawks, and you 'll see 'em arming Indians, as they did in 1812. Down at Astoria, Birnie digs day after day — don't tell me it 's a garden. I know better. There 's cannon buried down there at Tongue Point, and one of these days you 'll hear 'em booming."

Douglas went over to Nisqually and found the war-ships burnishing their guns in Puget Sound.

" Ah," said the officers, as Douglas dined on shipboard. "If we could only be sent to the Columbia we 'd take the whole country in twenty-four hours."

That Oregon question had become the battle-cry of a presidential contest.

" Fifty-four forty or fight."

" All of Oregon up to Alaska or war."

America listened for the drum-beat.

" A ' small meal' will be made of the troops of the 'free and enlightened,'" said an editor on the St. Lawrence.

" The crows will soon be picking out their eyes," said an Indian chief on the northern border.

With clear vision Dr. McLoughlin saw the inflamed public of both countries. More than once he was dis-covered on his knees, praying that he might keep the people quiet in the disputed territory.

" I saw blood flow in 1812," he said to the son of England's premier, " I stanched the wounds of com-rades at Sault Ste. Marie. As one born on the conti-nent of America I feel that no foreign power has the right to fling her peoples into conflict. Suppose you take a ride up the valley and get acquainted with the people."

Well mounted on the best Vancouver horses, Parke and Peel went dashing up the Willamette.

It was harvest-time. Men dressed in buckskin

trousers, "hickory" shirts, and moccasins, were cutting wheat with the reap-hook. Settlers jogged along in rude carts ironed with rawhide, hauling their deerskin sacks full of grain to the river, where it was heaped on great bateaux, big as the hull of a steamer, and paddled down to Fort Vancouver, to exchange for "black strap" molasses, dirty Hawaiian sugar, and ready-made clothing. That clothing was all of one size, made in England; said to have been cut to the measure of Dr. McLoughlin. The thrifty immigrant wives clipped off the hickory shirts that came down to the feet and over the hands and were thankful for the patches. There were no old chests from which to resurrect cloaks and dresses; the American stock was soon exhausted, and the Hudson's Bay store, not contemplating such expansion, had none to sell. Old coats were threadbare, old tent covers worn out. Members of the legislature canvassed their brethren for a coat to wear in public. The singing-master met his classes in a suit of buckskin.

"You must get looms," said Dr. McLoughlin. Two immigrants set out for the States for flocks of sheep.

Everywhere Parke and Peel were met with rude but unstinted hospitality. Men who had marked the trail to Oregon with their blood, slaughtered for them the fatted bullock and sat down to dine in their shirt-sleeves. Women ground the grain for cakes in the coffee-mill and baked it in a Dutch oven set among the coals. Brisk housewives brushed up their hearths with hazel brooms, set the table with tin cups and plates, and seated the guests in the best old-fashioned cane-bottomed hickory rocker that had banged its way across the plains.

Every picturesque feature of New England, Ohio,

Missouri pioneering was repeated here. To Parke and Peel it was a revelation. Never before had they seen a people whose handbook of history was the migrations of their ancestors, whose ideal statesman was George Washington, whose model parent was Uncle Sam, Daniel Boone the chief hero, and the American eagle the favorite bird. With great good humor they heard the tales around the fires and slept at night in the cabin lofts.

"Tell me how you crossed the plains," said Peel at the house of Applegate. He told the story of 1843.

"Such men would make the finest soldiers in the world," said Peel and Parke as they went riding on.

"How do you like the country?" asked a horny-handed pioneer.

"It is certainly the most beautiful country in the natural state that I ever saw," said Peel.

"Will England try to hold it?"

"Not against the wishes of its people," answered the nobleman.

Before Parke and Peel returned from their trip up the valley the autumn immigration came pouring in with "54° 40' or fight" blazed on their wagon covers. To eager inquiries, "Yes, that is the party cry, and Polk is elected."

Parke and Peel looked on amazed as three thousand dust-begrimed pilgrims came toiling in to stake out their claims on the Indian lands. Never before had they seen the building of a State. "Hopelessly Americanized! hopelessly Americanized!" was their frequent comment as the long line of occupation took up the country. "Ploughs are better than traps to hold a country, and farms are better than forts."

The story of 1845 has never been told, never can be

told. In the face of Parke and Peel and all the British warships Dr. McLoughlin sent succor to the famishing immigrants. Far up Des Chutes they met his messengers of mercy with shouts and hallelujahs. The settlers bestirred themselves, and hurried forward pack-trains of food and horses to rescue their brethren in the mountains. There were not boats enough in the country to meet the needs of transportation, and when at Christmas all were in, the population of Oregon had been doubled.

And yet the boundary was not settled. A rumor was current at Havana that the whole British armament was sailing for the Columbia. Commodores Sloat and Stockton off the coast of California cast many a longing eye toward Oregon, but the Mexican War demanded their presence South. The Provisional Government sent the Applegates to cut a road for United States troops to enter southern Oregon.

Senator Benton said in Congress, " Let the emigrants go on and carry their rifles."

But Rufus Choate made that clarion answer: " In my judgment this notion of a national enmity of feeling towards Great Britain belongs to a past age of our history. We are born to happier feelings. We look on England as we do on France. We look on them from our new world, not unrenowned, yet a new world still, and the blood mounts to our cheeks; our eyes swim; our voices are stifled with emulousness of so much glory; their trophies will not let us sleep. but there is no hatred at all, no hatred; all for honor, nothing for hate. If you will answer for the politicians I think I will venture to answer for the people."

Webster, too, made a great peace speech that was heard on two continents.

The brother of the Earl of Aberdeen fretted on his warship in Puget Sound: "McLoughlin is right. 'T is a beastly country, not worth a war. Nisqually plains are a bed of gravel. Curse the deer! They will not wait for me to shoot them. Curse the salmon! They will not bite with the very best flies and a patent English angling rod. I would n't give tuppence for the whole country;" and he sailed away.

Lieutenant Peel took the shortest cut to London. What he poured into the ears of his father, Sir Robert, has never been known.

Lieutenant Cushing, also, reported to his father at Washington. All at once Congress adopted conciliatory resolutions.

Said Lord Aberdeen, "I did not delay a moment, but putting aside all ideas of diplomatic etiquette I made a proposition of settlement that was immediately accepted by Congress."

With joyful countenance Sir Robert Peel announced to the House of Commons, "The governments of two great nations have by moderation, by mutual compromise, averted the dreadful calamity of war."

Word reached Vancouver in the autumn of 1846 by way of the Sandwich Islands. Douglas immediately sent the news to Governor Abernethy. The settlers fired their anvils, the bluffs flung back the jubilee. Canadians and Americans rejoiced together. "Now Congress will take us under her wing," was the joyful cry. "Now we shall have territorial rights. Now they will recognize the acts of our Provisional Government. Until then how can we be sure that we own a farm or that any transaction that we have made will stand in law?"

Then for the first time the United States began to

look out of her western window to the sea. But no one thought of the Indian. With news of the boundary settlement came news of the Mexican War and the occupation of California. The front of the world had changed.

But when the Oregonians learned that the line was 49° instead of 54° 40′ there was an outcry — "A third of Oregon gone? Polk has betrayed us. Oregon reached Alaska."

And the Hudson's Bay barque sailed as usual, with a million dollars' worth of furs.

As colonial treasurer Ermatinger gained so good an insight into the strength or weakness of the little colony — for no one knows on which side Ermatinger was working — that just after the departure of Parke and Peel he suddenly handed in his resignation and left with the March express for England, committing his young wife to the care of Dr. McLoughlin. There may have been a political motive for the flight at that time. If so, it failed, for before he could sight the hills of Cornwall the treaty had been proclaimed, June 15, 1846.

Ermatinger visited the scenes of his English youth. Of his old friends few were left, some were dead, some were gone, and all were changed. Homesick, he set out for his old post on the Columbia. At Montreal he met Sir George Simpson — "You will hereafter be stationed at Athabasca," said the autocrat of the fur trade.

"Athabasca!" gasped Ermatinger. "Good God, can't I go to Fort Vancouver for my wife?"

"You understand the terms of this service, sir." Sir George passed on as though he had brushed a caterpillar from his sleeve.

Ermatinger, the jolly Ermatinger, staggered from the door, white as a man in ague. Too well he understood "the terms of our service, sir." He felt it was a cold-blooded act to separate him from his wife because of some pique at McLoughlin. Too well he knew the military system that bound any man that accepted a commission to hold himself in readiness to starve in Labrador or freeze at the north pole. But this —

"Curse it! Why did I not take Catharine with me and dig like a dog in England? There, at least, the laborer has his home."

Well he knew the heart-break of that disappointed wife, well he knew the weary distance and the danger should she try to reach him. She could not even learn of the change until the November mail packet. Then the waiting till the next brigade in March, the moun-tains, the rapids, and a babe in arms — in anguish as never before Ermatinger felt the iron of the great monopoly.

"Perhaps Sir George has no personal feeling in the matter," thought Ermatinger; "it is the factor's duty to obey, but" — like a sheath-cut came the con-clusion — "neither I nor any one at Vancouver can ever believe it is anything less than premeditated cus-sedness."

Some of his comrades tried to rally him. "Don't give up the beaver so, Erma."

"Now you can amuse yourself talking Chinook with the Chippeways."

"Or joking with the Assiniboins."

But none of these sallies could rouse the sad spirit of the prostrate Ermatinger.

"Men!" exclaimed Ermatinger, bitterly. "Men are of trifling value provided he gets furs. Wives! Wives are encumbrances; men are not expected to have them; they interfere with the company's interests, no arrangement can be made for them. The employés of the Hudson's Bay Company, gentlemen, are tools, mere implements, machines, under Sir George."

XXXVIII

DR. McLOUGHLIN RESIGNS

1846

THE spies' report of Dr. McLoughlin irritated the London Board. "What right has a chief factor in our employ to meet those immigrants with boat-loads of supplies, to nurse their sick in our hospital, and to loan them seed and agricultural implements to open up farms on the Willamette?" Across the sea there came a call to halt, and an account was demanded of Dr. McLoughlin.

Strong in the consciousness of his own integrity the doctor answered: "Gentlemen, as a man of common humanity I could not do otherwise than to give those naked and starving people to eat and to wear of our stores. I foresaw clearly that it aided in the American settlement of the country, but this I cannot help. It is not for me, but for God, to look after and take care of the consequences. The Bible tells me, 'If thine enemy hunger, feed him; if he be naked, clothe him.' These settlers are not even enemies. If the directors find fault with me they quarrel with heaven. I have simply done what any one truly worthy the name of a man could not hesitate to do. I ask you not to bear these debts; let them be my own. Let me retain the profits upon these supplies and advances made to set-tlers, and I will cheerfully assume all payments to the company. All that I can do honorably for my com-pany shall be done. Beyond that I have no pledges.

Shall I leave these Americans to starve, or drive them from the country? Gentlemen, if such be your orders, I can serve you no longer."

And so, on account of assisting the immigrants, Dr. McLoughlin resigned his position at the head of the Hudson's Bay Company west of the Rocky Mountains, and thereby sacrificed a personal income of $12,000 per annum.

As sad-faced Eloise sailed home into the Columbia she saw a great concourse at Fort Vancouver. A beautiful young lady, escorted by British officers, was christening a new sloop for the infant Prince of Wales.

"Can that be little Cecelia?" said Eloise. "How quickly she has grown! How quickly I have aged!"

In widow's weeds, with an infant in her arms, the Lady of the Pacific Coast had returned to Fort Vancouver, to find her father dethroned and Douglas reigning in his stead.

Dr. McLoughlin brought to Oregon City the same spirit of enterprise that had made Fort Vancouver the metropolis of the fur-forts. He gave employment to immigrants, built the best house, built saw and grist mills, and his loud voice might be heard in the streets directing his Indian servants as they grubbed up the stumps. Many yet living remember the white-headed man in swallow-tailed coat and brass buttons waving his cane like a truncheon at the head of the Falls — "A canal can be cut from this basin to the gulch beyond the bluff, and this whole canyon can smoke with factories."

A certain element, however, could never forget that Dr. McLoughlin had been at the head of a foreign monopoly, and pointed the finger with the whispered, "Aristocrat! Aristocrat!"

He applied for a ferry right across the Willamette, but was denied. He applied for a canal right; as this great public improvement would cost the public nothing, the petition was granted, and McLoughlin's men cut the first race-way in the gray rock around the Falls. He wanted to build locks at his own expense — and again was checked. "Give him too much power," they said.

Late one autumn evening an immigrant unyoked his oxen under the bluff beside the Falls. As they were getting supper a venerable old gentleman came to their camp-fire. Seated in the only chair they had, he made some friendly inquiries.

"Doctor," said the immigrant, "I heard before I left the States that you were intending to put locks at the Falls, but I see nothing has been done."

"Tut, tut, tut!" said the doctor, "too much jealousy of me, too much rivalry; cannot do anything."

The doctor further endeavored to push development by giving more than three hundred lots for public and private uses, lots for squares and parks, lots for churches and parsonages, to Methodists and Baptists, to Presbyterians and Catholics and Congregationalists, eight lots for a Catholic School, and eight for a Protestant Female Seminary now used by the Oregon City High School.

In a certain sense Dr. McLoughlin was a genius, with the irritabilities of genius. He saw clearly what should be done and could brook no delay in execution. A busy man himself, he wanted all busy about him. Across the river an American held a claim. "Now there's X in his Robin's Nest up there!" the old doctor would exclaim. "Why don't *he* do something? No, there he lies, and lets the skunks gnaw his toes while he waits for the country to develop."

Eminently sociable, full of talk, full of detail and incident, the ex-chief factor could never be happy without a crowd around him. Despite his detractors, he
made friends with all the new-comers, stopped to talk
with the men that strode the streets in moccasins and
leather pantaloons whipping up their black oxen, and,
indeed, the old gentleman was quite a gallant in brush-
ing up his beaver and starting out, cane in hand, to call
on the ladies. His stately form might be seen in any
door, always joking, running his fingers through his
hair, and inquiring after the children.

McLoughlin noted the shabby hats of the early leg-
islators. In his own genial manner he presented each
with a tall white hat, " bell-crowned and peculiar." " I
would see every honorable gentleman well roofed in,"
he said. Then he handed to each a long-stemmed pipe
with ornamented bowl. " And " (says a survivor),
"the majestic law-makers meandered along the river-
side whiffing the calumet of peace, while jealous Americans scowled and said, ' See corporate influence,' and
hated McLoughlin worse than ever."

To the end he never lost his love of dress and dancing; decked in white kids and white vest, like a gentleman of the old school, he adorned the parlor of many
a gay assembly. One night he knocked at an immigrant
neighbor's door with a lantern in his hand. " I am
going to the party," he said. " I want you to see me."
Laughingly he held up the lantern from point to point,
exhibiting his ruffles and carefully combed locks, his
narrow-tailed coat and satin vest. " Will I do?"

" Ah, yes, you will do," said the laughing pioneer
mother as the good old doctor trudged away with his
lantern and a new pair of dancing-pumps under his
arm.

"He used to wear a long blue cloak thrown around him. To see him walking to church Sunday morning, it was really a sight," said ex-Governor Chadwick twenty-five years after, so out of keeping seemed the patriarchal figure with the modern world that was pushing in.

One of the most beautiful characteristics of the now famous doctor was his life-long devotion to Margaret, his wife of the old fur-hunting days. "He treated her like a princess," says a missionary of that day. "In public and in private he was as loyal to her as if she had been a daughter of Victoria. His gallantry to her knew no bounds."

It was well understood that a slight to the Madame was a slight to the doctor. When the "Modeste" was at Vancouver the people of the fort gave the officers a picnic. On their return the doctor perceived his wife walking alone, carrying a heavy basket. Turning to an officer, — "Tut, tut, tut! What do you mean by letting a lady walk alone and carry a burden like that?" he cried, as he hastened to her assistance. If a servant entered her presence with his hat on — "Your manners, sir, your manners, before ladies!" was the punctilious reprimand. Old Oregonians remember the two, sitting in their porch like the Dutch burghers of Amsterdam, greeting the passers-by. The Madame took the liveliest interest in the doctor's benevolences, going about hunting up sick immigrants and putting herself to no end of trouble to help them. Many a time she sent petitioners home with a great Indian basket full of provisions, and out of her own stores supplied needed clothing. "It is a duty put upon us by our Heavenly Father," the Madame was wont to say.

Across the hall from the Madame's room was the

reception-room. "Two sofas were there," says a lady of 1846, "and I seldom found them empty. Always the new-comer in want and in trouble was directed to the house of Dr. McLoughlin. Always the front door of McLoughlin's house stood open. 'We must never leave the house alone, mother,' he would say. 'Some immigrant might come that needed our help.'"

Dr. McLoughlin had a fondness for lawyers. "Doctor," said the first chief justice of the Supreme Court of Oregon, as they sat one day in his office, "Doctor, they say that when you were governor of the Hudson's Bay Company at Vancouver those who approached you were expected to do so with their heads uncovered. How is that?"

Reddening and running his fingers through his hair the doctor stammered, "The French! the French! A very polite people, a very polite people!"

"Of course, Doctor," said the judge, "but—"

"The French! very polite, very polite," said the still confused doctor. Then, casting aside his embarrassment,—"Well, I will tell you. I was at the head of the Hudson's Bay Company in this country. When I came there were many Indians here. The success of the company depended on the way the Indians were treated and controlled. The lives of all the servants and employés, and the property of the company, were in my keeping. I knew enough of Indian character to know that, if those around me respected and deferred to me, the Indians would do the same."

Whenever the doctor, lively, impulsive, sympathetic, heard of a wrong his eye would flash; he was likely to blurt out a sudden oath, then blush — "The Lord forgive me, the Lord forgive me," crossing himself with tears. The play of pain and pleasure on the handsome, fair, flushed face that seemed to never grow old was a constant study to his friends. The transparent, baby-like skin revealed every heart-throb as the hot blood ran up to the roots of his snowy hair. Like all generous natures, the doctor was quick-tempered— none regretted it more than he. "No, no, no," might be the irritable answer to some unlucky petitioner. Then, in a moment the doctor would turn and beckon, "Here, here; what do you want?" and grant the request.

He could not hear a tale of woe without lending assistance; the multitude of such stories would fill a volume.

"He was, indeed, the Father of Oregon," says an aged American. "He came into our colony and led the procession the next Fourth of July. Every New Year's Day he used to go up one street and down another and call at every house. If any one was in trouble he saw that necessary aid was despatched at once — he did not trust it to others, he saw to it himself. We would have died when we came had it not been for Dr. McLoughlin. He gave us seed and clothing and the very bread we ate."

Such was the doctor's humility that although weighed down with the responsibility of the unpaid debts of the immigrants, he never alluded to any particular act of charity, neither would he accept interest on any debt when it was paid.

XXXIX

THE WHITMAN MASSACRE

1847

STILL the procession was on the plains. Still echoed the crack of the ox-whip and the captain's call — "Close up! close up! Why don't you keep close together? The Indians could kill all in the forward wagons before you 'd know it, and then come back and scalp the last one of you fellows here behind."

In the morning they milked the cows and put the milk in the churns. Up hill and down dale they went, jiggety-jog, all day long, until at night the butter was come.

And the Indians on the plains? At first they watched the invading whites. Still there were buffalo, still they were rich. But scant and scanter grew the pastures under the tread of immigrant cattle. Farther and farther retreated the buffalo. The timber by the streams disappeared. Bare and more barren grew the land. Unrest, distrust, collisions came. The Indians on the plains began to scalp the invading whites. More and more the march from the Black Hills to the Dalles became a rout, a retreat, a flight from pursuing famine. The measureless plains stretched under the brazen sun. The stony mountains, the grandest and most desolate on the continent, rimmed in the distant sky. The sand scorched, the dust suffocated, the wagons went to pieces. Furniture was thrown overboard; claw-footed tables and carved oak bureaus, the relics of an ancestral time, were left to warp in the prairie sun. Sentinel wolves lay in wait to devour the lagging cattle; Indians hov_ered in front and rear and ambuscade. Killed by Pawnees, plundered by Dacotahs, scalped by Sioux, compelled by Cheyennes to pay tribute for passing through their country, corralled by Blackfeet, crossing the battle-ground of hostile Snakes, still on the immi_grant pressed with the same restless spirit that inun_dated Europe and broke up the Roman Empire. The migration of races ebbs and flows like the waves of the sea. What if men's hearts died and women wept by the roadside?—the tide swept on. Fever and cholera and Indian arrows decimated their ranks. The road to Oregon was strewn with graves. Some buried their loved ones at dead of night in the middle of the road, that no red man might discover and desecrate the tomb.

Guided at last into the Grande Ronde by Whitman's beacon, "the fiery banner of friendship," "the pillar of smoke by day and the pillar of fire by night," the weary immigrants for the first time in months fell asleep without a guard, leaving their cattle to feed at will.

Five Crows camped close beside the trail. Here and there he peered into the wagons, offering, offering everywhere horses and robes and blankets to buy a white wife. And others besides Five Crows were look-ing for wives. Spruce young settlers dressed in their best, gray-beard widowers, and grizzly hunters all went out to look for wives.

Immigration broke up the peaceful life at Whitman's mission. The Indians grew excited and distrustful. "I have been over to the Willamette valley," said an old chief. " The Bostons are as many as the sands of the beach. If something is not done they will overwhelm the whole country."

Past the open prairies of Illinois, past Iowa in her primeval verdure, past the American desert that since has blossomed like the rose, five thousand people came in the autumn of 1847. Happily the granaries of Oregon were packed with wheat, — thousands of bushels without a market. The lands of the Cayuses lay directly in the path of immigration. They realized as others could not the impending danger of annihilation.

Mrs. Whitman wrote to her mother: " The poor Indians are amazed at the overwhelming numbers of Americans coming into the country. They seem not to know what to make of it. Husband is wearing out fast; his heart and hands are so full all the time that his brethren feel solicitous about him. His benevolence is unbounded, and he often goes to the extent of his ability and beyond in doing good to Indians and white men."

Over in the valley the Willamette Indians shrank back and back as the settlers staked their ancestral pastures into farms. Their faces assumed an habitual look of grief and sorrow. There were some collisions.

" Pay me for my land," cried a Willamette chieftain.

The settlers went on and built their cabins, giving slight heed to " those rascally Injuns."

" Pay me for my land," demanded the chieftain.

He kept up such a disturbance that the people sent for Governor Abernethy.

" Just wait a little," said the governor, soothingly. " A chief will come out from Washington to pay you for your land."

" When ? " demanded the Indian chief.

"With the immigrants some time this fall," answered the governor.

"So you. said before," retorted the chief, crushing the grass with his haughty stride. "Wait, wait, wait. This fall, this fall, and *this* fall. We are dying. We shall soon be gone. Our game is gone, our camas gone. You take our land, but we get no pay, no food, no blankets."

There was friction from the Willamette to the Walla Walla. In fact, from St. Joe to the Pacific the Indians began to look upon the immigrant as lawful prey.

"Why don't government protect us?" cried the immigrants.

"Why don't they build that line of posts to guard these citizens of our country?" groaned Whitman.

"Oh, they are fiddling still at the nigger strings," sang a careless happy-go-lucky. "Only slave States are favored now."

So one great national question eclipsed another.

There was a fracas when the first wagons reached the Dalles. One immigrant was killed and two wounded. A chief and several followers fell. Governor Abernethy hurried up there.

"The Indians steal our horses," said the immigrants. "They insult and annoy us in every way."

"The white men destroy our pastures," answered the Indians. "They have driven all the game from this part of the country."

The governor settled the matter. He had scarcely reached home when news of a second outrage reached his ears.

"Why don't the government come to our aid?" cried all the distressed people. "An Indian war may break upon us."

Up in the mountains Dr. Whitman had a saw-mill. The Cayuses did not love toil, they were a haughty race of herders; yet even the Cayuses had kept to work until they had fenced their little farms. But now they frowned and threw down their tools.

There was sickness in the immigration of 1847, the sickness of moving bodies subject to privation and exposure, mountain fever, dysentery, and measles.

The measles is an aggravating disease even to the whites in their cool homes in the East, very aggravating indeed to immigrants; but to Indians — it is death. They tried the traditional sweat-bath and a jump into the river. Day and night Dr. Whitman visited their lodges, warning and watching, but the moment he turned his back, moaning and groaning in the height of fever, they jumped into the cold Walla Walla, to pop up — dead.

"The *tew-ats!* the *tew-ats!*" cried the old men. "The Great Spirit is angry because we have discarded the *tew-ats*." The *tew-ats* came, but the sick ones died.

"Doct' Whit 'n," said Tamsucky, "Indian say kill all medicine men. They say take big one first, take you."

Dr. Whitman went over to the Willamette valley to consult with Dr. McLoughlin.

"Leave at once," entreated the doctor. "A Cayuse chieftain never jests."

"But I cannot leave," said Dr. Whitman. "My house is full of sick immigrants. I cannot leave. Besides, 'the hireling fleeth because he is an hireling.'"

All the way back Dr. Whitman met the plundered immigrants. They noted his careworn, anxious look. War hung in the air.

Tom McKay and his Canadians were driving cattle up the river to Fort Colvile when the measles overtook him at Fort Walla Walla. He sent for Dr. Whitman.

"I am worried about you, Doctor," said Tom. "The Indians think you are the cause of their sickness. And now since the Catholic priests are come the Indians want you to move away and let the Black Gowns open a mission."

"I know it," answered Dr. Whitman, groaning in spirit. "My poor Cayuses are distracted by their troubles. And the large number of whites stopping at the mission increases their suspicion. But what can I do? I cannot turn the poor immigrants sick and impoverished away. Can you not come and spend the winter with me, Tom?"

"I cannot, Doctor," answered the sick man. "But you must leave the Cayuses."

Pio-pio-mox-mox came up from California in October with heart still sore. Elijah was still unavenged. But what is this? His warriors fall sick around him. Death, plague, contagion lurks on every passing breeze. In every lodge the wail is heard, and yet — the immigrants are pouring over the mountains.

The immigrants had warning. Far out on the foot-hills there came a letter from Dr. Whitman, — "Make haste, the Indians are rising. Keep close together and under arms." So into the Oregon country came the worn-out immigrants of 1847.

"Be careful," said Dr. Whitman. "I fear there will be trouble. Do not provoke the savages." So with bated breath they endured every insult and pushed on into the valley.

"Shall we arm?" asked Mrs. Whitman.

"I have not a charge of powder in the house," answered the doctor.

Tom Hill was not there; he remained with Fremont in California; Dorion was not there, but the seed of their sedition was growing in the hearts of the frightened Cayuses. "Let us go to war," said Chief Tiloukaikt in the Indian council.

"War not," said Pio-pio-mox-mox. "The Americans fight like eagles. I have seen them in California. You will all be killed."

"Dr. Whitman does this," said Jo Lewis, a half-breed renegade, who came that autumn sick and starving with the immigrants. Dr. Whitman took him in, doctored, fed, and clothed him, and gave him work. He heard the whisper of discontent; his evil nature delighted to swell and spread it. It puffed his pride to see the eager Indians hanging on his word.

"Yes," said Jo Lewis, in the Indian council. "Dr. Whitman has been writing for two years to his friends in the East for poison to kill off the Cayuses. It has just come. When I was lying sick in the doctor's room I heard them talking."

"That must be so," chimed in Nick Finley, another half-breed. "One hundred and ninety-seven Indians have died already."

"He wants to get your beautiful spotted horses," added Jo Stanfield, a third half-breed.

In a lodge on the Umatilla the conspirators whispered — not with Tauitau, Five Crows, and Pio-pio-mox-mox. "They would betray us," said the half-breeds.

"I am a Cherokee," said Jo Lewis. "A few missionaries came, then thousands of Americans came, and drove us away from our country."

"That is what the Delaware said," chorused the
Indians.

"Yes, yes, yes; so they do always," added Jo Lewis.
"Dr. Whitman writes to the Americans that this is a
vast country, with healthy climate, rich soil, and bands
of horses. Now, see how they come and bring the
poison. Did not Jason Lee kill off the Willamettes?
Who gave the smallpox to the Blackfeet?"

Tamahas snatched his battle-axe. "If this be true —"
said Tiloukaikt.

"Of course it is true. The priest said so," said Jo
Lewis, as ready to lie about the priest as about Dr.
Whitman.

"My wife is sick," said Tamsucky. "Let him give
her medicine, and if she dies —" the death-wail in a
neighboring lodge ended the conclave.

Over at Lapwai Mr. Spalding's little daughter was
ten years old.

"Eliza talks Nez Percé like an Indian," said Mrs.
Spalding. "Let us send her to Waiilatpu, where there
are more people."

Eliza, mounted before her father, rode over the trails
that terraced the hillsides. Behind them followed a
dozen packhorses laden with grain to be ground at the
doctor's new grist-mill. Half-way between Fort Walla
Walla and the mission lay the camp of Pio-pio-mox-
mox. Mr. Spalding stopped to rest with the friendly
chief. As he sat on the buffalo-rug a Cayuse lifted the
door-curtain. "Is Dr. Whitman killed?" he asked.

That night the niece of Pio-pio-mox-mox died. They
buried her at Fort Walla Walla in the morning.

"My heart shall ever be with the Americans," said
Pio-pio-mox-mox, grasping Spalding's hand as he set
out after the funeral.

Seventy-five souls were sheltered under the roof of Whitman's mission, — orphans, and sick immigrants, who had found here an asylum for the winter. Day and night, like an angel of mercy, Mrs. Whitman passed from couch to couch. Her face was thin and her cheeks white with long and incessant watchings and labors with the sick.

"Doctor, I have my doubts," said Spalding, "about your turning your house into a hospital."

"I have no doubts about it," answered the doctor. "Looking after the immigrants is a part of my mission. That's what I'm here for."

"I hear that the priests are going to open a mission near you," said Spalding.

"I know it," answered the irritated doctor. "They want to buy this mission."

Just then a messenger reined up at the gate. "There is sickness at the lodges of Five Crows and Tauitau," he said. "They want you."

"I will come," said Dr. Whitman. It was thirty miles to the Umatilla.

"I will go with you," said Spalding.

They set off about sundown, and rode all night in a heavy rain. The Indian cocks were crowing when, drenched and chill, they reached the lodge of Sticcas in a low ravine. Sticcas spread fresh blankets and piled fuel on the lodge-fire. The missionaries lay down and slept till dawn.

The morning hymn of worship broke their slumbers. There was an appetizing breakfast of potatoes, squash, fresh beef, and wheat-bread baked by Sticcas' wife, taught by Mrs. Whitman. There was deathly silence in the lodge and in the village. After breakfast Dr. Whitman went over the Umatilla to the lodges of Five

Crows and Tauitau. As he rode the red men peeped and whispered —

"Bad Medicine."

"Kills our people."

"Takes our lands."

"We ought to avenge Elijah."

"Black Gowns better teachers."

Mr. Spalding preached to the Indians at the lodge of Sticcas. At four o'clock Dr. Whitman returned, pale and weary. "I met the Bishop and two priests at Tauitau's house," he said. "They invited me to tea, but I had not the heart to partake. They want to buy my mission." He dropped his head in thought. It was very hard for Dr. Whitman to give up his beloved mission, and particularly to rivals. "I told them to come over Tuesday," he resumed absently. "Now I must go."

"Not to-night," said Sticcas.

"Oh, yes; there are many sick, and I am needed." So at sundown the good horse of Dr. Whitman bore him over the hills homeward. He was weary and disheartened. How still it was! How dismal the village dirges on the November night wind! Tamsucky's wife was dead.

As the horse's hoofs died away Sticcas sat on the buffalo-rug before the fire and shook his head. Days before he had said to Dr. Whitman, "My people have decreed against you." The doctor made no reply. To-night he said to Spalding, "My people have decreed against the whites," but not another word would the old man say.

Throwing himself upon his couch of skins, the missionary could not sleep. He felt apprehensive for that lone rider in the night. On either side of him an Indian woman rocked to and fro and chanted the death-song. "For whom do you mourn, good woman?" he asked. But they made no answer. Only the depressing death-wail broke the silence.

Two days later Mr. Spalding turned to Waiilatpu. An old Indian woman put her hand on his horse's mane and whispered: "Go not to Waiilatpu. Look out for the people there. They are bad people."

"But I must go, good mother; my child is there."

Fear made him fleet. The very air whispered. Across the Walla Walla he met a horseman coming to meet him. It was the priest who was to visit that day at Waiilatpu. Riding ahead of the interpreter and the son of Tiloukaikt, who were lighting their pipes, he motioned to Mr. Spalding.

Apprehensive of evil, "What is the news?" he asked.

"Dr. Whitman is dead," answered the priest.

"Mrs. Whitman?"

"Dead also. Killed by the Indians."

"And my child?"

"Is safe with the captives. Escape! escape!" as he saw the interpreter and the son of Tiloukaikt approaching. "Here is my wallet — there is bread in it. Go!"

"But where shall I go?" was Spalding's despairing cry.

"I know not. You know the country better than I. All that I know is that the Indians say the order to kill Americans has been sent in all directions." Dazed, stunned, the missionary took the bread and turned into a bank of fog, just as the interpreter and the son of Tiloukaikt approached Father Brouillet.

Over the sugar-loaf barren hills a messenger came riding post to Lapwai. He dashed through the mission flower-beds, crushing the bachelor's buttons with his moccasins as he passed. An Indian never knocks. He sets his gun outside, lifts the latch, enters edgewise, shakes hands, and sits upon the floor. This messenger did not shake hands, did not sit down; he sidled along the wall of the schoolroom to the fireplace. Mrs. Spalding was teaching a class. Resting his elbow on the mantel he clutched his fingers in his tangled locks and looked at her. There was excitement and glitter in his eye. Mrs. Spalding felt nervous. She sent the children out of the room. "What news?" she asked in the Nez Percé tongue.

"Doct' Whit'n killed. All killed. Injun coming. Hurry." The runner sidled out of the room, strode over the flowers, dashed over the sugar-loaf barren hills, and out of sight.

Although naturally nervous Mrs. Spalding was very wise, very quiet, and in an emergency calm. She turned to her assistant — "What shall we do?"

"Escape as quickly as possible," he answered.

"No," said Mrs. Spalding. "We will throw ourselves upon the sympathy and protection of our Indians. Call Jacob and Eagle."

The two friendly chiefs were close by. They took Mrs. Spalding and her children to their camp. Scarcely had they gone when a troop came tearing over the hills, led by their own Chief Joseph, the Nez Percé. The house was ransacked, beds and bedding were stripped and taken away. Every drawer was opened, and the precious little keepsakes, brought from home, were taken and divided among the pillagers.

"Chief Joseph!" exclaimed Mrs. Spalding in amaze. "I cannot think it. We trusted him more than any other. His conduct has been most exemplary. Alas,

indeed, I am confused! The more we know our Indians the less we know them."

Half crazed, worn and torn, on foot up the river Touchet (Toosha), in six days Mr. Spalding reached Chief
Timothy's camp. He listened. His Nez Percés were
calling his name in prayer. It gave him hope. He entered. His Indians leaped with joy, and bore him to
his wife, safe in the care of Jacob and Eagle. But his
daughter? —

There were dead people lying all around at Waiilatpu.
Narcissa Whitman's fair hair floated in blood. A few
escaped; the women and children were captives; the
rest, thirteen or more, were dead. There was a smell of
blood and powder in the air, the windows were broken,
the mission plundered.

"Mamma! mamma!" cried the parched lips of little
Helen Mar Meek, sick with the measles. But mamma
could come no more, and the sweet child died of neglect.

Narcissa, the snowy Joan, led all the host of women
to the conquest of the West, an innumerable train that
is following yet to this day. The snowy Joan led her
hosts; and, at last, like Joan of old, she ascended to
God with the crown of a martyr.

Pio-pio-mox-mox sat in his lodge. Again the Cayuse
lifted the door-curtain. "Doct' Whit'n is killed."

Pio-pio-mox-mox sat very quiet while the voluble
young man ran over that day of horrors.

"What part had you in it?" inquired the chief, fix-
ing his Egyptian eye upon the herald. Proud of his
exploits, intent only on making them great as possible,
the runner said, "Me? I wounded one, I struck one,
and I killed one."

"Take that young man and hang him to the nearest tree," cried Pio-pio-mox-mox, in a tone of thunder.

The attendants seized the boaster, and before he realized it was not a jest, the noose tightened about his neck. In a few moments a corpse dangled from the boughs of a rugged old cottonwood.

Five Crows heard the awful tale. Then he rode over to the mission. There was a beautiful girl there, a young school-teacher, with eyes like Mrs. Whitman's. She was just from the East, and sick with a fever. Her rose-and-lily beauty captured the heart of the savage who had tried so long to buy a white wife. They dragged her shrieking to his lodge. The rest were distributed among the Indians.

McKinley had removed to another post. The new man in charge at Fort Walla Walla seemed afraid to assist the Americans in this time of trouble. He turned away the few fleeing fugitives that struggled to his door. He did, however, despatch a messenger to Fort Vancouver.

The thunderbolt had fallen. Douglas at once sent word to Governor Abernethy at Oregon City. Chief Factor Ogden set out the same day with sixteen armed Canadians, in December snow and rain, up the inclement Columbia to ransom the captives.

The colonial legislature was in session when the panting messenger from Fort Vancouver landed at the Falls. All that morning they had been listening to the governor's annual message, treating chiefly of the embarrassments of the Indian question. When at two o'clock Governor Abernethy communicated the fact of an actual massacre, the excitement knew no bounds. Nesmith leaped to his feet with a resolution to despatch fifty riflemen to protect the mission at the Dalles. The session adjourned to call a mass meeting of citizens that night. Several members went over immediately to consult with Dr. McLoughlin.

"Dead? Oh, those treacherous Cayuses! I warned him, I warned him," cried the old doctor, pounding the floor with his cane. "Why did he not heed?" Presently recovering himself, "Yes, yes, if there is to be an Indian war the Dalles is your Gibraltar. Hold the Dalles."

In fifteen hours from the time they enrolled their names, the Spartan band of fifty were on their way to the upper country.

The governor issued a call for five hundred men to rendezvous at Oregon City on Christmas day. Those whom Whitman had befriended leaped to avenge his death; heroes who had toiled at his side in 1843, and immigrants of succeeding years who had hailed his mission as the first civilized landmark beyond the Rockies.

Applegate, Lovejoy, and Abernethy on their personal credit secured a loan at Fort Vancouver. The women of Oregon City baked and sewed and tore up their last sheets for shirts, and out of bits of bunting made a flag. Trembling fingers sewed the stripes and stitched on the stars. Farmers on horseback came packing through the woods old buffalo-guns and flint-locks, beans and bacon, and lead and blankets — whatever could be spared from their scanty stores. Joe Meek, the trapper, resigned his seat in the legislature to go overland as a delegate to Washington with despatches for aid.

The Indians regarded the settlers at Champoeg as their own people.

"Will they desert us? Will they join their Indian kindred?" queried the anxious settlers.

Happily Tom McKay solved that. Like a centaur he rode up and down the prairie. In French, in English, in Chinook he gathered them in: "Pierre, François, Antoine, come, come to the war!"

The snow proved too deep to get word over the Sierras to California. Shut in, Oregon must fight her way alone.

XL

THE CAYUSE WAR

1848

AT the peril of his life Ogden went into the Indian country and despatched couriers calling for a council. The chiefs came to Fort Walla Walla to treat with their old friend, the fur-trader, and if possible to ward off the retribution they feared from the angry Bostons. The great fire of driftwood from the Spokane forests roared in the chimney. The chiefs spread their palms to the blaze and waited. Ogden noted a troubled look in certain faces, but he was not there to secure the murderers. He only hoped to secure the unhappy captives before news came up from the lower country. His short, fat figure, in marked contrast with their tall ones, appeared still more rotund from his bulging, ample cloak. His otter-skin cap lay on the floor. With the grizzly locks trailing over his shoulders and his keen eye fixed on theirs, the trader began:

"Friends and relations, I regret to see that all the chiefs are not here. Repeat to them what I say. We have been among you for thirty years without shedding blood. We are traders, and of a different nation from the Americans. But recollect, we do not supply you with ammunition to kill the Americans. They are the same color as ourselves, speak the same language, are children of the same God. Their cruel fate causes our hearts to bleed. Besides this wholesale butchery, have you not robbed the Americans passing peacefully through your country and insulted their women? You tell me your young men did this without your knowledge. Why do we make you chiefs, if you have no control over your young men? You are unworthy the name of chief. You, hot-headed young men, you pride yourselves on your bravery. You think no one can match you. Do not deceive yourselves.

"If the Americans begin war, war will not end until every one of you is cut off from the face of the earth. Your people have died. So have others. Dr. Whitman did not poison them. God commanded they should die. We are weak mortals. We must submit. It is merely advice that I give you. I promise you nothing. We have nothing to do with your quarrels. On my return, if you wish it, I will see what can be done for you. I do not promise to prevent war. Deliver me the captives. I will pay a ransom. That is all."

Silence followed for a space of ten minutes. Then Tauitau rose up slowly and spoke with deliberation: —

"The — fur-traders — are — married — to — Indian — women. They — are — our — brothers. I — cannot — refuse — my — brother's — request."

Another silence; then Tiloukaikt rose, tall and dark, dignified and savage: —

"They are our brothers. They bury their dead along with ours. Chief, your words are weighty, your hairs are gray. We have known you a long time. You have had an unpleasant journey to this place. I cannot keep the families back. I make them over to you, which I would not do to another younger than yourself."

"I have nothing to say," said Pio-pio-mox-mox. "I know the Americans are changeable. Still, I agree with my brother. The whites are our best friends; we follow your advice. The captives shall be given up."

All day the council lasted, and at night they still talked by the flickering light of the driftwood fire. Outside, the snow beat up against the windows.

Blankets, shirts, guns, ammunition, to the value of $500, lay on the council floor.

"There," said Ogden, as an attendant displayed the tempting array, "these are for you. Hasten, now; bring me the captives and receive the ransom."

On Christmas Eve the messengers were speeding over the new-fallen snow to Lapwai, to the Umatilla, to every lodge where a prisoner lay waiting her uncertain doom.

What joy to the poor captives, terrified by old women fierce as Waskema, who came round flourishing their dull tomahawks, only too eager to put them to death; girls who had seen their fathers slain, women who had been snatched from their husbands and brothers, all to be dragged to lonely lodges, a prey to savage passion.

It was yet early morning when the chiefs came to the lodge of Five Crows. On a couch of costly skins lay the beautiful white girl. For a savage Five Crows had been kind to his white wife.

"Don't go," he pleaded. "All horses," he waved his hand toward the herds on the hills, "all cattle," feeding in the lower meadows, "all skins," they were heaped in the lodge of this rich Indian, "all slaves," there were dozens at his command, "all house," close by stood Five Crows' log house with glass windows, "all land," with a gesture toward the young woman — "yours."

She only shook her head.

"Then let me go with you, live with white people," begged the Indian suitor.

Still she shook her head.

He waved the staring domestics back. With his own hands the Cayuse chief broiled her venison, and brought her tea, and knelt before her couch of skins. Tradition says he was a handsome Indian, taller than his half-brother, Chief Joseph, and fairly educated. But the white girl dreaded his eagle plumes and raven hair; she shrank from the touch of his moccasined toe, the brush of his painted robe. She did not hate, she feared him.

The impatient chiefs outside kept calling and spatting their hands, "Oh, Five Crows! Five Crows! Five Crows!"

Those voices seemed her deliverance. Still flushed with fever, she tottered toward the door. Five Crows sprang to her assistance, pleading at every step. He spread a new blanket and a tanned robe on the saddle of her horse — and still he would detain her. His was a lover's parting, reluctant, seeking every pretext for 'elay. The chiefs interfered and ended the scene. Supported by her savage escort, the poor girl reached the fort.

Mr. Ogden came out. The tender-hearted trader lifted her in his arms as a father would.

"Thank God; I have got you safe at last! I had to pay the Indians more for you than for all the other captives, and I feared they would never give you up."

Scarcely were the captives in his hands when a rumor reached the fort — "The Americans are coming up the Columbia."

"Tell it not to the Indians. 'T will be our death," said Ogden.

It turned his hair white to think of the situation with all those suspicious Indians camped around the ill-defended fort. The Spaldings had not arrived. Dare he wait? They might be cut off. Two days and two

23

nights Ogden paced the fort and listened; he dared not
sleep.   Then came the Spaldings, escorted by their
Nez Percés from Lapwai. Ogden paid their ransom
and hurried them into the ready boats.

It was the morning of New Year's Day of 1848.

"The wind is cold; cover, cover," said old Sticcas,
taking off his cap for one of the rescued ones.   "Cover
ears," he said, compassionately tying his handkerchief
over the head of another.

"How fiercely yon Indian rides!" exclaimed Spalding, as the boats shoved off with their shivering passengers.

A howling horseman came into sight, lashing
his pony, white with foam, with the cruel double-
thonged whip tied to his wrist. Another came, and
another, fifty infuriated Cayuses dashed down to the
water and followed along the river's edge with angry
shouts. They had caught the rumor, "The Bostons
are coming." The trader and his ransomed had but
escaped.

Ogden prudently kept his boats on the farther side,
and his Canadians rowed for life. It was an exciting
moment.

"Sing," cried Ogden, in tense agitation.

The Canadians struck up the spirited —

"*Sur la feuille ron — don don don,*" to steady their
strokes as they shot away.

Outwitted, sold, the wrathful Indians jerked up their
steeds by the cruel horsehair bits.   Blood dripped with
the foam.   The usual Indian adieu is a gay yell.   This
was a taunting, scornful, satanic laugh, as they waved
their tomahawks and watched them, singing, glide beyond their grasp.   Then they turned to the lodge of
Pio-pio-mox-mox and threatened his life, because he

and his Walla Wallas would not arm to meet " the Bostons."

Even Tauitau said: " If the Bostons come to fight us I will not raise my gun. I will sit in my house. If they will, they may kill me. I shall not resist."

The Nez Percés refused to join them. Only Five Crows and the murderers were left to lead the hostiles.

Swiftly gliding down the Columbia the rescued ones met the fifty riflemen landing at the Dalles. Ogden was amazed at the daring of this handful.

" Go back with us, go back," he urged. " You can do nothing. All the tribes will unite against you. The idea of sending a party up there this winter is the wildest notion I ever heard of. You had better burn the mission buildings here and go back to the valley."

But the Americans firmly answered, " No," and proceeded to fortify the mission at the Dalles.

Worried, troubled, nervous from loss of sleep, Peter Skeen Ogden went on to Fort Vancouver. Douglas immediately despatched a letter to the anxious settlement at the Falls.

It was Sunday morning when the courier arrived and found the governor and his people at church. The welcome message was read from the pulpit: —

Mr. Ogden has this moment arrived with three boats from Walla Walla, and I rejoice to say he has brought down all the women and children from Waiilatpu and Mr. and Mrs. Spalding. . . . Mr. Ogden will visit the Falls on Monday. . . .

In haste, yours respectfully,

JAMES DOUGLAS.

Portland was but a village in the woods, but it fired a salute as the boats went by; again the salute rang out as the gray-haired old hero landed his burden of sixty-two souls at the city by the Falls. Governor Abernethy received the rescued ones, and in the name of humanity thanked the courageous chief factor for his inestimable service.

Many of the women were nervous wrecks. Dr. McLoughlin received some; Governor Abernethy some; the doors of every home were open, as borne on beds they were distributed among the settlers.

Fired at the sight, scarcely better equipped than the patriots at Valley Forge, the little army of five hundred pressed into the Indian country. Fort Vancouver looked on amazed as the daring boats went by.

"Wildest attempt I ever heard of," muttered Ogden, who had returned to the fort. "All the Indians of the country will be upon us. The Cayuses, the Walla Wallas, and the Nez Percés are so intermarried they will fight as one."

The old chief factor's hands trembled. More than anything else the company dreaded an Indian war. It meant the ruin and rout of their business, the breaking up of fur brigades, and the end of big returns to London.

"I hear that they have prohibited the sale of ammunition to the Indians," continued Ogden, shaking his disapproving locks. "They even found fault with me because I paid them a few handfuls for portage at the Dalles."

"Prohibited the sale of ammunition!" exclaimed Douglas. "That is a dangerous measure. It will only excite them more and more. They will starve without ammunition, and distress may drive them to dangerous courses. They will prey upon the settlements and slaughter cattle when they can no longer hunt the deer."

" Just so, just so," assented Ogden from his lookout on the porch. " If they tumble the nations down on their heads we are not to blame. There goes another boat-load."

With the whoops of the old voyageurs McKay's men dragged the only piece of artillery, a rusty nine-pounder, around the Cascades in a driving snow.

The painted Cayuses were out on their painted horses, galloping on the hills. It was a thrilling sight. Every eminence was filled with Indian men and women, as on a grand review, to witness the defeat of the Bostons. They looked with contempt on these immigrants. Had they not borne with meekness and patience the insults and robberies of the preceding autumn, and autumns and autumns before?

" Ho-ha-ha-ha-ha—a ! " laughed the demoniac chorus on the hills. " The Bostons are women. We will kill them with clubs. We will go to the valley and steal their women. Never shall the Americans drink of the waters of the Umatilla."

" Ho-ho-ho-ho—o ! " screamed War Eagle, chief of the dreamer-drummers, prancing out in face of the foe. " I am a great *tew-at*. I bear a charmed life. I can swallow molten lead ; powder and shot cannot harm me ! "

" Well, then, let him swallow this," said Tom McKay, raising his silver-mounted rifle. One click — the boaster headlong bit the dust. A shot from another shattered the arm of Five Crows. He dropped his gun — like smoke the Indian cavalry disappeared, demoralized by the sudden and unexpected loss of their leaders whom they had supposed invulnerable. In Homeric song the leaders fought the battles ; so here in this Pacific Iliad. The spectators melted from the hills.

"That is the Indian of it; they fight and flee," exclaimed the impetuous American, Colonel Gilliam. "They did it in the Black Hawk War, they did it in the Seminole."

Where hundreds had lately stood, now a barren and apparently unoccupied country stretched out in silence. But every rock and ravine and hillock and sand-hollow along the old immigrant road sheltered a foe. All day until sunset they sprang from their ambuscades in the masterly attacks and retreats of Indian warfare. All day the Indian fusees picked off the volunteers in their march to the upper country. At night for miles ahead the Cayuse signal-fires burned like sleepless red eyes on the hilltops. Without water, almost without food, without tents, and half clad, in the dead of winter, the little army hurried on toward Waiilatpu. Exhausted, famished, chilled, the Americans reached the camp of Pio-pio-mox-mox. The old chief came out to meet them. At his belt hung Siskadee's shot-pouch.

"We are not one with the Cayuses," he said. "We have no part in the war."

"We are glad to hear it," answered Colonel Gilliam. "We hear that you fought with Lieutenant Fremont in California and that you acted bravely. Your conduct convinces us that you are an honorable Indian. Have you beef to sell?"

Pio-pio-mox-mox drove up his herds. In an hour the savory odor of kouse and bouillon filled the camp. The old chief remained to watch proceedings, and smoked his pipe in a long and friendly talk. Over toward Waiilatpu a few thin lodge-fires rose against the sky.

"That is the spot," said the old chief, pointing. "My people were not there."

The volunteers found only a heap of burned adobes on the site of the Whitman mission. Torn letters, shattered glass and china lay among the trampled poppies. Even the orchard was tomahawked away. Wolves had uncovered the shallow graves, and the remains of the martyr-missionary and his household lay scattered on the wintry plain. Tresses of tangled gold identified the disfigured brow of the queenly Joan of the West.

The bodies were gathered up and reinterred, and above the mound of his little Helen Mar the old trapper, Joe Meek, swore vengeance as he hastened on to Washington. Six weeks later he met his old comrade, Captain Bridger, in a mountain pass.

"And my little Mary Ann?" he asked.

"She, too, is dead," said the trapper by the camp-fire.

Poor old Sticcas! evading the gibes and threats of his countrymen, he hunted up the doctor's cattle, and collecting what he could of the stolen property, delivered them to the volunteers, — money, watches, books, — and then with Tauitau left for the mountains to wait till the war was over.

"Stay a moment," cried the colonel. "Before you go, tell me, where are the murderers?"

With a frightened look to see that he was unobserved by his people, old Sticcas waved his hand and whispered, "Fleeing up the Tucanon."

Colonel Gilliam had thrown up a fort out of the burned adobes. Leaving his wounded there, he continued the pursuit. On the fifth day, after an all-night march, he surprised a camp at the mouth of the Tucanon. An old man came out with one hand on his head and one on his heart.

"We are the people of Pio-pio-mox-mox," he said in bad Chinook; "we are friends."

"He lies. It is a cloak," muttered the impatient volunteers.

The camp was full of painted warriors, apparently just making their toilet for battle.

Still the old man reiterated, "We are Pio-pio-mox-mox *tilicum* [people]."

The volunteers had their fingers on their triggers.

"Don't shoot," commanded the colonel. "Where are the murderers?"

"Fled to the land of Red Wolf," pantomimed the Indian.

"Fleeing, fleeing, fleeing," muttered the disappointed colonel. "Who can catch an Indian in his native hills?"

"This is their stock — take it," said the old man, waving his hand around toward the cattle — Tiloukaikt's cattle.

The hills were covered with herds. Riding up the precipitous highlands, the little army looked down on the winding Snake. It was full of horses and cattle swimming over by thousands and ascending the opposite bank.

"Collect the stock," commanded the colonel. Dark faces peeped and whispered in the shadow of the camp.

The volunteers set out to drive five hundred head before them to Fort Walla Walla.

A flash, a whoop; the land was alive with Indians in all the fury of savage warfare. The painted camp was out, the Palouses sprang from the very earth, the herds were lost in the fierce-running battle of the Tucanon.

For thirty hours the firing never ceased. At last the struggling, fighting, fleeing remnants of the almost entrapped Americans escaped beyond the Touchet. After the hand-to-hand struggle at the ford the confusion of battle gave way to the death-wail on the farther shore. Nothing but the superior arms and ammunition of the Americans saved them from utter rout.

"Something must be done, and done at once," ran the report sent to Governor Abernethy, "or we shall have the Indians in the valley in a month. There are one hundred and fifty of our boys in the very heart of the enemy's country almost without ammunition and wholly without bread."

Just then the United States transport "Anita" entered the Columbia, seeking recruits for the Mexican War raging below. The captain whistled when he discovered Oregon herself in arms.

"Our settlers are scattered throughout the valleys," said Governor Abernethy, "many of them isolated and lying in such a position that they could be swept off in a night, and the Indians be in the mountains out of reach next morning. Our policy is to keep the Indians busy in their own country, and by this means keep them out of the valley, but we have no money, no munitions of war. Our patriotic volunteers are destitute of clothing, tents, and provisions, even while in the field. Our powder is gathered up in half-pounds and parcels as the settlers have brought more or less in for their own use. This will soon give out."

The transport left the Columbia and returned to Monterey, promising to get word to the United States as soon as possible. Then more than ever isolated, Oregon felt itself at the end of the world. How long would it take for an envoy to reach the capital? How long for a ship to double Cape Horn?

The measles had followed the track of the immigrants and found a nesting place in the Willamette valley.

Whole Indian villages lay prostrate. Old Waskema in distress flitted from camp to camp; she squatted by every fire. With her knotted cane in hand she stood on the edge of the forest and pointed toward the settlements — "Skookum tum-tum gone. Squaw man stay. Quick in the night, quick, cut down the Boston people," hoarsely she whispered to Koosta, chief of the Molallas.

In old time Waskema told the fortunes of chase and of battle. Could she still divine? Koosta sat in his smoky hut and watched her with the luminous eyes of a hunted deer. But he made no move. The moans of his children filled the hut. Waskema flew wild, stamping her feet and tearing her hair. "Shame! shame! shame!" she cried. "Sick, all die. No medicine, no food, no powder. Boston take land, take game, poison us, starve us." Her frenzy was fearful to look upon. A sick baby stretched its thin hand for a wee little muskrat toasting on the coals. A skinny old man came in with a sack of bread, begged at Champoeg.

Old Waskema's *tamanowas* (spirit) had a strange charm for the young men. Down in the damp marsh grew the Oregon yew; they were shaping it into arrows. She sanctioned what they desired — bloodshed and plunder.

Eighty Klamaths came over the southern mountains, and camped at the head of Abiqua creek, a branch of the Willamette, near Koosta's camp. Another force camped in the passes of the Callapooias — waiting. The Warm Spring Indians hung like a cloud at the foot of Mt. Jefferson. The Klickitats were riding down the zigzag mountain passes ready to join them.

It was March, raw and windy and squally with snow,

when the howling Klamaths sounded the whoop on the hills. They began shooting cattle, raiding cabins, and closing round the house of the *hyas tyee*, the principal white man, into whose log house the frightened settlers fled. A postman came in sight; he put spurs to his steed and gave the alarm up the valley. Before sunset sixty men and boys had chased the Klamaths to their rock-walled, brush-covered camp on the Abiqua bottom. From a rocky ledge at early dawn there came a flight of arrows. The American rifles blazed. In the cold and drizzling rain lay the dead. Among the fallen warriors was an Indian woman, withered and shrunken, with a drawn bow in her dying grasp. It was old Waskema.

The Klamaths fled over the southern mountains. The rising in the valley was quelled, but the measles went on silently, surely, depopulating the camps of the red men.

Governor Abernethy issued a third call for men. With dismay the Indians beheld a second army advancing into the upper country. Already their herds were ruined, ammunition gone, their families scattered. The Cayuses as a people had no heart in the war. Every day at sunset the mothers lamented the act that had brought this trouble upon them. The opposition narrowed to the few who had participated in the massacre, and some sympathizers who had assisted their escape. In April the army summed up the situation:

"Where are the murderers?"

"Fled beyond the Rockies."

"Will you, Pio-pio-mox-mox and Tauitau, deliver them up on their return?"

"Yes, if you will give us peace."

"Where is Jo Lewis?"

"Escaped to the Mormons."

"Who are the Mormons?"

"Dwellers in a magic city that has risen on Salt Lake."

"Where is Five Crows?"

"Dying at the camp of Chief Joseph."

"Where is Chief Joseph?"

"Quiet in his own valley. He has taken no part in the war."

"And Chief Ellice?"

"Dead. He and sixty of his men went to hunt elk in the mountains and all died of the measles."

Declaring the Cayuse lands forfeited to the United States, and leaving a garrison at the Whitman Fort to watch for the murderers and meet the autumn immigrants, the volunteers gave up the chase and returned to their homes. But Colonel Gilliam came not back — he, too, was numbered with the dead.

An autumn immigration of a thousand people entered the country unmolested — but yet no word from Washington. Unaided the little colony had fought it out alone.

XLI

THE BARQUE "JANET"

1847

PASSING to and fro, Dr. McLoughlin noted the growth of the brisk young settlement of Portland. He decided to establish David there, and with a small fortune in gold McLoughlin's son became the junior partner in the rising firm of Pettygrove & Crosby.

The finest ship that traded on the coast in those days was the teakwood East India built barque " Janet," owned and run by Captain Dring, an Englishman. The captain was a tar of furious temper and iron will. His meek little wife sailed with him, and his lovely blond daughter, Trottie, the Queen of the Sea.

The " Janet" entered the Willamette for a load of wheat. The firm of Pettygrove, Crosby & McLoughlin despatched their junior partner to the ship. There David McLoughlin's eye fell on the captain's laughing daughter with her brown curls flying in the wind. Trottie, too, saw the young merchant with black locks waving on his velvet collar. The captain saw no flush, no blush of pleasure; the two had met and passed before, in rocking ships in an English harbor.

Gala evenings followed, as the teakwood ship lay in the Willamette. Whale-oil lamps flickered and lanterns were hung aloft when the deck was cleared for dancing. Grave elders sat around on tea-chests and bales of merchandise, beating time with their toes to the piping sailor's band. And under the Oregon stars Trottie danced with David. Trottie's mother smiled upon the young American, — he had travelled, he had read, he could sing, his dress was faultless, his manners Parisian. In the jig, the reel, and the Highland fling he out-stepped them all, and his contagious laughter was a tonic. People said, "David the heir will marry the captain's daughter."

Just then the Whitman massacre upheaved the Oregon world. All the men were hurrying away to the war. But David stayed and stood with Trottie before the captain.

"Good God, Trottie! What are you thinking of, — to tie yourself up in this unheard-of corner of the world, where Indians come in and massacre settlers without warning! I'd rather bury you at sea. And isn't that Frenchman waiting for you up there at the Islands? What will he say when I get back to Hono-lulu?" Trottie turned white.

David was thunderstruck, but Trottie clung to his arm, and the bluff captain dared not send him from the ship. The cargo was not complete; David could hold him a little. He must go to the Champoeg warehouse that day; he felt sure the captain would relent on his return. So David went tearing up the Willamette, revolving a thousand plans for winning his Queen of the Sea.

How impatient the young man was! How snail-like the Indian packers carried the wheat on their backs from the storehouse to the bateau! How slow the swift-glanc-ing paddles beat the foam! "Faster, faster," he cried.

"He is mad," said the Indians, as they tore back down the Willamette. All was hushed save the rapping row-locks and the rough breathing of the heavy working rowers. Some one hailed him at the Falls. He heard not. His father watched him with regret.

"Halt! Carry!" By main strength and awkward-
ness, under the Chinook moon the Indians transferred
the wheat to the barge below the Falls. All night he
flew; obstacles vanished; new hope filled his heart as
he neared the old familiar dock. He laughed. He
will greet her in a moment. He was opposite the
shingle camp called Portland, where the store of Pettygrove, Crosby & McLoughlin was most conspicuous
on the shore.

"The ship! where is the ship?" he cried.

"Gone," said an idler on the shore. "Sailed yesterday. Carried news of the Whitman massacre to the
Islands."

A few empty canoes rocked idly on the sea-green
water. He stepped into one; two fishing Indians took
the paddles. Without rest, without food, he gave the
word, "Vancouver."

But the wharf at Vancouver was vacant and deserted.

"Send out the 'Cadboro';' chase her. I must catch
the 'Janet,'" he cried to Douglas. But the "Cadboro'"
had gone the day before. He called to the voyageurs,
"Fifty beaver skins to the crew that makes the 'Janet'
to-day."

David's barque flew down the Columbia. He leaned
forward, glass in hand, to catch the gleam of a sail.
Oak Point, Coffin Rock, Pillar Rock, Astoria, a day,
a night, at last there, beyond the bar, with sails set,
the "Janet" stood leagues away at sea. And the crew
sang on —

> "Thy heart was made for laughter,
>   My heart's in tears to-day;
> Tears for a fickle mistress,
>   Flown from its love away.
>   I've loved thee long and dearly,
>   I'll love thee, sweet, for aye!"

Crouched in a berth, her long, overhanging 'curls swaying with that sea-rocked ship, lay Trottie Dring, her eyes hot and tearless, and her heart numb. Away into the great Pacific she went, never again to catch a glimpse of the Oregon coast. The surf-beaten rocks on the shore seemed not harder than the **flinty heart** that divided herself and her lover.

From that day the veneering of civilization fell off from David like an egg-shell. He lost all interest in the store. Indian impatience of restraint, Indian instincts and inherited tendencies triumphed over the Scotch in his veins. He roved continually. He gave himself up to dissipation, and was happy only with his red friends in the forest. He wedded the daughter of a chief.

XLII

THE DISCOVERY OF GOLD

1848

THE volunteers came home to their wives and sweethearts — the Indian scare was over. The old idyllic life went on, more united, more ideal after the tempest. Up and down the tributary valleys of the Willamette many a young couple staked out their square mile. Like shadows the Indians drew back into the forest, dumb, patient, vanishing. The volunteers put aside their buffalo-guns. The war-horse captured in battle was hitched to the plough. Harvest was at its height when a schooner from Yerba Buena came into the Willamette. Almost before his barque was moored the Yankee trader began to buy knives, spades, picks, pans, flour.

"What are you going to do with that sort of cargo, Cap'n?" inquired the settlers, handing over their unused picks and spades.

"Oh, hardware for the Spaniards," was the nonchalant reply as he stacked them away in the schooner. With lading complete and sails trimmed, the Yankee captain, by way of good-bye, held up a sack of gold-dust. "The hills of California are made of that," he said. An incredulous burst of laughter followed the retreating ship.

The brig from Newburyport came rushing in for picks and pans and flour. Douglas entered the Columbia from the Islands at the same time. "Pooh-pooh!

24

't is all a fake," he said, but certain letters dispelled all doubt. Marshall, one of those enthusiasts of 1844, had really reached the land where money grew.

The quietude of that summer was broken. The Cayuse pony and the Chinook canoe carried the news to the remotest settlement. The farmer left his plough in the furrow, his sickle in the wheat, crops remained unharvested. Women and boys took charge of the shops and stores in Oregon City, men left their wives to hold their claims, milk the cows, and keep the children. The editor ran off and left the paper, the blacksmith quit his anvil, the carpenter his plane and saw, the legislature adjourned for want of a quorum. Judge Burnett, the chief justice of Oregon, left the bench and said to Dr. McLoughlin: —

"What shall we do? Can we make the trip with a wagon?"

"Yes," said the doctor. "Get Tom McKay for a pilot. He has been back and forth with pack-trains for twenty years. He knows the road better than any one but La Framboise."

In eight days Burnett's "ragged regiment" held a barbecue feast, and one hundred and fifty men and fifty wagons rolled out on the California road, with provisions for six months and planks for gold rockers in the bottom of their wagons.

Pettygrove sold the site of the city of Portland for a pack of leather and left for the mines. In a few weeks the trappers' heavy trail became a broad and beaten highway, thronged every hour with men and boys on foot, in wagons and on horseback. The soldiers, fresh from the Cayuse war, rich in tales of adventure, passed their evening in song and dance around the camp-fires in the valleys, while the signal fires of Shastas, Rogues, and

Klamaths glowed on neighboring heights. The Indians, who had never seen such invading armies of palefaces, fled to their mountain fastnesses in consternation, or now and then, from behind some shelving rock, discharged a shower of bright reed arrows pointed with volcanic glass. One evening, as the sun sent his last lingering rays against the lofty range of the Sierras, the Oregonians camped in the shining valleys of gold. These sons of adventure, who had blazed the way to Oregon and had trounced the savage, now gayly raced the hills in search of the gilded treasure.

"What if the Indians should come?" said the women left in Oregon City.

"Don't be afraid," laughed the fatherly Dr. McLoughlin. "I set a watch on the bluff every night to look after the settlement."

Panthers howled on the bluff. Indians pitched their teepees in the dark wood, and once, some years before, they shot their arrows down into the village.

The lately silent river became noisy with commerce. From a village in the woods, Portland leaped to a city, with twenty vessels waiting for cargoes at a time, all paying in bags of gold-dust, and all heading for California. Provision stores opened everywhere, prices went up among the stars; four bushels of apples from the Willamette brought five hundred dollars in San Francisco. Tons of Oregon eggs sold for a dollar apiece on the Sacramento.

One hundred and fifty Canadians deserted Fort Vancouver in a body. Douglas and Ogden hired Indians to supply their places.

The rush from Oregon began in 1848, almost a year before the rest of the world heard of the find at Sutter's mill. After six weeks on the Yuba the Oregonians

were ready to return with their sacks full of gold-dust,
—but how? The harbor was full of ships rotting at the
wharves. As in Homer's lotus-land, every sailor that
touched the golden shore straightway forgot home and
friends and native land and longed ever to remain
eating the golden poppy.

In February a hundred Oregonians were waiting for
passage from San Francisco. Finally the captain of
the old East India ship, "Janet,' 'accepted $10,000 to
make a flying trip to Oregon. So the Argonauts came
home, bringing the Golden Fleece, bags full, tea can-
isters full, pockets full of the beautiful shining dust.
It was weighed like wheat or bran at $16 an ounce in
trade. Men carried gold-dust in pails through the
streets, women stored it away in coffee-pots and pickle-
jars. Milk-pans full of it sat on the shelves. Home-
comers on horseback threw sacks of it over the
fence into the tall grass to lie over-night, or until they
took a bite of supper. So great waste resulted from
continual measurements that the colonial legislature
concluded to mint it into dollars, and a missionary
mechanic hammered the dies out of wagon tires. Thus,
the Oregon colony exercised all the prerogatives of an
independent power, organized government, levied taxes,
coined money, raised armies, and carried on war.

Clerk Allen of Fort Vancouver was on that ship with
gold from Captain Sutter in payment of his almost out-
lawed debts at Fort Vancouver. As he came up the
Columbia the quick eye of Allen caught sight of Chief
Factor James Douglas and his family and servants in a
brigade of canoes just entering the Cowlitz.

A hurried colloquy ensued.

"I am removing to Fort Victoria," said Douglas.
"You will find Mr. Ogden at the fort."

The haughty Douglas stood in his canoe and watched the Argonauts go by. Nelia, his wife, never looked more matronly than on that spring morning of 1849 when sitting there, with her rosebud family around her, she looked her last on Oregon. Allen dropped off at Fort Vancouver, and with him some of the Canadian servants with their piles of $30,000 and $40,000 apiece. Ogden sat with his head on his hand; the fort was desolate, trade abandoned.

"Yes, Douglas is gone," he said sadly. "He saw how matters were going. He could n't stand it, he left; he was too strict a disciplinarian to stay and see the rack and disorder."

Allen had a conference with Ogden in the office, then he took $150,000 in silver coin, nailed it in little boxes, loaded it into a canoe, and followed Douglas up to Puget Sound. They reached Fort Victoria on Vancouver's Island in safety. Three years later James Douglas became the first governor of British Columbia, and his first official act was to summon all the Indians around Victoria and pay them in full for their lands. Sir James, knighted by the queen, ruled long and wisely. Settlers came from England and built their ivied halls and wayside inns, and for many a year Lady Douglas led the noble dames of British Columbia in graces of person, mind, and heart.

There were other passengers in that ship from San Francisco.

After infinite trials, Joe Meek, the trapper, had made his way to Washington, to find his own Virginian cousin the charming Lady of the White House.

He says: "When I heard the silks rustling in the passage I felt more frightened than if a hundred Blackfeet had whooped in my ear. A mist came over my eyes, and when Mrs. Polk spoke to me I could n't think of anything to say in return."

The White House was full of his relatives, from cousins and nephews down to the mulatto servant he played with when a boy. In short order the barber and the tailor transformed the unkempt, buckskin-clad Oregon trapper into a fashionable " Envoy Extraordinary and Minister Plenipotentiary from the Republic of Oregon to the Court of the United States ! "

The handsome trapper, no longer " old," returned to Oregon with the star of a United States Marshal on his breast. With him came General Joe Lane, the " Marion of the Mexican War," with the sword of Santa Anna at his belt, appointed by President Polk to be the first United States Governor of Oregon Territory.

That same month a company of United States troops were stationed at Fort Vancouver. At last the little colony had been heard, but it was only after Whitman was dead and homes had been desolated by an Indian war. The Whitman massacre awakened and united the settlers of the sparsely peopled valleys, it roused Congress from her dreams, and brought recognition to the first American settlement on the Pacific.

Congress admitted Oregon to territorial rights, and ratified the laws and acts of the Provisional Government the very day that schooner brought in the news of gold from Yerba Buena. Before the trapper-marshal could get back — presto ! change ! Gold brought in the world !

The Acadian days were ended. Governor Abernethy handed over the gavel to Governor Lane, and the technically illegal, yet efficient, Provisional Government was no more.

But the gold brigade went on. Even sleepy old Champoeg was roused; unquiet crept in as the serpent crept into Eden. In 1849 Canadians and half-breeds went to the mines. A strange epidemic swept among them, so that out of six hundred only one hundred and fifty returned alive. A dozen years later Champoeg itself was carried off in a flood.

The farms on French Prairie were sold to Americans. Little tow-headed Missourians sported in the barns and rifled the flower-gardens. Yankee boys and girls wondered what meant so many huts all in a row back of each Canadian manor house, — huts of the Indian slaves of the old Champoeg days.

One of the first acts of the new governor of Oregon Territory was to call in $50,000 of gold coin in five and ten dollar pieces minted at Oregon City. Every coin bore the stamp of a beaver — a reminiscence of the Hudson's Bay régime when the beaver-skin was legal tender. When the money was melted at the U. S. mint at San Francisco every piece was found to contain ten per cent more gold than government money. Oregon was honest as well as brave.

The last act of that same administration occurred one still and smoky day when Tiloukaikt and four accomplices of the Whitman massacre were hung in great solemnity at Oregon City. The United States marshal at the gallows was Joe Meek, the trapper.

XLIII

THE DEATH OF DR. McLOUGHLIN

1849-57

OREGON politics took on a vivid hue in 1849. A young fire-eater from the States, of surpassing oratory, espoused the anti-Hudson's Bay cause and rode on the popular wave to Congress. Congress, that had looked for some lean and bearded trapper from the far-away West, was startled by the youth, the beauty, the boldness, and the eloquence of Oregon's first delegate, a boy from Maine, scarce two years out. They leaned to catch the fiery invective of this brilliant but misinformed young man, who pictured Dr. McLoughlin, the "old monopolist," holding the savages in leash upon the trembling immigrants of Oregon.

Naturally prejudiced, it took but little to carry the tide. Every other settler in Oregon was confirmed in his title to land, but Dr. McLoughlin's was taken away. The old philanthropist, who had filed his papers for American citizenship, and had been the Father of Oregon, was left without a foot of land in all that territory that he had opened up to trade. When the news reached the Pacific, the Oregonians themselves were astonished — few had known of this conspiracy, and fewer still approved.

On the other hand, a great conflagration was kindled in England. Fitzgerald's "Hudson's Bay Company" was published to prove that the Hudson's Bay Company, and especially Dr. McLoughlin, had been inimical to British interests in America. All the old charges against Dr. McLoughlin as assisting Americans were re-cited here. A parliamentary investigation of Dr. John McLoughlin's conduct was demanded, and the fact that he was called "The Father of Oregon" was cited against him in the House of Commons. So in Congress and in Parliament the conflagration raged around one devoted old man, who had tried to keep the peace, and to do his duty to God and humanity.

In those days Dr. McLoughlin gave his heart to good deeds and to prayer. Only now and then did his quick temper emit a volcanic flash. Distrusted by England because he had befriended Americans, distrusted by Americans because he had been an Englishman, he exclaimed bitterly : —

"In my old age I find myself a man without a country. Having renounced my allegiance to Great Britain, now I am rejected by the United States."

The Klickitats came down from the mountains to trade for the last time. To their surprise they saw the "Bostons" picketed in the sacred enclosure at Fort Vancouver. They shook their heads and galloped away, riding like mad up the hillsides. Beaver had dropped to nothing.

"Furs?" said Chief Factor Ogden to a visitor. "Lord bless you, man, we lived in furs, dressed in furs, slept in furs. We purchased furs and piled up furs, until the presses were packed from sill to rafter. Five years ago beaver brought eight dollars a skin — now, since some pestilent fellow has invented silk nap for hats, it does not pay to transport the skins to London. It's all one, now, the game is up, the Americans hold the country.

"Lord bless you, man, I was the first white trapper on the lava plains of the Snake. Many a time have I entered a mountain pocket where never foot of white man trod before, and trapped my fifteen beaver in a night. Along the Missouri, twenty years ago, a good hunter could trap a hundred in a month. Many an industrious Flathead laid up six hundred in a season. It's a great business, a great business," continued Ogden, lighting up with his old pride. "The loss of Oregon is a paltry matter — all the North is ours. Our boats will carry British manufactures to the remotest wilds, and bring back furs, furs, furs. Wherever the smoke of a wigwam curls you will find our gay ribbons, and beads and bells and scarlet cloth."

Peter Skeen Ogden sat with hand clutched in his grizzly locks, while Bonneville, hero of Irving's tale, the very Bonneville driven back in 1834, came in, and right under his nose laid off a United States military reserve on the old Hudson's Bay ground.

At last the day came to give up the keys. The trapping clans gathered for their last banquet. Dugald McTavish came down from Victoria, and Donald Manson who had built the fort in 1824. Birnie came up from Cathlamet, McKinley from his farm in the Willamette, and Gagnier, who one time ruled the Umpqua. The old hall rang to the last bout and wassail. General Harney was guest where on the morrow he would be master. All night the puncheon floor sprang to the steps of dancers. When the fiddle-strings snapped and the candles flared, McTavish opened the window. The red sun rolled up like a wheel of fire beside Mt. Hood, gilding the dawn of United States possession of Fort Vancouver. By order from Washington, General Harney demolished the old fort, and to-day the prettiest military post in the United States covers the grassy greensward on the north bank of the Columbia, — six miles from the city of Portland.

Ogden died and was buried — under the stars and stripes.

Soon after, Dr. McLoughlin took to his bed. The chill of nearly fifty years before, in the icy Lake Superior, had never left his bones. Dr. Barclay had followed Dr. McLoughlin to Oregon City, and was his constant attendant. Mrs. Barclay, beautiful in person and character, ran over frequently from the cares of her young and growing family. Eloise was a true daughter in directing the servants, in consoling her mother, in watchings many at the bedside of her father.

" *Comment allez-vous ?* " asked the good old wife, as his end drew near. With an upward glance and smile he answered, " *A Dieu.*" It was his last word. In the still nights now and then a groan was heard. The long, white locks curled on the pillow, and silent tears rolled from the closed eyelids. So he died. The Father of Oregon sleeps on the banks of the Willamette within sound of the Falls he loved so well. Peace be with him.

The familiar form that had passed up and down the streets, thinking of others and never of self, had been laid to rest. Carlyle says the sceptic does not know a hero when he sees him ! Five years before McLoughlin's death the Oregon legislature had pigeon-holed a resolution thanking him for his generous conduct toward the early settlers. How could they thank him while they withheld his land ? In the mean time there had been a great talking and thinking among the people. Men paused when they heard his funeral knell, and women wept. The scales of party strife fell from their eyes.

" This was a good man," they said.

" He saved our lives."

" He gave us seed."

" He gave us food."

" His good deeds cannot be told."

" He has been foully dealt with."

"We have brought his gray hairs in sorrow to the grave."

The murmur for restitution grew high and higher, until, five years after his death, the State Legislature by special act restored the land claim to his heirs, — too late, alas! to gladden the philanthropic heart.

The peculiar circumstances under which he was situated, make McLoughlin's benefactions unique in history. It is a trite saying on the Columbia, that had any other than a John McLoughlin been at the head of the Hudson's Bay Company's affairs in Oregon, American settlements might have been crushed in their inception. With all the savages at his command, a single hint could have hurled the adventurous immigrants back across the Rocky Mountains, and the United States would never have carried a war of invasion so far from her frontier. The conduct of McLoughlin, his humanity and magnanimity, lift him above the range of common heroes into the sublimated realm of Christian ideals, where he and Whitman walk together, the Father and the Martyr of the Pacific Northwest.

Not in vain did Nathaniel Wyeth, the first American, knock at the gates of Fort Vancouver, not in vain did he sink $100,000 in his Oregon enterprise, not in vain did Whitman fall or the immigrants toil across the Rockies. Out of McLoughlin's semi-barbaric empire has risen the better empire of to-day. From the ceded territory Oregon had been cut, a part of Montana, Washington with her Mediterranean, and Idaho with her wealth of mines.   Now the summer tourist flies across the continent in a week.   From his palace window he catches glimpses of the old immigrant road, winding through alkali-sand and dust, a road that was lined with graves and wet with blood and tears.

"The Americans are mad!" cried Sir George Simpson, but it is the madness that has strung our cities from Plymouth Rock to the Philippines.

The moccasin age is past.   The evanescent fur trade is over.   Cavalcades of merry trappers wind over the hills and glide on the streams no more.   Those daring men, more worthy than many fictitious heroes of romance, have passed with the passing of the red man. Where the little " Cadboro'" and occasional ships from London fluttered the triangular pennon sixty years ago, the fleets of all nations come in, bearing away, like busy ants, their burdens of lumber, fish, and grain.

An interesting scene was enacted in Oregon's State House the other day, when the pioneers gathered to dedicate a portrait of the Hudson's Bay governor who befriended them on their first arrival across the plains. There was a hush, and few dry eyes, as they heard again the story of his virtues.   " And now," said Oregon's foremost judge, pointing to the face that smiled benignly from the canvas, " it is to be hung in the State Capitol, where you may look at it, and show it to your children, and they to their children, and say: ' This is the old doctor, the good doctor, Dr. John McLoughlin.'"

Lightning Source UK Ltd.
Milton Keynes UK
UKHW02n0827190818
327370UK00002B/120/P

9 780260 096487